DEATH ON A GRAVESTONE

The Newshound Mysteries
Book 1

M. K. Jones and John F. Wake

**Copyright © Mary Kathryn Jones
And John F Wake 2024**

Mary Kathryn Jones and John F Wake have asserted their right under the Copyright, Designs and Patents Act 1988 to be identified as the authors of this work.

This story is a work of fiction. Names and characters are the product of the authors' imagination and any resemblance to actual persons, living or dead, is entirely co-incidental. Where real historical persons, places and events are featured, they appear only as the authors imagined them to be.

All rights reserved. No part of this publication may be reproduced, stored in a retrieval system, or transmitted by any means without the prior written consent of the authors. This story is sold subject to the condition that it shall not, by way of trade or otherwise, be lent, re-sent, hired out or otherwise circulated without the authors' prior consent in any form of binding, cover, or other format, including this condition being imposed on the subsequent purchaser.

First paperback edition: 2024
Published by: Mary Kathryn Jones
Cover Picture: © Charlotte McAdam
Cover Design: © Alison Morgan at Ali-Cat Design

ISBN: 9781738504602

Category: Historical Thrillers/Police Procedural Mysteries

1

For the third time this month I enter the Cardiff Coroner's Court, notebook in hand, pen attached to notebook. I still think of it as the "Cardiff" Coroner's Court despite a local government committee having decided to site it in Pontypridd, twelve miles away from our capital city and half way up a perpendicular hill, with no parking. It serves the whole of South Wales, which means that some poor sods have to travel from as far away as Llandrindod Wells, miles farther north. Let's hope they don't have too many suspicious deaths up there. Bloody committees. What is a camel? A horse designed by a committee. Told that one when I was young and never forgotten it.

There we are. It's a nice building, I have to say, despite its location, Victorian ornate tiles and wood panels inside. I stop in the foyer to catch my breath from that sodding hill, then wheeze up the green tiled main staircase to a mezzanine where, halfway up, the stairs divide in two, left and right. It doesn't matter which one I take. They both lead to the main court on the next floor. There are three courts here. This case is in Court One, the largest of the three, which is no surprise. Sometimes you can hear a fly fart, but not today, not for this one. The room is already full and buzzing with activity. I pause for a moment, until my breath is steady again. I shouldn't be wheezing. I am fifty-six, not eighty-six. Once, I kept myself fit but that was before…

Three seats are reserved for Press, at the back of the room, one of which is exclusively mine. Woe betide anyone else who dares to sit there. The seat pad moulds around my ample backside. I have been attending this court for five years. It is my seat, from which I can survey the bench, the family, the police, the lawyers and the spectators.

All the usual suspects are present and waiting. Old Betty with her bag of toffees is in her regular place – spectator area, third row on the coroner's left, seat next to the wall, just in front of me so she can throw off the occasional comment, usually to the wall. I say old. She's probably in her late fifties. It's the headscarf, the grey perm and second-hand crimplene dresses that put ten years on her. Sid and Harry, definitely sixties or even seventies, homeless, and happy to go anywhere to keep out of the cold. Today they choose the back of the room, close to the radiators. Mary Anne Rafferty and her husband Terrence, Coroner's Court groupies, both in their eighties. They sit close to the door, and the toilets. Terrence can't hold it in like he used to, poor sod.

One seat away from Betty sits Cardiff's worst, most vicious gossip, Billie Everard. Everyone keeps away from Billie the know-it-all, who has a bad word to say about everyone. When unwelcome news arrives, Billie already knows about it, of course.

A much bigger crowd than usual today and no wonder. This is an odd one. Suicide, supposedly.

The family troops in, gloomy, shocked, sits in the front row directly in front of the clerk, and solicitors if there are to be any, and the coroner. You can see their bewildered thoughts on their faces, *'how did we end up here?'*

My colleague from The South Wales Recorder dashes in, sits next to me. 'Thought I'd find you here Trevor. Weird one, this, isn't it.'

I grunt. I know more than he does but I'm not letting on, not yet. He's just a lad, no idea how to work the system.

The courtroom is light and bright, unlike its inhabitants. More spectators drift in, taking up all of the remaining seats, attracted by the publicity this case brings with it. Ghouls, with morbid curiosity about how a woman died in such a bizarre way. Some may have known her in a professional capacity. I can tell from a group of three suits whispering to each other, grimacing, their eyebrows jiggling up and down as they exchange hushed comments, that they are from the Council. One grins, but another whispers roughly to kill the grin. They didn't like her, much like most of the people whose paths she crossed in her fifty years. Much like most of the city.

This is an odd one, though. Of all the people who might take their own life for whatever reason, poor sods mostly, Agnes Hunter would be at the bottom of the list, if she were on the list at all. Yet, she did. Today is the re-opening of the inquest, initially opened and adjourned six weeks ago to give the police more time to investigate. I am expecting to hear the details of their investigation today. It will have been extensive: after all, Agnes was a well-known public figure, hated, but in the public eye. If you wanted to compile a list of suspects who might have murdered the old bitch, it would take more than a ream of paper and headed by the Leader of the Council with the Chief Constable not much further down.

Agnes is – was – a professional politician. No-one's sure how she got into the party, but once in, she was determined to take over from day one. She'd only been on the Council for five years, but her lack of empathy – except of course towards her personal voting constituents – combined with her spite and compulsion to gain revenge for slights real and imagined towards her colleagues, made sure she wasn't on anyone's Christmas card list. Nor was she invited to any social event where her presence wasn't mandatory. She'd turn up anyway, oblivious to the disgusted looks of her colleagues and – I heard on the council gossip grapevine – was on one occasion ordered by the head of a committee to get out of the room. He lost his position not long after. Agnes wasn't averse to using gossip and spying to get what she wanted.

Agnes Hunter, nee Dole – tall, thin, upright with a stance always ready for a fight, never seen casually dressed, nor in anything other than a designer suit. She had a sharp pointed face, thin lips whose smiling muscles had atrophied away, and well cut, short grey hair coiffured by a military stylist. The idea of this woman lying down on a flat gravestone in Cathays graveyard, putting a gun under her chin and blowing the back of her head off, splattering her brains all over the nice upright Celtic cross that stood behind the flat stone was, as my colleague had said, weird.

'Trevor bach, are you with us?' Mary Anne stands and walks down the couple of rows to stand in front of me. 'You look like you're a million miles away.'

I nod. 'Just thinking. Odd one, this. Did you ever meet her?'

Terrence joins her – he's as keen on the gossip as his wife – and answers for both of them. 'Came across her once, we did, down at the Bay, saw her put some poor little devil in his place. Reduced the lad to tears she did, all in front of a crowded foyer, loud enough to make sure everyone heard. Bitch.'

'Terrence, language,' Mary Anne chides. 'Although Trev, I must say she wasn't nice. My neighbour met her once, tried to shake her hand and—'

'Here they come,' I say, not wanting to get into a gossipfest with Mary Anne. She would get around to asking me about Nia, a conversation I couldn't cope with, not yet. Terrence and Mary Anne hurry back to their seats.

We all stand as the coroner, with his clerk and usher, enters from a side door, steps up onto the dais and nods to the crowd to sit. Once we the audience settle, he looks around at the full house and shakes his head.

He goes through the usual procedure, explaining what the court does, the process and so on. I've heard it so many times I tune out. I watch the family: the husband and teenage son. Husband – angry, arms grabbing the sides of his chair, position upright, tense. Son – bewildered, sunk down into the seat. I doubt he'll be giving evidence.

Jim Bowen is a good person to take on the role of a Coroner. He's been a top-notch barrister and is kind enough, on the whole. I've never known him lose his grip. He'll need that skill today. Reginald Hunter is now as red as a bottle of ketchup. The son is green, looks like he's going to puke. Jim notices, calls the usher and whispers. The usher fetches a bucket.

He begins with the police officer who found the body, rather was called to the scene by the shocked dog walker who'd wandered past shortly after eight thirty. The officer is brief. She found this member of the public puking up against the nearby chapel wall. She touched nothing but immediately called her uniformed sergeant, Gareth Roberts, who attended with a senior paramedic, who confirmed life extinct. Sergeant Roberts got the show rolling, with CID and CSIs and, of course, the pathologist. Tony Millbank, the pathologist was the first one to recognise Agnes and inform the CID attendees of her identity. The latter, a couple of Detective Constables, being of lowly rank and pissed off by being called out for what they thought was just a random suicide, recognised the name at once, glanced at each other, then put in a call to their own Chief, the dreaded Detective Inspector Harry Morgan.

Sergeant Roberts's next call was to me, at nine. We go back a long way. I hopped into an Uber and headed up to the cemetery. He told me to make it quick, as Harry Morgan and I do not get on. I strolled past, just before the police tape went up to cordon off the area and had a quiet word with the sarge.

'What's this all about Gareth?'

'That's Agnes Hunter. Lay down on a flat stone and blew her brains out. You can see the gun, and her brains decorating the Celtic cross.'

This was the first odd thing. From what I saw when I arrived, the gravestone Agnes laid herself down on, next but one to the path, had once been ornate and large, surrounded by an ankle high iron fence. The details and identity of whoever's grave it is had worn away with time, and weeds had begun to take over. I think the first name might have been Charles. It's one of the more noticeable graves, even now, so Agnes must have thought it suited her own station in life. Typical. She couldn't even kill herself without a final bit of snobbery. But why this particular one?

Still, I was stunned. 'You sure she did this herself Gar?'

'Pathologist will report after his examination and the CSIs' report, but it looks like it. There was a note.'

'There'll be an investigation anyway,' I said, shaking my head. 'Big one, this. It'll be front page news on The Cardiff Sentinel tonight, and on the telly news. Look, TV van arriving already.'

The van had pulled up on the road, blocking the entrance to the cemetery. A crew jumped out and immediately rushed forward, with a constable trying to push them back. Reporter, too. Agnes was definitely going to be the star of the show on the six thirty news. The reporter was trying to get the Sergeant to confirm it was Agnes. No chance. He snapped at her that a statement would be given later.

The appearance of the next witness brings me back into the room.

It's Inspector Harry Morgan, who had taken over, and who had visited the family: father and son but not daughter, who was away at University in Oxford he explains. She's not here today, either. Odd, but a Coroner's Court isn't for queasy people. The Inspector reports that Agnes Hunter had left for work that morning at seven thirty, which was early for her. She was thoughtful, not talking much. Father and son sensed she had something on her mind, something heavy, but absolutely no hint or suggestion that she was planning to take her own life. She was not depressed or anxious. She said she had an early meeting before going to the Bay.

Now comes the revelation. 'There was a note. It was lying on top of her,' the Inspector says, 'tucked into the lapel of her jacket.' He reads it out. *"I understand now. This is the end. I will die like you died".*'

'This is something I will discuss with Mr Hunter,' says Jim Bowen, but first I would like to hear about the gun and your further investigations.' Reginald Hunter looks down. His hands are clasped together.

'Please tell me about the gun,' Jim says. The Inspector replies, 'Neither father nor son had seen it before, were quite certain it had never been in the house. It's an old pistol, WWII Walther Pistole 38.' He goes on to describe in minute and lengthy detail, the investigation he and his team have undertaken. They have not found any history of ownership of the gun.

'My team have found people though' – he pauses for an embarrassed cough – 'who didn't like Agnes Hunter, people with whom she had had run-ins in the past months, and we've checked out and verified the alibis of all these people.'

He explains that The Team have been through the Council, her previous jobs, her family, and her neighbours – the latter said she rarely spoke to them and when she did it was to complain about something, plus she had an ongoing dispute with next door over a hedge – until there was no-one else left to talk to. The only person they could find who might have had a solid grudge against her was her clerical assistant, a nineteen-year-old girl by the name of Cerys Hughes. He says Cerys was waiting anxiously in Agnes's office at seven thirty, having been summoned to a meeting. She was expecting to be sacked for an error she'd made. She saw Agnes drive up in her car, park it, glance up at the window of her office but then get into an Uber and leave without entering the building. The police have concluded suicide by reason of an issue in her professional life, for which the rationale may never be known.

'What did she mean when she said, "I understand now" in her note?' Jim asks.

'We have not been able to establish the meaning,' Inspector Morgan replies. 'It meant nothing to her family, nor to anyone to whom we spoke.'

'Did anyone hear the shot?'

'No, Sir, we checked with the residents of houses close to the perimeter, but as I am sure you know, Cathays is the biggest cemetery in Wales, if not in the whole of the United Kingdom. We found a couple of locals who thought the noise might have been a car backfiring, around eight twenty-ish, which corresponds with the pathologist's report about time of death but didn't think any more of it.'

Do modern cars "backfire"? I haven't heard one for years. Typical Harry Morgan. Thought probably never occurred to him.

'Thank you, Inspector Morgan. You may step down.'

He does so. Harry Morgan can't help looking pleased with himself. Every appearance before an audience gives him an opportunity to preen. Six feet three, twenty stone, most of it flab these days. I know him of old. He's a monolithic, self-serving prat, a bully, a tyrant and an arse-licker, who likes to weed out anyone who appears to fear him and make their life a misery. He won't come near me, though. The history we share is long and bitter.

Finally, Reginald Hunter. His face hasn't changed colour, still beetroot red.

'Mr Hunter, I understand how difficult this is for you, but there are questions I must ask before I can pronounce a verdict. Can you give me any idea about the meaning of the note?'

'None whatsoever,' Reginald replies, his voice carrying around the room and outside.

'Was it in your wife's handwriting?' Jim asks.

Reginald takes a deep breath, brushes his comb-over smooth and flat. After a pause he says 'Yes, it would appear so.' Emphasis on the "appear". Then he asks permission to read out a statement. He says that Agnes was a respected and well liked – who is he kidding – Councillor. He is one hundred percent certain she did not take her own life, she wasn't that kind of woman. She ploughed through life with a determination to overcome obstacles and achieve results for her constituents. *'And God help anyone who got in her way'*, I think. He finishes by saying that the note might have been a forgery, a clever one, but still a forgery. He can't believe his wife killed herself but was killed by someone still out there and is outraged that the police have stopped looking for her killer. He sits down. The son remains seated, visibly shaking.

Jim Bowen asks if Reginald knew of any enemies. Reginald stands again, shaking his head, and I think he blushes, but he's so red in the face already you can't really tell.

Jim sums up, summarises the evidence, the reports from the police, the pathologist and the CSIs. He says he remains puzzled by Agnes's suicide note, but her husband has confirmed it was written by her own hand, albeit he thinks it might have been a good forgery. He is also sorry that the police have not been able to find who might have been the person she went out to meet on the morning of her death, as Cerys Hughes had a proven alibi. However, given the thoroughness of the police investigation he is satisfied that his sad, but inevitable conclusion is that this was a suicide, for reasons that may never be known. He extends his heartfelt sympathy to the family, then stands and leaves the dais and the room. Reginald and son also leave in a hurry.

The chattering starts at once. It was not an unexpected outcome, but still enough food for gossip.

I stand and start to move through the crowd, to get out before anyone can speak to me when a hand catches my arm as I reach the door. It's Gareth Roberts. 'Quiet word Trevor.' I nod and we walk to the top of the stairs, where we can lean against the wall.

'What did you think?' he asks.

I open my mouth to reply, and in that moment, everything changes. A crowd of the public walks past, chit chatting in lowered voices. And I catch a whisper, so low it's like a feather brushing my ear, two words, *"justice, again."* I glance around. No-one is looking my way.

'You going back to Cardiff Gar?' I ask.

The sergeant nods.

'How about a pint later, in The Rummer, about seven?'

He nods again, then descends the stairs.

I follow him out into the slashing rain, head back down the steep street and around to the station, for the train to take me to Cardiff Central, from where I can walk home. My head is full of that whisper. Did I really hear it? If it was real, who said it and what does it mean? Never mind the "justice." My interest is in the "again." A tiny seed has been planted in my head and is sprouting – that Agnes Hunter might not have killed herself after all.

2

When I reach the pub, Gareth is not alone. He has a young woman with him. I don't know her but suspect she's a colleague. They're sitting at a table in a corner, away from other customers. I buy my usual pint, then go over to join them.

'Trevor,' Gareth says as I sit. 'This is Hayden Wilkins. She's been a member of the CID team investigating Agnes Hunter's death.' I note he doesn't say "suicide". Hayden nods. She's drinking G&T. Typical CID. She can't be more than twenty-five. How did she get into CID? Fast track? Know-nothing University graduate on the quick path to management?

She watches me staring at her, with amused eyes. 'I'm thirty-one, single, and been with CID for a year. I'm not a high-flyer, simply good at my job. I started as a constable on Gareth's team. Gareth says you have doubts about how Agnes Hunter died.'

'Did he now?' I reply, taking a long sip of beer.

'Yes, as does he,' she replies.

'I can speak for myself,' Gareth mutters. 'But she's right, that's why we're here, isn't it Trevor?'

'You weren't in court today Hayden,' I say.

'I'm inconvenient,' she replies. 'But I was there. You didn't notice me.'

I stare again. She's tall, with a good figure as far as I can tell given she's sitting down but she's not an attractive woman, nose too big, thin lips. You'd pass her in the street without a second glance. But she would notice you. She'd notice anyone. The deep green eyes are sharp, the kind that take in everyone. I glance around. She could probably tell me how many people are in the pub right now.

'Seventeen,' she says. 'Fourteen men and three women, including me.'

She is unnerving me. 'They don't like you much on the murder team, then?' I reply.

She laughs and what looked like a permanent set of frown lines is gone. She releases her black straight hair from the elastic band holding it at the back of her head and it falls on either side of her face down to her shoulders.

'What do you know about me?' I ask.

'Trevor Jones, age fifty-six, a bit overweight, tubby, I'd say, don't take care of yourself. Your rather lovely shade of russet hair is turning grey and thinning. You have a nice face, handsome, would be better without the double chin, though. You're a reporter for The Cardiff Sentinel. You once had dreams of Fleet Street, good enough too, but never left Cardiff. A widower. Your wife Nia—'

'Stop there,' I say in a clipped tone. 'Don't talk about my wife.'

'Sorry, Trevor. That was insensitive.'

I nod. 'Apology accepted. Before I say anything more, I don't understand why you're here, talking to me, in public. If anyone sees you and reports you to Harry Morgan, he'll make sure you're suspended and disciplined, if not outright fired.'

'I know,' she says, glaring at me. 'Harry Morgan is the reason I'm here.'

'You'd better explain, and it'll have to be good.'

She looks at Gareth and he shrugs. 'Up to you, Hayden. If you don't tell him everything, he won't be convinced enough to speak to you. Trevor and I go back to school days. Everyone knows that. But you're different.'

She stares into her drink. Gareth and I wait. After a long wait she takes a deep breath. 'There are two reasons I'm here. One is personal, the second is professional. The professional reason is that Inspector Harry Morgan was economical with the truth on the stand at the inquest today. Like I said, I was – am – an inconvenience to him. He hates women, especially gay women. I mean, he hates all gays, but especially gay women. So, he left me to vegetate in the office during the investigation into Agnes Hunter's death. One day he brought a file in during the investigation, which he put into his desk drawer, then locked it. I opened it. I'm a good lock picker.' She stops here to blush and cough. 'It was a file of correspondence taken from Reginald Hunter. In it there was a letter, a very odd letter, threatening to expose Agnes for who she really was, but there was no further detail, so I didn't know what the anonymous writer was threatening to expose. I returned the letter to the file, put the file back in the drawer and locked it. I should have photographed it. My own stupid fault I didn't. The next time Morgan came in, I asked him if there was any evidence that might point to something other than suicide. He verbally lashed out at me, told me the case was a suicide and if I tried to make waves, I'd regret it. Thank God, the office door opened, and Del Smith came in. I managed to push my chair back from where Morgan was leaning over me. Del gave me a funny look but didn't ask any questions.

'His eyes hold a story, if you know what I mean. He disgusts and revolts me and I know he disgusts other women officers too. I've talked to a few. He'll brush against them in the corridor, then apologise, he'll start telling a dirty story, then stop, saying "oops, sorry lads, ladies present". Taken one case at a time it doesn't amount to anything. But most of the women in the station avoid him if they can, and definitely avoid ever, ever being alone with him. He's careful, he never crosses a line that would get him into real trouble.'

'Did you report him?' I know the answer already.

She shakes her head. 'One woman sergeant did report him, about six months ago. I don't know what he said or did, but she resigned when the investigation couldn't find independent proof, and a sidekick of his said he was elsewhere at the time, and the woman was known to have a vendetta against Morgan, because he was promoted to Inspector ahead of her. So, I hate the bastard with every bone and sinew in me and if I can manage to find something against him in terms of this investigation, then I'll use it. Knowledge of that letter is all I have right now, but I'm willing to sacrifice my job because I can't take much more of him. He keeps winking at me then he licks his lips.'

Now it's my turn to shudder. I believe her. Morgan is a monster, I've always known that, but this is beyond anything I've heard before.

'I'm so sorry,' I say. 'But you have to know what you're risking. And yes, whatever comes out about Morgan, you could still lose your job if anyone finds out you're speaking to me. I've never attempted to work with any police before, apart from Gareth, and that's only barely tolerated.' I pause. 'Right, let's get to it. We're here because we're not convinced Agnes Hunter killed herself. But I'm assuming that, like me, neither of you has any idea if it was murder and if it was, who did it.'

They both nod. Gareth starts. 'I came across her when I worked down at the Bay. She was a nasty piece of work. I never looked her in the eye. She looked at you like she was trying to find a way to do you harm.' He shivers. 'Like you see on those vampire programmes on the telly, thinking of a way to launch into your neck.'

Hayden takes over. 'I never crossed her path personally. The boss assigned me to background work, so I spent my time during the enquiry sitting on my ass at a computer, trying to find out as much as I could about her life and background.'

Gareth takes a long swig of his pint and says, 'Hayden saw me talking to you at the inquest. Afterwards she had a quiet word with me.' Here he turns to her, and she nods. 'She believes, from everything she learned during her research, that Agnes Hunter was murdered and there's someone else's agenda at work here. Far as I'm concerned, you've heard what Hayden is going through. I trust her and I believe her motivation, not just the personal stuff. She agrees with me and wants to know what led up to this death, because when Agnes Hunter set out that morning, someone was waiting for her at Cathays, and we've never been able to find out who that person was.'

I drink slowly, thinking about how to tell them what I thought I heard as I left the court. I'd asked myself on my earlier walk to the station how – why – do I care if Agnes Hunter was murdered or not? The police have done a thorough enquiry. But the thing is, I'm a reporter. All my life I've been after a big story. I've covered murders: mostly domestic, sometimes accidental, manslaughter, minor crime, Coroner's Court cases. But never the big one. Now, today, something in my gut is urging me to pursue this, telling me this is it – "the big one", the one I've waited for. I don't know why, but I think these two people sitting here with me have it too. Only one way to find out.

I turn to Gareth. 'Does she have it?'

He grins and taps the side of his nose. 'She has it.'

'Good enough,' I reply. 'Then we need a plan.'

'What is it you suppose I have?' Hayden interrupts.

'A nose for the big one, the special one, not just out of the ordinary, but well into the extraordinary. In court today, my colleague from The Recorder said, "this is a weird one". He was right. Do you have the feeling there's a whole different story here, that no-one's even touched on yet?'

Hayden slowly nods her head. 'I found out stuff about her past, but Inspector Morgan didn't think it was relevant or didn't want to pursue it. I wanted to explore further, but he said no. He had an agenda to make sure the verdict came out as suicide'.

'Probably suited the brass,' Gareth puts in.

'Then that's where we start,' I say. 'You know you'll have to work on this with me and Gar without anyone else knowing? It'd be the sack for you if anyone on the force finds out.'

'No problem,' she says. 'Morgan is looking for a reason – any reason – to get rid of me from his team, so it might as well be for consorting with a reporter. I've been thinking seriously about packing it in, anyway. I get a thrill from investigating, but all I've been allowed to do in the six months since I've made sergeant is to sit in the office and compile statistics and other reports. How and when do we start?' She's sitting forward on her seat, looking like she's waiting for the starter's gun to do a hundred metres dash.

'Tomorrow,' I say. 'Gar, are you in on this?'

'Much as I can be,' he says. 'Which may not be much, given my shift patterns. I'll more likely be background, and devil's advocate in case Trevor gets carried away. I'm going to have to leave it to you two and do what I can, when I can.'

'I've nothing big on at the moment,' Hayden says. 'I'm working nine to five for the foreseeable, unless something else comes up.'

'In that case, my place tomorrow at six.'

'Works for me,' she says.

'Sorry, I'll be on shift,' Gareth says.

'Then I'll catch you up later in the pub.'

'You'll need my address,' I say to Hayden.

She grins. 'I know where you live.'

'Of course you do,' I say followed by a sigh. 'Right then, see you both tomorrow. I have a room to clear out, ready for an investigation.' I turn to Hayden. 'Try not to be alone with Harry Morgan.'

I leave them in the pub. I am walking with a bounce in my step, a sense of excitement in my stomach, something I haven't felt for months, not since – not since Nia died. She'd have approved. Pity she couldn't have been with us to join in. Nia loved a mystery and I'm going to get to the bottom of this one. See if I don't.

3

Before I start anything at home I pay a visit to my paper's Editor-in-Chief. I filed my copy when I arrived home, before the five o'clock deadline and she had already approved it so I enter her office without fear of her displeasure.

'This is a surprise Trevor. Nothing better to do?' I'm used to the sarcasm, so I go straight into my pitch, at the end of which she grins, folds her arms and sits back in an enormous chair. 'You must be fucking kidding.'

I pause, tilt my chin up to the ceiling then back down to her eye level, and tell her about the "justice again". She sits up. 'How do you know it wasn't just some local with a grudge against politicians, who's been threatening all and sundry they don't like in the world of politics. There's plenty to choose from.'

In response I tap the side of my nose, and nod. She bites her lower lip then sucks in her cheeks. I know I've got her. 'All right, you've got a week. I want a daily update.'

I know when to stop and I leave her office before she can change her mind, on the "out of sight, out of mind" principle.

I spend the rest of the morning compiling a list of all of the newspaper cuttings I can find since Agnes Hunter died, including anything I can find about husband Reginald Hunter. I'm not bad at searches. I can work my way around the internet, although I don't have access to any of the police databases, more's the pity.

The news articles are the same. They have no more information than I have, except for one. This interests me.

It's an obituary that looks back at Agnes's life. She was an only child born in Cardiff to a single mother, Hannah Dole. Her place of birth was Whitchurch. Hannah and Agnes moved away shortly after Agnes's birth, to London where Hannah had family. Agnes moved back to Cardiff to complete her University Degree in History, met Reginald Hunter – doesn't say where or when – married him and set up home in Swansea, where he ran a family accountancy business, which she joined. They moved back to Cardiff in 2000 with young daughter. Elected to Council 2015, member for Selwood Ward. Head of Governance and Audit Committee in 2023, rumours she would soon be Deputy Leader. She and Reginald lived in Lisvane. That's posh, voted the poshest area in Cardiff in a public vote held by The Cardiff Sentinel. Most houses there fetch over a million.

My first set of questions: why did Agnes end up in Cathays, at that particular entrance? Was there any CCTV around the cemetery? Was her car still down at the Bay? Did the police appeal for witnesses there? Is there anything more we need to know about Cerys Hughes?

My follow up questions: Reginald said Agnes left the family home saying she had a meeting before heading down to the Bay. He was clear about the "before". Was this the Cerys Hughes meeting? Couldn't be, but if Reginald is right, there was another meeting. What was it about? He hinted that she was "thoughtful" that morning. Was she usually a thoughtful person? What I know of her would say she wasn't, not in the kind, considerate way. She was a straight in swinging brutal punches type. Why did this "thoughtfulness" not get more attention? It should have done. Did Morgan deliberately suppress it? Did the police investigation even make enough inquiries? This is a mess, in my opinion, and will be until I get more information.

My final questions, for now: Why choose that particular grave? Is there any special significance to it, other than it's a poorly kept but high-end one? It's fenced off from others around it by an ankle-high ornate iron fencing with gold tips on the railings. Must have been someone very posh, once.

I think of more, write them up on the white board I have purchased and erected on the back wall of the defunct dining room. I had to take down one of Nia's favourite pictures. I have pushed the dining table up against the wall where it fits nicely just under the bottom of the board. We can spread out papers on it. It's still only midday. What else can I do before Hayden arrives at six? I can't just sit around, thinking. I stare at the questions and decide there is someone who might be prepared to answer some of them. I will pay a visit to Reginald Hunter.

I don't drive so I'll order a taxi. What do they call them these days – an Uber? I have an app installed by one of my younger colleagues. The car arrives in ten minutes – very efficient. I give the address in Lisvane. The driver's eyes pop for a second, then we set off. It takes almost twenty minutes to the front drive of the Hunter home, out of the bustling mass of the Cardiff metropolis up to the quiet streets of this suburban millionaire's dream. To my surprise, the houses around that of Reginald and Agnes don't look particularly special or interesting. They are on a small private estate of about ten or twelve houses, each fortified with high electric fences and CCTV cameras, sufficient to keep out Vladimir Putin's army, or any nosy passerby. The house in question is a sixties build, a boring heap of random bricks. Thousands of bricks, no soul. Lisvane has an historic significance, an old, interesting village, characterful old pubs, and a reservoir close by, used for sailing. I sigh and turn to the ten-foot-high gateway. Someone has left it slightly ajar. Good. I slip through the gap and march up to the front entrance, immensely relieved there is no sound here of the deep, menacing barking I hear from the house next door. I ring the bell. Of course it couldn't just ring. It plays an operatic overture. A shape arrives. The door opens a few inches. Reginald Hunter.

'Good afternoon, Mr Hunter,' I say in my best non-Cardiff accent. My name is Trevor Gwyn Jones — I rarely use the double barrel but it might come in useful here — from The Cardiff Sentinel. I was present at your wife's inquest yesterday and was intrigued by your assertion that your wife did not commit suicide. I wonder, might I talk to you about what you think may have happened? I won't take up too much of your time.' I give him my sympathetic smile. It doesn't work.

'Get off my doorstep, you trash reporter scum, or I'll call the police and have you arrested for trespassing.' He slams the door in my face, leaving behind in the air a strong whiff of whisky.

I stand for a moment. I hadn't expected a warm welcome, after all the man is grieving — supposedly. I didn't expect that reaction, though. I'm puzzled. He ranted about the police not doing enough to find out who killed his wife, thus suggesting unlawful killing, but when someone arrives to ask him what he meant, he shuts them out. I am not reporter scum, like the London redtops and similar tabloids. The Cardiff Sentinel is a respectable newspaper, which reports actual news.

As I turn to walk back down the drive and go to order up another Uber, a boy enters through the gates. He wears the uniform of the top private school in Cardiff and carries a satchel. He is tall and thin, slouching in the usual manner of a sixteen-year-old. His black hair is slightly too long and he constantly pushes the sideways fringe back as it falls forward to cover his eyes. He stops dead when he sees me. He walks slowly up to me. Am I to expect another heap of insult? I hold my ground until he is a foot from me.

'You were in court.'

'Yes, I was. I'm a reporter from The Cardiff Sentinel. Trevor Gwyn Jones.' I hold out my hand and he takes it. His handshake is firm for a boy his age. 'I came to ask your father about what he meant by his statement, but he's thrown me out.'

The boy glances up at the entrance to the house, then back at me. 'David Hunter. I'll talk to you,' he says. 'But not here.'

He turns and walks, quietly and quickly, back down the driveway, out of the gate and around a corner to a small green with benches at intervals around its perimeter. I follow, slightly out of breath, and sit beside him. For a few minutes he stares at the green, not speaking. I know not to fill the silence. He will talk when he's ready.

He shuffles on the bench, then says, 'My mother received threatening letters. They frightened her.'

That didn't come out in court. What might have been in them to frighten the likes of Agnes Hunter? I wonder if the police know. I'll be sure to ask Hayden as soon as she arrives later exactly what she found in Harry Morgan's locked desk.

'Do you know what was in them, David?'

'No, she burned them.'

'All of them?'

'Yes. I was there when the last one came, the day before she died, and I saw the edge as it lit up. It said, "*Pay the price*." And I also saw "*your family*". There were strange markings on the paper.'

'What sort of markings David?'

'I only saw one, a goat's head with "Satan" in cut-out letter above it.' He pauses here. 'And I think someone has been following me, on and off, ever since my mother died.'

'Have you told your father?' I ask.

'No.' He blushes and turns his head away from me. 'He's too drunk most of the time. He's scared too. He saw that one and he's not sure if it meant him, or just my mother's family. He's had a lot of calls with his lawyer. He thinks I don't notice, but I do. I've overheard the calls. He asks when he can get access to mum's will.'

'Has the person you think is following you ever approached you?'

He shakes his head. 'Which paper did you say you were from?' He is suddenly wary. I give him my business card. He checks it out and puts it in his satchel.

'Have you talked to anyone about this David?'

'Only my sister, Louisa. She's a Professor at Oxford. She's twenty-eight – one of the youngest Professors. She's married with a little boy.'

I hear the pride in his voice.

'Once I've done my AS levels, I'm going to live with her. I'll be seventeen next week. Then he can't stop me. I'll finish my A levels in Cambridge. He stares at the green again. His head suddenly jerks towards me. 'You aren't going to print any of this, are you?'

I feel a rush of compassion. Adults would have asked this question up front. 'No,' I say, 'not a word of it. I've been compelled since the inquest to find out what actually happened to your mother. David, this is a difficult question, and I'll understand if you don't want to answer it. Did you like your mother?'

He blushes a deep red. 'I hated her,' he says in a whisper. 'She was cruel.'

'Physically cruel?' I ask, dreading the answer.

'No, mentally. I'm not as clever as Louisa, although I work hard. Louisa did her A levels when she was sixteen, two years ahead of normal time, and went to Cambridge when she was seventeen. She took a Double First and then a PhD based in Cardiff. My mother always criticised my school reports, said I was stupid and an embarrassment to the family. She wished she'd never had me, she said.'

I could see his hands shaking. 'But you aren't cruel or nasty. I can tell, reporter's instinct. Does your sister hate her too?'

'They haven't spoken in years.'

'Might Louisa have any idea of what was frightening your mother? I have to say, Agnes never struck me as a woman to be frightened by anything.'

He grins, for the first time. 'No idea,' he replies. 'I have to be going now. Should I tell the police I think someone's following me?'

I think for a moment. 'I'm meeting a police officer tonight. Do you want me to discuss it? Your call.'

He nods. 'I'm OK with that. Can I call you?'

'Any time. You can always leave a message at The Sentinel office. They'll let me know' I say.

He stands and walks away, brushing hair out of his eyes. There is so much more I want to ask him, but his mother hasn't been buried yet. I'll have to wait. No wait, just one thing.

'David,' I call out and he looks back. 'Do you think your sister might be willing to talk to me?' He stops, considers. 'She might,'

'Could you give her my number. Tell her I'm willing to go up to Oxford, but only if she's willing. She should call me.'

Once he is out of sight I order an Uber. Back at home, I write up the notes of the meeting and convo with

David, then I wait for Hayden, who already has background information. My gut is telling me that Agnes Dole Hunter has a secret history integral to her death, that needs to come out.

4

Hayden arrives dead on six. I can see her through the glass, bouncing on her toes, waiting for me to open the door. She rushes in and I show her into my "investigation room". She stares at the white board for a while, then reads my notes, all without speaking. When we met in the pub she had been seated. Now she's standing I see she's about five feet eight, or one metre seventy-two if you're born after nineteen seventy. Her hair is loose again. She brings an elastic band out of her parka pocket and pulls the hair falling over her eyes and impairing her direct line of sight back into an untidy ponytail. Underneath the parka she's dressed in scruffy jeans and an old t-shirt. Even for CID I think this might be a tad too casual. She sees me looking.

'I've been on street surveillance,' she says. 'We're trying to catch a gang of teenagers, three of them, who've been robbing old ladies around the back streets of the town centre. One really nasty incident earlier today. The woman tried to chase them and fell and hit her head on the curb. She has a brain haemorrhage. She's in hospital and it's not looking good.'

'How many of them?' I ask.

'Robberies or old ladies?'

'Robberies.'

'Six robberies so far, so six old ladies. Always older women. Nasty little shits. We'll get them,' she says in a voice of quiet but absolute, non-negotiable confidence. 'They'll get too cocky. Is your paper covering the story?'

'Yes, The Sentinel is covering it. Not me, though. What about my board and my notes?' I say. 'What have I missed?'

She turns her back to the table and leans on it with her hands back, palms down. 'I have more. I was bored when the rest of the team was out questioning all the wrong people, so I did some deeper searching on our databases.'

'Why didn't your Inspector try harder?' I ask.

'Because he was looking to confirm suicide. That's the outcome *they* wanted.' She emphasises *they*, jerking her head up.

'They?'

'You know who I mean,' she says, staring ahead. 'Agnes was a bloody nuisance to the police, a dangerous interloper to the Council and a virago to everyone else, pushy and threatening. She was hated and feared in equal measure. Which made me think, after I saw that letter in Morgan's drawer, what was it that Agnes didn't want anyone to find out? Everyone has a skeleton in their closet. So, I dug.'

'What did you find?' I ask.

Before she answers, the doorbell rings. Muttering an oath I would never have dared to use in front of Nia, I exit the room, hurry down the corridor and fling open the door, ready to tell whoever it is to piss off. It's Gareth, out of uniform and with a large bag of steaming Chinese takeaway.

'I swapped a couple of hours with Billy Davies. Thought we might need this,' he says in his usual grumpy tone, raising the bag, walking past me and into the dining-now-investigation room, where he stops and stares at the wall and table.

'We'll have to eat in the kitchen. Let's go.' He already knows where everything is so I leave him to set us up.

'What have I missed?'

'Let's eat, then I'll catch you up on my day. I've made notes.'

'I'll read the notes later,' he says through a mouthful of sweet and sour chicken balls and rice. 'I have a couple of questions. Hayden, what did you find out during your clandestine searching?' 'I was about to tell Trevor. Some family stuff,' Hayden replies. 'Agnes Dole was born on the tenth of September 1973, to Hannah Dole of Porter Street, Whitchurch.

'No father named. She was christened on twentieth of September in Whitchurch, Church of England. Her godparents were Hannah's sister, Gwen and – this is the interesting one – a man called John Harries, Gwen's husband, a policeman. Almost as soon as the ceremony was over, Hannah travelled to London and lived with relatives, her brother and his wife, David and Susan Dole – living in Hackney. I don't think it can have been a happy household, because within a year Hannah had become a drug addict. She has a record as long as your arm of drug abuse related offences, you know, shoplifting, theft, prostitution, threatening behaviour. Eventually it killed her. Agnes was five when her mother died. The brother and his wife didn't keep her after Hannah died. They put Agnes into the care system where she remained until she was shoved out at sixteen. A lot of kids like Agnes end up on the streets at this point, but not her. She went back to Cardiff, found herself somewhere to live in the city with the help of social services and went to college to do her GCSEs then her A levels.'

'Was Hannah known to us here before she had the baby?' Gareth asks. 'What else do you know about her?'

'Very little,' Hayden replied. 'No record whatsoever here in Cardiff. Youngest of three children. Model citizen. She had respectable parents. She went to Cathays Girls School but left when she was sixteen after her GCSEs. She passed five, all at "C" grades. My impression was that her head had more empty spaces than brain cells, but she was an exceptionally beautiful girl. She was an enthusiast about beauty pageants. She became Miss Wales at seventeen. When she was eighteen she married a man called Joshua Spencer. He was an accountant. She tried out for several more beauty pageants but didn't win any more. Last record I have is of her at twenty, coming third in Miss Great Britain.'

'She must have done something in between marrying and having Agnes. That's eight years,' I say. 'She was twenty-eight when Agnes was born. No record at all, for anything? Then next thing we know she's pregnant, has a baby and runs away to London, with the baby but without the husband. She becomes a drug addict and dies at thirty-three. Something must have happened. That's a massive change.'

'Probably a man, or something to do with a man,' Gareth says. 'Perhaps domestic violence?'

'Why a man?' Hayden replies, rather aggressively in my opinion.

'Could have been a woman,' I say. 'Does it matter?'

'These days no it doesn't, at least not to broadminded sensible people. But back in the nineteen seventies, well, you know. It was illegal.'

Gareth glares at her. 'That was for men; it was never illegal for women. I don't care which side you bat for, and I didn't back then either and I wouldn't have arrested anyone for just being what they were meant to be.'

'You weren't on the force in '73 Gar,' I say.

He has red spots on his cheeks, which is not unusual for Gareth. He's known as grumpy Gareth and everyone keeps on the right side of him, because of his temper. I'm one of the few people who know him well enough to understand why he snaps so easily. It's lifelong disappointment, to the point now where he's given up on the career that once both excited and drove him and is serving out his time until he can get his pension, six months from now.

'Not CID material', they said each time. Bollocks, I say. Gareth's a solid man, clever and thoughtful. He's a big bloke, a fraction over six feet with a head of thick silver hair. He has two faces.

The face itself is long and even, with big blue eyes, and a wide smile; the sort of copper the public automatically trusts.

This is his public face. The professional face never knowingly smiles. That's grumpy Gareth, who has little respect for senior police authority. On the whole his colleagues and subordinates are fond of him, but careful to keep on his good side. At fifty-six he still goes to the gym and runs at weekends with his girlfriend Tracey, twenty years his junior and a fitness fanatic. I wouldn't like to take him on in a fight. Then again, I'm five-foot eight of wobbling flab with a dodgy hip, a big bum and a receding hairline. And I wear a scruffy mac like Columbo.

'Let's get back to the matter in hand,' I say. 'Hayden, anything else from your databases?'

'No, nothing else.'

'What about the car?' Gareth asks her.

'That was one of my questions Gar,' I say.

'That's an interesting one. She drove straight down to the Bay, parked in her usual space. She had pre-booked an Uber to take her straight back to Cathays, where she arrived at 7.55am. She told the driver she'd book when she was ready to come back.'

'Did he see anyone waiting for her?'

'No, but as he was waiting to turn around, he saw her in his rear-view mirror. She walked up the path to a junction, looked both ways, then went left. That's when he lost sight of her.'

'Remind me Gar,' I say, 'what time was the sound of a shot heard?'

'Around eight fifteen. The dog walker found her at eight twenty. She called 999. We arrived at eight thirty. I called you at eight forty-five, after I'd called CID.' He didn't look at Hayden as he confirmed this last part. 'There was nothing significant from the dog walker. She had come in from a different entrance.'

'Apart from the gun, was there any other clue Hayden?'

She pauses for a moment. I sense something coming. Then she shook her head. 'The gun was lying next to the body, on the right-hand side. Agnes was right-handed, according to her husband. The only other thing in the close vicinity was a glove. An old looking leather glove. We took it, checked it for fingerprints and DNA. There were none, of either.'

'Do you mean you didn't get a hit on either or there was nothing to test or check?'

'That's what first made me suspicious, when I heard,' Gareth said. 'If it was just a lost glove, there should have been some of both, but it did seem old, so DNA might just have degraded.'

I sit back. I've finished my sesame beef.

'There's always something left behind when a murder's been committed,' Hayden says. 'But the Inspector decided it was just an old, degraded glove that someone probably dropped. I didn't agree as it was inside the grave area, and it wasn't dirty, in fact it was pristine clean, despite its age. I didn't agree with the Inspector's decision to ignore it but got told to just stick to my research and let the people who know what they're doing get on with deciding what's important and what's not.' She bristles, and she's right to do so.

I ask, 'Was it right or left-handed and where exactly was it?'

'It was wedged behind the cross that stands behind the flat stone. Right-handed.'

'So, inside the iron railings surrounding the grave?'

'Exactly!' she says and plays a drumroll on the table with her fingers. 'How did it get inside the railings?'

'What about shoe marks?' I ask.

'Strangely, none, not even Agnes's. She was wearing flat pumps, size six. She should have flattened the grass. But there was no sign of a shoe print.'

'What do you think about that?' I ask.

'I think, Trevor, that someone took great care to remove any potential clue to their own presence and in doing so, took Agnes's too. That's all I have.'

'It's why I called you that morning, Trev,' Gareth says. 'I just didn't like the look of the thing. To me it looked posed.'

'And?'

He grinned. 'Something in the deepest valley of my unconscious memory is trying to take me to a different story, I think about a glove, but I can't get it to come out.'

'It will,' I say. 'Best leave it to work its way out on its own. Now, are we all agreed that Agnes Hunter did not kill herself?'

They both nod.

'She told the Uber driver she'd book a return when she was ready,' Gareth says. 'Put that on your board.'

'Good, so, what do we do next? We might get something about Agnes's past from her daughter in Oxford and from the relations in London. I'd like to visit the daughter in Oxford,' Hayden says.

'I can do some research on the relatives in London. And on the policeman John Harries. He interests me,' I say.

'Leave that one to me,' Gareth replies. 'I don't know him, he may be retired, but I can ask discreet questions in ways you can't. And don't go looking him up on the police database Hayden. It'll push up a red flag somewhere and you don't want anyone coming to ask questions. Not yet.'

'Two more things,' I say, turning to Hayden. 'Agnes was getting threatening letters that talked about her family. Did you know that? Was there any reference to them in the file Harry Morgan took from Reg Hunter?'

She sits bolt upright in her chair. 'No, we didn't. There was only that one letter I told you about, threatening to expose Agnes for something or other. How do you know about other letters?'

'I went to visit Reginald Hunter this afternoon. He wouldn't speak to me, threw me off his doorstep, in fact. As I was leaving, the son, David, arrived home. We spoke. He told me. And he thinks someone's been following him.'

'Does he know who?' Gareth asks.

'No, it's more of a feeling he has. I asked him if he would speak to his sister Louisa for me, see if she'll speak to me about her mother. I said I'd go up to Oxford. I thought she was a student, but it turns out she's a professor. Fine if you go instead Hayden, once the contact's been made.'

'Does the lad know anything more about the letters?' Hayden asks, 'like how many, how often, did they come by regular post?'

'I don't think so,' I reply.

Hayden huffs, sits back, arms folded.

'Dilemma for you' I say.

She glares at me. 'If I tell the boss he'll want to know how I found out. If I tell him the boy told you, he'll have you in for approaching a minor without parental permission, or he'll find some other excuse. Then he'll want to know what I was doing talking about the case to you, and that might involve Gareth, which will give him the opportunity he needs to suspend and probably fire me. Gareth could get suspended too, and potentially get fired, which would mean he'd lose his pension.'

We all three sit back, thinking. Hayden's phone rings. She ignores it. It rings again. She takes a quick glance, frowns and answers. 'Boss?' She listens, her eyes widening, putting a finger to her lips. 'Right away boss,' she says, ends the call and stands. 'An anonymous call came in, giving the name of a boy not involved in the thefts from the older women, but the caller says this boy knows who the culprits are. He's being brought in for questioning.' She shakes her head. 'It's David Hunter. I have to go.'

5

Hayden rushes out before I can speak to her. I run into the hallway and hear a mumbled 'call you later', before the front door slams. Gareth is standing in the open kitchen door.

'Am I in trouble?' I ask.

'Depends on what she tells the boss,' he replies, frowning.

'When was the attack on the woman who's in hospital?' I ask.

'Around two this afternoon.'

'Then it wasn't David Hunter. He was talking to me around that time.'

'It's not about him being involved, it's about his knowing who they are.'

'If he does know he'll tell Harry Morgan, and you'll be called in to confirm you met with him yesterday, if he mentions it. That's where you might get into trouble. If there's any suggestion he told you, Harry Morgan will have you for it.'

'He didn't say anything to me about it.'

We both sit back at the kitchen table, and I get up again to clear up the detritus of our takeaway. I stop for a moment. 'I think Hayden should tell him everything, except our plans. Depends on what he wants to do,' I say over my shoulder as I tip everything, food and cartons, into the bin. 'If he thinks it's still suicide then we should carry on.' I throw the cutlery into the dishwasher and sit again, facing Gareth. 'But if he thinks it might be something else, then we'll have to back off. How well do you know him these days, Gar?'

'Inspector Harry Morgan – you saw him on the stand at the inquest. He's still a lazy bully, never changed from when we knew him back in the day. Hayden can keep herself out of trouble if she's wily with what she says and what she leaves out. She can read him like a book. We'll have to wait for her to come back.'

He's right. We can only wait. 'OK, let's watch some telly.'

'Fine with me, so long as it's not a replay of that bloody match last Saturday.'

**

Hayden arrives back just before ten. Gareth is asleep. She grins as I shake him and he jumps up, with that puzzled expression of being woken suddenly from a deep sleep with no idea where you are.

'Hayden's back,' I say. I turn to her. 'Well?'

'You're wanted at the station tomorrow morning at nine sharp to give a statement to support David's story of talking to you when the attack took place yesterday, just to be certain David wasn't one of them. Other than that, Inspector Morgan lost interest, as soon as David insisted he had no idea who the three boys are. He was adamant he knows nothing about any of it and couldn't say why anyone would have said he would know. Morgan's moved onto the woman who fell and hit her head. Her name is Maureen Henslow. She died at five today.'

'Did you tell him about the letters, and someone following David?'

'Of course,' she says, leaning against the wall. 'I had to. He demanded to know how I knew. I said he left the file on his desk and I saw it. It was a real face-off. But in the end, he backed off. I don't know what he's done with the rest of the papers in that file, and I'll take a bet he destroyed the letter to Agnes, and he definitely doesn't want it known that he had it in the first place, if he can avoid it. He dismissed a stalker as David's imagination, never even asked me how I knew, but he's suspicious of me, so I'll have to take even more care. Now for the good bit. David's father was with him, and he said the letters weren't for Agnes, but for him. He did say he'd given the file to Morgan, though, and confirmed David's story about the letter the day before Agnes died.' She pauses for a moment. 'Can we go into the kitchen and make a brew? I'm parched.'

As the kettle boils, I say, 'Did you suggest to Morgan that there might be a connection between the stalker and Agnes Hunter's death?'

'Of course I did. I had to cover my own ass. He ripped me off, told me to leave it alone. It would mean another bloody murder incident room. I said I still had doubts. He said I should keep them to myself. If we have to investigate this too, there'll be no more coppers left on the streets. I said I'd like to do a bit more checking. He said "whatever", but my primary focus is on the street gang and I'm back on surveillance first thing tomorrow and all day, so I can't do much on checking the databases until tomorrow evening.' I hand over her tea, she takes it from me without looking up and mutters 'thanks' but I sense her focus is elsewhere.

'What else?' I ask.

She smiles. 'Perceptive bugger, aren't you.'

I smile back. 'What else happened in that interview Hayden?'

She raises the cup to her lips but doesn't drink. 'David's father. He was lying about the letters. I don't think they were for him. He said they were probably from some disgruntled employee that he'd had to fire, but the signs were there. He was lying.'

'How did Mr Hunter behave?' I ask.

'He was angry. I suspect as soon as he gets home, he'll be giving his son the third degree about exactly when and what you discussed with him. The boy defended you, Trev, said he'd approached you and asked to talk to you.'

'It was sort of fifty-fifty. Anyway, I'll be there in the morning at Cardiff Police Station. Who's likely to take my statement?' I ask. 'Will Harry Morgan be there?'

'It'll be a sergeant from the case squad and no, Morgan won't be there. He'll be in a strategic gathering with the Deputy Chief Constable about getting young hooligans off the streets.'

I breathe a sigh of relief. 'Once I'm done, I'm going back up to Lisvane to have another go at Reginald Hunter. Now his son's off the hook he owes me a favour. Let's see if he'll let me in this time. Right, I'm off to bed. I'll see you both tomorrow night. See yourselves out.'

I hear them both leave ten minutes later. As soon as I'm sure they've gone, I go back downstairs and clear up. I go to sit in the office room and stare at the board. I'm thinking about Reginald Hunter and the right questions to ask, once I get into the house.

**

I am awake at seven the following morning. I dress up in my best suit, which is tight around my waist. I last wore it to Nia's funeral. It must have shrunk at the dry cleaners. I decide to walk instead of taking the bus, help the trousers to stretch back out to a better fit. It's a sharply cold but bright morning, mac and scarf weather despite being almost May already. I can hear the gulls screaming above the roar of the tail end of the rush hour traffic. I think I can smell the occasional whiff of the sea on the sharp breeze that whips in from Cardiff Bay. The castle looks fine this morning, standing proud on its ancient mound. I love this city.

Sergeant Rhod Thomas is waiting for me. He doesn't look more than twenty. Policemen are definitely getting younger.

'Odd one, that, wasn't it?' he says as I finally sign my statement.

'Is there anyone in this station who believes Agnes Hunter shot herself?'

'The boss,' he replies. 'Good luck.' He gives me a wink and I leave.

Back outside the station I book an Uber. This one arrives in five minutes. I tell the driver to take me up to the address in Lisvane. The traffic through the city and out into the countryside has subsided so it takes less than twenty minutes to reach the Hunter house. On the way we drive past Cathays cemetery, which is less than half way to the house and only a third of the way down to the Bay and I think again as we pass one of its entrances how odd it was that Agnes drove all the way to the Bay then took the Uber back here.

The driver drops me at the gate and zooms off. Damn! This time the gate is locked. I hit the entry buzzer, aware that there's also a camera, so I can't pretend to be the postman. I'm in luck. David Hunter answers. He lets me in and is waiting at the front door. I just manage to get a foot inside when Reginald Hunter comes out of a door at the end of the hall.

'Get out!'

'Too late Mr Hunter. I'm in.'

He comes charging down the corridor, red faced and fists clenched. Before he can reach me, David stands in front of me.

'Stop it dad,' the boy says in firm voice. 'If it wasn't for Trevor I might still be at the nick.'

Time stops for a few seconds as I prepare myself for the inevitable pushing aside of the boy and the punch. It doesn't happen. Reginald Hunter has stopped, sagged, almost fallen. I'm not sure if he had a change of mind or just tripped, as David is holding his arm. Father and son stare at each other for a long minute, then Hunter says, 'You'd better come in.' He turns, opens a door to our right and leads me into the living room. It's a long room with windows at the front and back, the latter being French windows leading onto a patio, with a view of a well-kept garden. Hunter points to an armchair for me and David sits next to him on the settee.

'I am grateful to you,' he begins stiffly, clasping his hands on his tightly held knees. 'You made sure that whoever has been doing this to us didn't succeed this time.' He falls back on the settee.

My reporter's senses are on steroids, '*doing this to us*', and '*this time*'?

'Do you want to explain to me?' I ask in a quiet voice.

Reginald nods. I get out my notebook.

'No notes.' He says. 'This is a private family story.'

I shake my head. 'Sorry Mr Hunter. Your wife died, in my opinion and I think in yours, in suspicious circumstances. If that's true and it can be proved, it will become public. There's nothing you can do to prevent that.'

'I want to do my best to protect my wife's good name.'

I sigh. 'Look, Mr Hunter—' He interrupts me with 'Call me Reg, please.'

'OK, Reg, the only way we can go forward and find out the facts around Agnes's death is by telling the truth and I'm going to start here and now. Sometimes, the truth hurts.

Reg, your wife didn't have a good name. She had a terrible reputation; she was hated and feared in equal measure.'

The man leans forward and puts his head in his hands. After a few minutes of awkward silence he looks up at me. He is crying, his eyes red and swollen.

'She wasn't always like this, like she's been over the past five years. She enjoyed politics, and yes, she was ambitious, but she had kindness in her too.' He turns to his son, who nods. But she changed, suddenly. She found out something about her family's past. The woman you know of, as a spiteful, nasty, vindictive virago, is not the woman I married.'

I think quickly. 'Reg, I can't and won't make promises about privacy but, depending on your story, I might be able to not make it a public scandal. Will you tell me your story?'

'Yes,' he says. 'I'll tell you the truth.'

6

David, having been sent out to make coffee for us, gives me the opportunity to look around the perfectly groomed, sterile living room with not a single family photo of any generations of Hunters, arrives back with three exceptionally fine china mugs, a cafetiere of coffee, a jug of milk and sugar in a bowl. I pour myself a mug, milk, no sugar, sip – it's excellent bespoke coffee – and put the cup back on the small mat that has been put out to prevent drips from the mug. The boy goes to sit next to his father, but Reg Hunter puts up his hand.

David is having none of it. 'I'm seventeen next week. I'm going to hear this.' He sits upright on the settee and pushes back the lick of long hair out of his eyes in an unconscious gesture.

Reg sighs, then begins. 'I met Agnes when she was nineteen, at University in Cardiff. We had a couple of dates. I didn't exactly warm to her right away, but she could be funny. She liked rugby so I bought tickets for games at the Arms Park, that kind of thing. I'm not sure how it happened, but we fell into a pattern of being friends, spending time together, you know. I never loved her, but I liked her. It was the same for her. I proposed when we were twenty-one. She accepted. It was convenient and lazy, and a big mistake, which we both knew, but the deed was done and neither of us would admit it wasn't really working, on any level, you… get what I mean?'

I nod. His cheeks are burning, his hands twisting together in his lap. No need to go into detail in front of his son.

'Louisa arrived quickly. Agnes wasn't cut out to be a mother, because of her own experiences.'

'I understand,' I say.

'I don't,' David says. 'Please explain.'

Reg turns away from both of us but carries on. 'Your mother was born in Cardiff but she actually began life with only her mother, whose name was Hannah, who moved them both to London when Agnes was about three weeks old, to live with her brother and his wife, who didn't want either of them and made that clear but let them stay there. Your grandmother soon turned to drugs, leaving your mother with her brother and sister-in-law for longer and longer periods of time. Eventually her mother walked out one day and never came back. Turns out she died from a heroin overdose. The brother, David Dole, called in social services and Agnes was taken away and put into the system. She was five and what they called a "difficult" child. She went through a series of children's homes and foster parents; all of the foster families returned her. At sixteen she was let out into the world.' He stops and coughs. 'Agnes was a clever girl. She got herself into a hostel, went to college, achieved brilliant results and got a place in Cardiff University to study accountancy.'

'Why Cardiff?' David asks.

'Because, like I said, she was born here,' Reg replies. He turns to me. 'Her first birth name was Veronica: Veronica Agnes Dole. There's no father listed on the birth certificate. To answer your question, she wanted to know who she was.'

'Did she find out?' I ask.

Reg hesitates. 'Not until six months ago, when she discovered who her father was. That's when the anonymous letters started to arrive. She'd found out a lot about Hannah before that, but not about her father.'

I lean forward. 'You know his name?'

'No,' Reg replies. 'She wouldn't tell me. Agnes and I haven't communicated properly for years. By unspoken agreement we went our separate ways. I haven't been a faithful husband, but all she required from me was discretion.' He glances at his son, whose expression is hard to read.

'What happened five years ago? You said she began to change around that time when she was co-opted onto the Parish Council.'

Reg nods. 'She was taking a stand against the Parish Council, over some issue with a pathway. I can't remember what the issue was, but she won, and she liked it. Then a seat became vacant on the Parish Council. No-one stood so she put her name forward and was co-opted on. Within six months she was the Chair. Then a few months later the Cardiff Council elections came around. She decided to stand. The party incumbent was old, pretty useless, and never envisaged being beaten. She ran a campaign against him, and she won again. That's when her personality changed. Or did it?' He looks directly at me, his eyes boring into my face, with a look of fierce intensity. 'It was like something sleeping inside her came alive – like releasing a monster from a deep sleep.' He shakes his head with a look of disgust. 'The more people she upset and hurt, the better. I remember she came home ecstatic one night, about six months ago, when she became Vice Chair of the Finance Committee. I'll never forget the cruelty in her words that night, delighted she had destroyed a man's reputation.'

'What did she say?' I ask.

He takes in a deep breath. 'She said, "Cardiff chased us out. They'll regret that." That's when I guessed it was about some kind of perverted revenge, for her mother, But for what? I think by that time Agnes knew more about her past than she'd ever told me.'

'But she left when she was a baby,' I say. 'Let's say something or someone did force her mother to leave. They'd be incredibly old or dead by now.'

Reg nods, then puts his hands up both sides of his face, rubbing his temples with the tips of his fingers. 'It wasn't rational. I can only think she must have learned something about her childhood, something about her mother maybe, that explains why they left and made her want revenge. Perhaps it was someone on Cardiff Council at the time. I don't know.' He shrugs.

'We'd had arguments over the years, she'd throw back in my face the fact I'd had a happy childhood, and I had no idea what it had been like for her. I stopped speaking to my parents years ago, because she hated them. We became estranged—'

'You told me my grandparents were dead,' David interrupts.

'My mother is still alive,' Reg says, reaching out to put a hand on David's arm. The boy pulls it away. 'Does Louisa know?'

Reg nods. David jumps up and leaves the room.

'Back to Agnes,' I say before I lose my grip on why I'm here. 'Just a few more minutes, please Reg.' I'm rushing my words out, knowing he wants to go to his son. 'You said she found out her father's identity. Was that when the letters started?'

'Yes, just vague stuff at first, but when she became Vice Chair of the Finance Committee, they became more frequent and more vicious and threatening. She stopped letting me see them and burned them all. I lied to the police; said they were for me.'

'And the final one?' I ask. 'What do you know about that?' He is standing now.

'The day before she died, and I don't know what was in it, only that it was about a meeting the following morning. I didn't see the contents, but I caught a few words when she put it on the fire.' We are walking out of the room now. 'I could make out that it said, "you know who I am…" and "you and your family… plus the strange markings". Please leave now. I must speak to my son.'

He is at the foot of the stairs. I stand in front of him, blocking his way. 'Reg, you know whoever sent that last letter killed her. Is there anyone else who might have known about any of these letters? Do you have a housekeeper, or cleaner, or have you spoken to a close friend, someone you trust?'

He hesitates, then nods. 'We do have a cleaner, but we never spoke about anything personal in front of her. And, as I told you, Agnes burned all of the letters. There's just one close friend who knows, someone – a woman – I've been involved with, but I trust her implicitly.' There's a small hint of red in his cheeks. This is probably the woman with whom he's involved, but I can ask more later, if it becomes necessary. For now, back to Agnes.

'Reg, are you really protecting her alleged good name, which you know she didn't have, or was Agnes threatening you and your woman friend. I'm guessing you'd asked Agnes for a divorce?'

His face drains. He leans forward. 'Leave my house now,' he snarls.

'Reg, I couldn't care less about you and this woman, whoever she is. But Agnes didn't commit suicide, no matter what she was being threatened with and who was threatening to expose it. You believe she was murdered. You know that. Why haven't you been back to the police with this information?'

He pushes me out of the way and runs up the stairs.

I let myself out, walk down the path to the gate. Outside I order an Uber and for once don't chat to the driver on my way home. I ask him to drop me at City Hall, then walk the rest of the way. I had agreed with Reg not to take notes. What he doesn't know is that I have an eidetic memory. I can recall every word, but I need to think about more than the words. I need to think about the body language, the expressions, the hints and clues. And I will wait for David Hunter to call me, which I know he will.

7

To say that Hayden is fed up is beyond any boundary of normal, everyday fedupedness. She has been trawling streets in the Splott area of Cardiff for five hours, her feet are killing her and she is soaked from the earlier heavy downpour. Her bobble hat, that Harry Morgan insisted she wear to *"blend in"*, is dripping and her hair is now so wet it's allowing water to run down the back of her neck. At least the shops will be closing soon, so any vulnerable older ladies will be safely tucked up in their houses and she will be able to clock off. Morgan has at least given the evening bingo and pub shift to DC Del Smith, the squad's human cannonball, with twenty-three-inch biceps and a three-inch brain, according to one of Morgan's so-called "funny" jokes, which Del takes good humouredly. He's rarely offended. If the boy gang try anything within Del's reach, they will find themselves running into a human man mountain.

Hayden has had a feeling all day, that she's close to something that's making her draw in her gut. The end of this shift will be a blessing.

She has one more street to take in, either via the end of this long street and around the corner, or through the narrow alleyway she has just reached. *'Go around Hayden'* her sensible brain tells her. *'Just cut through'* her feet say, *'it's only a hundred yards.'* A few seconds' contemplation, a glance around to make sure she isn't being followed, and the feet win. She turns into the alleyway. She picks up speed, trotting. The alleyway is unlit and the walls too high to allow light from the windows of the backs of houses intersecting the high gates and walls of the back gardens, to throw out any illumination to help her. She stumbles, one knee reaches the ground; she picks herself up and pulls in a deep breath then picks up her speed again to a faster trot, glancing around to see if anyone is following her. She can't see the end of the alleyway where she entered and there are no sounds of footsteps, yet she has an uneasy feeling. She checks her pocket for her baton, takes it out of the inside pocket of her coat, then stops. There is a sliver of light from a broken plank in a gate she has just passed, and she sees a fleeting shadow. She stops, looks around again. A cat appears, runs across the alleyway and jumps up onto the high wall. Hayden grins as her heartbeat slows down. She turns to walk again. As she looks up towards the end of the alleyway, now in sight, she just has time to see something large, square edged and dark, heading towards her at great speed. A terrible pain in her head, then – nothing.

**

After my journey back to the city centre, I am finishing my lunch in my favourite café, when my phone rings. It's David Hunter.

'Trevor, can we meet?'

'Of course David. Does your father know you want to meet me?'

'Yes,' he says. I catch the reluctance in his voice.

'Good,' I reply, 'best there's no secrets. Where? I'd offer you lunch but I've just finished mine.'

'How about the Central Library? I have to go there to research a project for one of my A levels. They have a small seating area near the entrance.'

I glance at my watch. 'It will take me twenty minutes to walk there. How about we meet at two.' The boy agrees and the call ends.

When I reach the library in the centre of the city – a beautiful, modern tall building in an open square – I see him waiting outside, hovering from foot to foot. Why do teenage boys always hunch their shoulders? My reason is deterioration towards old age, but I guess his will straighten up once puberty has moved onto another victim and he develops confidence, although some never do.

We nod in greeting, enter the library and head to the seating area on the ground floor. We're in luck, it's almost empty.

I take off my raincoat. David wraps his tighter around his twig-like body.

'Thanks for coming,' he says from beneath the lick of hair, his eyes on the floor.

'What is it you want to tell me David?'

'My dad told me mum's problems stem from discovering her father's name. He did see some of the letters, before she burned them. The one naming her father came a couple of weeks before she died, although he thinks she already knew. He said it was terrifying. It was made up of letters cut out of newspapers, with words like "liar", and "monster" and "murderer" scribbled all over the rest of the page, with numbers and pictures of demons. He says it was from someone completely mad, more than mad; someone psychotic.'

He has rushed this out in one go. Now he scoops in a long breath. I wait. He lifts his head up. 'He says we're in danger from this person, that's me and Louisa. I called her to tell her. She's coming down to Cardiff tonight. She wants to meet you tomorrow, down at the Bay.'

'Why didn't he go to the police with all of this?' I ask. 'This is serious. He should have told them.'

'He did.'

'What!' I shout, loudly enough for the people on the opposite side of the open area to look up. 'Who did he tell?'

'An inspector, called Harry Morgan. But he said it was just some loony constituent and as my mother had burned the notes, there was nothing the police could do. He said that lots of politicians get death threats and hate notes these days, but nothing ever comes of them.'

I shake my head in disbelief. Inspector Harry Morgan: a man who's never met a corner he couldn't cut. 'Did he do anything at all?'

Now it was David's turn to shake his head. 'He asked dad who he thought it might have been, but dad couldn't give him names. Dad offered to go through mum's correspondence file, but Morgan took the file himself, said he would check through it and get back to dad.'

'And did he?' I know the answer before I ask the question.

'No, not before the inquest.'

I thought for a moment. 'Does your father want me to follow up with Morgan?'

'No.' David's answer was fast and emphatic. 'But he is willing to give you the name of my mother's father. He said to tell you that he's ok with you investigating but it has to be below the radar.'

Damn! I knew Reg Hunter was holding back. I think about this. 'I'll have to tell my editor, but she'll keep it quiet until I know more. What was the name?'

'It was Joshua Spencer.'

'I know that name,' I say. 'He was Hannah Dole's husband, which makes sense. I'll check it out.' I pause. 'David, I don't want you or your sister to be involved in this. How can I contact your father if I need more information, or if I need to let him know about anything I find out?'

He gives me his father's number. 'I have to go now. I really do have some research to do here.' He smiles and stands up, slinging his satchel over his shoulder. 'Thanks, Trevor.' He slouches off towards the stairs to the research room on the upper floor.

I make my way slowly home, to my terraced street behind the old Cardiff Infirmary. The rain has stopped but the wind is biting. By the time I get home I can't feel my nose. Gareth and Hayden should be here around six and I'm hoping both have news. I decide I will cook. No more takeaway. I'll do a spag bol, one recipe I learned from Nia. It's a long time since I cooked for anyone.

It's just about ready by six. I pop garlic bread in the oven and boil the kettle ready to cook the spaghetti. By six fifteen I'm tutting a bit. By six thirty I turn everything off. By seven I'm worried and pace back and forth to the window in the front lounge looking up and down the street. By seven thirty I know something is seriously wrong and am about to try Gareth's number for the umpteenth time, when there's a knock, or rather a thunderous banging on the door. It's Gareth. His face is red and he's panting.

'Trev, someone's hit Hayden over the head with a plank of wood. She's been taken to A&E.'

I don't say anything. I grab my mac and run to his car, and we speed off through Cardiff, blue lights flashing and siren blaring.

We arrive at the A&E department and jump out of the car. Inside it's chaos, like most NHS emergency departments, but we find a nurse who says Hayden's been taken up to the High Dependency Unit. We head up there, to find Harry Morgan and his crew in the waiting room off the corridor outside the entrance to the HD Unit. As we push through the doors, I catch what Morgan's saying to the crowd around him.

'She'll be all right, just a massive headache. What the hell she was doing in that passageway God only fucking knows.'

'You bastard,' I say, below my breath, so no-one else can hear. 'I know who you are, Harry Morgan. From now on, you start looking over your shoulder.'

Two of his team move forward. 'This isn't for the press,' says DS Ahmed. 'How did you find out?'

'Not much happens in this city without my finding out.' I want to add *'usually before you'*, but I decide I've antagonised Harry Morgan enough for one day. 'Do you have a comment, Inspector Morgan?'

'Yeh. Piss off.'

He's prevented from adding more by the arrival of a doctor.

'We'll be keeping her for a couple of days. We're going to sedate her for now, you can speak to her officially tomorrow.' He looks around. 'Which one of you is Sergeant Roberts?'

'That's me,' Gareth replies.

'I'll talk to her,' Morgan says. 'I'm her boss.' The doctor shakes his head. 'She's asked specifically for Sergeant Gareth Roberts.'

Before Morgan can object, Gareth, who looks puzzled, is taken away by the doctor.

'You,' Harry Morgan shouts at me, 'get out of here.'

I leave the waiting room but remain in the corridor outside.

Meanwhile, the doctor leads Gareth to a room where Hayden is lying. He returns without the doctor ten minutes later.

'Well?' Harry Morgan asks. 'What did she say?'

'Very little, Sir. She's sedated, but she said to tell you she thinks it was a woman.'

Harry Morgan makes a humph of disgust. 'Did she get a good look at this woman?'

'No Sir.'

'That's not much use is it. When will she be able to tell us more?'

The doctor returns and takes Gareth aside. 'She'll be all right, she's been lucky, there's no fracture but there's some swelling on her brain, so we'll keep her sedated for now, then slowly reduce the sedation. She'll need a couple of weeks off work. I take it you're her boss?'

'No,' Gareth says. 'I'm a colleague. I'll let our other colleagues know so they can start an investigation. Where was she found?'

'I don't know. That information would have been given in A&E by the ambulance paramedics.'

The doctor nods and leaves the department. Gareth returns to the waiting detectives. 'She's going to be OK,' he says, 'but she'll stay sedated for the time being.'

Morgan grunts. 'You should have told him to speak to me. I'm in charge here. Right, nothing we can do tonight. Go home, all of you.'

Del the man mountain is one of them. 'But boss, shouldn't we start—'

'I said go home,' Morgan barks, as the entrance doors swing open again and a uniformed man walks in. All present, including Gareth, stand to attention. He walks straight to Morgan, stares at him with intense gimlet eyes.

'Inspector Morgan, how is DS Wilkins?'

Morgan's back is rigidly straight in front of his Chief Superintendent. 'She's going to be OK, Sir. No skull fracture, just a small wound and a bad headache.'

'Have you spoken to her?'

'Barely Sir, she's sedated.'

'But the CSIs are at the scene with some of your men?'

Morgan blushes. 'Not yet, sir. I'll get on to it right away. Evans, Khan, come with me.'

He leaves, scowling. The others trail out slowly. Del, the man mountain gives me a wink as he passes by, whispering, 'She'll be OK.'

I go back into the waiting room.

The Chief Superintendent nods at Gareth then turns to me. 'Why are you here Trevor? This is police business, nothing to do with the press.'

I hold out a hand. 'Long time no see, Jimmy.'

He stiffens but before he can try to throw me out, I say, 'Hayden is a friend of the family, Nia's family, that is.' Small lie. Nia wouldn't mind.

'This attack is off the record Trevor. That's an order.'

'For now,' I say, 'although there was another reporter in A&E who's probably picked it up already. It won't make the morning paper, but it'll be out on the internet already.'

He scowls. 'Sergeant Roberts, what happened?'

'I don't know, Sir,' Gareth replies. 'I heard a call come in and I, um, rushed here. Inspector Morgan will have the details.'

'Only if he's down in A&E now, collaring some doctor or nurse, which he should have organised as soon as he got here,' I mutter under my breath.

'Sergeant, please go down to A&E and ask Inspector Morgan to come to my office at seven tomorrow morning. Tell him I need full details to prepare for a press briefing.' He turns to me. 'That's assuming he can find a doctor or nurse in A&E to collar.' He walks out of the HD Unit.

'Nice to see you again, too, Jimmy,' I mutter.

'Come around to mine,' I say to Gareth, once Chief Superintendent James Malcolm is gone. 'I'd made a meal for us. No point letting it go to waste.' Gareth nods and heads off. 'I'll give it five minutes then meet you down in A&E.'

We reach home at nine thirty and warm up the food. Gareth sits silently in the kitchen. When we have eaten – not much, neither of us has an appetite – I tell Gareth I have a lot of news. I go through the meeting with Reginald Hunter and David and then with David this afternoon at the library.

'What time are you meeting with Louisa Hunter tomorrow?'

'I'm not sure yet. She's staying at the family home tonight; first time in years. David's going to call me to say when they're on their way.'

'I'll come with you, I have a day off tomorrow,' Gareth says. 'If this person really is psychologically ill, and is a woman, like Hayden was trying to say, I can hover in the background and look around, see if I can spot anyone looking at you.'

'Fair enough,' I say. 'Presuming this is connected to the Agnes Hunter case. Right now, I can't think who would know that Hayden's involved in our clandestine investigation. Anyway, I'll call the hospital first thing in the morning, to see how she is. Can you give me a lift? David wants to make the meeting as early as possible, so Louisa can be back in Oxford before it gets dark.'

'No problem Trev.' He pauses, sitting back, arms folded for a couple of minutes while I clear up the plates and leftover Bolognese and put it in the fridge, then plates in the dishwasher.

'Joshua Spencer,' he says. His eyebrows crinkle together in the frown that appears when Gareth is thinking and remembering at the same time. 'I know that name, but I can't remember the context.'

'Perhaps you arrested him?'

He shakes his head.

'I was going to ask Hayden to work on the name, but now we're without access to the police database, we'll have to have a go ourselves.'

'Not me,' Gareth says. 'You try. You're better than you admit.'

'If I had a starting point, that would make it easier,' I say.

'Why don't we try just googling him?' Gareth says. 'Let's do it now, see what comes up. It's still early.'

'It's almost eleven,' I protest. 'Alright, just a quick look.'

We go into the dining-now-investigation room and I start up my laptop. I google "Joshua Spencer, Cardiff," and we both sit back in amazement at the list of sites that produce his name. They tell of a suicide in 1973, of a body found on a gravestone in Cathays cemetery, of a manhunt for Spencer's business partner, who turned up dead on a beach in Bognor Regis, and of the total failure of the Cardiff police to find the killer. It is now a cold case.

'Fucking hell,' Gareth says, then points to a particular site. 'Open that one.' It's a bigger article, with a photograph of the gravestone on which Joshua Spencer's body was found, with a gun lying next to his right hand. It is the same gravestone on which Agnes Hunter's body was found six weeks ago.

8

At first, neither of us speaks. We are both stunned. This is no co-incidence and will change the way we approach everything about this investigation. Any previous ideas, assumptions, guesses, whatever, are off the table and we have to re-think where we go next. Something we don't understand – yet – is going on. We continue to stare at the grainy black-and-white photograph. Then, I say the first thing that comes into my head. 'Was Harry Morgan involved in the investigation?'

'How am I supposed to know?' Gareth replies. 'Why are you asking?'

'I don't know. Something about his behaviour is bothering me. Let's leave it here for now. It's late and there's too much to process. You go on home, get some sleep and I'll see you early in the morning. I'm expecting a call from the paper about the press briefing, which won't be until later as the Chief Superintendent is seeing Morgan at seven. That should give us time to get to the hospital – I want to visit Hayden – then down to the Bay, before it starts.' I have another thought. 'Gar, don't pick me up. I'll make my own way to the hospital and down to the Bay. If Hayden's attack was to do with this case and she was being watched, then it's possible we are too. When I hear from David I'll suggest the Sunshine Café on the long pier out towards the barrage. Afterwards, I'll go to the briefing and then we can meet back up here separately. Use the back gate, it's locked, but there's an electronic entry pad. The code is 180456. Here's the key for the kitchen door.'

'Sure you aren't being paranoid?' he says.

'Quite sure. Bugger off now. I'll see you back here as soon as the briefing's over.'

He takes his coat and leaves. I know he will be doing the same as me when he gets home – sitting up and writing a lengthy list of rhetorical questions. Tomorrow we will compare the lists and work out what action we're going to take first. This discovery of the bodies being on the same gravestone has astounded me. There's another agenda at play here. But whose? This is going to be a big case for me and The Sentinel. Big.

**

Having had only three hours sleep, I jump in terror until I realise the jangling noise is the alarm, it's six am and I have to get up.

I'm at the hospital at seven, tentatively entering the main building and looking around at length to check for any random police presence. There is none and on the eighth floor there's a pleasant surprise. Hayden has been moved out of the High Dependency Unit to a side ward. The nurse agrees to give me five minutes, Hayden being a close member of my departed wife's family and without any close family of her own. Hayden is awake, just. She's pale, with two black eyes. 'It's all so hazy,' she says without me asking, 'but I'm sure in the flash of a second before I blacked out, the face I saw was a woman's.'

'Any recognisable characteristics?'

'Not really. Grey hair, so an older woman, crazy eyes. That's it. Sorry Trevor.'

'I have a lot of news, and a name, now. It's Joshua Spencer. He was Agnes Hunter's father. Mean anything to you?'

Hayden nods her head and winces. I grin. 'Big headache. How long are they going to keep you here?'

'They should let me out tomorrow, but they're worried I don't have anyone to be with me for a few days at least. Joshua Spencer was Hannah Dole's husband.'

I make a quick decision. 'How about you come to stay with me? I have a spare bedroom you can use.' She frowns. 'Just for a few days and it has to be better than staying in here.'

Thanks for the offer Trevor. I'll think about it. I couldn't let anyone on the team know.'

'Do give it some thought. I'm going down to the Bay to meet Reg Hunter with his children: both of them.'

Hayden's eyes widen. 'You've been busy. Sorry I never got to do the research. I was going to go back to the office and make a start.' Her eyes moisten.

'Yes, and I made a spag bol, so you missed that too,' I say, wagging a finger at her. 'Gareth ate your portion. After I meet with the Hunters I'm going to the Chief Superintendent's press briefing. You're the star of that show. Then, I'll come back here, see how you're doing.'

She puts out a hand and I take it, give it a quick squeeze. 'See you later.'

**

The cab drops me off as close as he can get to the Welsh Assembly Building, where the Welsh Parliament or Senedd, meets. There's no session today and there's little activity inside the building, as some of the everyday administration work goes on up in North Wales, in Llandudno Junction. The text arrives from David, saying they will meet me at the Sunshine Café at ten. I have an hour and a half, so I decide to take a walk along the barrage trail to where boats can enter and exit from the Severn Estuary.

It's almost the last day of April and the weather has suddenly turned gorgeous, although the usual wind is blowing in off the water, ruffling the sea into small wavelets, agitating the few boats tied up to the wall. I walk slowly along, past the Norwegian Church, breathing in warm air and soaking up the smell of the sea. The estuary reaches the Bristol Channel here, which eventually leads to the Atlantic somewhere near Cornwall. There are many attractions along the way, but I'm too busy thinking. Thinking about Gareth, and about how the conversation will go with the Hunters, thinking about how much danger I might personally be in, if I continue to pursue this story. And about Gareth and Hayden, who are both risking their careers.

The idea that consolidated in the night, as I made my list of rhetorical questions, is that someone is taking revenge. There is no way Agnes Hunter being shot on the same gravestone on which her father was found is a co-incidence. But revenge for what? And by whom? Damn, we need that research. We have to find out about Joshua Spencer, details about his life and death, the kind of stuff that doesn't reach a newspaper obituary. There's a hint in one of the reports that the man's accountancy firm was in trouble. So, it might have been an unhappy client. No, if it were, his suicide would have been the end of it. Agnes would not have been involved. One of my questions is about the timeline, between Joshua Spencer's death and Agnes's birth, assuming she really was his daughter, which is yet to be verified to my satisfaction. She was born on the tenth of September 1973 and christened on the twentieth. She was christened as a Dole, not a Spencer. Sometime shortly afterwards her mother left Cardiff and went to London, posing as a single mother. She must have deliberately removed any mention of Spencer from her life. Why? The newspaper articles didn't give the actual date of Spencer's death. It's going to be imperative to find out everything we can about the life and death of Joshua Spencer.

I have reached the end of the barrage. I glance at my watch. Nine thirty. Time to turn back to meet up with the Hunter family. The Sunshine Café is half way back to the Senedd building, so I have time. I reach the venue before the family, take a table for four outside – it'll be difficult for anyone to overhear us – and take out my notebook and pen. Gareth is already here, sitting three tables away with an unobstructed view of people walking from each direction. He has taken his role to heart with sunglasses and a peaked cap. He is reading a paper and has a coffee on the table. I stop myself smirking.

Five minutes later the Hunter family arrives. I am introduced to Louisa, who is tall, in looks favouring her mother with a short sharp haircut and green eyes. Louisa too has an upright, defensive way of standing, but the hand she reaches out to me, accompanied by a wide, soft smile, is nothing like the way Agnes would have greeted me. We go inside to order drinks.

She cuts to the chase. 'Are we in danger, Mr Gwyn - Jones? I have a young child at home.'

'Honestly, I don't know, but I'm going to err on the side of caution. A policewoman was attacked last night, hit on the head. It turns out her injury isn't as bad as it first looked, it's not life threatening, but she thinks it was a woman who attacked her, not a member of the group of delinquents she'd been looking out for.'

Louisa looks puzzled. 'But the news this morning said she was attacked by a gang of boys the police are trying to find, who've been attacking and robbing old women. The latest one died yesterday.'

I shake my head. 'She was patrolling but it wasn't those boys did it.'

'How do you know that?'

'I'm a newspaper reporter. I have sources.'

'So why are the police saying it was a gang of boys?'

'I don't know, yet. There's a briefing at midday. I'll be there and I'll find out.'

The barista takes our order, and we go back out into the sunshine. Davd and his father are sitting next to each other, both looking around nervously.

'Don't worry,' I say. 'There's a second pair of eyes on us. Please don't look.' Reg is pale. His hands are twitching. He reaches into the inside pocket of his coat and produces an envelope, which he puts in the centre of the table.

The barista arrives with our drinks. Her pleasantries are met with silence as we stare at the envelope. As soon as she's gone, Reg says, 'There are two items. One was hand delivered by her solicitor last night. It's a letter from Agnes. It's short and to the point. Also in there is a fragment of the letter Agnes received the day before she died. Please read both.'

I pick up the yellow A4 envelope and take the items out. I look first at the burned fragment. I can make out the words "you and your family", surrounded by scribblings of "murderer", etcetera, as David had described, plus what I think may be quotations from the Bible, numbers and demon drawings. 'This person is psychotic,' I say. And dangerous.' They all nod their heads. I turn to the letter. He's right about the short and pointed.

"Reg, something has come out of my past, that frightens me. My father, Joshua Spencer, was a bad man, bad but not so terrible. He died violently for reasons the police never discovered. My mother was threatened and ran away. I am the next target. After me, one or both of our children. I am going to meet the person who has been stalking me and sending me increasingly violent letters. If I am right and this is some kind of vendetta, I may not come home today. I am going to deposit this letter with my solicitor with specific instructions. Please find

out who is carrying this out and why. The police will not help you. I know we never loved each other, but please protect our children. Agnes."

I read it through twice, then look again at the fragment of ranting. 'You must take this to the police,' I say. 'It should convince them, even Inspector Morgan, that Agnes's death wasn't suicide.'

'I'd rather hear what you find out first,' Reg says. 'I don't trust that man. Can we give it a couple of days?'

I shake my head. 'It might take longer than that.'

'We'll risk it,' Louisa says. I look at the family and decide to tell them what started me on this journey.

'After the inquest, as I was talking to a sergeant I know, a crowd of people passed me. In a second of time, no more, I heard a whisper, that said "justice, again". The "*justice*" is subjective. The "*again*" is not. My colleague and I decided to take a further look. When you gave me the name, Joshua Spencer, who I knew only as Hannah Dole's husband, I took a look on the internet. The man committed suicide in 1973, a week before Agnes was born. I assume you looked him up too?'

Reg nods. 'There wasn't much from the newspaper reports at the time. After an initial search, the trail went cold.'

'Did you find the photograph?' I ask.

Reg looks puzzled. 'What photograph?'

'There was a longer piece. You have to go down about four pages into the google search to find it. Reg, Agnes died on the same gravestone as her father, Joshua Spencer. Vendetta, or vengeance, or revenge is what this is about, I'm increasingly convinced. It's not about unpopularity with colleagues, or about being found out for something she did. What we've learned between us confirms the "*again*" that I heard following your wife's inquest.'

They are all dumbstruck.

'I showed the fragment of burned letter to the police,' Reg says eventually. 'Why haven't they done anything?'

'I did wonder at first, if Harry Morgan, the Inspector you spoke to, was involved in the investigation into the death of Joshua Spencer, but he wasn't, he's not old enough. But this time he was under pressure to deliver a result of suicide. I don't know why, but I'll try to find out. In the meantime, you all need to take steps to protect yourselves. Reg, I suggest you drive David to and from school until this is over. Louisa, can you take your family away somewhere?'

Louisa nods. 'I'll tell my husband tonight. His parents live in Cornwall. We can go there. Henry's too young to question why and he loves the beach. How long do you think it will take to find out who's doing this to us?'

I shake my head. 'I hope we can find out quickly. I've been given a week by my editor, who's the only person who knows about this under-the-counter investigation, apart from us. We have something solid to go on now.' I glance at my watch. 'I have to get off to the Chief Superintendent's press briefing, to see what spin they're putting on the attack on the policewoman. Reg, I'll keep in touch, let you know of any progress we make.'

I stand and leave them. As I walk back to the centre of Cardiff, I have time to think about this new piece of information. The indomitable Agnes was frightened that last morning, knowing she might not win this time. The answer lies somewhere in the past. We have to begin with the suicide of Joshua Spencer and why it was never understood. I hope Hayden improves quickly. She's our best bet on accessing the information.

**

On the way back, outside the Senedd, I see Betty, she of the inquest groupies, strolling towards me. I can't avoid her, so I wave to her and she hurries over to speak to me.

'What are you doing here Trevor? Some business in the Chamber?' She looks at me with wide, hopeful eyes, as if expecting me to drop some exclusive political scandal.

'Just out for a stroll and a coffee with friends Betty. Nothing going on today.'

She nods, mouth turning down, then says, 'Look, isn't that Agnes Hunter's husband with his children?' Her eyes are gleaming, must be her gossip radar on high alert.

I glance over. 'So it seems, Betty. They must be enjoying the sunshine too. I must go. I'm attending a press briefing.' I hurry off, as she continues to stand and stare at the Hunters as if they are superstars.

I have to call in at home to change into my best suit and tie. It's only a briefing but I need to look like one of the more respectable members of the press. At the station I show my credentials and am early enough to take a seat in the front row which I know will annoy Harry Morgan. There's a good turnout; TV and radio as well as press from around South Wales.

The Chief Superintendent enters with the press secretary and Harry Morgan, ignoring the flashes from the photographers. Morgan preens in their direction. He thinks he's looking important. He looks like a smug asshole. Chief Superintendent Malcolm succinctly describes the attack on Hayden, says she is doing well. He blames it on the boy gang and hands over to Morgan to say what action is being taken. Morgan describes house-to-house interviews with the residents on both sides of the alleyway, which are ongoing. He asks for anyone with information to come forward and says a special tip line has been set up. *'That'll keep them busy'*. I think.

Question time. A reporter asks if there is a description of the attacker? Morgan answers no, the DS didn't have time to see her assailant. It seems Morgan either hasn't asked her yet, or if he has, Hayden has been economical with the truth. Another question about progress on catching the boy band. Morgan replies that substantial progress has been made – liar, liar, pants on fire – but that older women must still be vigilant. I decide to throw a stick of dynamite into the fire.

'Are you certain the attack on the detective sergeant is connected to the beatings and robberies?' I ask. 'If the DS couldn't make any identification, then it could be something quite different, couldn't it?' All eyes turn to me.

Morgan goes to answer, but the Chief Superintendent gets in first. 'We're concentrating on the group of boys first and foremost,' he says, 'but there's always the possibility it might be unrelated. That's another line of enquiry.' He gives me a hard stare. I'll have to exit quickly when this is done. Jimmy Malcolm isn't a fool, like Morgan. He knows I know something.

As soon as the briefing is over the Chief Superintendent and Morgan are grabbed for TV and radio interviews. Morgan laps it up, but out of the corner of my eye I see Jimmy Malcolm watching me as I scuttle out. I have a feeling he and I will be meeting again… soon.

9

From the police station I head up to the hospital. My head is so full of thoughts, ideas and plans I think it's going to burst.

I'm hoping to be able to have a few words in the HDU area with Hayden, but to my surprise she's now in a general ward, sitting on a bed, and fully dressed, although in the same clothes, which are blood smeared from the wound on her head.

'They say I can go, as long as I have someone with me for a couple of days, so I've decided to take up your offer and damn the consequences, Trevor. Let's get out of here before Harry Morgan arrives. I'll have to tell him what I saw, but I don't trust him, and I want to talk to you first.'

'And I want to talk to you. I have a lot to tell you.'

'You'll have to be patient with me,' she replies. 'My head is still woozy and my brain is slow.' She rises gradually from the bed. 'I have plenty of pain meds and I'm likely to be sleeping a lot. First, can we go to my flat to pick up some clean clothes? I have to get out of this bloody mess.'

I find a wheelchair – there's no chance she can walk downstairs – and we leave. Her flat is down on the Bay, a beautiful two-bedroom apartment overlooking the Channel. She disappears into one of the bedrooms, leaving me in the open plan lounge kitchen where the sun is streaming in. It has what looks like a comfortable balcony but there's no furniture on it. After a few minutes admiring the view, I look around the living room. There's a wall with one of those imitation gas fires, above it a huge TV set. The furniture is all white. It's very smart. On a sideboard is a picture of Hayden and another woman, together, dressed up and looking joyful.

As I'm looking Hayden comes out of the bedroom with a packed bag. 'My wife,' she says. 'She died eighteen months ago; brain tumour.'

'I'm so sorry,' I say. 'What was her name?'

'Angela. She was a doctor at the University Hospital. We have something in common Trevor. We're both mourning a loss. We look at each other directly for barely a second but I see it in her eyes as she does in mine: the devastation of grief, so deep that some days it's paralysing and getting out of bed on those days and functioning as a normal human being is a superhuman act. 'What was your wife's name?' she says in a hushed, gentle tone.

'Nia,' I reply. It's still hard to get the word out. 'She had cancer. We were childhood sweethearts, from school. Married when we were seventeen, didn't quite make the forty years.'

'Ange and I were married for five years. It's still… well, you know what it's like.' She gives her head a quick shake. 'Let's go, then.'

Back at my house Gareth is sitting in the kitchen with the patio doors open, still reading the paper, but has lost the dark glasses and cap. He stands up when Hayden and I reach the kitchen.

'Hayden, I didn't expect to see you.'

'I'm a lot better and avoiding Harry Morgan,' she replies. 'Trevor told me the news on our way back from my flat. It was beyond a shock about Agnes's body being on the same gravestone her father was found on. Sinister, but we need more about Joshua Spencer's death. I'm sorry I can't get into the office for a few days. There might be something on public computer records, if I dig deep enough. Old records are being digitised, but it's more likely to be in paper files.'

'I can take a quick look tomorrow,' Gareth says. 'I might at least be able to find out if the files still exist.'

'Good. I could do with sleeping for a couple of hours,' Hayden replies. 'Then, if we can get together for dinner, we can plan more. Trevor, do you have photos of the fragment and letter Reginald Hunter showed you this morning?'

'Of course. I'll print them out, ready for when you wake up.'

There is no dinner. Hayden's medicine knocks her out and she doesn't wake until the following morning. She arrives in the kitchen at ten thirty, dishevelled and confused.

'You slept longer than you planned. I did look in, but you were out for the count. Breakfast?'

'Just tea and toast please Trevor. What are we going to do today?'

'You'll be mostly sleeping. When you're actually awake, I'll go over again what I learned from the Hunters. How much can you remember of what I told you?'

'Not much,' she admits. 'I'd like to hear it again if you don't mind.'

'Let's sit outside,' I say. 'It's sunny and warm.'

I tell her again as she eats her toast, and I show her a printout of the photo of the letter and fragment. She reads them several times, wincing.

'My vision's off,' she says. I loan her my glasses. 'That's better.' After another read through, she says, 'This is a dangerous person Trevor, a mentally ill psychotic person. Could Agnes have been afraid of this person? If the woman who hit me over the head thinks we're onto her – and I'm going on the supposition it's connected with Agnes's death – we're all at risk.'

'I agree Hayden. I think it's likely it is connected, but I can't think how, except that maybe someone saw us together at the pub and is watching us. Gareth's on an early shift today. He'll be finishing at two and he's coming straight here. For the time being he's coming in through the back gate, so no-one sees him at the front too often.'

She pushes back her hair from her face and closes her eyes.

'Why don't you rest until he gets here,' I say. 'Fingers crossed he's been able to track down the Spencer death investigation files.'

She nods and I leave her to it. I go into the kitchen and phone my editor with the update. She's excited. This would be a great scoop for The Sentinel. She warns me to be careful, not to put myself in any danger, joking that the paper isn't insured if I do anything reckless or stupid. I laugh, but I'm not sure she's kidding.

She's also worried about not revealing the "co-incidence" of the two bodies on the same gravestone. 'This is sensational,' she says. 'But if another paper finds out first, we're screwed. What are the chances Trevor? Could anyone else find out?'

'Unlikely,' I reply, 'fingers crossed. The Sentinel hasn't had a story this big in its existence. To begin with, whoever it might be would also have to be suspicious about Agnes's death being murder, not suicide. The young chap from The Chronicle thought it was weird, but he seemed satisfied with the outcome of the inquest. I've checked his piece and it's short and accepting of the verdict. Look, I'm asking you to take a big chance on me. I just know – reporter's gut – that there's a much bigger story here. If someone else does go to the police with this information, that means it's all they've got. They'd have to chase the history, like I'm doing, and I think we're well ahead there. Of course, the police would set up a Murder Investigation Team and we'd be limited to what we could find out. But I can carry on regardless. I wouldn't necessarily have to share what I dig up about the past beyond Agnes's father. Well, I suppose I would, but only if I'm asked.'

She's thoughtful. 'OK, but you keep in touch with me every day and if you pick up so much as a sniff that anyone else is investigating, we go to press and to the police – in that order.'

I lift up my eyes to the sky, then close them. My nerves will be frayed having to account for everything, every twenty-four hours, but she hasn't stopped me.

Outside, Hayden has fallen asleep again.

Five minutes later, my phone rings. It's Chief Superintendent Malcom's secretary. He wants to see me later this afternoon. Not unexpected. I explain I have a work commitment. She says I don't; the Super has spoken to my editor. I agree to be there at four.

The phone rings again; my editor, of course, who warns me to be careful about what I disclose. As if I don't know. So far there's just Agnes's letter to her husband that should be handed over, but it's Reg's decision to withhold it for a few more days.

Gareth arrives at two thirty. I wake Hayden up.

'Good news or bad?' I ask him when we're settled with tea and sandwiches.

'Both,' he replies. 'I couldn't trace the files. They've been archived, so I put in a request, but the clerk couldn't find them. But then, during my canteen break I was talking to Dicky Pruitt, don't know if you remember him Trev, he's one of the desk sergeants. I asked if he's heard the name Joshua Spencer, in connection with an old crime back in the seventies. Dicky isn't one to enquire why I was asking. He hadn't heard the name, but he said if I wanted to know about old crimes I should contact a man called Norman Price. Norman's retired now, in his eighties. Dicky meets him occasionally for a pint. Norman's a bit eccentric, like, but Dicky told me Norman is writing a book about the most notorious unsolved crimes in Cardiff. It's worth asking him if he knows anything about the Spencer death. He said to be careful, Norman is a talker and prone to having an inventive memory when it comes to "*the old days*", so not to tell him too much local gossip, because the man can't keep anything to himself.'

'Worth a try,' I say. 'How do we find Norman?'

'I have a phone number,' Gareth says. 'You'd better set off to your appointment. I'll ring this man to see if he'll see us and talk to us.'

I hope Norman's "talkativeness" hasn't extended to telling anyone else about the relationship between Agnes Hunter and Joshua Spencer.

**

I reluctantly set off and by four I'm sitting waiting outside the Chief Superintendent's office. He keeps me waiting. The secretary apologises, says he's been detained in another meeting. She says this with no sincerity whatsoever. The man arrives at four twenty, apologises and invites me in. His desk and chair are impressive. I sit in front of him. The visitor chair is lower than his. What a cliché, especially given how we know each other.

'Trevor, why did you suggest the attack on DS Wilkins might have had another reason, other than her pursuit of the teenage gang?'

No small talk, then. 'I did no such thing Jimmy. She was patrolling at the time, not pursuing. There was no suggestion of the boys being in the same area, there had been a report of a group of three boys on the other side of the city a couple of hours earlier. I just put forward an alternative thought. And my being here tells me you think I might be right.'

'What do you know?' he asks, leaning forward.

'About the boys and the attacks? Nothing. It was just a suggestion, nothing more.'

'Two days ago you gave an alibi to David Hunter. What do you know about the Hunter family?'

I need to keep as close to the truth as possible. I sit back in my chair, going for a relaxed posture. Unfortunately, the chair is so low I can only see the top of his head so I sit up again. 'I wanted to do a piece on Agnes Hunter, so I approached her husband for information. He didn't want to speak to me and threw me out. On my way down the drive, I met his son. He didn't have much to say either. I gave him my card and asked him to call me if he thought of anything more I should know. The attack that ended in the death of Maureen Henslow was at the same time I ran into David Hunter. I was happy to confirm that. That's all there is to it. If David knows who the boys are, it's up to him to tell you. I promise he hasn't said anything to me.'

I maintain eye contact as he sits back this time, folding his arms and saying nothing. Then he leans forward again and says, 'I don't believe you Trevor.'

'Everything I just told you is true Jimmy. If there's nothing else, I'm leaving.' I stand and walk to the door. As I open it he says, 'If I find out there's more to this, it will go badly for you and your paper.'

I smile and leave. Harry Morgan hasn't reported up the line that Reg has already given him the file of Agnes's papers and letters. I am starting to consider alternative motives for Harry Morgan's behaviour. Is he part of a cover-up, or am I getting paranoid? Jimmy's going to be furious when he finds out, but it's not up to me to tell him, no matter our long-standing relationship. Outside the building I phone my editor and re-assure her. I tell her that anything I find out that might impact the police investigation I will share with them, and that satisfies her.

It's six by the time I get back to the house. Gareth and Hayden are still sitting on the patio, both dozing. Gareth wakes up. 'How did it go?' he asks.

'Fine,' I reply. 'Nothing for you to worry about. He doesn't know Hayden is staying with me nor that you're involved too. You'll have to keep coming and going by the back gate. Any progress with Norman what's-his-name?'

'Yes,' Gareth replies, 'And it's Norman Price. He says he has something to show us. He practically jumped down the phone when I mentioned Joshua Spencer's name. We're going to his house in Whitchurch at nine thirty tomorrow morning.'

'Excellent,' Hayden says.

'You're not coming,' I reply. 'You can hardly get out of that garden chair and besides, you can't be seen in public for a couple of days yet.

She goes to argue, then sighs. 'You're right. Can we have some dinner? Then I'm going back to bed. By the way, Del rang me earlier, told me Harry Morgan is looking for me, quite urgently, apparently. I told him to tell Morgan I've gone away to stay with a relative and will be back in a couple of days. I also told him to say my phone will be off for the time being and anyway I have nothing to tell him, no memory of the attack and no idea who did it.'

'I've been out and bought her a burner,' Gareth says.

'A what?'

'A new phone, SIM only, not registered,' he replies sheepishly. 'That's what they call them on the TV cop shows. It only has two numbers programmed in – yours and mine.'

'I've added Del,' Hayden adds, 'just so someone from the office knows how to get hold of me.'

'Whatever,' I say with an eye roll. 'I'll make dinner now. You staying, Gar?'

'No,' I'm meeting Tracey for a run, then dinner out. See you in the morning.'

'You can drive,' I say. 'Pick me up at the end of the alleyway at the back at nine thirty.'

'Who's Tracey?' Hayden asks when Gareth's gone.

'His latest girlfriend,' I reply as I cook spaghetti and make a sauce for a carbonara. 'Since his divorce he's had a few, all a lot younger than him. He says they keep him young. His ex-wife Vera said he was boring. This one won't last long either.'

'Poor man,' Hayden says.

I'm not sure if she's meaning his divorce from Vera or new exercise-mad Tracey. Probably both.

**

The next morning Hayden is still asleep when I leave by the back gate to meet Gareth at the end of the lane. It will take around half an hour, given the tail end of the city's rush hour traffic, to reach the suburb of Whitchurch. I like leafy Whitchurch, with its own village-like environment, its trendy shops and avid environmentalism. I once suggested to Nia we move up there, but it was too far out of the city centre for her. We began our married life in her parents' house and I'm still here.

We arrive on time at Norman's house. It's at the end of a lane, a small, whitewashed cottage with roses starting to put out buds over an arch covering the front door. The frontage is small but heaving with tulips and other late spring flowers. We knock. Norman must have been waiting, as Gareth has hardly let go of the brass knocker when the door opens.

Norman is in his eighties, spare in form, face and hands wrinkled, almost bald, dressed in a threadbare shirt covered by a faded cardigan with a hole in one elbow, baggy old trousers, and carpet slippers, but his voice is strong as he greets us and shows us into a room at the back of the cottage. He has done to his dining room what I have done to mine – turned it into an office, but his is permanent. After introductions, he says, 'Joshua Spencer, eh! That was quite a case. He's in my book.'

'That's smashing news,' I say. 'Can you tell us about him?'

'I can,' Norman replies, but first, tea, coffee?'

We both nod. It's only polite. He returns with a tray of tea and biscuits. 'You can eat and drink as you read.'

'Read?' I say.

'I'm going to share my manuscript with you boys,' he says. 'You can't take it away, though. I'm waiting for a publisher to get back to me.'

'Have you had any luck with a publisher yet?' I ask.

'No, not yet,' he replies enthusiastically. 'But it will come. It's not just a dry old account of what happened, see. I've used some "creative licence", as they say in the publishing industry. I've imagined what the main actors would be thinking and doing.' He sees me frown and glance at Gareth.

'It is almost like a novel, But don't you worry, all the facts of the case are in there.' He stands up and walks to his messy desk, picks up two sets of papers and hands them to us. 'Off you go, then. Read it all. I've written the account of the investigation exactly as it would have happened in the seventies. It was different then, I can tell you. No computers or mobile phones, just footwork and everything written down and typed up in triplicate. And the police interaction with the public was different too. Tell me what you think. When it's finally published, an endorsement from the police and the press would be most welcome. I shall continue my work.'

He turns away to sit at his computer. We look at each other, shrug and begin to read.

Cardiff's Most Notorious Unsolved Crimes

1893 to 2000

**True Life Tales
By
Norman Price**

Chapter IV

The Strange Death of Joshua Spencer, Found on a Gravestone in 1973.

Part I

The first of September 1973 was a red-letter day for John Harries. It was to be his first day-shift as a full Detective Constable, after having completed three months as a Temporary Detective Constable at Clifton Street police station, Roath, Cardiff. His immediate supervisor would be Detective Sergeant Rob Rayer. Next up the line came the Detective Inspector, whose office was along the corridor from the general office where DC Harries would work, and in local CID parlance, he was God. DI Wyn Jones was a "man's man", demanding that his day staff go for a drink with him at the end of their duty; no-one ever argued with him. He didn't suffer fools gladly. He was always immaculately dressed, with razor sharp creases in his pin striped trousers, heavily starched shirt collars, and a diamond studded tie clip with a little chain dangling beneath, which he always wore. 'Look smart, be smart' was his motto, often snapped at his officers. Next in the hierarchy came Detective Chief Inspector John Wall. At the top of the chain of command as far as John Harries was concerned was Chief Superintendent Hawkins, a man rarely seen unless there was a particularly brutal murder or a complicated investigation.

This was going to be a day that DC John Harries would remember for the rest of his service. 'He certainly leapt in at the deep end,' according to Sergeant Rayer, referring to what was about to start.

One of the two phones in the general office rang. 'Extension 363,' said Harries. It was the Detective Chief Superintendent screaming for DI Jones. Harries found him emerging from the toilet. 'Super wants you Sir. It's urgent!'

The DI spat out an expletive and dived into his office, slamming the door shut with a bang that must have been heard all over the Victorian police station. 'Jones here Sir. Yes Sir, yes Sir, yes Sir' he repeated to his senior officer before placing the phone back on the receiver. He opened the door and called out for his Detective Sergeant in the next office. Rob Rayer, quick as a flash, was in with his DI and ready to listen.

'Get all the staff ready downstairs, there's transport on the way.'

'What's up Sir?'

'Death incident up at Cathays cemetery'.

Smiling, Rayer replied, 'Really Sir?'

'They've found someone shot dead there. Incident room is being set up at Rumney nick. You go straight there and take your day team with you.'

Rayer informed his shift officers who rapidly made their way downstairs to the front office to await the cars. This was to be the first incident for the newbie, John Harries.

**

At Cathays cemetery, the incident was already under investigation, the local police having been quick to the scene. The local officer in charge of the immediate discovery of the body, Detective Inspector David Jones, was inside the canvas sheeting tent used to surround the scene, watching while the photographic team were at work.

At 7am, a few hours earlier, a cemetery worker, David Powell, had been making his way across the vast field towards the dedicated chapel, when he noticed, just off the pathway, a man lying on top of a grave. His feet were facing towards the path with his head against the grave's memorial stone, behind which stood a tall Celtic cross. He lay flat out on the gravestone. Powell approached the man, who he initially thought was a tramp asleep, but as he got nearer, he observed that the man was well dressed. Then, to Powell's horror, he saw that the man's skull was blown away, his brain exhibiting, and his mouth disintegrated. A firearm was lying close, down to the man's right side. Powell ran for the nearest phone box and dialled 9-9-9.

As a result, teams of detectives were on their way from various city police stations to the quickly assembled incident room at the Rumney, Cardiff Police Station. The initial reaction of senior officers was: "suicide", but if it transpired to be a murder, they would have to show their professional intent at the earliest – with an incident room, as directed by Chief Super Hawkins.

John Harries reached Rumney station and then with others made his way to the "room". There was a perverse excitement, he felt it strongly: his first day as a full detective constable and a major incident. It was not new to him, he had worked on "rooms" before, but usually as a uniform runner, not as a detective and integral member of the team. A few minutes after he arrived one of the Serious Crime Squad sergeants spoke to him.

'John, go and see the Detective Chief Super'.

'What, me?' he said.

'Go on, he's waiting!' exclaimed the sergeant, who went to the front of the room to the chalk board. John

Harries stood for a moment before making his way along the corridor to the Super's office, knocked on the door and entered.

On entering he saw his Detective Inspector Wyn Jones standing by the window next to the Detective Chief Superintendent. They acknowledged one another. 'Sit down', said DCS Hawkins. 'We don't know what we've got up at the cemetery, suicide or murder, early days, but we do know the man's name.' He paused, and staring directly at his new Detective Constable, said, 'It's Joshua Moses Spencer.'

John Harries jumped out of his chair. 'What? I know him! That's my wife's brother-in-law.'

'Yes, we learnt that only half an hour ago. Sit down, please, I know you must be surprised, but we need a proper identification.'

'What about his wife, my sister-in-law? Does she know? If it's him, I must be with her when she's told.' He shook his head. 'I don't get what's going on.'

'John, we only have proof of identification via a wallet found on him. His injuries are such that identification is going to be difficult. We'd like you to go down to the Cardiff Royal Infirmary mortuary with your DI here and attempt a formal identification.'

John thought fleetingly of his wife Gwen, but it was his sister-in-law Hannah who took up most of his thoughts. Her husband Josh Spencer, he wasn't a fan of, and now the man was dead. "*What point good looks and money now, Josh, he thought*". Hannah, his Gwen's sister, had married a man from the famous Spencer family. Big business, monied. John was in awe of them. He stared at the Super, then at DI Wyn Jones and nodded in agreement.

'What about Hannah? What's going to happen to her?'

'First, we must ID the body, then cause of death, which is obvious, then…' He was interrupted by the stunned John Harries.

'What was it, what was the cause of death?'

'He was flat out on a gravestone. Shot from under his chin, blew the top of his head off. There was a gun lying by the side of the body. Sorry to be graphic but you have to know what you're facing. The gun he, or someone used, was there, and an old glove was found nearby. It'll go to forensics, but probably produce bugger all. The main thing is we must get the ID before we can move on. To all intents and purposes, it appears a suicide. Why would he do that?'

'He wouldn't! He was top man in his firm, he had it all. Money, status, beautiful wife…'

'We'll get you a coffee, then you go to the morgue.' He picked up the phone and ordered a tray of coffee to be brought to him at once.

Harries walked down the stairs via the incident room to the foyer of the police station. The desk was manned, and, as usual, by an officer chatting to a member of the public. It appeared the woman had her car broken into. "*Everyday crime, getting too common*", Harries thought, as he leant over the woman's shoulder and said to the desk man, 'Will you ring the incident room and tell them I've nipped over to the scene of the shooting. I want to see it before I go to do the ID.' The officer nodded then continued to write down details of the visitor's crime complaint.

Harries wanted to go alone to the scene, to see it, to understand it, and more importantly, to help his sister-in-law and his wife understand it. Within twenty minutes he was parking in the cemetery's dedicated car park. There were crowds of onlookers milling about, chatting in small groups, for whom this was an unusual and exciting event. Harries made his way to the grave. He stepped over the police cordon tape, as the grave was situated away from the path. Scenes of Crime officers had been working the main path for several hours and had cleared it for public use, having moved on to concentrate on every square yard of land within fifty yards of the murder location inside the cordon. Uniformed officers, armed with notepads, were questioning people wandering the path.

A man with a small child caught Harries's eye. He was pointing towards the grave location and, oddly, he was smiling and giggling. This initially annoyed John. Bloody smiling at poor Joshua, he thought, but quickly forgot, as he made his way gingerly to the murder scene. There was a yard wide tape marked "clearway" to the grave. His presence was noted in a book by a Scenes of Crime female officer. Harries looked at the grave, saw the blood-spattered upright cross, then turned and retraced his steps back to the car and drove away to pick up the Detective Inspector.

At the mortuary the DI, who had done this many times before, walked directly into a small office, where behind the desk, already gowned, was pathologist Ken Rees.

'What's this? A new boy initiation?'

'Yes and no Ken. He's a DC at Clifton Street, but on this occasion he's a witness: an identification witness.'

'Hope he knows the man well, and he's not a "fainter", is he?'

'It's his wife's sister's husband.' Rees stood up and offered his hand to Harries who took it, albeit it his own hand was damp and shaking. The morgue smell had already affected him. Even though he'd been in one before, this time everything was exaggerated. All his senses were on high, and the comment "fainter" had upset him; he hadn't thought of that before entering. The description of his brother-in-law's injury was going to test him.

'Let's get it over and done with,' he said. The pathologist made a note in his folder, asking for name and address.

'Put him down as Clifton Street police station, not his home address,' Jones instructed the pathologist, who called out a name.

A mortuary assistant came in the office. 'Ready Sir.'

'Ok, let's go,' Pathologist Rees said, getting up and exiting the room followed by Harries then Jones. In the short walk along the continuous plastic viewing window, Harries noted four "slabs", the CID jargon he had picked up, but the view he was about to see, was his first "bad 'un". The body lay just the other side of the viewing window. The main part of the torso was covered with a mortuary blanket, leaving just the head on display. Even Jones turned away from the view; he didn't have to stare at the man, but Harries did. He closed his eyes, but the mortuary smell penetrated his consciousness, causing him to open them and then stare grimly at what was left of the body's head. The face was reasonably intact.

'Yes, yes. It's him!' he snapped, before turning and walking along the corridor and out into the fresh air, which he took in, in huge gulps. My God what's Hannah going to say? She's expecting, you know,' he said to DI Jones who had walked up beside him.

'Positive identification? Was that man you saw Joshua Moses Spencer? Yes or no.'

'It was Josh Sir. I recognised what was left of his face.' Jones walked back into the mortuary building, turning on the way to shout to Harries, 'You'll have to do an Identification Statement. Do it down Clifton Street. Get yourself a pot of tea or something,' as he walked up the short ramp and disappeared inside the building.

Part II

When Detective Chief Superintendent Hawkins shouted for quiet, the officers in the incident room did so immediately.

'You've been put into your twos. You've got your vehicle allocation, and these are the tasks. Number one team: graveyard, trawl for witnesses, anything you can get on the movements of anyone, perhaps wandering through, perhaps regulars. Team two: trace the origins of the weapon. Photographs and details are with the photography office in Central. Go to the morgue and get a statement from the pathologist, cause of death, etcetera. Have that glove looked at. Probably nothing, but you never know. Team three: that includes you, Shirley, the family; mother, father and wife, Hannah, once identification is confirmed. I want statements. Ok?'

There was a general shuffling and mumbling in the room while the Super spoke to DI Jones who had joined him at the top desk.

'I've just been told that Harries has given a definite ID on the man as Joshua Moses Spencer. Now we can move. Team four: look at Spencer's business dealings, friends, associates, anyone who can give us some reason why he should kill himself, or alternatively, anyone who may want to kill him. Team five: man the phone lines. Keep in touch with the other teams, update when necessary, and keep me constantly in the loop. Team six: stay in reserve, general enquiries either static or out on the streets. Just to clarify, in my opinion, due to the strange circumstances, the position of the body on the old gravestone, the position of the weapon and the lack of any other evidence, we have a suicide. A strange one I grant you. Grave E1784w, is an old one, so why that one? Well, why any of them? Thousands to choose from, he chose that one. Off you go.'

Whilst the orders were being given out, the details were being written on the chalk board, with car call signs of the teams, by a civilian typist. Her work would commence soon, with all the written statements needed to be typed out, usually in triplicate, via carbon paper. Within five minutes the room was empty; the Super and DCI Wall had adjourned in the canteen, with a pot of tea and sandwiches.

Detective Constable John Harries had been given special dispensation to visit his wife. He had been told by Detective Inspector Wyn Jones it was for compassionate reasons, but in truth, as they both knew, it was to see if any light could be thrown on his wife's brother-in-law's frame of mind. Shirley Evans's team would be seeing Gwen Harries soon, but Jones thought she might tell her husband some facts she wouldn't give to an unknown police interviewing team.

No-one could have possibly known how true that 'logic of experience' was soon to become.

Part III

The Press briefing was held at 3pm and passed without incident, meaning in police jargon, no derogatory comments and no awkward questions. Not too many media outlets turned up, and all were local. 'We are not looking for anyone else in connection with this incident, at the current time,' Detective Chief Superintendent Hawkins informed them, leaving the media in no doubt he thought it was suicide.

The teams returned to the incident room at 6pm for the debriefing regarding their assigned actions.

'Team one, what you got?' snapped DCS Hawkins.

'We've produced a few locals who heard what they thought was a gunshot. They'd seen no-one. We've seen pub landlords and told them we'd be back in this eve to do a "mix" and see if we can find anything—'

He was stopped in mid-sentence by Detective Chief Inspector Wall, 'and the best place to hang out is by the bar…' The comment received a few laughs before he continued, 'you've got £5 beer ex's. Use them wisely.'

'Team two, what you got?' asked the Super, hoping for more positive news.

'The gun is a Mauser Luger PO8, 9mm, handheld, dusted for prints,' the Scenes of Crime lead officer replied. 'There were a few, but all belonging to the dead man. Photography's got good shots at the incident. We found out from the gun shop in town that it's not a rare weapon, in fact quite a common one, as it was apparently German soldiers' favourite in WWII. As far as where it came from, the task, we are told, would be impossible, unless someone identifies it as theirs. We found out it's riddled with serial numbers on all of the removable parts, or at least the last two numerals of the four-digit number are all over it. We also found out the magazine's number didn't match the gun's number, but according to our informant, that was common. There's no way of checking who last owned the weapon, unless a gun shop sold it and made a note of the numbers on the paperwork. That'll be our next task, probably phone calls, or telex to all the area's police stations as an action. That's it.'

'Ok, you get on with that tomorrow—'. The DCS was interrupted by Liz Williams, the 'room' typist who entered, and after muttering something to the top desk trio of Detective Chief Super, Detective Chief Inspector and Detective Inspector, they stood and followed her out of the room. 'Give us a few minutes,' said DCS Hawkins, before pulling the door closed behind him.

**

The expressions on the faces of the returning senior officers were enough to tell the waiting room detectives something was up, and things weren't going according to plan. They waited whilst the three men sorted out their seats and the papers in front of them. 'There's been a turn up', began DCS Hawkins. 'You all know that young John Harries's sister-in-law was married to the dead man. Before I continue, I want to tell you that the latest info is bloody confidential. Get it? If anyone of you blabs to a journo, and I find out, your feet won't touch, whoever you are. Do I make myself clear?' There were the usual nods, umphs and tuts.

'John Harries has found out that things were not as they should be at the Joshua Moses Spencer household. Spencer's business was apparently in trouble, and to add to the mix, Harries's wife has told him that Spencer's partner, David Hennessey, has gone missing. Harries says he hasn't been seen for a week or so. Gwen Harries was understandably reticent to say much, that's even if she knew much more, and then wasn't the time to push her. It's his wife for God's sake and passing some confidential family stuff to her husband was delicate. This now changes the whole bloody thing. We're booked to do another press release at 7pm, and I'll do a "things are proceeding ..." memo, but I will have to give them much, much more tomorrow. Most of you can go off now, and all start tomorrow morning at 8am, and expect a full day. Ok? The incident room commander, Detective Chief Inspector Wall will detail the tours of duty.'

Within half an hour the room had cleared, except for the detective sergeant and the detective constable from Team one. Their duties were what they had expected, doing the pubs around or near the cemetery and near the deceased man's home. Any snippet of information would be eagerly gathered up and perhaps linked, all ready to report back first thing to the incident room the next day. The detectives would be asking questions, finding new witnesses, listening to rumours. They would also be the officers "on call", should an incident room "new info" call be received. One officer would be designated "driver", and the others would have a small "drinks allowance", to be claimed at the end of the working month.

**

Later that night, after the final briefing and press release, the coroner's officer, Constable Page, had telephoned Chief Super Hawkins, asking for an update. It was he, Page, who had to arrange the Coroner's Court, and its jury. Page had come on duty at 8am and gone through the list of sudden deaths in the previous 24 hours. Nearly all foreseen, with Doctor's verifications. The standout death was that of Joshua Moses Spencer, currently not known if suicide, murder or accident. It had to be one of them. Page was aware there was an incident room on the go so he, representing the coroner, would be informed at the earliest opportunity of the facts. Page booked the courtroom at the Central Police Station in Cardiff, for the following morning at 10.30am. It was probably going to be a quick one. The Detective in charge would ask for an adjournment. Page had already had the word via the grapevine that the Super thought it was a suicide, so if he thought it, so would constable Page.

**

At 8am the following day, DCS Hawkins re-convened the Spencer Death incident room, this time with specialist officers from the Fraud Squad, an embryo department, with two detectives, a sergeant and a constable.

'DHJS Limited, who we've probably all heard of, is one of the biggest chartered accountancy firms in South Wales. I just found out what the letters stand for, which are David Hennessey and Joshua Spencer, the senior partners. There are several more junior partners in the business, and it's city centre based. FRC, the Financial Reporting Council, is a port of call for you Fraud Squad boys, so get all you can on what's going on at DHJS. They have loads of staff so someone's going to blab to you.' DCS Hawkins expected some quick answers, and as with all detectives, a quick answer was a mark of respect to the senior officer.

The usual question and answer session didn't last long, but there was a renewed enthusiasm tangible within the group. It had been heading for a suicide verdict and a small local media story, but the new input had lifted the incident a few rungs into a story that the nationals might get hold of. Detective Constable John Harries was informed that his sister-in-law now had to be formally interviewed as an action by Shirley Evans's team, preferably in a police station. Whatever the outcome, a comprehensive statement had to be taken from her, relative to her husband, his business, his business partners, and everything else she could think of, no matter how trivial.

'If David Hennessey has been missing, why the hell has he not been reported as such?' snapped Hawkins. 'Is he missing, or has he gone off with some floosy? Who knows where he is? Or could he be on a private holiday or some dedicated business enquiry?'

Everyone could tell the bosses were in danger of losing control of the incident as the story unfolded.

'We have one dead partner shot on a grave, one partner allegedly missing, and nowt else! I want answers. The bloody press may do their own snooping and I want to know more than them. Get it?'

DCS Hawkins was rattled. At the end of the briefing, the teams lined up for their action papers from DCI Wall. John Harries was posted to incident room duties, it being diplomatically unwise to have him at the sharp end any more.

Part IV

On Monday morning DCI Wall and DI Jones were driven down to the Coroner's Court at the Central Police Station. It was proposed to put DI Wyn Jones in the witness box. Wall had ratified the prearranged spiel. The driver parked up in the basement and the men took a lift, up to the Coroner's Court on the ground floor. In the police office Constable Tim Page was going through the papers for the day, but immediately stood up as the two senior officers entered his room. After a short conversation, Page left the room to update the coroner, who, exactly at 10.30am, entered the small court room. All stood. In the court were not only the police officers, but five members of the media in their set seats. It was not often you had five reporters in court, usually just one or two, sniffing around for local news.

Wall turned to Jones and whispered, 'They've heard, someone's blabbed.' There was a nod in return, but this was not the time for conversation.

The Joshua Moses Spencer case was the first called, there only being one more that day for the coroner and that was later that afternoon. Jones got to his feet and crossed to the witness area. After "swearing in" and introducing himself, he addressed the court.

'Yesterday at the Cathays cemetery, the body of a man was found lying on an old grave, near the central pathway. He was lying flat out on the gravestone, with his head at the memorial stone end, exactly how you would imagine the body underneath to have been laid. He was dressed in a dark suit, a white shirt and a patterned tie, with black leather shoes and black socks. It appears a firearm had been discharged from under his chin and up into his head causing the skull to fracture and parts of the brain to be exposed. We are not sure at this time whether he was sat up when the shot was fired, or even standing. The Luger Mauser PO8 weapon was found on the edge of the gravestone. The body was later identified as that of Joshua Moses Spencer, twenty-nine years of age, and residing at Whitchurch. Our enquiries have commenced into the incident, and, at this time, detective officers are undertaking antecedent enquiries as well as investigating pertinent business and family connections.'

The coroner asked, 'When do you think your enquiries can bring a substantial brief to this court?' The reporters stared straight at the witness, hoping for an answer that could initiate a dramatic headline. They got one.

'We have, at this time, an open mind on the death of Joshua Moses Spencer. We are examining various scenarios. We are not ruling out any causality and are currently assessing new information that has come to us in recent hours.' Detective Chief Inspector Wall, sitting at the back of the court, thought his DI had got it about right, and the activity in the press seats guaranteed some lively questions as headlines, which subsequently appeared in the first of the evening editions:

HEAD OF DHJS, JOSHUA SPENCER FOUND DEAD
Was it suicide or murder? Police unwilling to comment

DEAD ON A GRAVESTONE. WAS SPENCER MURDERED?
Police have new leads on Spencer shooting

The coroner gave the police a few days before they had to report back and appear again, with a substantial evidential brief. All left the court.

**

Back at the incident room, enquiries re-commenced, and the detailed teams left with their various actions. The most important, according to the senior officers, was the comprehension of why, and if, David Hennessey had gone missing and had it any link to the discovery of his partner's body in the graveyard?

The Fraud Squad officers visited the office of the Financial Reporting Council, where they expressed their interest in the work of DHJS and were told to apply officially via letter, in accordance with standard practice. However, they were given the "wink", indicating problems were already known about at this company. Reporting this back to DCI Wall, they were actioned to the head office of DHJS Ltd, Chartered Accountants, a firm which carried out numerous financial undertakings on behalf of their local Wales based customers, as well as multi-million-pound international audits. The front entry to the five-storey building was glass encased, with a male receptionist on duty when the officers arrived. They had not signalled their intention to visit the firm, but they were soon to discover they were expected.

'You're police,' the receptionist said, before either of the men had said a word.

'You're expecting us then Mr…?' answered Detective Sergeant Hicks.

'Michael Rhodes, please call me Michael. How can I help you?'

'I'm DS Hicks and this is D cMumford,' both men lifting their warrant cards towards him, 'We'd like to talk to a senior partner or whoever is in charge here today.'

'That would be Carys Williams. I'll tell her you're here. It will be no surprise.' His phone call was answered immediately and, acting on instructions, he asked the officers to sit in a visitors room, just a few yards from the reception desk. Within a few minutes the lift bell sounded, and a woman led the way out, with another younger woman walking in her wake. Carys Williams was about forty-five years of age, slim, and smartly attired. The other woman was younger and carried a briefcase. The two men rose to their feet as the women walked into the glass office, and after pleasantries, Carys Williams asked, 'Sergeant, how can we help you?'

A detailed conversation began, with notes being made both by the Fraud Squad officers and Nancy Breckon, Carys Williams's assistant.

The initial questions by the detectives and answers by Carys Williams, soon changed into a tense conversation, with Carys Williams swiftly coming to realise that things were serious, not just for her but for the whole DHJS Ltd organisation. Her initial defensive answers having done her no favours, she loosened up. Hicks had warned that if there was any suspicion of illicit practises, she would be cautioned.

The officers ascertained that David Hennessey was thirty-seven years of age and lived in a penthouse apartment in an exclusive building in Cardiff Bay. He was single and enjoyed the company of women. He was a free spender, a "lover of life" as Carys Williams put it, a man addicted to expensive cars and lifestyle. Hennessey had not been seen for almost two weeks, which in itself was not unusual for a man who used his home as a work base with a fax machine, telephone and hand written notes which were faxed to the office to be typed up. He attended high level meetings in the office boardroom when his presence was required, but lately had missed two important ones. Joshua Moses Spencer seemed quite the opposite of his partner, a serious family man, with a work ethic that put most others to shame. Joshua Spencer had been spending increasingly long days in his office, his usual calm temperament interspersed by loud outbursts and bad language.

After half an hour of conversation, the relationship between the four persons entered, as was always the way, into a more affable mode, with Carys Williams beginning to use the "off the record" scenario. Assistant Nancy Breckon had stopped writing, placed her notebook on the table and sat back, listening to the conversation.

'We have problems here Mr Hicks, big problems. We are a multimillion-pound business, with substantial assets, yet the bank is on our back. I'll explain.'

The two officers were wise enough not to use their notebooks and pushed their pens away. The feeling was that if Carys Williams had something crucial to say, she might be put off by the men scribbling in front of her. They could, if necessary, take a formal statement later.

'Everyone in this building had a massive shock when we heard that our Chief Executive and Head of Finance had shot himself; it made people fear the whole business could come crashing down with him. Josh, as we called him, was a popular man, a good boss to work for, but in recent months his worry lines were becoming noticeable. There were rumours that the top two, Josh Spencer and David Hennessey were progressively arguing, with numerous private meetings behind closed doors, which never used to happen before. I also found out that our bank was increasingly worried about large withdrawals, and clients were becoming disappointed in the service they were getting. I spoke to both Josh and David, but they brushed everything off, with some talk of a new "super deal" they were setting up. I didn't believe them. It got to a state where the two men hardly spoke to each other. We're carrying on as normal, but without both of them, the other directors are talking of calling an extraordinary meeting.' She stopped, as though she had said too much.

'Go on,' said Hicks, but Carys just stared; the conversation obviously upsetting her. 'It's all going to come out in the wash anyway. Tell me a bit more about David Hennessey, and where you think he is. Any ideas?'

She ignored the question but spoke quite deliberately about another matter. 'We have financial irregularities, and I'm left to handle it on my own. With Josh gone and David missing, the situation is becoming horrendous.' She appeared near to tears and the detectives looked at each other, with 'a *what do we do now*' challenge.

'Could we start with Hennessey?' asked DC Mumford. 'You say he's missing. Is it a regular occurrence, have you any idea where he is, or where he might go? It's important, we have one senior partner dead, under strange circumstances, and now we find another missing. Who knows he is, in your words," missing"?'

The two women looked at one another before Carys Williams said, 'I think I've said enough now. I really have to consult senior board members. There are serious problems with the business, and I don't want to say anymore until I liaise with our solicitors. I hope you understand.'

The officers did understand. Both smiled at the women and stood up. 'It's likely we'll be back,' Mumford said.

After gaining the address and telephone details of Hennessey, the officers left the room. 'It's going to have to be a warrant,' Hicks said to his fellow officer, 'and that's a bloody minefield.'

Their next stop was going to be the incident room and a chat with the Chief Superintendent, but as they were about to exit the foyer, they heard footsteps behind them, speeding in their direction. They turned to see Nancy Breckon hurrying towards them. 'I think you ought to know this, and I'd rather you didn't say where you heard it,' she said as she reached them. The officers nodded agreement. 'There'd been numerous arguments between David and Josh. David was accusing Josh of stealing a hundred thousand pounds from the business.' She turned and disappeared through one of the many doors leading off the foyer.

Part V

It is 7am on 3rd September 1973, and Constable Nicholas Bailey is booking on the morning turn at Bognor Regis police station, in West Sussex. His fellow officer had been granted two hours off, and therefore will be coming on duty at 9am. Sergeant Dawkins is the day supervisor, his turn is 9am to 5pm, enabling him to manage both the morning and afternoon officers, as well as the most important part of his job – paperwork.

The mop-carrying cleaner is on duty first thing, and one of her most important tasks is to make a pot of tea. Usually, she sits down with the officers for a few minutes, parking her mop and bucket up against the lockers, before carrying on with her functions. This day is no different. At 7.45am PC Nick Bailey dons his coat and his accessories, handcuffs, truncheon etc., and places his helmet on his head. A mirror, placed just inside the main front door, is for the beat officers to check their dress, to ensure smartness, before entering "the fray" as Dawkins puts it.

Bailey wanders down London Road in the direction of the front and the sea. It's a fine morning, bright sunshine, clear blue skies, a gentle breeze whipping up only small waves, and everyone in Bognor's foremost shopping street is reassuringly happy, or so it appears to Bailey. The usual nods and acknowledgments are accompanied by smiles, *'but who knows what's going on behind those smiles'* is the usual thought of Nick Bailey, who has dreams of being a detective. He window-shops as he wanders; the reassuring sight of a constable in uniform is what everyone wants to see. He turns right at the end of London Road and walks past the old bus station. It's then, from across the road, on the sea front, he sees a boy running towards him as fast as he can.

'Hey, policeman, come quick, they want you!' The urgency on the lad's face, his pace, his words, shake Bailey out of his soporific state.

'What's wrong?' he says as he holds the boy's lapels to calm him down and draw him in.

'There's a man floating in the sea. He's jammed on the pier. Some people are swimming out to him.'

The officer puts his hand up and stops a passing van. The driver screeches to a halt. 'Take me down to the pier. Quick, it's urgent!' The driver waits for his new passenger to clamber in, then turns around and makes his way down to the Esplanade. 'Some bloke's drowning. Thanks for the lift. I don't know any more about it.'

'No problem,' exclaims the excited driver, who sees in his mirror a panda car coming up fast. 'Your mates are behind us'.

Bailey pulls his personal radio from his pocket, presses the side button and an aerial pops up. He tries to contact his London Road wireless room, but there's no answer, because the battery's flat. Within a minute the van and the panda car arrive at the scene. There's a small group of people on the beach, some with their dogs, all watching a couple of men in the sea, swimming towards the end of the pier. A small rowing boat is being pushed out by a local angler. Bailey rushes down with his fellow officer, Spence Thomas, and asks, or in truth, demands, they be taken out to the scene of whatever incident is occurring. There are a number of people standing at the end of the pier looking down and over, in an attempt to catch any sight of the ongoing incident happening below them.

The angler, struggling to breathe, finally arrives at the far end of the pier. His efforts have made him sit, puffing for air; the extra weight of the officers in his boat, having been too much for him. Two men, both in swimming trunks, have climbed onto the framework of the pier, and are attempting to lift the prostrate figure of a male from one of the cross members. Nick Bailey being the most agile, and fittest of the three men in the dinghy, clambers onto the pier's metal work and makes his way to assist the others.

By now a large crowd has gathered on the beach, albeit the incident is a long way away, eager to find out exactly what's going on. More persons have run up the long pier to gain a better vantage point. In the distance a small motorboat can be seen powering its way, from the Pagham end of the long beach, the two crew, from the local yacht club, having been asked by officers at Police Headquarters to assist.

Nick Bailey, minus his jacket and helmet, and armed with Spence Thomas's personal radio, reaches the two men, who are by now standing on a cross member, and holding onto the pier's vertical framework. Draped over a part of the horizontal framework is a man, only dressed in what appears to be his underpants, his arms falling towards the sea on one side of the framework, legs on the other side.

'He's dead,' shouts one of the two men. 'When we got here the tide was in a little more and he was washing about in the sea. We draped him like this, otherwise he may have drifted off.'

**

At the Cardiff incident room, senior officers were having a briefing from the two Fraud Squad detectives, and they didn't like what they were hearing. A reasonably straightforward suicide was now turning into something *'a darn more bloody serious',* thought Hawkins.

It was Detective Sergeant Hicks, Fraud Squad, who summed it up. 'This ain't going to be easy boss. We've got two senior partners of DHJS, one dead, one missing. We've got reports of financial chaos within the business, but we don't know how much chaos. Is there false accounting on an industrial scale going on? It'll take a warrant and a team to sort it out. It does appear, though, that there has been serious mismanagement, if not criminality at the firm.'

'Bloody hell!' cursed Hawkins, 'my overtime budget is already dangerously low!'

The phone rang. DI Wyn Jones picked up the receiver. 'Phone call for you sir, it's the coroner's officer'.

'Bloody hell, give us a break' thought Hawkins as he grabbed the receiver from his DI. He listened, gave out a few 'umphs', then put the receiver down. 'Coroner wants the inquest asap, witnesses, the lot.' He looked to his DCI John Wall. 'You deal with it!' His order was met with a mild nod. All four men then left the office and entered the main incident room. Hawkins needed some good news. He was soon going to get news, but not of the "good" variety.

It had to happen. The papers had got hold of the information that David Hennessey was missing. It was obvious for them to link it to the Joshua Spencer death. One reporter was waiting in the foyer of the Rumney police station, just sitting, a ploy he had used often before. If a cop he knew walked in or out, there would always be a greeting between the two, and more often than not he would get some titbits of what was going on behind the scenes. All he had to do then was clarify it in the form of a question at a press conference.

The Press Office at Headquarters had been batting away constant callers, including some reporters from the Nationals, and they had told the Chief Constable plainly that the press must be given a credible update. The Chief spoke to his clerk and the message percolated down the system to John Wall, in the incident room. 'What the hell is going on?

Keep the media updated,' was the communication that came to the ears of DCS Hawkins via Wall.

The top table of three senior officers addressed in turn the other ranks sitting in rows of chairs facing them.

DI Jones spoke first, 'If any officer is seen in the company of a newspaper reporter, he better have a bloody good reason. If you must be in their presence, make sure your partner is with you. They're out for blood, and we have none at present to spill for them. DCS Hawkins is the man who authorises releases.'

Wall then continued, 'We have to get the coroner up and running. Team Three, you'll work with me and get it arranged. See me after.'

DCS Hawkins then stood, which didn't happen too often, and said, 'We have to find David Hennessey. Fraud Squad boys will go back into the firm and take with them as many officers as they need. Detective Constable John Harries will make further enquiries, in a formal interview, regarding his wife's sister-in-law's knowledge of her husband's recent movements and whatever she knows about the financial problems at his firm. He'll take a detective sergeant with him. Family values don't come into this now, we have to go in hard. We want you all to ring in to this room often for updates; we'll try to get to you all via personal radios. More have been issued from headquarters for our use. The key to all this is Hennessey. Get him and job done. Mr Hicks, if you want more men, just ask. Got it?'

As the room cleared, he turned to his fellow senior officers, 'Is Hennessey really missing? If so, he should be circulated as such. It's down to the family to do that. Find them and shake them up! Get on with it eh?'

'Yes Sir', came a sharp reply. The room stood down.

Part VI

'Dead on arrival,' the doctor verifies to the Bognor police. He has taken possession of a semi-nude male person's body at 10am. There is no cause of death given, but the likelihood is drowning. A post mortem is booked for 4pm that afternoon and until that time, cause of death is "unknown". The men dragging the body away from the pier supports noticed bruising but put that down to the actions of waves pushing the body against the metal framework.

Sergeant Dawkins, Bognor Police, requests a Scene of Crimes officer go to the hospital and take the fingerprints of the deceased. CID are informed, and asked to organise checks of missing persons records in the area, and to undertake usual enquiries into the incident. It is ascertained at an early stage, that there are no outstanding missing persons in the south of England area, and therefore the man's description will have to be circulated to all other forces. Even to the eyes of Bailey and Thomas, the first two officers dealing, it is obvious the man could have been in the sea for as much as a week. The only odd thing to them is why he was in just his underpants? They are aware, as suicide was not an unusual cause of death along that coast, that the man may have stripped off and simply walked into the sea, swam away and drowned.

At 4pm Detective Inspector Pierce and PC Bailey attend the hospital mortuary and witness the post mortem. 'The man is exactly five foot, ten and a half inches in height, weight 11stone 7pounds,' the pathologist says. 'Fair to brown hair. Only one real identifying mark, a half inch penetration wound on his left buttock, which has permanently scarred.'

Bailey makes some quick notes.

The pathologist continues. 'I would guess the body had been in the sea for a week or so, but there is one worrying aspect. We have found here,' he lifts the head and points to the rear of it 'a wound, which is the type of injury that I would expect to have been caused by an intentional blow. It may very well have caused him to become unconscious. It doesn't look like the type of wound that could have been caused after the body had entered the sea. I would say therefore that he either fell or was pushed into the water'.

Both officers think the same thought: '*murder*'.

'You'll let us have your official note soon Sir?' The pathologist nods and commences the clean-up, supported by his mortuary assistant. Both officers are glad to get out and into the fresh Sussex sea air. 'I think a pint later,' says the senior officer to Bailey, who enthusiastically nods his agreement.

**

Telex machines are active, sending details to the New Scotland Yard record office for distribution, and ultimately via the Criminal Records Office daily paper circulation. This includes a photograph of the man's face, such as remains of it, and full physical description. The circulation has a confidential stamp on it, indicating it is for police eyes only and not to go outside police stations.

In Cardiff, the name and description of David Hennessey have been circulated locally, and via telex to the CRO, but only as a "suspect" in fraud, which will be subsequently escalated to "wanted", which means any officer in Britain has the power to arrest the man and hold him until the police force concerned arrives. In addition to his name, date of birth and physical description, there is always a "when last seen was wearing" entry. In the case of Hennessey, it is a blue suit and white shirt. Visible attributes are none, except for an old incision scar on a buttock.

**

Detective Constable John Harries got home at 9pm on Monday night, expecting his dinner on the table, and was surprised and angry to find nothing waiting for him. His wife informed him she had had enough of the constant harassment by the press and questions regarding her sister and brother-in-law. 'She's worried sick and you expect me to cook? David goes missing, just disappears off the face of the earth, then Joshua is found dead. Where the hell is David? Do you know something you're keeping from me?' John shook his head at his wife and walked out of the house. 'Where the hell are you going?' she shouted after him.

'Down the fish shop. I'm bloody starving,' he replied as the door behind him slammed tight.

**

At 2pm on Monday, Maria Van de Meer came on duty at the Western Criminal Record Office in Cardiff. Her afternoon duty was, as civilian enquiry clerk, to answer and deal with telephone enquiries, and file the CRO and Welsh CRO circulations, then forward them on to various local police departments.

At 6pm she was the only person left on duty in the vast record office when, whilst logging and filing the circulations, she noticed an image of a man's face on the reverse side of the CRO national paper circulation. It had been circulated by the Sussex Constabulary as "Unidentified Man Found Drowned". The man's face, even though distorted in death by the action of the sea, had some likeness to another image she had seen recently on a local circulation. She flipped through the crime circulation file and there, on yesterday's sheet was the same man. "Wanted. David John Hennessey. In connection with False Accounting and Theft". The officer circulating was the officer in the Spencer case, Detective Inspector Jones.

DCS Hawkins had just finished his meal and was looking forward to an evening in front of the television. His hours had been long, and this was his first evening at home for some time. The phone rang. 'Darling, it's for you,' his wife called.

**

A Commer van, dark blue with a blue light, pulled up outside DHJS in Cardiff at 9am on Tuesday morning, driven by a plain clothes detective. The back doors of the van were thrown open, then a steady procession of boxes and files were brought out of the building and stacked in the back. There was, of course, the obligatory newspaper photographer, standing on the pavement outside the building, taking snaps of the activities surrounding the van, and anyone who walked in or out of the building, who looked official.

The Spencer and Hennessey families were well aware of what was going on, and their frustrations were growing. The internecine blaming and counter blaming were frustrating the investigation: Spencer's shooting, the finding of Hennessey's body, and the enormous DHJS losses. Hundreds of thousands of pounds was the initial estimate of monies missing, but it was sure to rise. It was one detective constable working from DCS Hawkins's incident room that put it all into context: 'My God, what a bleedin' mess.'

**

The newspapers were becoming hyper critical; reporters attendance at the Coroner's Court, just for adjournments, was wearing a bit thin. One headline read:

'WHAT IS GOING ON MR CHIEF CONSTABLE?'

This was intended to hit at the very heart of the South Wales Constabulary. Blaming the Chief Constable was designed to fire a rocket straight into the centre of the establishment, causing the Chief Constable to fire his own back, but not at the paper in question. His rocket was directed straight down, from the top to the bottom of his force.

Part VII

At 8am on Friday 7th September, at the morning briefing in the DHJS incident room, as it was now called, DCS Hawkins walked from behind the table, and stood in front of it. He was facing twenty-five detective officers.

'First of all, I would like to thank you all for your efforts regarding the incident. It's the spade work that creates results. As the days have passed, a much clearer picture has emerged as to the sequence of events that led to the deaths of the two senior men from DHJS. Some of you may not endorse the finding, there is always room for other suggestions, but it appears tragically straight forward.

'The search of the Spencer house has, as you know, found a used rail ticket, in the pocket of a jacket owned by Joshua Spencer, a day-return ticket to Bognor Regis in Sussex. The ticket had been used, as it had been punched. Why did Joshua Moses Spencer go to Bognor Regis on 27th August, five days before his own death? Not the obvious place for an exceptionally long day trip, even if it was Bank Holiday Monday?' Hawkins stopped and shook his head. 'We have the date stamped on that ticket. We have had confirmed by both his wife and work colleagues that Joshua Spencer was showing signs of depression and worry just prior to his death. We know from the Fraud boys they couldn't find evidence that Spencer had monies stashed anywhere, so if it was he who had stolen the firm's money, where is it? We also know from Hannah Spencer that Joshua had suggested a holiday abroad, but she said they had to wait, referencing her pregnancy. He, though, seemed very keen. Why was that? Teams have spoken to Spencer's friends and associates, as well as business clients, and none of them had knowledge of any of their money, or indeed anyone else's, being missing. Apparently, there's now a lot of anger out there.

Mrs Hannah Spencer has given us nothing, claiming total ignorance of her husband's business dealings. I believe she knows more than she's letting on, but given her condition, we can't question her further.

'Thank you also to Team Five who attended the Bognor Regis and Chichester inquests and arranged the statements from all concerned down there in Sussex. I sent them down Tuesday and late last night they gave me an update on the result of their extensive investigations. Hope you enjoyed your little break, all paid for by the firm. Whilst you were sunning yourself on the Sussex beaches, the teams here were tying up numerous loose ends.' Laughter and rude comments ensued in the room until Hawkins called for quiet.

'The main thing we asked our boys to do, was to find out if there had been sightings of the two men together: Hennessey and Spencer. They went to town on that, ensuring that the local paper asked the same question. So far no witness has come forward to report seeing either of the men, separately or together. We've spoken to the guard on one of the trains heading to Sussex from Cardiff on the day Spencer bought his ticket, but he could not remember the man. I probably wouldn't either.

'Police and witness statements are being typed up, and very soon we can present a full file to the coroner regarding Joshua Spencer's death. There are negatives, though. We've failed to trace the owner, and the history, of the weapon found on the gravestone on which Spencer died. There are prints, but not enough to categorically state they were the deceased's. The weapon has been sent to another lab, but they have stated it's pointless, as, if one lab has failed there is nothing much more they can find or do. There must be an answer out there, and to that extent one team still has that action on their list. Another item we received into the investigation, was the left-handed leather glove found adjacent to the grave. The glove has been forensically examined and has thrown up nothing. It is therefore deemed superfluous and coincidental. The position of the body on the gravestone appears to be a typical suicide arrangement, meaning, pick a convenient spot, convenient gravestone and let yourself have it. Seems straightforward, doesn't it? The new information gleaned only yesterday may have put paid to that theory. What was Joshua Moses Spencer doing in Bognor Regis five days prior to his death? That's the big question, and what I am sure you are all thinking: *"Did Spencer kill Hennessy then take his own life?"* 'But, if Hennessy was killed to stop him talking about the firm's irregularities, perhaps they were already emerging from other sources and it was too late for Spencer to stop the flood of information that was coming, all of it not to his advantage.

There was silence in the room as Hawkins paused to look at his papers.

'Now, I turn to the Sussex incident again. Hennessey had been missing for some time, yet no-one, family or business colleagues, thought to inform the police. Why was that? It would appear there was some reticence to do so. The business was in turmoil, and they probably thought he just made off. There have been no sightings of him, and the hotel registers, the local police appeals, the Sussex newspaper appeals, have given us nothing as to where he had been for the whole period of his absence. There is no abandoned car either. Did he travel by train? We do not know. The other concern for the Sussex police, and therefore us, is why was he found just in his underpants. Where were his clothes?

Appeals for those have been negative also. The feeling by the Sussex lads, is that his clothes went with him into the sea and simply drifted off. Could be over in France by now. One thing we have to note is that Hennessey had been missing for at least five days before Spencer's body was found.

'We know of no other person who had a grudge against or hated Spencer. His partner had made off, he was on his own. He got the gun and shot himself rather than face the embarrassment of police and fraud. That is, until we heard he had travelled to Sussex and back. Why?

'The body of David Hennessey, as you all know, is back in Cardiff and awaiting a funeral.

'The Chichester Coroner has deemed Hennessey's death as "Unlawful Killing", the wound on the back of his head being the cause. At this point we're all thinking: *'Spencer had something to do with his partner's death.'* As far as we're concerned, we are going to present to our coroner that at the culmination of proceedings, we believe that Joshua Moses Spencer took his own life, having killed his business partner to try to stop him revealing the truth about what he, Spencer, was doing. But, he was too late and had to acknowledge that. There was no-where else for him to turn. We believe that after listening to all the witnesses, the background evidence, and the facts, the jury at the Cardiff Coroner's Court will come to the same conclusion as we have: Suicide. It was down to the Sussex coroner and jury to come to their conclusion about Hennessy. Most of you can now go back to your stations. We have left a team to work with the Fraud boys. We wish them luck.'

John Harries put up his hand, stood and spoke. 'It can't be an open and shut case that Spencer had something to do with Hennessey's death, and we can't be a hundred percent sure that Josh shot himself. There are no witnesses in either case. And why didn't he do a runner, even without

Hannah. We haven't even looked at that possibility.' He sat back down, noting he was being ignored by the top table, apart from a severe scowl from Super Hawkins.

The incident room was stood down.

On 14th September 1973, the result of the Cardiff Coroner's Court was headlined in the first editions, with more clarifications in the eagerly awaited follow ups, with photographs of both men.

SPENCER TRAGEDY SUICIDE VERDICT
Spencer's business empire was crumbling

THE LAST REMNANT OF A COLLAPSING EMPIRE
Spencer shot himself in the head.

WHO KILLED SPENCER'S PARTNER?
'Unlawful killing' verdict in the Bognor tragedy.

POLICE REVEAL THAT SPENCER HAD GONE TO SUSSEX IN THE DAYS BEFORE HIS DEATH.
Sussex police working on theory that Spencer may be responsible for Hennessey's death.

In the weeks and months that followed, both in Cardiff and Sussex, the case investigations were wound down. It was the Welsh police who were the most satisfied with a "good job done". They had a definitive verdict at the Coroner's Court, that, on the balance of probabilities, it was most likely suicide, and "Suicide" was their ultimate verdict.

The Sussex police found themselves with an "Unlawful Killing" on their patch and enquiries continued in the normal way, with appeals to the public via the media for more information, witness tracing and sending teams to the Welsh capital to gain more information on the business dealings, associates, and family life of David Hennessey. Their prime suspect, Joshua Moses Spencer was dead. He had committed suicide after potentially murdering his partner Hennessey, but ultimately it could not be proved, as there was no evidence other than circumstantial.

Over the years the death of David Hennessey in Bognor Regis was forgotten; the case papers lying on file in the Criminal Records Office, where they probably still lie today.

10

Gareth and I finish reading at about the same time. Gareth takes out a notebook. I have no need to do so, as I have committed everything I've read to memory, but will need to write down some of the more important points I want to follow up.

I am the first to speak. 'Norman, this is quite a job you've done here,' I say. 'I'm guessing you were part of the investigation team, although you don't mention yourself. You must have an excellent memory.'

Norman spins round in his office chair, smiling with pride, his hands held together, fingertips connecting. He bows his head in thanks. 'So, can I expect an endorsement when I'm ready to publish?'

'No,' Gareth says flatly. Norman's smile fades and I'm surprised. Gareth is normally abrupt but this time he knows something. 'I was in the archives the other day, looking for the files on the Joshua Spencer case,' he says. 'I get now why I couldn't find them. Never mind your excellent memory. You stole those files. Hand them over now and what you won't get is, arrested.'

Norman's face is a picture. He is amazed, furious, his brow furrowed, with red flushes on both cheeks. He opens his mouth to berate Gareth, then changes his mind, opens a deep drawer on one side of his desk and pulls out a pile of old manilla folders, at least a foot deep. Gareth stands up to take them from him. 'What I will do, Norman, is see if I can get these back into the archives without anyone knowing they were missing in the first place. This case could blow wide open and I'd have to put myself in the firing line, knowing you nicked them. I have no intention of doing that.

Anyway, it seems to me you have everything you need already.' He pauses. 'Are there more?'

Norman doesn't reply. He sits back and folds his arms, face pouting like a recalcitrant child.

'I'll take that as a "yes",' Gareth says. 'I'm not going to ask for them now, but you'll find that any likely publisher will run a mile if, or rather when, they discover you stole police files to write your book.' He turns to me. 'We should go.'

I feel sorry for the old man, but Gareth is right.

'Don't you even have any questions for me?' Norman asks in a plaintiff voice.

'If we do, I'll come back to you,' Gareth says, already heading to the door.

Norman follows us out into the hall. We exit without a word.

I glance back as we walk along the road. Norman is leaning against his front door, smiling. 'See you soon,' he shouts.

'Why would he think he'll ever see us again?' I say to Gareth.

'Because he's kept something back,' Gareth says, 'something we need to know.'

**

Before we left, I had promised Hayden we wouldn't discuss whatever we learned until we reached my house, which is hard because I am bursting with comments and questions. Hayden is awake, sitting in the shade of the patio. She looks excited and gets her news in first.

'I got a call from Del, they've caught the three boys, right in the act. They're interviewing them now. All three of them, trying to overpower a woman of sixty-eight. This time they chose the wrong woman. She'd been taking self-defence lessons for years, in kung fu, or whatever, so she was more than a match for them. Apparently she laid one of them out cold, maced another one, and the third ran for it, but was caught in Queen Street, running in terror and easy to spot.'

She is laughing and I can't help joining in.

'I'll have to get onto the story,' I say. 'I'll go straight out. I shouldn't be more than an hour. Gareth, let Hayden read the files and tell her about Norman's story before I come back,' I say as I leave via the front door. 'There's something significant in there.'

There's much excitement at the Central Station. I spot Harry Morgan once or twice, yelling orders, as he sets up his investigation team. There'll be a lot to do, processing the ones who aren't hospitalized, then interviewing them with their solicitors, once the parents have been found. I pick up that they are from what are considered "good homes" and did, in fact, attend the same school as David Hunter. What is the world coming to? I wait in the foyer, and spot two sets of parents rushing in, plus one irate mother. I decide not to head up to the hospital. There, no-one is going to sneak a few words of info to an investigative reporter. I hear there will be a short briefing at twelve. It's now after eleven so I decide to wait, and call Gareth and Hayden to let them know. After the briefing, I'll have to go to the office to file copy, then I'll go straight home so we can discuss what we've learned about Agnes Hunter and her criminal father. And my editor and I have to have a seminal discussion again what we release about the co-incidence of the bodies of Agnes and her father being found on the same gravestone. I'm hoping I can still convince her to hold off for a few days more, as I think we're nowhere near the heart of the story, yet.

In the meantime, I get out my notebook and begin to write questions about Joshua Spencer. As I recall Norman's manuscript, it occurs to me that John Harries was a newbie in CID that day in 1973, so he couldn't be that old. Perhaps he's still alive. If so, we need to find him and speak to him. I doubt Norman will help, so I go looking for Dickie Pruitt. He's on duty and raises at eyebrow at my request.

'First Gareth looking for old files, now you trying to locate a detective from 1973,' he says. 'What's going on?'

'Maybe something, maybe nothing,' I say. 'I'd like to know if he's still alive and if so, where. Come on Dickie, help me out here.'

I've done him favours before, now he returns one for me. John Harries is indeed alive. He's seventy-nine and living in Penarth in a flat on the seafront. Nice. Nia and I loved to go down there on a warm Sunday. You can park on the front if you're lucky, stroll down the pier and along the seafront. The sea is the colour of mud in Penarth and there's no beach, but you can see the two islands in the channel, Flat Holm and Steep Holm, and there's often a clear view across to Somerset.

The briefing at midday is brief. Three boys have been caught and arrested on suspicion of a range of charges, including involuntary manslaughter. They will be in court tomorrow morning. As all three are minors, reporting of names will not be allowed.

I go back to the office, complete my piece, promise my editor I will be in court, although we both know that in youth court reporting restrictions will be in place, so the little shits cannot be named, nor their families. Should there be a conviction, the judge has the power to lift that restriction. We'll see how it turns out. Then we have our discussion. She agrees to give me three more days, but if anyone gets the story out first, she'll fire me.

'No-one else can get the story out first,' I reply. 'Since it's been ruled a suicide, I don't believe anyone else is looking closely. Like we agreed, I've been checking my sources, and no-one is asking questions related to Agnes Hunter's death.'

I head back to my house where Gareth and Hayden are waiting. Hayden has read the files and Gareth has filled in with his notes.

Hayden makes me a cup of tea and a sandwich and says, 'Where do we start Trevor?'

'With a precise summary of the case,' I say. 'Let's sit out. I'll tell it and Gareth can add anything I miss and correct me if I go wrong.'

It takes around fifteen minutes for me to go through the salient points.

'Let me summarise,' Hayden says. 'Agnes Hunter's father was a murdering, embezzling crook, who was probably shot by someone whom the police never discovered. The verdict was declared suicide, but we think it should have been an open verdict which would now make it a cold case. His wife scarpered because she possibly knew something the police didn't know, that frightened her sufficiently to change her name to Hannah Dole and run.'

'That about sums it up,' I say. 'It's certainly one explanation for why Hannah got out of Cardiff so quickly. Problem is, that doesn't help us find out who killed Agnes.'

'It gives us a couple of important leads,' she says, frowning into the air. She turns to me. 'Is John Harries still alive?'

'Yes, he's living down in Penarth, on the waterfront. We need to talk to him. He might know more than he let on at the time, more than ever got into a police file, or that was considered worth recording.'

'I wonder why Norman mentioned Harries seeing the giggling man with the child?' Gareth says. 'Hardly seems to me something to bother with.'

'Let's see if we can pin down John Harries,' I reply. 'That's our next step. There's something missing from that 1973 story and he's the only source can fill in the gap.'

'Are you suggesting we doorstep him Trev? He's an old man now.'

'No Gar, but there must be some way of finding out his mobile number.'

'I already have his number,' Hayden says.

'Please don't tell me you hacked a police database.'

'No. I used my ingenuity. Not everyone can only be contacted by mobile phone. I used the phone book. He still has a landline.' She holds up a piece of paper with a phone number on it.

'Smug git,' I say, dialling the number on my mobile.

John Harries answers just as I'm about to give up waiting. 'Harries speaking. Who is this?'

'John, my name is Trevor Jones. I'm a reporter with The Cardiff Sentinel. I'm here with a couple of friends, both of whom are police officers. I – we'd – like to talk to you about your memory of the death of Joshua Spencer, if that would be OK with you.'

There's a long silence at the other end, but he hasn't put the receiver down. Then, 'Why?'

'I've been troubled about the death of Agnes Hunter; you've probably read about her in the papers and heard the story on the news recently. Agnes was Joshua Spencer's daughter.'

More silence. I know not to speak. He either will or won't or will ask more questions.

'What makes you think I have anything to add?'

'We've been to see Norman Price. He's writing a book about…' I pause for a few seconds, as I don't want to say "murder", not yet, 'about deaths in Cardiff that the police never properly resolved. I know your wife and Spencer's wife were sisters. Norman said that you went to see the site of the death and you saw something. Please, could we come to speak to you?' I can hear myself begging.

'OK, I suppose. You can come to my place, I live in Penarth, down on the front.'

I resist the temptation to say, "I know where you live" and allow him to give me the address.

'Thank you, John. Two of us,' I look at Hayden and she nods, 'will come down tomorrow morning at eleven, if that's OK with you.'

'Yes, but this isn't for going in the papers. That's my condition.'

'No problem,' I say. 'We'll see you tomorrow, then.'

'I have to be back by three,' Hayden says. 'I have an appointment with the doc. If I'm signed fit, I'll be going back to work next week.'

'We'll be back well before then,' I say. 'Will you have to see Harry Morgan?'

She nods. 'I'll be in trouble for avoiding him, but I'll give my statement, see what he says. If I am fit, I'll be on desk duty for at least a week. He'll enjoy that, keeping me desk bound while he runs around looking like "action man".'

'It'll give you access to the databases,' I say. 'In the meantime, let's hope we get something useful out of John Harries.'

11

It being a Saturday, Penarth is busy and it takes some time to find a parking spot. John Harries is waiting at his door at eleven. He welcomes us in, and I introduce Hayden. His apartment is built on the side of what was once a steep cliff. He takes us down a level to his open plan kitchen and living room, then outside to the balcony. The front wall of the living room is all glass, giving a magnificent view of the Channel across to Somerset and Devon in all weathers. On the balcony is a small table ready with drinks paraphernalia and three chairs. We sit and he disappears back into the apartment via a side door.

Whilst we wait, I take in the view, the sunshine and the warmth. I close my eyes for a few seconds, remembering a time of complete contentment when Nia and I would bring a picnic to eat on the pier as the water ebbed and flowed beneath us, then walk along the front, gazing across the channel to Somerset. I open my eyes when John returns with a pot of coffee. He pours for each of us.

'Thank you for agreeing to speak to us John,' I begin. As usual I need no notebook. 'I'm not writing anything down nor am I recording what you say.' I am, of course, in my head. 'We've been looking into the death of Agnes Hunter. Can I ask, did you know she was Joshua Spencer's daughter?'

'I had no idea,' he says, somewhat taken aback. 'She was born a week or so after his death and still a month premature, probably the shock.' He shakes his head. 'Poor little Hannah. She was the youngest of the three. My Gwen was the eldest, then Paul, then Hannah. Did you know her full name was Johanna?'

'No,' I say. That could explain why we struggled to find the marriage between her and Spencer. 'John, we found a birth certificate for Agnes – I gather her first name was actually Veronica – and her baptism details name you as one of her godparents. The birth certificate didn't name a father and Hannah is named Hannah Dole, not Spencer. Do you know any of the history behind this?'

He nods, slowly and reluctantly. 'I'm taking your word for it that none of this gets into the papers Trevor, nor that the police will be involved,' he says to Hayden.

'Definitely not the papers,' Hayden says, 'but depending on where this goes, the police may eventually have to be involved. You see, we don't think Agnes committed suicide, as the inquest concluded, so these discussions are off the record, for now.'

'I never thought she did, even though I didn't know she was Joshua Spencer's daughter,' he says. 'Woman like that, doesn't kill herself.' He pauses, nodding. 'Not unless there's something going on the police didn't know about. Yes, that's possible.'

Hayden and I both sit forward, putting cups back on the table. 'John,' I say, 'in Norman Price's manuscript he says that you saw something that made an impression on you. Can you tell us about that?'

'I'll tell you what I remember and what I know. Best you hear the whole story.' He sits back, takes in a long breath and closes his eyes for a few seconds. When he opens them, he is looking out to sea.

'I didn't like Spencer from the start. He was slick, and handsome and a smooth talker. He was also clever, unlike our Hannah. She was a pretty girl, more than that, she was a real looker, Miss Wales at the age of seventeen, but not much up there.' His pointed finger taps the side of his head. 'She fell for him, big. He married her because he liked a beautiful girl on his arm, but he soon got fed up with her. Used to hit her, a lot. But she always made excuses for him, as they do. In those days, police didn't get involved in domestics. Whatever happened behind closed doors between husband and wife was none of our business. She had a couple of miscarriages; Gwen suggested Josh beat her in the early stages. When she fell pregnant for the fourth time, she left him and came to stay with us until she reached her twenty weeks. He tossed her aside and found another woman, then another. My Gwen was beside herself, tried to persuade Hannah to leave him permanently, come to live with us, but she wouldn't do it. She was convinced he would love the baby once it was born.

'Hannah was so dumb it was quite incredible at times, but nonetheless she knew something had gone wrong at the company. She told Gwen Joshua had too much money and was always in a foul temper. They had moved from a small cottage in Whitchurch to a big fancy apartment in the centre of the city, paid for in cash. When Hannah asked him where the money came from, he gave her a punch so hard it knocked a couple of her teeth out. Of course, he paid a good dentist to put a plate in. Then his business partner disappeared, Hennesscy his name was. Hannah told us he came around a few times and he and Josh had big arguments.'

'Can you tell us when that was, in relation to Spencer's death?' Hayden askes.

John scrunches up his face, trying to pull out a memory. 'About a month before Josh died, I think. Then Josh shot himself, on that grave. It was mayhem, I can tell you. Because I was his brother-in-law, I was told to go down to the morgue to do the ID. Pretty nasty, I can tell you, with half his face missing, but there was enough left for me to recognise him. We never let Hannah near him.'

My turn now. 'John, before you went to the morgue you visited the scene of Spencer's death, and you saw someone in the crowd watching, who made an impression on you. Do you remember that?'

'Of course,' he says, 'the giggling man. I remember because I saw him again.'

I hold in a burst of surprise. 'When was that John?'

'You know the coroner's inquest brought in a suicide verdict?'

We both nod.

'The police kept looking, because the DCS, Hawkins, never quite let go of the murder theory, but they couldn't find anyone who might have wanted to do it, you know, the people he'd robbed, but they all had alibis. After a couple of months, he announced they weren't looking for anyone else regarding the death, so he wound down the teams and moved on.'

'But you knew something else?' Hayden prompted.

'Once it was announced we weren't looking any more, and Hannah had taken off for London with baby Ronnie, that's what we called her then, I couldn't let it go. The image of that grinning, giggling man with the small child was in my head. On Christmas Eve I went back to the site of the death. It was snowing, I remember. I walked through the cemetery for a while, before I headed to the particular gravestone. I was at the end of a long row when I saw, farther on down, a man at the grave. At first, I didn't think anything of it, but as I got closer he looked up. It must have been the crunching of my feet on the snow that alerted him. He had a small child with him, who was dancing on the grave. He looked up and saw me coming. He grabbed the child and ran, but not before I saw that same grin as he raised up his shoulders, giggling. I chased after him, but I'm embarrassed to say, I slipped and fell in the snow. By the time I got up, he was gone. I looked around for about ten minutes, but you know how big that cemetery is. So, I walked back to the gravestone. It was better cared for than when Josh shot himself on it. There was a fresh wreath of Christmas roses laid up against the cross.'

'John, whose grave was it?' I ask.

'The man was called Charles Cadence. I hadn't seen that first time around, but now someone had cleared the blood off.'

'Did anyone called Cadence come up during the investigation?' Hayden asks.

John shakes his head. 'Never. There's a couple of places named after this Cadence. He was a big noise back in the 1890s. I did a bit of research, not much. He died in 1893, shot. A man called Tarr was arrested and tried for murder, but turned out he was innocent, as he had an alibi. No-one else was ever caught.'

'So no relationship to Joshua Spencer's death, you're sure of that?' Hayden asks.

'Well, never say no, but at the time, in '73 as I say, no-one called either Cadence or Tarr ever came into the investigation. And that's what I know.'

'John, why do you think Hannah ran away?'

He gives it some thought. 'She knew more than she let on. There used to be dinner parties over the years she was expected to attend. She never had to say much, well she couldn't, could she. She told Gwen she didn't like the men who attended, thought they were villainous. She got it into her head they were the Mafia, and we couldn't talk her out of it. Really, as if. They could well have been crooked businessmen, but Hannah's flights of fancy had them as Mafia business men who would have hired assassins to come after her after Josh died. She used to talk to Gwen after each dinner party and couldn't even remember their names or which firm they represented. But it was enough to send her running to London with baby Ronnie.'

'Thank you John,' I say. 'We'll have to give this some thought.' Hayden and I go to stand up when he says, 'There was the letter, of course, but we never thought that was important.'

We stop. Hayden falls back into her seat. 'What letter John?'

'Hannah found it when she was clearing out. It was made out of newspaper cuttings, with lots of weird scribblings. It was addressed to Josh.'

'Did you see it?' I ask, holding my breath.

'Yes, Hannah showed it to Gwen and me. It said stuff like "spawn of Satan" and "killer family". It didn't threaten anything or anyone, like. The stuff scribbled around was drawings of devils with horns and weird symbols and letters and numbers. I showed it to DCS Hawkins, but he said it was some nutter who'd read about Josh.'

'He made no attempt to follow it up?' Hayden says, her voice dripping with anger and contempt.

'No', he threw it into a file. He'd made up his mind by then to accept it was a suicide. You'll probably find it, if you can find the files.'

'Confirmation bias, perhaps,' Hayden says. We both look at her. 'Bad decision made after he had already decided it was suicide, so he no longer wanted anything that suggested a contrary outcome.'

'We'll find the file,' I say. I can't wait now to get back home to go through the files we have. Gareth has left them on my investigation room table. I'm deciding whether or not to tell this man that Agnes Hunter received a similar letter. I'm biting my lips when Hayden, who can read my mind, gives me a piercing stare and shakes her head. She's right. He's given us vital information, but he's an old, retired man.

No need to involve him further, certainly not in the story I'm going to be writing. I stand up. 'Thanks for your help John. This has been interesting.' I hand him my business card and ask him to call me if he thinks of anything else that wasn't recorded at the time.

'What are you thinking?' Hayden asks as we walk to her car.

'I'm convinced now this is a strange vendetta. Who is carrying it out I don't know, but it goes back beyond Agnes's father. I want to go through that box of files more thoroughly. If that letter is in there, I want to show it to Reginald and David Hunter. If not, I'm going straight back to Norman Price and ask him, with my hands around his throat, where it is.'

12

Hayden parks at her flat down on the Bay. I'm going to walk home. She's going to get ready for her meeting with the police doctor, outsourced of course, and she needs to look the part because she wants to go back to work. She'll go straight there. I am going to go to the next police briefing at five this afternoon. Hayden thinks she should be there, if she's given the "all clear" to return to work, but we won't acknowledge each other.

This gives me a couple of hours to begin reading through the Joshua Spencer files in detail, making notes as I go. There are twelve paper files altogether, dealing with various aspects of the investigation. Let's get going.

After two hours I'm becoming frustrated as I plough through. The story is just as John Harries told it, but there is no mention of the giggling man, when John first saw him, or later. Much of what's in the files I can ignore: copies of claims for expenses, notes from meetings with informants. Interesting that not one of them could give any information. Then, at last I reach it, in the eleventh file. It's an A5 sheet of paper with, as John Harries described, the words "spawn of Satan" and "killer family" and "you will pay for your sins". The drawings around it are disturbing and frightening. As well as the devil and goats with horns, there are strings of numbers, strange symbols I don't recognise and stick men with daggers in their torso. The ink is all black. This is very ugly and the product of a deranged mind, just like the Agnes letter. I look at the paper for a long time, thinking there's a message in it, that could help us move forward. I finally get it. It's the phrase, "spawn of Satan". It's like hearing the "justice, again" at the Coroner's Court. The message is that we must go further back into the history of the Spencer family. But how far? When I look up, almost four hours have passed since I began reading. I have to start heading up to the Central Station for the five o'clock briefing.

I arrive just in time and out of breath. My colleague has thoughtfully kept a seat for me on the front row. I see Hayden at the back of the room and give her what I hope is a discreet but meaningful nod. Gareth isn't there. He isn't on the murder team.

Chief Superintendent Malcolm introduces everyone then hands over to Harry Morgan, who is, naturally, in his element. The man loves an audience. He confirms three boys have been arrested and variously charged, including involuntary manslaughter. They will be appearing in court the following morning, but with the usual restrictions for fifteen and sixteen-year-olds. No further information is given that could identify them. There is confirmation that one of the boys was armed with a knife. A few questions are asked, with the expected vague replies: enquiries still ongoing, witnesses being sought and interviewed and re-interviewed, evidence being gathered, etcetera.

Afterwards, I find Gareth on the front desk. He can come round for an hour at about seven and he'll let Hayden know. I walk home and get out my computer to write and file my copy for the morning paper, which my editor approves. Then, I set out some of the more interesting papers from the Spencer murder files on the table. There's still half an hour before Gareth and Hayden are due, so I begin a search on the BMD free site, to see if I can find the birth of Joshua Spencer. If he's the "spawn", I want to know who "Satan" is, in the words of our deranged nutter. I find the reference to his birth in 1944 and am about to go onto the General Register Office website to purchase the birth certificate when Gareth and Hayden let themselves in at the back gate and walk up through the garden. They head straight for the "murder room", as we are now calling it.

'Are you cleared to return to work?' I ask immediately.

'Yes,' Hayden replies, 'but it took some persuading. The doctor wanted me to wait another week, but I said I was already stir crazy and bored, so he gave in. So, what have we here?'

They both examine the letter. Hayden pulls a face. 'This is a crazy person,' she says. 'beyond psychopathic. I wonder what Joshua Spencer made of it?'

'If I'd received that, it would have scared the shit out of me,' Gareth says. 'I would have gone straight to the police, but of course, he couldn't, could he?'

'Then how did this end up in the file, do you think?' Hayden asks.

'John Harries told me that Hannah showed it to him and Gwen. She gave it to him and he passed it on to Hawkins, but Hawkins thought it was just the word of a deranged nutter. It looks like he must just have thrown it in the file. He also raise the issue of the giggling man, but the Super didn't want to hear it. DCS Hawkins had made peace with himself about the suicide outcome, so this would have been inconvenient. He put it down to some crazy investor who had heard about Josh, and who had lost money, or something like that,' Hayden says.

'I want to take a look at Spencer's family history,' I say. 'Whoever wrote the letter refers to his father, or grandfather or whatever. Spawn of Satan. This "Satan", whoever he is – and it's definitely a man – is somewhere in the past. I'm about to get a pdf of Spencer's 1944 birth certificate.'

I carry on with my GRO certificate purchase and within minutes it appears on my screen. We all three lean in to look at the result.

Joshua's father is Captain Gabriel Moses Spencer, Army Captain, mother: Teresa Spencer, nee O'Halloran. Joshua Moses Spencer born 19th June 1944. Address: 138 Dean Street, Cardiff. Birth registered by mother, who confirms home birth. Father is deceased.

'I wonder if Joshua's father was killed in the Normandy landings in 1944? Whatever, father and son would never have known each other. Perhaps the mother married again. I'll find out,' I say.

'Why?' Gareth asks.

'Because someone hated Joshua Spencer enough to send this, and hated his father too, so the answer to who killed him must lie somewhere even further back in his past,' Hayden says.

'What's worrying me,' I add, 'is that we know it didn't stop with Joshua, because Agnes received identical letters and was killed in the same way, in the same place. This may be a wild and weird theory, but someone is carrying out an old vendetta against the Spencer family. To work it out, we'll have to keep going back until we find the trigger, the incident, that started this off. That means finding out everything we can about every member of the direct history of the Spencer family, and any offshoots, like wives, siblings, cousins and so on.'

'That's a lot of work Trevor,' Hayden says.

'It's a reporter's lot,' I reply. 'We have to do whatever it takes to get the story, and this is what it's going to take. But I have two concerns, and they're both about safety. One, our safety. Hayden, someone has already attacked you. This tells me, and I've said this before, someone knows what we're doing and we three are targets, meaning we'll have to watch our backs. Who could that someone be who knows that we're still looking into the case of Agnes Hunter's death. I've wracked by brains. It could be another reporter, but I don't think so, because I know most of the leading reporters in Cardiff and beyond, and none of them has ever said anything remotely psychopathic to me in the pursuit of a case. Two, if this really is a vicious vendetta, then it's not over. As well as Reg there's still David Hunter and his sister Louisa and her family. They have to be informed of what we're finding out.'

'There's another clue in there for us Trevor,' Hayden says, looking through the papers. 'The name, "Moses" in two generations of Spencer men – I'm betting when you find out the name of Gabriel Spencer's father, it'll include Moses. If I'm right, that'll be the key to identifying how and why this started.'

'That's if he's right,' Gareth says, with a note of scepticism. 'What if Trevor's theory is wrong?'

'I'm going to be thorough,' I say. 'I'll annotate everything I find along the way. If anything happens to me, one of you will be able to pick it up.'

'Nothing's going to happen to you,' Gareth says. He's not quite shouting.

'I'm going to carry on with this line of research,' I say. 'I'll work from here. If I need anything that I can't get from public records, I'll call one or other of you. Hayden, are you OK down in your flat on your own?'

She nods and Gareth huffs. 'I have a door entry code on the ground floor and the same on my apartment. I don't use keys,' she says.

'Gareth, you should be OK at home, too.'

'Of course I will be,' he says. 'This is stupid.'

'I don't think it is Gar. Whoever hit Hayden – and it wasn't a random event – I say again knows we're investigating. I can't figure out their reason for singling out Hayden rather than you or me, but they probably know by now we've been to see both Norman Price and John Harries. We have to be careful.'

Gareth looks doubtful.

'We'll see,' I say. 'In the meantime, I'm going back up to Pontypridd on Monday, for the inquest of Maureen Henslow, the woman who died after the attack by the boy gang, which I expect will open and then be adjourned for the time being. Will you be there Hayden?'

'No, Del's covering it. He'll say police enquiries have made progress but are ongoing.'

'OK. I'll let you both know if anything of interest comes up, but I don't expect it will.'

We leave it there. Hayden is tired and wants to go home. Gareth is meeting Tracy in the pub.

I am going to continue for a couple of hours on this family history research. Truth to tell, I'm enjoying it. I haven't honed my investigative skills like this for some time. I'm excited and hoping something will come of this. Let's see what I can find out about the Spencer dynasty.

13

After working on for a couple of hours last night, I wake up exhausted. It doesn't take much to wear me out these days. I need to get fitter. I'm not a runner, but I used to box a little in my youth, and when Nia and I first married. As the years went on, the intervals between the use of my punchbag grew longer as my paunch grew bigger. I still have the bag. It's lying in the corner of the shed, behind the mower and other detritus. That reminds me, I must cut the grass. Nia liked it always short and neat. On an impulse, I go out through the garden and unlock the shed. Yes, it's still there, covered in cobwebs, and the hook on which it hung is still there, too. I re-enforced the roof to take its weight. I move the mower out of the way and drag the punchbag to a spot under the hook. I manage to stand it up, but I can't lift it. Have I become such a lump of lard? Rhetorical question. I find my old gloves on a shelf. A couple of spiders, who have taken up residence, are soon removed to the garden. That's enough exercise for today. I'll think about how to hoist the bag up and re-attach it later. I might still have my old shorts, vest and shoes, somewhere upstairs. Actually, no point looking. I'll have gone up at least two sizes. Maybe, if there's time, I'll visit one of those sports shop places and get some new kit. I won't tell Gareth, though. He'll laugh his bollocks off.

Maybe the punching will help to ease my frustration in not being able to find out more about the Spencer family, in particular, in relation to any event that might account for a vendetta, if this is what it is. I have discovered that Gabriel Moses Spencer, father of Joshua, died on 6th June 1944, on Gold Beach, Normandy. He was a member of the South

Wales Borderers. He was thirty-one years old when he died. I have sent off for his war record but am assuming he was a victim of enemy fire, although he was in the second wave of the Borderers landing on Gold beach that day.

I also found out that Gabriel was born on 28th September 1913, the son of Joseph Moses Spencer – Hayden's prediction was one hundred percent correct - and his wife Eluned, nee Thomas. They lived in Whitchurch in Cardiff. He had been to University in Cardiff and joined the army when called up in 1940. I couldn't find anything unusual about this family. So far, so good. I wondered briefly about whoever was the original Moses, but I don't want to get sidetracked. Lots of families carry a family name through generations, for some special reason only known by them. And that's when it all went wrong, as I will explain to Hayden and Gareth as soon as I see them.

They're both on shift today, which gives me only an hour at lunchtime to update them on where I've reached in my research. I begin with Gabriel Spencer's father, the next man up the family line. Joseph Moses Spencer. But this is where I'm stuck, because he just appears out of thin air. There's neither birth, nor baptismal record. I checked the Cardiff census records and found the first record of a Joseph Moses Spencer on the 1901 census where he's an eleven-year-old schoolboy at Friars school for Boys, the son of Captain Nathaniel Spencer of the Purple Star Line, a sea captain, and Mrs Lilian Spencer. His school record is also online but there's no more information than that he was a pupil aged twelve in 1902. Next is the 1911 census. Again, born in Cardiff and now twenty-one years old. He's a Sea Cadet. He doesn't appear on the 1921 census, so I thought perhaps he was at sea. However, the real answer for what happened to him comes from the next set of records – WWI. A great many of these have been lost but Joseph's survived. On joining up in 1914, he gave his age as twenty-four, so more confirmation he was born around 1890, but when I check back he does not appear on the 1891 census. In 1911 he is single, but on his war record he names his next of kin not as one of his parents, but as his wife, Eluned. I check back to the free BMD site. Joseph and Eluned were married in 1912. He joined up in 1914 and attained the rank of Captain. When I reach the end of the record, I discover that he died at the Ypres Salient in 1917. His name is on the Menin Gate, which means his body was never recovered. Gabriel was the couple's only child. So the question that remains is, where did Gabriel's father, Joseph Moses Spencer, come from?'

'I was right about the name Moses,' Hayden says. 'It has to be significant. There has to be a plain Moses Spencer somewhere.'

'I agree,' I reply. 'but there's no Moses Spencer born or died in Cardiff, nor in South Wales anywhere between 1850 and 1890. Joseph's father was Nathaniel Spencer, the sea captain who was born in Somerset. I haven't found any further reference to Joseph's parents anywhere in his personal history, but I'll keep looking.'

Which I did, to no avail for the rest of the day. I gave up around ten and, my head full of ideas on how to track down Joseph bloody Spencer. Nevertheless, I fall asleep immediately.

**

We are all too tired and feel in need of a break, being as it's Sunday, the proverbial day of rest. I don't know what Hayden and Gareth are doing, but I decide to have a go at putting up my punchbag before I go out to buy myself the appropriate clothing. It takes me over an hour to get the bag into position and secured, and by the time I'm finished I've exhausted my entire supply of residual energy and need a cup of tea and some breakfast. I cook myself a "full Welsh", which is exactly what I'll need to stop eating if I'm to get fit. I get dressed and walk to a city centre sports shop where I buy a full set of boxing gear from a young lass who looks barely out of her teens, if she is out of them at all, and is doing a Sunday job. She is speechless as she stares at me throughout my visit to the store.

As I leave the store, I bump into Betty who is just coming in. 'Hello Trevor, fancy meeting you here.' She's blushing. I hope she's not stalking me. I know she's been alone for a long time, but I'm not ready for a new relationship and anyway, it would never in a million years be Betty.

'Just buying some boxing gear Betty,' I say. 'What about you?'

'Boxing, eh? I've decided to take up yoga, so I need an outfit.' I think about Betty in a leotard, then immediately banish the imprint from my mind. 'Well, nice to see you, I say,' and get away as quickly as possible.

'Do you have time for a coffee?' she asks. 'I was about to buy some new swimming goggles too, but they can wait.'

'Sorry not today. Work to do. Just on my way to my office.'

Strange co-incidence.

From the centre of town, I walk down to the Bay and wander around with my bag of goodies. Again, it's a lovely day and there are crowds out walking, admiring the amazing Welsh buildings, dating from the days when Cardiff was a major coal port. I salute those that have transformed this former wreck of a place into, in my opinion, one of the greatest cities in the UK. I stand, as always, in front of the smooth curved shape of the Millenium Centre, with its motto carved into the stone in both Welsh and English: "Creu Gwir Fel Gwydr O Ffwrnais Awen", accompanied in

English by, "In These Stones Horizons Sing." I once asked what the poet meant and was told that's not the actual translation of the Welsh, which is: "Creating truth like glass from inspiration's furnace".

I think about that motto as I continue to walk past the Welsh Parliament building, the Senedd, and farther along the walkway to the Norwegian Church. I stop here, enter its café and have a coffee, all the time thinking about the motto on the Millenium building – "Creating truth like glass…" It gives me hope that I can find the truth about the death of Agnes Hunter. I need the inspiration, but not today.

I spend the afternoon gardening and thinking. After a couple of hours, I have the garden looking how Nia liked it, but there's still no clarity to my thoughts. I know that the journey still has a long way to go. Later, once there isn't another weed to dig up, I carry on with the research well into the evening, my frustration increasing.

**

I spend Monday morning trying various genealogical sites looking for the birth of Joseph Moses Spencer, again to no avail, then remember I have to attend the inquest into the death of Maureen Henslow.

The inquest is due to begin at two. I have to hurry as I lost track of time in the researching. I decide to make my way up to Ponty on the train and begin the long trek up the hill to the Coroner's Court building. It's raining today, or is that just in Ponty? Does it ever actually stop here? Cardiff was fine when I left. Halfway up the hill there's a café. As I pass it I see the usual inquest crowd sitting at a table in the window: Terrence and Mary Anne, Betty, Billie, Sid and Harry, today with Marcus, their dog, whose head seems permanently cocked to one side when he's sitting behaving himself. He has a way of looking at you with big brown soft eyes that persuade you to give him half of whatever you've ordered. The scruffy mutt will eat anything.

Mary Anne sees me and beckons me in. I check my watch; still half an hour to go. I decide to join them as they're always good for a bit of local gossip.

'Surprised to see you all here today,' I say as I sit next to Betty. 'It's only going to be an open and adjourn.'

'We know,' Terrence replies, 'but Mary Anne and I knew Mo Henslow, so we're here out of respect.'

'Nasty little shits,' Billie says. 'Prison's too soft these days. They get TVs, you know, in their cells.'

The others all shake their heads. I know it's not true. I've been inside Cardiff jail several times to interview prisoners. These people here have no idea what it's like, and I can't be bothered to educate them. It would go against what they've convinced themselves of and they probably wouldn't believe me, so I ignore the remark.

'What can you tell us Trevor?' Betty asks. 'You must have the inside story.' She leans forward and I catch a whiff of too strong, stale old perfume.

'No more than anyone else,' I say. 'I went to the briefing, which was very brief, last Thursday afternoon. "Enquiries are ongoing," was the message. That's what we'll hear later. Police aren't giving anything away, not yet.'

'I blame the parents,' Billie says, preening. 'Not enough discipline. Now, in our day—'

'Time to go, I think, if we're going to get our seats,' I say, to stop an onslaught of boring reminiscences that bear no resemblance to whatever actually used to go on, although I wouldn't be surprised to hear that Billie was hit on the head quite a lot as a child.

'What about that young policewoman they hit over the head? Betty asks.

'Police think it might have been those boys and as far as I know, she's fine,' I reply, 'and soon back at work.'

'That's lucky,' Betty replies. 'Friend of yours, isn't she? Could have been a lot worse.'

'Indeed, Betty. And no, she's not a friend of mine. Whoever did it must have hit her on the wrong side of her head,' I say with a grin.

'Is there a right side?' Sid asks. He looks indignant.

'Joke Sid, let's get going.'

**

As expected, the inquest is opened, Del on behalf of South Wales police does his bit and Jim Bowen confirms the adjournment for two weeks.

The oldies stay on to sympathise with Maureen Henslow's sister and other relatives who have attended. Betty sidles up to offer me a toffee, which I refuse, and I wonder for a few seconds why Betty thinks Hayden is my friend. Maybe she's noticed something, which means that we aren't being careful enough, so I'll have to warn Gareth and Hayden tonight. If Betty thinks we seem friendly, then who else has noticed? They invite me to join them at the weekly pub quiz on Friday. Sometimes I go, sometimes I don't. I say I'll think about it. I make a quick getaway, reach the station just in time for the train, then take an Uber up to the Hunter house where I have an arranged appointment with Reg and David.

They are waiting for me in the garden, sitting under their pergola, with untouched glasses of lemonade in front of them, looking shocked and vacant. I wonder if Reg's drink is laced with vodka; he's got that glassy eyed look of a man who's been over-imbibing.

'Has something happened?' I ask.

In reply, David hands me a piece of A5 paper. Before I take hold of it, I can already see what's on it. I recognise the drawings and the numbers. I pull in a deep breath and take it from his hand. 'When did this arrive?' I ask.

'This morning,' Reg says. 'As you can see, it's addressed to me, but it's about David.'

It's a horrible thing, with just one sentence: "Your son is next".

David's hands are shaking. 'Is someone going to try to kill me?' he asks me in a trembling voice.

I don't reply, but turn to Reg. 'You have to take this to the police now. These days they can recover fingerprints from paper. No more waiting.' He sits up and I see his hands start to shoot up and his head shake.

'Reg, this is too serious now, it's a direct threat to David's life.'

He sinks back down in his chair, nodding, tears in his eyes. 'Who is doing this to us Trevor?'

'I don't know yet, but I've discovered a link to the past. You already know Agnes's father died in the same place as she did, in the same way. We all think she was murdered. This confirms it.' I glance at the crude picture drawn in the centre of the page, a goat's head with David's name annotated underneath, and below that: "You are next." 'This is sick,' I say, 'from a sick, mad mind. It's my belief someone is conducting a vendetta against your family.'

'Is Louisa safe?' Reg asks. I hear panic rising in his voice.

'I don't know Reg. This must go to the police. Do you want me to take it?'

He nods. 'It's Agnes's funeral tomorrow. Can you take it now? We might need a police presence there.'

'Of course,' I say, standing up. 'and give me the one from Agnes's solicitor, which says she's frightened and in trouble. Could you drive me down to the station?'

**

When I reach the Central Station, I ask for Chief Superintendent Malcolm, telling the desk sergeant it's a matter of extreme urgency and probable danger. He gives me a strange look but makes the call. 'Sorry Trevor, he's left five minutes ago. Gone to a meeting in Swansea.'

'Then he needs to come back,' I say, holding up the letter. 'This is an imminent death threat related to an ongoing case.' He looks at the letter, frowning, and hears the agitation in my voice. 'OK, I trust you. Let me see if I can get him on his mobile.' He succeeds. I can tell from the way he winces, the Chief Super is not amused. 'He says this had better be beyond fucking good. He'll be here in ten minutes.' The old relationship still works.

I go outside to tell Reg that Chief Superintendent Malcolm is on his way back to the station and it might be advisable for him to come in with me, to give more details about how the note was delivered. Reg is clearly not keen – probably the vodka – but he doesn't drive away, although he does tell David to come to sit with him in the front passenger seat.

Twenty-two minutes later the Chief Super steams in through the door. I wince at his expression. 'Come,' he says, and I follow.

Once we've reached his office, we both sit. 'Urgent and dangerous, is it Trevor, enough to come straight to me and bypass Inspector Morgan?'

I could say something about what might have happened if I'd gone to Harry Morgan, but instead I hand him the letter, which is now in a plastic folder, plus the letter from Agnes. He picks them up between two fingers, skims through them then throws them on the desk. 'The Hunter boy receives a note from some lunatic, and you pull me out of an important meeting?'

I pull the Josh Spencer letter out of my pocket and hand it to him. At first he's puzzled.

'Sent to Joshua Spencer in 1973,' I say, 'just before he died. He was Agnes Hunter's father. And in the Agnes Hunter file you'll find another identical one, that's if Harry Morgan has handed it over yet. He may have destroyed it.'

His expression changes. 'How long have you known about these?'

'The one to David Hunter – today, an hour or so ago. The Agnes Spencer copy, a couple of days. Harry Morgan dismissed it as the work of some lunatic.' I emphasise the last words to make sure he gets the point. 'The Joshua Spencer letter came out of a police file from 1973, which was taken from here and has now been returned – not by me in either case. It was also dismissed by the investigating Detective Chief Superintendent, Hawkins his name was, as the work of some lunatic.'

Jimmy's face has lost most of its colour, as he closes his eyes and takes in the implications of what he's just heard. 'Are you one hundred percent certain about all of this Trevor? I'll need to see the research you've done, defining the relationship between Agnes Hunter and Joshua Spencer. I know a little of the Spencer case, although it was before my time. It had major financial repercussions in Cardiff.'

'Naturally Jimmy,' I say. 'I can show you everything.'

He nods. 'This changes things. I'll have to call the investigation team back together.' He stands, frowning in thought as if forgetting I'm still here. 'This must remain completely confidential until we investigate and confirm it's all true. You can go now.'

'No,' I say. 'I'm not done. Reg is angry, David is terrified. Agnes Hunter's funeral is tomorrow. I have more, much more on what happened to Joshua Spencer, and I have a theory.'

'You can tell it to Inspector Morgan when we re-open the Agnes Hunter case.'

'Not a chance,' I say. 'Hayden Wilkins and other women in this station are wary of Harry Morgan and don't trust him. I know because I asked. And he's no person to be questioning a terrified sixteen-year-old. Harry Morgan is an arrogant, sexist, misogynistic racist, as we both know and don't pretend you've forgotten. If you'd bothered to look closer, you'd have seen most of his team dislike him. And he didn't tell the whole truth at the Agnes Hunter inquest. He already had a letter like one of those, given to him by Reg Hunter.'

Jimmy Malcom has moved to stand in the doorway, scowling at me, but he doesn't tell me to get out. 'You'd better be certain about what Morgan has said and done.'

'I am,' I reply. 'Ask his team. And don't ask me how I know what's going on inside this station. I will not reveal my sources.'

'In other words, it's Sergeant Roberts.'

'No,' I reply. 'He may have made the occasional offensive comment in relation to Harry Morgan, but so have others. You should check with them.'

'Whom I decide to speak to is none of your business Trevor.'

'Reginald and David Hunter are outside in Reg's car. They gave me a lift here.'

'Tell them to go home. I'll have a FLO allocated. You say the funeral is tomorrow?'

I nod.

'Very well. Someone will attend on behalf of the police. Immediately afterwards, the investigation will begin. Now, get out of my office before I have you thrown out.' He pauses. 'And just remember Trevor, I owe you nothing. All debts are paid.'

This time I leave.

Reg and David give me a lift home. As I expected, Reg isn't happy about a family liaison officer taking up residence in his house, but David is grateful. I WhatsApp Gareth and Hayden to tell them what's happened. There are no immediate replies, but I guess CID will likely be in uproar, which makes me smile.

There's a letter waiting for me on the doormat. It's the record of Gabriel Moses Spencer's military service. I put the kettle on, then sit down in the murder room. It takes ten minutes to read the contents of the envelope and fully take in the facts and the consequences, which are that Gabriel Moses Spencer was yet another of the Spencer family to have been murdered. There is a note with the record, asking me to call the writer. In a state of shock, I make the call immediately.

14

Hayden Wilkins stands in front of Chief Superintendent Malcolm. She knows the rest of Harry Morgan's team have already been spoken to but has no idea what they've said. She has a suspicion as to what's going on, since Gareth managed to tell her on her way in, that Trevor has spent time with the Chief Super, who elected to come back from a meeting in Swansea to speak to him. She feels a shiver of hope, but suppresses it, in case she's over optimistic.

'Sergeant, are you aware of being referred to in a pejorative way by Inspector Morgan?'

'Yes Sir, if you're referring to his suggestive behaviour, and saying women like me should never be allowed to join the force.'

'Has he ever said that to your face?'

'Not exactly Sir, but I did overhear him telling other members of the team not to bother with me, as I don't have either the intellectual capacity or the stamina to be a detective, that I'm a "token gesture to inclusivity".'

The Chief Super swallows. 'I see. Is anyone else on the team referred to in pejorative terms, within your hearing?'

'Yes Sir. I once overheard him refer to Sergeant Khan as "Pakki Boy", and Constable Smith – that's Del Smith – as "the brainless hulk". Of course, it would be his word against mine.'

After a few moments, the Chief Super says, 'In light of evidence the reporter Trevor Gwyn Jones has supplied – and none of it had better have come from you or your job will be gone – I am re-opening the Agnes Hunter case. I will inform the coroner. There will be a new team, headed by Detective Chief Inspector Evan Broderick from Swansea. Fresh pair of eyes. He will report directly to me. You will be his Acting Inspector for the purpose of this investigation.'

'What about Inspector Morgan Sir?'

Malcolm coughs and ignores the question. 'DCI Broderick will be here tomorrow and he'll want to meet with you to go over everything about Agnes Hunter's death. That's all.'

'Thank you Sir.' Hayden leaves the Chief Super's office and bounces down the corridor to where the team are waiting in the CID room.

'Hi guys, meet your new Acting Detective Inspector,'

'Don't get too big for your boots, Wilky,' Del says with a grin.

'Not me. Don't have the big boots yet, but I must go out and buy some. But seriously, the real boss will be here tomorrow. Just for today, it's me. So, let's get ready and be well prepared to provide a thorough update. Gather round, people, let's talk through what we know.'

No-one asks about Harry Morgan, although a rumour has spread that he has been returned to uniform in another area of South Wales Police.

**

Later that evening, Hayden arrives at my house at seven, accompanied by Gareth. She's bouncing like Tigger. I can see they are both fired up. I want to tell them my news, but I let them speak first.

'I've got you to thank for it,' Hayden says, kissing me on the cheek. She's brought fish and chips with her, and we are sitting outside to eat. 'What's that lovely smell Trevor?'

I sniff the air. 'Jasmine,' I say, pointing to the wall where it's coming into bloom. 'It's especially pungent in the evening. What happens now?'

'First of all, I'm meeting the new man at eight tomorrow morning. I'll be taking him through the story from the time you and Gareth began to talk at Agnes's inquest, right up to today, and the note to David Hunter. I won't leave anything out Trevor. I'm going to tell him that you've been vital to getting this case to where it is.'

'What if he wants to thank me for my involvement then tells me to piss off and leave it to the police?' I'm thinking about whether or not I should say something to her about what Norman Price is doing with his book, whilst leaving Norman's involvement out of the story. I fork up my last few chips, then put the fork down, sit back and fold my arms.

'I'm hoping to convince him your assistance has been essential, because I'd like to keep it going,' Hayden says.

'No chance,' Gareth says. 'Never met a senior officer yet who'll let a civilian, never mind a member of the press, get anywhere near police work.'

'We've used consultants before,' Hayden says.

'But not reporters,' Gareth replies.

'I don't intend to get involved in police work,' I say.

'He'll find out soon enough,' Gareth says.

'Find out what?' Hayden asks, leaning forward. 'What is it you two aren't telling me?'

I glare at him. 'Something from the past, the long-forgotten past.'

'It never goes away,' Gareth says. 'Why don't you just tell her?'

I think for a minute. I suppose she has to know, now this is likely to be a major investigation. 'When Gareth and I joined the Cardiff force together, there were three of us on the same training course who knew each other from school.'

'You? You were a copper?'

'For twelve months,' I reply. 'It wasn't for me, I didn't like the grunt work. I wanted to be a detective, but apparently I got the nod I wasn't "suitable material". So, I resigned and became a reporter. Detection is in my blood.'

'Why weren't you suitable material?'

I don't answer.

'Because he went off looking into a case on his own,' Gareth cuts in. 'A woman was killed, a hit and run by a drunk driver, but Sherlock here thought there was more to it. Turns out he was right. The "accident" was not an accident, it was paid for by her husband. But the brass were angry about his involvement.'

My turn. 'I didn't know too much about procedure back then. I was so proud of myself. Turned out I didn't do enough on the case to get a conviction, and the husband got off, got away with it. After that, I quit.'

'I'm sorry Trevor. So, you became a reporter,' Hayden says.

'I did some training. I had the idea I might become a top investigative reporter for one of the big nationals. Got a job, too, on The Daily Globe as a cub reporter. I used to go up to London Monday morning and come back on a Friday afternoon. Nia and I were married, and she hated me being away.'

'Couldn't she have gone with you?' Hayden asks.

'She was a Cardiff girl. We moved into this house with her parents when we first married and here we stayed until the day she died.'

'And you didn't resent that?'

'Not for a moment. You see, she had a miscarriage, and I knew after that I couldn't keep going up and down to London. I resigned from the Globe, just before the culmination of a big case I'd been investigating, too. Whatever, Nia came first. I started to work in Cardiff.

There've been a few big cases, but honestly, they're few and far between here. Now I just trot along. Thanks to Gareth, I get the word when something's going down, so I have a good relationship with the police and a good name and respect in return. It keeps me satisfied.' I sit back, not sure that was all of the truth, but it's good enough.

'Did you ever have children Trevor?' she asks.

'No Hayden. Nia had three more miscarriages before she was thirty. That was enough.'

'I'm sorry.'

We're all quiet for a few minutes, as the sun goes down, the garden slowly descending into slumber, and the solar lamps beginning to light up the pergola.

After a few minutes I notice Hayden is far away.

'Everything OK?' I ask.

'Two things. You said three of you joined at the same time. Who's the third?'

'We were all at school together, all the same age. But our careers have gone down different paths,' Gareth replies. 'I wanted to be CID too, but never made it. I tried a few times for Inspector, but never got that either. The third one did, and higher.'

'You don't mean Harry Morgan?' she says.

'No, although he was at the same school, just two years below us. He was a bully. A big bully and I mean in size as well as gang leadership. He used to pick on our third man something terrible, a skinny, runty kid, but with a big brain. Trevor and I set Harry right one day after which he left our mate alone.'

'Who was it Gareth?'

Gareth glances at me, laughs, then says, 'It's our boss, Chief Superintendent James Malcolm: our mate, Jimmy.'

Hayden looks somewhere between amazed and horrified. 'You were in school with the Chief Super? You beat up Harry Morgan?'

'Yes and yes,' I reply. 'Jimmy may hate my job now, but he hasn't forgotten. You can't tell anyone, ever. Anyway, he told me today all dues are paid.'

'Of course I won't,' Hayden replies. 'Ah, now it's all becoming clearer. No wonder he agreed to come back to hear what you had to say. I don't think he'd have done it for any other reporter.'

'I would hope not,' I reply. 'He's a good man and a tough bugger, but he usually does everything by the book. Instinct must have told him to take this one seriously.'

'You said two things,' Gareth said.

'It's something else you said Trevor,' she replies. 'Something we haven't looked at yet. And I think we should consider it.'

'What's that?' Gareth asks.

'Did Agnes leave a will?' she asks. Not the question I was expecting.

'I've no idea,' I reply. 'Reg hasn't mentioned it. Perhaps it'll be read out to the family tomorrow, after the funeral. He told me his solicitor wants to meet with him, David and Louisa tomorrow around four-ish.' I pause. 'You're right, I've been so intent on following up the meaning of the letters I haven't taken the time to think about the financial aspect.'

'We'll have to,' she replies. 'Now we have to look for murder suspects.'

'I have more news,' I say. 'You know I've been looking into the history of the Spencer family. I've taken a deeper dive into the death of Joshua's father, Gabriel and I've come across some fascinating information.'

'Is this something I can tell the new DCI tomorrow?' Hayden asks.

'I think so,' I say, 'but I don't know if it'll be of any use to you. To recap, he died in WWII.' They both nod. 'He died after the attack on Gold Beach in Normandy.'

'After, not during?' Gareth asks. He was always quick to pick up on a nuance.

'Yes. He survived the landing and the initial advance. He and part of his platoon of men were almost clear of the beach. They'd reached the land at the top, when Gabriel was struck down by a fatal bullet. Only, it wasn't a German bullet. He was shot in the back, by what the Army calls "friendly fire." There's a story behind it, and that may – I'm not sure yet – provide us with a clue.'

'How so Trev?' Gareth asks.

'The report of the incident says there were four men following Gabriel, close behind him, who were all questioned. They gave more or less the same story: the landing itself had been terrible; so many mown down by machine gun fire; they had their weapons out and had had to shoot, sometimes blindly at what they thought was a target. There was a great deal of shouting and screaming, and the smoke coming off the canons and machine guns made it difficult to see. None of them said they could see the Captain at the moment he was shot. In the end, the army put it down to a tragic accident.'

'But you don't think it was?' Hayden asks.

'The notes I received had a post-it note stuck on the top, with a telephone number. I called and spoke to a chap who's a volunteer at the records office, Jack Hamilton his name is. His interest was piqued when he saw the request for the record of Captain Gabriel Moses Spencer. Turns out, his father was one of the four men and told him a story. Jack told me there was a Sergeant – his father, John Hamilton Snr

– and three privates. All four were pretty shaken up. Captain Spencer was something of a martinet, but popular and trusted. The men wanted to rest for a few minutes but Spencer said no, they had to push on and find the rest of the platoon, to see who had survived. Jack's father, Sergeant Hamilton, argued that what they had just been through was terrifying and the men needed just a few minutes to gather themselves. Two of the privates were squaring up to each other and he needed a few minutes to calm them down. They were two Irishmen, from Cardiff, who had been at loggerheads with each other since before they left England. They were called Collins and O'Hara. Seems they had a long-standing feud. The fourth man, called Vincent Credance, sat apart from the others. He had his head in his hands and Jack Hamilton said his father was worried about Credance because when he called Credance's name, the man looked up and smiled, didn't seem at all fazed by what they had just witnessed. He was the one who stood up, ready to move on. My dad said Sergeant Hamilton got between the other two and ordered them to pull themselves together and get ready to move. Collins began to argue with him, when there was a sudden burst of machine gun fire, but they couldn't tell where it was coming from, or from whom. The soldiers dropped to the ground, except for the Captain and Credance, who ran forward, gun in hand, following the Captain. As the machine gun fire paused, the others jumped up and ran after them, with their weapons held out and firing wildly around them. They had lost sight of the Captain and Credance in their panic to get away from the machine gun fire. A couple of minutes later they found Captain Spencer, lying dead, shot down, with Credance standing over his body.

'Sergeant Hamilton checked, but Spencer was dead. They assumed he had been caught by a bullet from the machine gun. They picked him up and carried him forward, found the platoon and the body was eventually taken away. Later, they all told the same story, but leaving out the fight between Collins and O'Hara. Jack said his father told him there had been too many deaths to think much on Spencer's, but later, when he did have the time to think about it, he couldn't reconcile the difference between where he thought the machine gun fire came from and where they found Captain Spencer with the bullet in his back. Anyway, Collins died a couple of weeks later, during the attack on Caen. O'Hara got home, as did his father. Credance was wounded during the fighting at Caen and dad heard he died of his wounds in the nineteen fifties. O'Hara was eventually dishonourably discharged. He had been caught stealing from a house in Caen. Back in England his father reported his concerns about Gabriel Spencer's death. The army investigated and it turned out it was a British weapon that killed him. They concluded it was "friendly fire", an unfortunate accident by men who were themselves under fierce attack. Jack ended by telling me his father never forgot the smile on Credance's face as he ran in the direction the Captain had taken. That's it. What are your thoughts?'

'Did Jack's father think Credance killed Gabriel Spencer?' Gareth asks.

'Yes, he did. But he didn't want to know why and by the time the army made its decision, Credance was back in Cardiff, disabled by his wounds.'

'So that's three generations of the Spencer family killed in suspicious circumstances,' Hayden says. 'That's a pattern, and it gives us a name,' she adds.

'You don't know it was this man Credance,' Gareth says.

'No, but I'll do more investigation. I want to find out if he was from Cardiff.'

Hayden stands up. 'I must go. The meeting tomorrow morning is at eight. I want to write some notes. Thanks Trevor. This has been invaluable.'

'Me too,' Gareth adds. 'He's meeting the rest of the team after he's met with Hayden. I don't think I'll have anything to add, but… just in case.'

I watch them leave, walking fast down across the grass and out of the gate, animated and chatting as they walk. I feel flat, left out, unimportant, unwanted. *'We're not a team any more',* I think. *'They have another team now.'* Then I give myself a metaphorical kick up the ass. I don't need a team, and I still have a lot to do, whatever the new DCI decides, which I know will be to remove me from any involvement with Hayden and Gareth. I started this off and I'm not leaving it alone now. Besides, my editor would kill me if I even thought about it. This is my story, continuing tomorrow with Agnes Hunter's funeral. Let's see who turns up.

15

Agnes's funeral turns out to be a collection of the good and great: her family, a few neighbours, a few police officers and the nosy and gossipy, ie. the inquest crowd. I'm as surprised to see them here as they are to see me.

'What're you doing here Trevor?' Betty whispers. She is wearing a black dress and coat and a lacy fascinator with a small black bird attached, which looks ridiculous, perched on the side of her head. The bird looks like it could drop off at any moment.

'We wanted to see the turnout,' Betty says. 'Look, here they come. Ooh, the Mayor's come in his official car.'

'I'm here for the paper,' I reply. 'There's a photographer around somewhere.'

The cortege is turning into the churchyard. It stops for a moment to allow the funeral director to get out, put on his top hat, take his cane and begin a slow walk at the head of the procession. It's long and impressive, headed by the funeral director, walking at a slow pace. The hearse is the first vehicle and I can see as it passes that Reg has forked out on the priciest coffin. Just the one wreath, that says "MUM". Then come two family cars. In the first one are Reg and David, Louisa and the man who must be her husband. No child. Then another family car. Must be Reg's family. They are followed by the Mayor's official car. With him are the Deputy Chief Constable and the Leader of the Council. I smile at what the latter must all be thinking. *'Bloody good riddance'*.

I am interested in the crowd. Apart from the inquest crowd I don't see anyone I immediately recognise. Then, I spot John Harries keeping well back. Of course, he didn't know Agnes as an adult, only for a brief period as a baby, being her godfather, but he knew her father. And her mother Hannah. There's also a well-dressed woman in a large hat, keeping her head down, at the back of the crowd. She's watching Reg Hunter.

There's another group keeping together, a few of whom I remember from the inquest: colleagues and people who worked for Agnes. I wonder if Cerys, the girl Agnes was about to fire on the day she died, is here.

A couple of what must be the neighbours nod at Reg as he exits his car with David, Louisa and her husband. The coffin is removed from the hearse and the family lines up to troop in, in its wake. The church is small, I'm surprised Reg didn't opt for the cathedral; but Agnes was the showy one, not him. It's a rather nice, old Norman church, on the outskirts of the city.

'She's going to be buried here,' Betty whispers, making me jump as she has crept up behind me. 'Wouldn't do to park her in Cathays, would it, under the circumstances.' Betty's eyes are gleaming. She does so love a good gossip. And she's still looking at the grieving Hunters as if they are local royalty.

I'm one of the last to enter the church. It's a simple service, all about Agnes's virtues. Mostly lies, although she must have had some merit as a mother because Louisa is crying. I think she's the only one.

It's family and friends only at the burial, which is in the overflow cemetery in a wooded pasture next to the church. I go to walk away, when there's a tug on my arm. I turn and am surprised to find Reg.

'Trevor, can you come over tonight? We're going to hear Agnes's will this afternoon. I've been told by the police that the investigation into her death is being reviewed. That's thanks to you. The children and I are having a quiet meal, and I'd like you to join us.'

I'm shocked. 'If you're sure Reg. Why me?'

'Because you're the only one who believed she didn't kill herself, despite what everyone else thought and said.'

'But surely you want to be alone with your family?' I say.

He shakes his head. 'Let's not fool ourselves Trevor. It'll be a quiet family meal. David and Louisa both like you and you can meet her husband, Justin. My family can't get away quickly enough.'

'In that case, I accept. What time?'

'Seven, if you can manage that,' he says.

'I'll be there,' I say, then add, 'I've been doing some more digging, so if you're up to it, I can bring you all up to date on what I've found.'

'Excellent. I must go. We'll see you later.'

**

This is unsettlingly puzzling. Why do they want to talk to me? Is there some hidden agenda? I can't think at this moment what it might be, but if they don't have one, I certainly do. This is going to be my big break, at last. Dinner with the family. Bring it on.

I arrive on time at seven. I wondered if I should bring a gift. Wine? Whiskey? I decide neither is appropriate and bring flowers, made up by a proper florist, not the garage or supermarket kind. Trevor opens the front door to me. I am about to say something when I see the expression on his face. He appears to be in shock, his mouth is hanging open. He beckons me in. 'Is something wrong?' I ask. 'Is your family OK?'

He nods and points to the living room. I enter to find the others: David, Louisa and Justin, to whom I am introduced formally, as Doctor Justin Miller, all looking the same. Their faces are mostly white, but they are not unhappy. What the hell has happened?

'Take a seat Trevor. I know you're a newspaper man, but what I'm about to tell you is family only. I'm only telling you because of the bearing it might have on what happened to Agnes. Can you please promise me you will not, absolutely not, print this news.'

'That's difficult,' I say. 'If it's newsworthy, I must think about it.'

'I don't think it is particularly newsworthy, and eventually—' he glances round and each of the three nods. 'Eventually, we won't mind, but only after Agnes's killer is caught.'

I have to make a quick decision. If this news, whatever it is, will help catch the person who killed Agnes, then it will form an excellent part of my eventual story. 'OK, I agree,' I say. 'Tell me what's happened.'

Reg sits up. 'This afternoon, after everyone had gone, our solicitor came to visit, to tell us about Agnes's will. I hadn't expected too much. I know she had some savings, but we kept our finances separate. I didn't expect anything myself, but assumed she would have left whatever she had to Louisa and David. I was right. I do well enough for myself. This house is in my name, and Agnes and I had been leading separate lives for some time now, as I told you already.' I nod. I had seen the "bit on the side" at the church.

'Agnes had fifty thousand pounds in her savings, and half each is left to Louisa and David. Then came the shock. There's a separate trust fund, nothing to do with Agnes's will. It was set up by Agnes's father, Joshua Moses Spencer, specifically for his grandchildren, should there be any, after their parent, his child who turned out to be Agnes, dies.'

'It's valuable, I presume?' I ask.

'It's worth five million pounds.'

Now, my mouth is hanging open.

'We only found out an hour or so ago. We don't know what to make of it,' Justin says.

My mind is in a whirl. Is this the money Joshua Spencer hid, his firm's money, squirreled away for such a long time? But why didn't he leave it to his unborn child? That's easily answered. Basically as the Fraud Squad was already onto him at the time, they would have found it. It would have gone via Hannah who would have told Gwen and inevitably back to the police. Where was the fund, in the UK or overseas? Then the final one hits me with a bang in the head. Was the person who killed Joshua Spencer expecting to get the money, and killed him when he wouldn't hand it over, and was it the same for Agnes?

'Did Agnes know about this?'

'I think not,' Reg replies. 'She learned that whatever money her mother might have had, went mainly up her nose. When Agnes was put into the care system there was no money.'

I think for a few more moments in the pregnant silence. 'We can't know what he was thinking,' I say, 'or what were his intentions. He may have left something accessible at the time for Hannah and the baby but he wasn't expecting to die. He might just have been hiding the money until the heat died down, then he was going to revoke it. I'm not sure, but he could have cancelled the trust fund. We'll never know.' I'm thinking tomorrow I'll be calling again on John Harries to see if he knew anything about it, but I won't tell this family, for now.

A bell rings in another room. 'That's the food ready,' Louisa says. 'Come on, let's go and eat, and Trevor, perhaps you can tell us more about what you've found out about mum's ancestors.'

**

I am still in a state of shock when I leave the Hunter house just after ten. We have discussed so many things. I tell them they must tell the new DCI about this trust fund. I know nothing about the legalities of such matters, but it adds an extra layer of danger for David and Louisa. David has already had a threatening note. I had looked at my copy again and saw what I didn't see the first time in amongst the hieroglyphs and other nonsense: pound and dollar signs. Whoever killed Agnes knows about this money. And they want it, believe they deserve it, even. But for now, that's just wild speculation on my part.

16

The following morning, I begin again on the search for "Satan", whom I don't believe was either Gabriel or Joseph Spencer, now I know a little more about both of them. A gut feeling tells me it wasn't Captain Nathaniel Spencer either. There's someone or something else, an event or a person, that I'm still missing.

I don't know what to do next, so I search around the internet and come across a site that gives details from the 1939 War Register of England and Wales. This gives me an idea. I pay the subscription for a month's worth of access – the least I can get away with – and begin to look for the four soldiers who accompanied Gabriel Spencer from the sea up and beyond Gold Beach. If they hadn't already enlisted or been called up, they should be on that 1939 register, in Cardiff.

I give up quickly on the Collinses and O'Haras – there are too many without more information and the War Register only contains name, address, date of birth and occupation – and return to the army regimental records. There, I discover they were Patrick Collins, aged 23 and James O'Hara, aged 24, when they were called up in 1940. That makes them much easier to find on the register. However, I can't find Vincent Credance. Not only not in Cardiff – not anywhere in the country. I check the surname only. A few called Credance but none near the right age. I check the name Vincent. No, too many to know which one he might have been. Thirty-seven men in Cardiff alone called Vincent and around the right age.

I haven't heard anything from either Hayden or Gareth. I try not to be disappointed. Next, I call John Harries. I can't be bothered going back down to Penarth, despite it being another lovely day and perfect for a walk along the front. Bugger that. I need information. I tell him the Hunters have come into some money and it appears it might have come from Joshua Spencer. Good try. He immediately cottons on to what I'm really saying.

'You mean he hid the money and it's turned up?'

'Maybe, maybe not John. If you know anything you'll have to speak to the police. It'll soon be public knowledge that the death of Agnes Hunter is being reviewed as a potential murder.'

'I don't want to talk to them,' he says, too quickly in my opinion. 'It was too long ago. I don't want to get involved.'

'I won't tell them about your connection to Joshua Spencer,' I say, in a way that I hope he takes as threatening. 'But I will let you know if anything comes of it.' He finishes the call, suggesting in the nicest possible way that he'll be happy if he never hears from me again.

It's lunchtime. Still nothing from Hayden or Gareth. I take a walk around the garden, trying to focus my mind on something else I can do, another lead I can follow. Then, I remember. It's that name – Moses. Hayden thought there might have been something connected with the name. I go back in and google Moses Spencer. Nothing. I am angry and frustrated. Joseph Moses Spencer did not appear from under a bush. I try a marriage for his parents. I know their names from an obituary in the Cardiff Globe when he was killed on the Ypres Salient – Captain and Mrs Nathaniel Spencer, with a comment from Mrs Lilian Spencer. I try the Births, Marriages and Deaths free site again. Nothing. Damn it! They were married. Why can't I find it? A thought occurs, a daft one, but who knows? What if they were married at sea? Is there a separate place to look? I can't find one. I am about to give up, when I think of one more person I can speak to: Norman Price. I wonder if he might know something about the Spencers? I might as well try; there's no-one else left to ask. I dial his number.

'I knew I'd hear from you again, old boy.' His enthusiasm mixed with condescension is irritating.

'Norman, this is just on the off chance, but do you know anything about a family called Spencer, the head of which is a Captain Nathaniel Spencer?'

'I wondered if it would turn out to be the same family,' he says.

'Norman, don't mess me about. What family?'

'Why, the family involved in one of the most infamous murders in Cardiff, of course. You'll be able to read about it in my book.'

'I'll be able to read about it this afternoon,' I snarl down the phone. 'Don't even think of saying no. I'm guessing you've got more old police files. For your information, there's a new DCI on the case of Agnes Hunter and he's keen to solve what may now be her murder. Either you give me access to what you've got, or I'll report you, and not only will you be arrested, but I'll also make it my mission to ensure your book never sees the light of day.' I'm shouting by the end and have to stop for breath.

'OK, OK,' he says,' his voice trembling. 'You can read it. There's a lot on the internet, you know, but not everything. I had to do a lot of research to uncover the full story.'

'I'll be there in twenty minutes, and you'd better have the manuscript ready for me to read.' I hit the "end" button so hard I drop the phone, curse and pick it up. Not broken. I order an Uber, then go to leave a message for Hayden and

Gareth but change my mind. OK, childish, but sod 'em. I'll fill them in when I get to see them.

I arrive at Norman's cottage twenty minutes later. I am so intent on what I will find at this time, as I walk along the road I barely notice another Uber pull up at the end of the lane, close to the entrance to Whitchurch cemetery. Its engine is turned off. There is a passenger inside. No-one gets out.

Norman is waiting with the cottage door open. He doesn't welcome me in, but points to his living room. A small table has been placed next to an armchair. On it, sits a pile of printed paper.

'Give me a brief, a very brief synopsis Norman.'

'Very well, if you insist. It's about the murder of a man called Charles Cadence, by Moses Tarr.'

'Charles Cadence?' I say, catching my breath. The man on whose gravestone both Joshua and Agnes Spencer were found? 'I've heard of him,' I say as normally as I can to Norman. 'Who was Moses Tarr? And what's he got to do with anything?'

He was the brother of Lily Tarr. She married Captain Nathaniel Spencer. She gave Moses an alibi and—'

'Stop there,' I say. 'I know the name Captain Nathaniel Spencer. I want to read what you've got here.'

'Let me know when you're done,' he says in a quiet voice.

I settle myself down. I have no idea what I am about to read, how it fits into the Agnes Hunter case, but I have that feeling a reporter gets sometimes, not often, but when he knows he is on the brink of a huge discovery. I have that feeling now.

Cardiff's Most Notorious Unsolved Crimes

1893 to 2000

True Life Tales
By
Norman Price

Chapter II

The Murder of Charles Cadence 1893

Part I

This infamous murder took place in 1893 and has remained one of the greatest unsolved murders to take place in our city. Charles Cadence was a prominent citizen of the day, tipped for Mayor and possibly Member of Parliament. He owned properties around the city, like many of his fellows, and let them to the poor and indigent.

The trigger that began the series of events leading to this murder happened in Stanley Street, which is now long gone. What was Stanley Street like? Here's a description, printed by The Cardiff Post, in 1892.

'Stanley Street is almost a cul de sac from Bute Terrace, only a few feet wide, having in its centre a narrow channel into which is poured all the liquid refuge, slops etc, from the houses on each side. The stench from the outer portion of this open gutter in summer is often abominable.

The street, or rather pitched footway, forms the drying ground for the occupants of the houses. A clothesline, common to all, extends from one end of the alley to another, and this in fine weather is constantly in use.

In Summer the street forms a kind of general wash house, and women, in a state of semi nudity, whose clothes are often nothing but a collection of dirty rags, sit with old earthenware pans on broken chairs, to occupy the day trying to gain an appearance of cleanliness to their children's clothing.

There are about 40 houses in this street, many consisting of two rooms, one over the other with a tiny back door in the back wall to give ventilation and access to the toilet sheds in the narrow back lane, shared by the houses onto which it backs.

There is scarcely a house with a window in which a number of panes of glass are not broken and the aperture filled with old rags.

There is not a house in which the lower half of the outer door is not honeycombed with substantial portions eaten away by rats which, in the early morning, make the street and houses a happy hunting ground for their species.

The bedroom in each house is reached by a staircase rising from the lower room or rooms and entering the upper room through an opening in the floor like a trap door.

Police recently found a woman and her baby sharing a wooden projection to a house which sheltered a donkey, and homeless children are often found sleeping under carts.'

Moses Tarr had left his parents' Stanley Street home in 1885 for work in the tanneries of Ceredigion. He was twenty years of age. The death of his father whilst cleaning the hold of a French Barque in the West Dock, left only Moses and his younger sister Lily to provide for their grieving mother. His father Thomas Tarr had been a sufficient breadwinner, and with the money from various lodgers passing through the docks, the Tarrs managed to exist well enough. They had been a handsome family, albeit having had a further four children die shortly after birth, with a larger house, two up, two down, and with domestic etiquette far above those of their close neighbours. Tommy

Tarr had been a disciplinarian; he had to be. Their terraced home was in a squalid row of houses. He had been planning to move. He wanted his son and daughter to achieve something in life and not fall in with the dull and wanting lifestyles of most of their Stanley Street neighbours. He was a smart man, and demanded the same from his family, even though finances were sometimes a problem.

Their largest weekly outgoing was the rent. It had to be paid, even though landlords scarcely ever put things right in their houses. Slates falling off roofs were left where they fell, the holes left behind adding to the problems of slum living. The shared toilet sheds in the back lane were commonly overflowing with effluent, the ditches and pipes underneath blocked, and hardly ever cleaned.

Moses was desperate for a better life, and, after his father's death, had made the selfish decision to leave his family. It reduced his mother to tears. She saw no wrong in Moses, and as the new 'patriarch' of the family he would have provided for her and his sister, but he was gone. Fanny Tarr never got over the loss of her husband and now her son was gone, albeit promising to find a job and send money home. Her health was poor. The damp, the vermin, the washing and scrubbing had left her a feeble woman.

After Thomas Tarr died, Lily had obtained employment as a maid in a rich house in Windsor Place, up town. It was a 'live-in' appointment, meaning she could only visit her mother on her very few days off, or a Sunday. This street was full of "up and coming" business people who enjoyed the dynamic economy of one of the fastest growing, and greatest coal ports in the world.

Lily was an attractive young girl. At seventeen she had all the attributes of the upper classes. Her auburn hair was the crowning glory to her beautiful, engaging face. She was five feet eight inches in height, slim, and together with deportment, attitude and articulation, her back street upbringing was invisible, all thanks to her father's care and determination.

She had watched in Stanley Street how the other girls sold their bodies in prostitution, got drunk at an early age on gin, and teased the men coming out of the beer houses, acquiring their money off them with ease. Lily's father had kept her away from it all. He had raised his daughter with schooling way above the accomplishments of others around the Tarr family, which in truth was zero. It was, though, to the detriment of his son Moses. who saw the protection and guidance of father towards daughter as something to be jealous of. It was left to Fanny Tarr to educate and direct their son's life; a job which an ailing woman, no matter how loving, under these circumstances strained to do.

Part II
March 1892

Charles Cadence walked to the Stanley Street junction with Bute Terrace, away from the site of the day's evictions. His coachman parked the family landau out of the sight of the ruffians who inhabited the street. Alongside Cadence was David Donaldson, Chief of Police, and alongside him Idwal Collins, Chair of the town Finance Committee. The five terraced house block Cadence owned was easily identifiable, even from the end of the street, by the row of bailiff's men and three Borough Constables standing outside. Some furniture, if that's what you could call it, was already on the cinder pavement. Two or three small children were playing outside, too young to comprehend what was happening. Neighbours had started to gather, leaving their homes, many of which had been built and were owned by Borough Councillors, and Aldermen including Idwal Collins.

An elderly lady stumbled from one of the houses, her long dress swirling among the pavement cinders. Dreadfully unkempt, she had thick and platted brown hair riddled with lice. For balance she used a broken tree branch. She pleaded with the bailiff's men for compassion. None came; they were doing a job for which they were paid handsomely, and the boss was watching.

Fanny Tarr looked up the street and saw the assembled officials. She hobbled towards them, prompting the Chief of Police to recommend Charles Cadence remove back to his landau. Cadence climbed up and sat in the rear, followed by his fellow Alderman, Idwal Collins, who sat next to him. The old woman shouted, 'Please, your Honour, please Sir. Don't put me out, I'll get money from somewhere. Please Sir, please…'

Her words were cut short by Cadence who turned around, and from the moving landau shouted, 'It's the Workhouse for you. Go and beg off them!' Smiling, he turned and ordered the driver to 'make speed' as he had an official lunch to get to.

Chief of Police Donaldson watched as his officers supervised the seizure of the furniture and its placement onto a cart. The five houses where the evictions were authorised, were cleared of furniture and people. Other residents in the street were loath to get involved, fearing their own homes might be next. Times were hard and money tough to come by. One of Fanny Tarr's neighbours in Stanley Street had a total of twenty men living in the house and paying rent. It was done in a work pattern, according to the men's particular shift patterns. Any spare money, after rent was paid, went on whisky and gin.

Fanny Tarr had fallen to the ground, her screaming pain heard by all who had watched the eviction. But she was just one of hundreds evicted from their homes over the last year by Charles Cadence. His housing empire included many of the south town back streets, and when it came to non-payment of rent, he was ruthless, giving no time to let the miserable residents attempt payment. If they missed two payments he went straight to the court where his fellow Aldermen sat as magistrates. He always acquired his eviction notices.

Proud of his father, was twelve-year-old Humphrey Cadence. In return, Charles was a doting pater, a father who wanted his son to become like him: rich and successful. He was already looking at the legalities of a future business: 'Cadence and Son'. As far as his daughter Clarissa was concerned, a rich husband would look after her. At eighteen years of age, she was already turning heads at the Town Hall balls.

NEWSPAPER HEADLINES 1893

GLOOMY SCENES IN STANLEY STREET
Cadence evicts – children left homeless
Woman of fifty-eight put onto street by Alderman Cadence

'THE LAW IS THE LAW' SAYS CHIEF DONALDSON

HUMPHREY CADENCE SPEAKS OUT
'These people are only too willing to rent my father's houses, but quite unfairly defame him when it is their own fault. In some cases, even the Workhouse is too good for them!'

Part III

The brutal days scouring skins, and the use of toxic chemicals, had taken their toll in the tannery. Moses Tarr's leather gloves, issued by the tannery, were pointless, as for most of the constant scouring and manipulation of the skins, his gloves got in the way. His breathing was laboured, the sound of his wheezing a constant reminder of the damage the chemicals were causing. Moses initially drank beer as a way of clearing his chest and relieving the dryness in his throat. The beer had evolved to whisky consumption, this time not as an antidote to the wheezing, but as diversion. His marriage to a Cardigan girl, Branwyn Davies, then in servitude to a local Parson, had failed. His constant alcohol abuse caused her to leave home to enjoy the solace of the parsonage, although she was already "with child".

She gave birth in an ante room to the church, with the assistance of women from the parish. The boy, Joseph Moses Tarr, was taken in by Branwyn's benevolent employer, Parson Algernon Williams, an extremely rare event in Ceredigion society at the time.

Moses Tarr attempted a reconciliation, promising he would stay away from alcohol, and at the beginning of 1892 Branwyn Tarr moved back into a 'one down – one up' dilapidated cottage with Moses, in Llandudoch village, not too far from the old Abbey. It did not go well for Branwyn; only her strong Christian belief had forced her to give her husband another chance. Moses continued to work at the Tannery, resulting in his wheezing and coughing becoming worse, and visits to the alehouses soon became the norm. His constant battle with whisky caused bouts of violent behaviour, always followed by howls of remorse. Branwyn became sickly and often bedbound. She died on the table in the cottage scullery, at the birth of their second child, which was "still born". The local women did their best, even sending for the doctor from the Cardigan surgery. When he finally arrived Branwyn was dead, as was her daughter.

Following these losses Moses Tarr became ill, and, incapable of worthy employment at the age of twenty-eight, was pensioned off with a few shillings. Homeless, he entered the Cardigan Workhouse, where alcohol was banned outright, which at first caused Moses a problem, but with the assistance of Workhouse staff and the daily visit of the Workhouse doctor, he began to stabilise. Moses would sometimes visit his son Joseph at the parsonage and put a few pennies in the church collection box. By this time, Moses had become stable enough to accept that little Joseph would stand more of a chance in life if he remained with Parson Williams and his wife.

Moses's breathing was still a concern, and his skin showed advanced signs of ageing, although he was only twenty-eight years old. He was aware that the tannery chemical agents, the smells and the leather wastewater had affected his ability to think straight; he forgot people's names, forgot the most obvious of things, yet there were still occasionally some wonderful days when his head cleared.

His feelings of guilt following Branwyn's demise, and his longing to see his mother and sister back home in Cardiff, sometimes manifested in anger. Around late May 1893 his fall from grace became pronounced when, after a bout of insolence aimed at a Workhouse cook, he was charged before the local court with being a Cardigan Refectory Pauper. The local media, whose reporter had been present in the courthouse, described his behaviour towards the cook as disgraceful, which Moses saw as injustice. After all, the cook was a disgrace, a loudmouth, and dirty to boot, someone had to 'put her right'. He was described on the front page as a 'layabout, drunk and beggar'. The words hurt. He saw himself as none of these, but now he was branded, and had to get away.

On completion of his sentence of seven days hard labour, he decided to make his way to Cardiff and home to his mother, and sister Lily. He hoped she was married to a fine working man. He had heard that she had gone into servitude, within a "superior house".

Little Joseph Tarr, now twelve months of age, had never left the confines of the Parsonage, and was becoming an inherent part of Parson Williams's family life, in all aspects other than name. Moses was a man on a mission, a mission to get home, see his mother and hopefully sort out his life. *'She must be around sixty'* he thought, *'and sis just two years younger than me.'* He had become desperate for some loving arms, someone to trust, someone to care. He informed Parson Williams that, as soon as he had put everything right with his family, he would return for Joseph.

Moses Tarr arrived in Stanley Street, on 10th June 1893, two weeks after leaving the Parsonage. His nights had been spent in barns, having worked for basic amounts of money during the day on farms. Moses was not scared of hard work, his physique showed that, but he was scarred, deeply damaged, hated the world and everyone in it, except his mother and sister and little Joseph. More than anything, he despised injustice. Losing his father, losing his wife, losing his child, losing his Cardigan home, all took a toll on his mind. He had prayed to the Lord that his mother was well and enjoying some form of satisfying daily life, although he occasionally he had dark thoughts that she may not be still around. He dreamed of their meeting when he would finally see her, of throwing his arms about her, promising he would never leave again. The guilt that had grown over the years hung heavily on him, his dream of coming home to Ma with wife and two lovely children was gone. All that remained in Cardigan, was Joseph, his son. But he knew his sister Lily was a lovely girl, and she would have cared for her mother. He wanted to say sorry to her, too, for leaving, and vanishing for so many years.

His guilt was deep, boundless. He had not even written a note to his mother. Now he was almost alone in the world. He worried that his mother had moved, but if she had, neighbours would know where to. It was a tight knit community in Stanley Street, mostly of Irish origin, where hard times for one, led to good deeds from others.

**

Moses stood at the southern end of Stanley Street, tired and with a hope that nothing had changed. His walk to his mother's house was slow, even though it was hardly fifty yards, as he had to avoid children with skipping ropes, women in groups talking, and old men sitting on windowsills in clouds of pipe tobacco smoke. Moses recognised no-one, he didn't really expect to after eight years. When he reached number twenty-four, his old family home, he stopped. The door was open, showing the little flagstone corridor with the almost vertical wooden stair planks leading up to the bedrooms. He half expected to see his mother ghosting out of the front room. But that was not what happened. A red headed woman, around 35 years of age, hurried towards the man standing at her front door. 'What you want?' she snapped.

'Where's Fanny Tarr?'

'Who's Fanny Tarr when she's at home?'

'My mother. She lives here or used to live here.'

'Well, she don't live here now. I've been here for over half a year.'

'My sister Lily lived here too. Where'd they go?'

'How do I know?' The woman was joined by a man who had come running up the street. 'Here's my man. He doesn't look happy.'

The man, rough and shabbily dressed, pushed himself in front of Moses at the front door. 'What's he want?' he snapped.

'Looking for a Fanny Tarr, says she used to live here.'

'She don't live here now. Now go on, bugger off!'

'How long have you lived here then?' Moses asked.

'I just told you and it's nowt to do with you anyway. Go on, bugger off, or I'll put a knife in you!' His aggression was enough to cause Moses to walk backwards along the pavement, but as he did so he lost his balance and tripped over a bucket of effluent. The laughter that followed did not come only from the new occupants of number 24, but others in the street.

Still standing at the front door, the woman shouted, 'If Fanny Tarr was the old cow that lived here before, she's six feet under, died in the Workhouse.'

Her words initiated an immediate response from Moses. He dived at the woman but was prevented from knocking her over by her husband, who threw Moses down onto the pavement, turned him over and rubbed his face into the cinders. Moses screamed in pain but managed to get to his feet. Both men then fell into the front passageway, knocking down the woman, who fell under them. Her screams and the vicious altercation between the men brought the whole street out. Within a minute the sounds of police whistles screamed out and Borough Constables lunged into the skirmish. Fighting in the street was not an unusual occurrence, with no-one usually taking a police officer's side, but this was different. It was Moses Tarr who was the unknown troublemaker, and all watching cheered as he was dragged off by several officers. He screamed insults as well as shrieks of agony, as he was truncheoned.

'I'll kill you, I'll kill you all, I'll kill the bastards who killed my ma. I'll shoot you all dead!' His threats were cut short as a truncheon hit the side of his head and he lost consciousness.

Charged with violent behaviour and threats, Moses Tarr appeared at the Police Court the following morning, 11th June 1893, where he was fined £2 on each charge with 14 days incarceration with hard labour as an alternative to not paying. His small savings contained in a belt pouch saved the day and he was released. He had given his address as Priory Street, Cardigan which was entered into the records.

The magistrate, Harold Herbert, on seeing Moses Tarr stand down from the dock commented, 'Go back to Cardigan Mr Tarr. Nothing for you here'. The comment, if heard, was not acknowledged by Moses Tarr.

Part IV

On leaving the Town Hall courtroom, Moses had one thing on his mind: to find his sister Lily. The only way he was going to do that was to return to Stanley Street and ask questions. It was barely a five-minute walk to the northern end of the small, terraced street. The bright June afternoon sun shone on the score or so of children playing in the roadway, keeping away from men leaning against the walls of houses and what appeared to be an alehouse. Most of the children were dressed in rags, with no shoes on their feet.

He did not hang around on that busy street corner. He knocked the first residential door he came to. He noticed the windowpanes virtually adjacent to the door were all broken. Pieces of rags had been stuffed in to keep out flies, or harsh weather, or both. It was opened by a woman, around twenty years of age, with bright ginger hair, and dressed in a long swirling dress covered over by an apron, heavily stained with weeks of food and ale swills. Moses put on a pleasant manner, raised his cap and said, 'I'm looking for Lily Tarr who used to live down the road there, in number twenty-four. I'm her brother, Moses Tarr. The woman noted his dishevelled and foul appearance, but it was the norm in that street.

'Why don't you ask at twenty-four?' the woman said.

'I have. They don't know her. She lived with her mother, Fanny Tarr.'

'Oh. yes, I remember them. The old woman Alderman Cadence chucked out. She had a daughter, about mid-twenties. She used to visit regular. She was a "posh un". Used to be brought in a trap to the end of the street by some gentleman.'

'Why did Mr Cadence chuck her out?'

'Usual thing. Non-payment. Cadence owns all the houses along here. He chucks you out if you miss a week or so and when you do, you're gone. Don't matter if you're ill, old, got kids, anything. If you don't pay, you're out on your arse. Don't deal with Mr Charles Cadence. He's a posh un, and we aint.' The woman glanced around, realising she may have said too much, and went inside and slammed the door shut.

Moses Tarr turned and made haste to his next location, the Workhouse. His thoughts were focussed on two questions. Did his mother die in the Workhouse as the woman in Stanley Street had shouted, and who was the posh woman who called to see his mother? Could that really be Lily? If not, what had happened to her? She would be twenty-six already.

He knew the location of the Workhouse. His route took him through various town centre thoroughfares and streets: Bridge Street, Union Street, Queen Street; in front of the castle he passed through Angel Street. One minor plate glass shop window caught his eye: Septimus Chambers, Gun Dealers. Nothing mattered anymore to Moses, other than gaining revenge for his mother's mistreatment. He would need protection, though. He couldn't fight hand-to-hand against groups of men, but brandishing a weapon would scare most of them away.

The shop was small and narrow, as was each house in the row of terraced houses in which the shop was located. A small weasel of a man stood behind a counter. He slammed a cupboard door shut when he heard Moses Tarr enter. The caller was not an expected one; most visitors were sent in by the Marquis or others of his ilk, to purchase weapons for containment of poachers on their land.

Lying on the counter in front of the weasel-like man was a revolver he had just shown a customer. It had just been loaded, but he had slammed the cupboard door before placing the revolver inside it. He had barely looked up before Moses grabbed the revolver and ran out along Angel Street towards the main river bridge. The man shouted, but in the time he took to secure other cupboards and run into the street, after locking the door, Moses Tarr was gone. He shouted at once for a runner. The first he saw was a lad of about twelve years of age, leaning on an adjacent wall. 'Go get a policeman. I've been robbed.' The boy held out his hand and the proprietor put a penny in it.

Within a minute a police whistle sounded, then from two separate ends of the street, Borough Constables approached.

The proprietor's story was quickly digested, but the most important constituent of any police enquiry at the time was missing: a good description of the offender. The proprietor told the constables the man had grabbed a loaded revolver from the counter, then run out. The description he was able to give was basic to say the least: male, about forty to fifty years of age, a street ruffian appearance and unshaven. That was it, except for one thing. The man said he was wearing a stained jerkin, and he thought some of the stains appeared to be blood.

Moses Tarr had tucked the revolver deep into his breeches, slowed his run to a casual walking pace and made his way to the Workhouse, a quarter of a mile from the bridge. The Workhouse was an impressive building, should you enter via the main door. Not so for the unfortunates who were in residence; theirs was a different entrance into another world.

Moses was aware of his appearance, but he was devious, learnt during those long hours in the tannery, where excuses were the only way one could get a break from work, or get outside for the pure air of Cardiganshire. At the front entrance, he was at once ushered outside by a burly man dressed in a guernsey smock and leather breeches.

'I only want to visit my mother. I've been away for years. Please tell her I've come home.'

'Who's your mother?' came the snapped reply.

'Fanny Tarr.'

'Stay there,' the man said and disappeared inside. Moses sat on a wall, where he was not alone. There were several old men and women shuffling about, some sitting on walls, and some leaning. He imagined his mother would have been one of them.

After about fifteen minutes the man reappeared at the entrance gateway. Moses crossed to him.

'Dead.' The man used just the one word, the word Moses was both expecting and dreading.

'How?' replied Moses.

'Just says 'Visitation of God'. She must have been locked somewhere, room or cell, or even sent to prison. I ain't got time to go searching no more for you.'

Moses felt anger rising, an anger not directed towards the ice-hearted man standing in front of him, but towards Mr Charles Cadence, the man who had killed his mother with his heartless behaviour.

'Oh, yes,' said the man, 'I remember now: Fanny Tarr. She was the one who used to get money given her every few weeks by a posh lady who called. She used to send her coachman to bring it into the office. Didn't do much good though; Fanny Tarr was raving mad. Straight jacket suited her,' he laughed.

'What was the posh lady's name?' asked Moses.

'How would I know? Now go on about your business. I got work to do.' The man disappeared inside the Workhouse entrance.

Moses's mind was in turmoil, a mixture of loathing towards authority, and passion towards his sister, whom he must find. Twice now people had told Moses about the superior woman who would call and give money. It had to be his sister, but where was she? If it was her, where was the money coming from to give away for his mother's wellbeing so easily?

He walked away to his next visit, with just one intention in mind – to confront Alderman Charles Cadence.

Part V

On 15th June 1893, Detective Scott walked the short distance from his Westgate Street police office to the entrance of the Town Hall building where the coroner held his inquests. His regimented gait temporarily departed as he avoided a dung heap, deposited recently in the roadway. He was aware there were onlookers, and he wanted to give the appearance of a man totally in charge of himself and his world. The police station's austere look, and equally austere huddle of humanity gathered outside, summed the day up for him. Another Coroner's Court appearance, another conclusion, another man going to his grave, and more lurid headlines.

1892 had been a good year for promotion, but it had meant endless visits to dead bodies, the results of murders, manslaughters, and accidents. It was the murders he dreaded, long days and unbridled criticism if the perpetrator was not caught swiftly. He had hoped 1893 might bring an upturn in his life and his career; nothing else mattered. He was not a married man. His life was devoted to his work.

He stood with his back to the external wall of the old Town Hall, just out of sight of the gathering of people and the media news men. He went over his lines, his words for the coroner and the jury. He had already decided on how Charles Cadence had died, and why. The police surgeon was in full agreement; they had discussed it together during the post mortem the previous afternoon. Scott never read from his notebook, even though he would have it held securely in his hand. He began to walk slowly back and forth alongside the wall going over his evidence. He knew the coroner well and knew how much trust the coroner placed in him. Scott's reputation was the highest and therefore his word was sacrosanct.

*'I am Detective Benjamin Scott, Cardiff Borough Constabulary. At eight o' clock yesterday morning, I came on duty at the Town Hall police station. A few minutes later I was undertaking administration duties when I was called out to the foyer to speak to a runner. The lad told me that there was a man dead in the Cathays graveyard, which I thought at the time was not unusual, (*Scott liked to bring wit into his evidence*) but the runner went on to say that the man had shot himself. I called for the assistance of Detective Hayward, and we hailed a cab to take us to the scene.'*

This was his standard introduction to evidence in the Coroner's Court. The narrative from now on would become more exciting to the media but more distressing for any family present.

Waiting for the coroner, he continued to practise his lines: *'As we arrived at the gate I noticed a number of men, women and children in an excited state, who surrounded us as we alighted. One man, the witness Bert Humphries, took me through the yard and within a minute I saw people gathered around one of the graves. On seeing me they dispersed and detective Hayward hurried them on out of the way. The grave in question was located some twenty feet from the thoroughfare pathway.'*

Scott had now reached the part of his evidence everybody would be waiting for. The media men would have their notebooks opened ready to write down every grizzly detail that emanated from his mouth. He knew the more the grizzly, the more publicity he would get. The more publicity, the more promotion.

'I observed, lying on the gravestone, with head against the memorial stone, the dead body of a male. It was as though mimicking the position of the body that had lain dead beneath him for many years. He was well dressed. I could not make out his face at the first time of looking. A service revolver was lying on the gravestone on his left side as

you looked at him. His head was thrown at an angle against the stone, his face was contorted in death. I saw that his skull was open to the top with a portion of his brain showing and much blood and brain matter defiling the stone. I leave the exact picture of death to Doctor Buistin, who undertook the post mortem. I looked closer at the face of the deceased and was shocked to recognise its owner, Alderman Mr Charles Cadence.

Good: he was ready. At this point Inspector Scott heard the distinctive voice of Constable McKenzie, come to warn him the coroner would be soon starting his court, and Scott was required to show attendance. He followed the officer around to the entrance and up the stairs to the grand court room. The top table chairs were empty, but the male jury were in their places. They had been chosen from local businessmen, many of whom were known to Scott. The jury members were trawled the previous evening by court officials, as the court usually sat the day after the event. The court clerk shouted 'Stand!' Coroner Tibbett walked in and sat.

Scott had assembled the witness list, from the finder of the body to the Cadence family, to Doctor Buistin who undertook the post mortem. He gave his opening speech, then came the witnesses. As each witness gave evidence, the reporters consumed their words with morbid glee, considering the sadness of the proceedings. With the fame of the deceased dominating the thoughts of all present, there were two questions that kept Detective Scott busy in the witness box. The first "why?" The second, "where did he get the gun?"'

Police surgeon Buistin had an easy ride through the proceedings, his evidence straight forward: death via a single shot under the chin from a revolver, the bullet entering the brain, ensuring instantaneous death. The reasons why the deceased would do such a thing the doctor could only guess at. It was not unusual, he stated, that a suicide came as a shock to a family. 'Who knows the state of mind of anyone at a particular portion of his life,' were the words with which he ended his evidence.

The deceased's wife, daughter and friends could give no reason why Charles Cadence would kill himself. Suggestions such as 'rapid melancholia', or 'delirium tremens' were laughed at. The young Humphrey, in his evidence regarding his father's state of mind, took those possible suggestions by Dr Buistin as "insults".

Evidence of alcohol was found in the body and the fact was verified by Cadence's daughter, Clarissa. 'Just one or two whiskies last evening,' she told the court. His walk would have been the usual early morning one: through the graveyard and back to his mansion home via the adjoining lane. No-one had seen anything or anyone untoward that morning

It was Scott who used persuasion on the jury in an attempt to ensure a suicide verdict, saying, 'Revolvers are easily available, should one want one.'

He added that there were gun shops in the centre of Cardiff town which had been checked on yesterday. Cadence did not get a gun from there. He was so well known they would have remembered him. Scott did not want a murder enquiry when it was in all probability a suicide. He told the court of a suicide case he knew of where a knife was plunged deep into a man's heart. The subsequent murder enquiry found that the man had asked an associate how much force would be needed to punch a sharp dagger into one's own heart. It was thought that it was the dead man himself who placed the dagger at his heart and punched it in. That murder enquiry resulted in a suicide verdict.

It was almost over, but as Coroner Tibbett was about to address the jury, a door opened to the left of him, and a local police officer entered. It was curious to all present, as to why the officer had entered, and why and what he had whispered so quietly into the coroner's ear. Tibbett nodded and the officer left the room. He looked towards Scott and then to the jury.

'Members of the jury, I have just been updated on newly discovered relevant information. Because of that information I am going to adjourn this hearing.'

The jury all nodded to one another and to Mr Atkins, who had been chosen by them to be their spokesman. Atkins, after exchanging positive nods with each of his fellows, addressed the coroner telling him, 'All agreed Sir'. Tibbett rose and exited. The court room cleared, leaving the reporters, and indeed Detective Scott, in the dark as to what was the information that had made Coroner Tibbett adjourn the hearing.

Scott left the court and entered the police office. His face was enough to warn the desk constable that he was not happy. 'What the hell is going on?' he snapped. He was aware that Charles Cadence was an important part of local life, a dignitary, albeit a very controversial one, so an adjournment like this was unusual, to say the least.

'It's that man over there Sir. He's a gravedigger. Says he's found something.'

'What?' snapped Scott. The elderly man stood and handed Scott a leather glove.

'I found it, not too far away from the place where Alderman Cadence was found.' Scott took the glove and placed it on the station counter. 'If you look just inside the glove there's a burnt-in name, M. TARR.'

'Was this why the coroner stopped the hearing?'

'That is exactly why Sir,' answered the constable, 'This man here, Tom Glazier, was working in the same spot the day before the body was found and that glove wasn't there.'

'Why didn't we find the glove?' snapped the angry detective.

'Nothing to do with me Sir.'

Scott left the station office to be confronted by two men, both reporters for the Gazette. Behind them were members of the coroner's jury. There was only one question being asked, 'Why was the hearing stopped?' That was exactly the question asked of Scott by reporter Luke Jones. Scott ignored the question and walked back inside the police office. He wanted to question the gravedigger further and get to the bottom of who missed the glove, why wasn't it found? More importantly who was M. TARR? This was embarrassing.

Worse was to come Detective Scott's way, new information that caused the officer to explode with rage. He had returned to the detective's office in the main building where a uniformed officer was just exiting. The men nodded to one another. 'What did he want?' asked Scott of Detective Hayward, who was sitting at his roll top desk in the far corner.

'He had some information which he thought may be… of interest.' His words came to a stop.

'Go on, what information?'

'A loaded revolver was stolen from Septimus Chambers, the gun dealer in Angel Street, the day before Cadence's body was found.'

Scott turned and kicked the door shut. The noise must have been heard around the old building. 'How the hell—?' He stopped; the words just would not come out. It was as though a dagger had been stuck into him.

'Hayward, I've just told the coroner and his court that I thought it was a suicide. I look a bloody clown. A right bloody clown.' He sat in his usual chair and stared at his fellow detective. 'We've now got a glove which our searchers failed to find, a bloody gravedigger found it. We've just learned a man stole a revolver the day before, and I'm told about this after the Coroner's Court has commenced. Now I'm going to have to inform the bloody family.'

The door of the office opened. 'Mr Scott', said a youthful, uniformed constable, 'The Chief wants to see you'.

Part VI

The following day's newspapers screamed out the headlines and they still hadn't got the full story.

CADENCE DEATH – CORONER ADJOURNS COURT
Blew his own brains out

HORRIFIC SCENE DISCOVERED IN GRAVEYARD
Controversial Alderman and businessman blows his brains out
Did Cadence shoot himself on early morning walk?
Wife and family in shock

WHY DID ALDERMAN CADENCE DO IT?
Humphrey Cadence claims Criminality!
Detective Scott Claims Suicide!

WHY WAS THE HEARING STOPPED?
Detective Scott refuses to speak to The Sentinel's Reporter

Mrs Emily Cadence, wife of Charles, was hardly ever seen, nor ever known to have given an opinion. She was happy to live in the large mansion, adjacent to the Cathays graveyard and its church, with her servants taking up the chores, leaving her to crochet and knit.

Clarissa Cadence, however, was the new "belle" of Town Hall balls. Her father bestowed monies and gifts galore on her. Clarissa wanted for nothing. In return, Clarissa adored her father, adored the ground he walked on. She knew he was not popular among the south of town inhabitants, nor with many of the news journals, but she knew he always acted within the law and had the respect of fellow Councillors and Aldermen, and the Chief of Police. *'What more could a daughter want from her father?'* was a thought that oft crossed her mind. In return her father adored his beautiful daughter.

Clarissa was never convinced her father shot himself and took it upon herself to address the waiting crowd and the reporters.

CLARISSA CADENCE CLAIMS FATHER MURDERED
My father was the happiest man in the world, why would he suddenly shoot himself?

OUTSPOKEN CLARISSA CADENCE EXPERIENCES THE WRATH OF CORONER TIBBETT
The young lady, though obviously grieving, needs to cease her comments

'M. Tarr? Who the hell is M. Tarr?' queried Inspector Scott of the three plain clothed officers he had assembled in the police station. He jabbed a finger at Detective Hayward and said, 'Put out a paper to all officers. Ask if anyone knows who M. Tarr is. Check our records, court records, everything.' Constable Hayward nodded, stood, and left the office. Another officer was instructed to check out the beer houses and the hotels. It was methodology used often by police attempting to trace suspects or witnesses in serious cases. More often than not, enquiring officers were met with blank faces, negative answers or ridicule and hate. But Scott knew it had to be done, someone must know who the hell M. Tarr might be. The glove was the only clue he had relating to the death of Charles Cadence.

His blanket enquiries were cut short by the sudden appearance of Chief of Police Donaldson. He was accompanied by a young man known to Scott: Humphrey Cadence, son of Alderman Charles Cadence.

'Scott, you want to know about an M. Tarr? Listen to what Master Cadence has to tell you.' Scott stood rigid in deference to his superior officer; the other police officers had already sprung to their feet, and to attention. There were no salutes. Nobody was in uniform. Hayward, who had returned, also stood to attention.

'My father had to evict a wicked non-payer from one of his houses in Stanley Street. Her name was Fanny Tarr. She was kindly taken in by the Workhouse authorities who took pity on her. I am not sure I would have given her pity, as the money she should have paid to my father she used to buy gin.'

Scott pulled a chair up for his Chief to sit. The scowl and nod he gave to one of his officers intimated he should do the same, this time for Humphrey Cadence.

Scott intervened with a question. 'Whom was she living with in Stanley Street?'

'The woman Tarr lived alone. Her husband had been killed on the dock. Her son left home years ago, that son was a Mr Moses Tarr. I am aware of all aspects of my late father's business and I was with him on the day the Tarr woman was removed from her home.'

There was silence. Donaldson slowly raised his head staring straight at his top detective. 'There you are Mr Scott; we have found your M. Tarr for you.'

Scott felt humiliated and embarrassed. His theory of suicide at the Coroner's Court had been well documented in the news sheets, and now it wasn't he who had found the main suspect, but his own Chief.

'Who gave this Fanny Tarr money to buy gin, then?' was the first question that Scott could come up with.

'Mr Scott, perhaps you should also listen to this.' Donaldson moved to sit next to Scott and spoke in a calculated and objective way, 'If you were to knock on the door of the Magistrates Court and ask to speak to the clerk who was present on 11th June, he will tell you that Moses Tarr appeared in that court and was fined for violent behaviour, then released.' The last words were said with venom to a red faced and baffled detective. 'It's your problem now Scott. Sort it!'

'He killed my father. It was Tarr who killed my father,' shouted a tearful Humphrey Cadence. Chief of Police Donaldson put his arm around the boy and led him out of the office. Turning before he exited, Donaldson said, 'Get him Scott. What more evidence do you want? Suicide? Bunkum!'

Scott looked at Hayward and said, 'A comedy of errors, or a police force of buffoons?'

'You came to a conclusion too fast Sir. All those signs were out there, you just weren't told about them. No fault of yours.'

Scott could only stare at Hayward in disbelief. 'You are of course correct,' was his softly delivered comment.

On 17th June 1893, Scott returned to the adjourned Coroner's Court. Everyone present, including the reporters, was eager to hear what was happening. Rumours had circulated that the Coroner's Court was about to hear fresh, evidence. Coroner Tibbett's courtroom officer made sure his court was ready at the exact time, his last duty to message his chief, stating the court was waiting. Coroner Tibbett walked in, the gentlemen of the jury stood, the male reporters stood, and like a well drilled military, sat at the instant they were ordered to. Sitting together on a public bench in the court, were Chief of Police Donaldson and Humphrey Cadence.

There was only one person called to give evidence – Detective Scott. With the swearing and identification formalities completed, Scott was asked for an update to the police enquiry. The silence in the court was palpable as Scott laid his papers out on the witness box shelf.

'I am the senior officer in the Borough Constabulary charged with the investigation of the death of Mr Charles Cadence on 14th June this year. His body was found lying on an old grave some twenty feet from the main path through the Cathays graveyard. The jury has already heard the details relative to the discovery of the body and the police enquiries up to the adjournment of this court some two days ago. The court had been paused as a focal piece of evidence had been discovered, which has thrown an entirely different light on these proceedings. We are now looking at a murder enquiry.'

There were gasps and shuffling by the jury, and reporters raised pencils in readiness.

'We are searching for a twenty-eight-year-old man in connection with the shooting of Charles Cadence. Information has come to light which was not readily available to me at this court's first sitting. As a result of that information, and further critical evidence from witnesses, I will name the man we are seeking. I do this, as I fear he is dangerous and still at large within this town. The man we are seeking is called Moses Tarr.' He waited until the gasps and murmurs had died away. 'He has contacts amongst the community in the Ceredigion area, near Carmarthen.'

'Thank you Inspector,' the coroner interrupted, 'This whole sorry incident has taken on a new presence. We do not know, of course, whether the man Moses Tarr is guilty or not, but we appreciate the update you have delivered to us. I am sure you have numerous enquiries to make, and the newspaper men sat in this court will want to speak to you regarding the man, Moses Tarr. May I say to the court, and especially the public who are noting these proceedings, that the man Moses Tarr has not been convicted of anything. He is a suspect, just a suspect. We do of course recognise why the police have named him. They regard him as extremely dangerous, and any apprehension should be left to them. I adjourn this court until a future date, not known at present, but you will be notified'. He stood. Everyone else in the courtroom stood until he had left the room. Scott was soon surrounded by persons anxious to get a description of the wanted man, Moses Tarr.

Sitting at the rear of the court was Humphrey Cadence. His stare at Detective Scott was penetrating. The detective's immediate assumption that his father had committed suicide was humiliating, distressing to him, his sister and mother, and he was not going to rest until he saw Moses Tarr swinging on the gallows. He left the courtroom an angry young man, seething that his father had been murdered by a street ruffian. He was going to laugh when they hanged Moses Tarr. Just desserts for shooting a great man.

The reporters had somehow – Scott assumed through a policeman – found out about the gun theft and he winced, ready for the following days' headlines.

REVOLVER STOLEN FROM
SEPTIMUS CHAMBERS GUN DEALER

CORONER'S COURT SENSATION!
Scott admits he got it wrong

SCOTT NAMES THE MAJOR SUSPECT – MOSES TARR
Warning! This man is dangerous and armed!

POLICE ISSUE WARNING REGARDING MOSES TARR
Wanted for questioning re Charles Cadence death

HUMPHREY CADENCE SPEAKS TO OUR REPORTER:
I would willingly pull the gallows lever on my father's murderer

Part VII

On 18th June 1893, Moses Tarr walked slowly and aimlessly through the peaceful High Street of Cowbridge. It was around noon, and he was hungry. The last few nights sleeping in barns had taken a toll on him, always on edge he might be discovered by a farmer and shot. His change of clothes, stolen from a cottage on the Tumble, were ill fitting, but it gave him the rustic look of a local labourer. He was desperately hungry. For sustenance, Moses had chewed on, and in many cases eaten, rye and barley that covered the floors of the barns.

He was in a state of instability, his mind closed, his thoughts frightening. He felt fastened to a new normality. He did not know where he was. Confused, he stood at a rail head and watched as a one carriage train puffed its way out. He vaguely remembered Cardigan, the tannery, the heat, the pain. Moses felt strange, his mind could only see, and he could only feel the heat of the boiling vats of hides.

He sat on a bench at the doorway of an old hotel called The Bear. Next to him was an elderly gentleman, richly dressed, his appearance crowned with a fine top hat. He was holding a newspaper with the front page almost pushed in Moses's face. The man was engrossed, but it was the headline that caused Moses to stand abruptly,

POLICE SEEK MOSES TARR AS CADENCE MURDER SUSPECT

and

CADENCE DEATH – NEW EVIDENCE

Glancing around, he screeched out the words, 'Me? That's my name.'

The gentleman looked up from his newspaper. Moses managed to bare his teeth in a smile, which seemed to pacify any thought of astonishment in the man, who looked back down to read. 'That's my name,' Moses shouted out again. 'Moses Tarr, that's my name.'

The gentleman rose from his seat and made his way briskly up the road where he crossed, but not before he turned and noticed some people from The Bear had come out and were watching Moses. The top hatted man entered a building on the High Street and stood at the desk. An elderly, grey-haired constable got up from his seat behind a ledger-ridden desk. 'What's up, Mr Benjamin?'

'You know that Cadence murder? There's a man down there, a crazy man, who says he's Moses Tarr.'

'Moses Tarr? That's the man the Borough boys want, isn't it?'

'Yes. You better get down there quick. He's acting very strangely.'

The officer pulled on his tunic, and bellowed, 'Sarge. Trouble!' The words were shouted with such power that a door flew open on the far side of the office, and a giant of a man appeared, hastily pulling on his coat. His stripes of power, emblazoned on the tunic arms, were nothing compared to the power emanating from his giant moustache, his gnarled face and huge frame.

'Where?' he growled.

'Outside The Bear. May be Moses Tarr, the murderer.'

When they reached the street, the sergeant pulled out his whistle and gave three long blows. There was one other officer out there somewhere and he would hear the call.

By the time they arrived at The Bear, they found a crowd surrounding a man who sat quietly on a bench. His face was red, his eyes unfocussed in an unintimidating stare, and a curious smile on his face. The sergeant pushed his way through the gathering and with one arm lifted the man to his feet.

'Are you Moses Tarr?' he thundered, as he held his prey against the hotel wall. Moses, both scared and excited, kicked out at the sergeant causing him to lose his grip on Moses who punched at the first person who blocked his way. It was a woman, a servant in The Bear Hotel. She fell to the ground. Two women dropped to her assistance, and Moses, running around them, pushed some elderly locals away, and ran for his life.

He didn't know where he was going, but there was an inner stimulation which propelled him at great speed along the cindered roadway, knocking over anyone who got in his way. The sergeant and constable were not far behind, and behind them a crowd was eagerly following the chase. Moses careered around a corner from the High Street and found himself at a little terminal railway station. There was just one platform. He jumped down onto the track and with leaps and bounds, jumped from sleeper to sleeper, in an attempt to escape. He tripped and went down face first into the cindered slag between the rails. The searing pain in his face increased when two constables jumped on him and dragged him to his feet. A punch to the face from the sergeant was the last thing he remembered.

Moses was unceremoniously dragged into the High Street. One of several stationary pony and traps was hastily demanded as transport by the sergeant. The crowd, having wind of the rumour that a murderer had been detained, started to 'boo' and angrily shout towards the half-conscious captive. The trap, with the sergeant squeezing Moses in a neck grip, drove to the nearby police station, the constables and others following on behind. Moses was dragged through the front door and to the small cell block where he was thrown onto the floor. The heavy wooden door was slammed shut. The sergeant opened the observation hatch, saw his man attempting to get to his feet, which proved he was in a fit state to be incarcerated, then slammed the heavy hatch shut. The metallic clank resonated right through the police station. Moses Tarr was at last in police custody, the main suspect for the murder of Charles Cadence. In truth, there were still some in authority who thought it was suicide. One rather low-level accounts clerk in the Town Hall was said to have whispered to his colleague, 'That Cadence, he'd been fiddling. Too clever to get caught though.'

Later, Moses was transported to Cardiff.

**

On the morning of 19th June, Detective Inspector Scott walked into Westgate Street police station enquiry office. At the desk was a woman in a tattered bonnet, and an even more tattered long dress. She signed a ledger presented to her by Constable Davies, the reserve officer. She turned and exited but not before firing an expletive towards the officer who had just returned her property. Her arrest the previous night had not been taken to court. *'Just an in and out'* thought Scott. Davies stood to attention as a mark of respect to his detective superior.

'Where is he?'

Davies knew who Scott was referring to. 'He's in the cell Sir.'

Scott said, in a manner that left no cause for ambiguity in the uniformed officer's mind, 'He stays here until I say he goes. Got it?'

'Yes Sir,' the junior officer replied. He lifted up the counter flap, and Scott walked through into the small cell block. He took the key hanging on the hook and opened the main block door, then handed the key back through the small opening at eye-level in the door to Davies. In return Davies handed the detective the key to number one cell.

Scott opened it, but not before peering through the hatch, to note that Tarr was sitting on the wooden bed. Twisting the key he pushed the heavy door open.

'Moses Tarr?' No answer. 'Moses Tarr. Are you Moses Tarr?' No answer. Scott lifted Tarr to a standing position. 'You're going to play the dumb act, are you Moses?' Still no answer. Scott shoved the prisoner back to the sitting position, then sat down next to him. It was a situation he had encountered many times before, and sometimes the social approach worked. 'Now come on, Moses. I'm here to help. My name is Detective Scott, first name Benjamin. May I call you Moses?' The prisoner replied with a nod. 'Good. Now I know I'm speaking to the right man. Are you hungry?' Moses shook his head back and forth. 'Good, they're feeding you, then.' Scott stood up and leant against the wall opposite the bed. 'I'm going to take you out of here to sit in a cozy room where we can have a little chat.' Moses nonchalantly nodded in agreement. 'Good. Come on then.' Moses was lucky. If he had not agreed, Scott would have dragged him out of the cell.

The ante room to the cell block was not constructed for large gatherings, the table able to take only five chairs. Near the door was an iron ring attached to the wall by a chain. This was used to secure troublesome prisoners before his or her court appearance. Moses Tarr sat with Detective Scott sitting opposite. On the table in front of Scott was a large ledger style book, its hard covers showing years of wear. Scott waited, lit his pipe and stared. Moses did not react, only to be glad to be out of the tiny cell. A long white smock had replaced his dirty, stained clothing, these being examined for evidence. Blood, though, was always a difficult one for the constabulary, as animal blood and human blood could not be separated. It was just blood.

After a few minutes of silence, the door opened, and Detective McCormac entered. He, too, sat at the table. Nothing was said, the only sounds heard were clip-clopping of horse drawn carriages and carts outside.

Scott pushed the heavy ledger-style occurrence book to McCormac who pulled out a small, lidded bottle from a leather case, and then a pen. He snapped open the lid, pushing the pen nib into the black ink. He looked at Scott, who leaned in towards Moses and said, 'Moses, you are in big trouble, aren't you.' There was no answer. 'We are going to get you a friendly solicitor later, if you can afford it, but first I am going to ask you some questions. Do you understand?' Moses kept his stare directly at Scott, but still didn't answer. 'Detective McCormac, show Moses the glove.' From his case McCormac withdrew the leather glove found near the grave. He pushed it towards Tarr. 'Is this yours?' Moses looked towards the glove then back to stare at Scott.

McCormac asked again, 'Look at the glove. Is it yours?' There was still no answer. Scott held the glove up in front of the prisoner, pulled the edge over to reveal the name burnt into the material. 'It says M. Tarr. That's you, isn't it?'

'Used to be,' Moses whispered. 'A long time ago.' Scott glanced at McCormac who retrieved the glove and put it back into the case. He made a note in the book.

'What do you mean, "used to be?"' snapped Scott.

'Used to be,' Moses repeated, 'When I was younger.'

Scott looked at McCormac with a grin, before once again leaning right into Moses's face. 'You are annoying me!' Scott held his position.

'Sorry,' whimpered Moses, 'my wife used to keep my gloves for me.'

'And where is she?' asked the detective.

'She's dead,' Moses answered. Scott sat back in his seat and there followed a period of silence. It was McCormac who broke it.

'It was you who stole a revolver from Mr Chambers' shop, wasn't it?'

'No.'

'It was you who used the revolver to shoot Alderman Charles Cadence.'

'No.'

'Is your mother Fanny Tarr?' At that question Moses stood and attempted to throw a punch at Detective McCormac. In the ensuing melee, both detectives managed to lie Moses on his back on the floor of the room. The door opened, the reserve constable entered, and between the three of them Moses was pushed back into his cell and the door slammed shut.

'That's our man,' said a breathless Detective Scott. 'Callous bastard! One more for the gallows.'

'Now to prove it,' answered McCormac.

'He's trying for a Broadmoor,' replied Scott, 'an insanity plea. We've enough evidence to hang him. I'll put more to him later, then I'll charge the bugger.'

Both men returned to the interviewing room, taking turns to make notes in the ledger. They were aware that their notes could be examined by any defence solicitor, if Tarr could afford one. Together, they made notes for their personal pocket books. 'We'll have to go in on him again,' said Scott, 'If we can get a guilty nod, it'll be the black cap. No time like the present.'

He left the room with McCormac following and walked the few steps to the cell. Looking through the hatch he saw Moses sitting in the cell corner with his back to the wall. Both men entered, in the prime position of looking down on a suspect, to show they were wholly in charge.

Scott said, 'Moses Tarr, admit your crime and go to your maker an honest man, a man that will be welcomed into heaven, or risk the wrath of a living hell after you die. Now tell me, why did you shoot Charles Cadence?'

Moses looked up at the two faces leering down into him and said, 'My dada dead, my mama murdered, and all you care about is a blackguard called Cadence. You go to hell!' The last words were shouted, as he jumped to his feet and attempted to push his way past the officers to the cell door. McCormac grabbed him and pushed his forehead against the stone cell wall. Moses fell to the floor, blood seeping from a wound. The two men left, and after slamming the door shut went into the main front office where they ordered the reserve officer to get the services of a doctor to his charge.

'He thinks he's heading for an asylum. I have news for him. It's the gallows, no straight jacket in a padded cell. Lying bastard!' The frustration of not getting an admission of guilt from Tarr was getting to Scott.

Part VIII

The following day, at the re-opened inquest, the jury, after hearing the evidence of witnesses and the physical identification of Moses as the gun thief, concluded that Charles Cadence had been murdered. They named Moses Tarr as the culprit.

The Magistrates, three days later, brought Moses Tarr before them, after hearing the coroner's decision, the witnesses' evidence, and the subsequent police enquiry. He had been charged with the murder of Charles Cadence and was soon to be arraigned. The Magistrates committed him for trial at the County of Glamorgan Midsummer Quarter Sessions and to be kept in custody on the following charge: "For that on 14th June 1893, Moses Tarr did feloniously kill and slay one Charles Cadence." He would not have to wait too long to learn his fate.

The Midsummer Quarter Sessions took place at the Cardiff Town Hall during the month of July 1893. On Tuesday 2nd July, the usual displays of authority and respect were on show with the Judge arriving in his horse drawn carriage with a mounted policeman leading the way. The red-cloaked clerks formed a "welcome line" to escort him into the building. Respect for rank then was at its highest.

During the first two days, the majority of cases heard were 'guilty' pleas, with implorations of mitigation accompanying each case, as long as the defendant was represented. Few were.

On the third day of the proceedings, the mood and logistics of the Crown Court underwent a marked change. Various factions had appeared. It was the first day of the Moses Tarr trial for the murder of Charles Cadence.

Everything was prepared. Police, legal gentlemen, witnesses were all ready and waiting. The factions, predominantly outside the Town Hall in the High Street, were groups of men and women. The largest group, of about one hundred men and women, were supporters of Moses Tarr. They saw him as a hero for dealing with the tyrant Charles Cadence. Another group, about twenty strong, wanted the killer of Cadence to be hanged, and good riddance. Ironically, the members of both groups thought that Moses was guilty of the murder; it was their interpretation of justice that was conflicting.

Moses Tarr stood bolt upright in a jaded wood dock at the Cardiff Town Hall Court. The activity in the court room was distinctly different to what it had been the previous two days. The public gallery was full soon after the court had opened at around 9.30am. Scores of people who had failed in their attempt to gain access, milled around outside, being joined every minute by many others, all keen to get the news as soon as possible to the question, "Did Moses Tarr kill Charles Cadence?"

On either side of Moses stood a moustachioed police officer, both attempting to pull him down onto the bench. He did not want to sit, seemingly unaware of the gravity of the situation. Trial for murder is the ultimate dramatic stage. There was no need to stand, Recorder Williams had not entered the court room yet and all around were the sights and sounds of a major court trial. Shuffling onlookers in the public gallery, reporters jostling for position on their dedicated bench, court ushers moving witnesses and onlookers into designated places, clerks shuffling mountains of paper and arranging exhibits on the main court bench. The barristers and their clerks moving paper bundles around and practising their submissions; after all it would be headline news soon.

Moses Tarr still refused to sit down, preferring to be able to see the comings and goings. His warders looked to one another in resignation at the man doing what he wanted. One barrel-chested officer shook his head and tutted, 'He's a no-hoper and guilty.'

'Stand up!' bellowed the Clerk of the Court, as the Judge's door opened and Recorder Isiah Williams entered. He walked to his chair at the centre of the bench, bowed to the Court, watched the officialdom bow back, then sat.

At the beginning of Moses Tarr's trial, the usual submissions and court procedures, including the Prosecution's opening statement, took up most of the morning. After the luncheon break, Recorder Williams stood down for the afternoon, stating to his clerk that he was feeling unwell with a headache. Not one of the hardened police officers, or indeed any of the other regular officialdom at the court, believed he was unwell. Scott commented to the Cowbridge sergeant who had arrested Tarr, 'Off to some "do" or a posh luncheon somewhere. Imagine us trying that?' He explained to his witnesses they would have to come back tomorrow, in essence the first real day of the trial. The reporters rushed off to their HQs, describing the atmosphere and the reality of the courtroom and the street outside, rather than the court proceedings. But their headlines did not hold back. Both the evening and morning editions carried banner headlines.

TARR STANDS TRIAL FOR CADENCE MURDER

THE CHARLES CADENCE MURDER TRIAL BEGINS

THE TRIAL OF MOSES TARR BEGINS

The Crown Court packed and crowds outside
To some Tarr is a hero – to others a scoundrel

Part IX

Lily Spencer, nee Tarr, stood in the window of her grand Windsor Place home. Lily's husband, Captain Nathaniel Spencer, had been gone for months, skippering his ship from Cardiff to various South American ports. Although she had received several telegrams it was still not known when he was due to return. Lily lived her life with all the trappings of wealth, not a London-style highborn wealth, but a wealth much envied by her acquaintances in Cardiff society. Her monthly allowance provided her with enough money to cover the costs of running the house, plus extras to allow any comfort she desired. Her husband had risen up through the ranks of a local shipping company, and with the rise in status and responsibility, came financial reward.

Lily didn't often bother with the newspapers, but today she glanced at the front pages of yesterday's late afternoon copies, which her maid had left in the parlour last eve. They carried the headlines she never believed she would see.

MOSES TARR STANDS TRIAL FOR CADENCE MURDER
Events in earnest start tomorrow

The opening day of Moses Tarr's trial took up the whole front page of the Gazette, and Lily Spencer devoured the content, discovering that, as yet, no witnesses had been called, but that the opening statement of the prosecutor, outlining the case to the Grand Jury and press, had been eagerly swallowed up by all present. The trial was due to commence again today, at 10.30am. Although she hadn't seen him for years Lily knew, from certain passages in the prosecutor's opening statement, that this had to be her long-lost brother.

Lost in shock and surprise, she didn't hear the maid knock and enter with a tray. 'Your tea ma'am,' was spoken quietly, as she placed the cozied pot and fine china cup and saucer onto the reading table.

'Thank you, Edith. Can you take it into the drawing room?' replied Lily, not even looking up. She heard the door close quietly as the maid exited the room.

Lily was aware of her back-street background, her mother's awful demise, and her brother's absence, but now he was back, and in serious trouble. Lily felt fine pins and needles run up and down her back, as she sat in a state of distress. She was sure Moses could not have committed murder, so a terrible mistake must have been made; there must be persons attempting to blacken his name. She noted it was reported he was not represented by a solicitor, also that he hardly spoke in court, using nods to signify "yes" or "no". She had not seen her brother for eight years. It appeared, from the newspaper reports he was alone in Cardiff. No solicitor nor friend to speak for him.

Lily was well aware of the opinions and attitudes of the upper and middle classes towards the poor and working class. She had crossed the divide and lived a life away from the streets and people she had come from, but had never forgotten her past, and always spoke highly of the people from "the south side". Lily found it hard to accept the drinking, violence and criminality of the back streets, but knew among the nasty element there were genuine, hardworking and God-fearing people. She pushed herself to her feet and took deep breaths, then stood still, knowing she must do something to help her brother, if that's who this accused man was. If no-one else would, or could, it was she who had to give him assistance. She stared out of the window, watching the tradesmen and domestics scurrying around, employed with their work and chores, the pony and traps and horse cabs delivering supplies to their masters or mistresses, to their business premises or to the up-market shops of St Mary Street.

She crossed the drawing room and stared at the fine china teapot, the porcelain cups and saucers. Her stare at those everyday objects was long and hard. She thought of Moses languishing in a cell, facing alone the wrath of the judge, then walking to the gallows, again alone. She remembered her brother in their bedroom in Stanley Street, he at one time lying on a palliasse, letting her sleep on the mattress. She shivered, gained her composure, and called out, 'Edith, Edith, would you come here for a minute please?' Whilst she waited she went to sit on a comfortable sofa by the window.

The maid knocked, then entered. Edith Collins was in her mid-twenties, smart, well turned out, with an air of elegance about her. Lily had found it hard to use the services of a maid, wanting more of a friend than a servant. Edith was trusted implicitly by Lily Spencer. In truth, Lily and Edith were good friends, each well aware of their position, homeowner and servant, but in their long conversations a deep friendship had developed. That was unusual, but not as unusual as a girl from the back streets making good.

'Edith, when were you last in the basement?'

'Not for a few weeks, ma'am. I gave it a brush and clean. Do you want me to do something for you ma'am?'

'No, it's fine, thank you. I was just checking. I want to ask you something.'

Edith came nearer to Lily, who gestured her to sit down. This would have been an astounding incident in a house where maids worked in servitude, but Lily ran a different kind of house.

'Do you remember a month or so ago I had to go into the basement?' Edith looked puzzled.

'You must remember. I mentioned my brother to you, too.'

'I think I do ma'am.'

'You do, Edith.' The words were said with a nod of the head.

'Yes ma'am, I remember. I'm sure I remember.'

The two women stared at one another for a short period of time before Lily spoke again. 'You did not see my brother I know, but you probably heard him, didn't you?'

'Yes, I did hear him ma'am. Whatever you say'.

'It is important Edith.' Lily smiled, then spontaneously they hugged. Their bond was strong, and soon it would be examined in the most severe of situations.

The following morning, before even the postman had called, Lily Spencer took to her dressing room. Once her hair was done, and she was robed in her Sunday best dress and bonnet, she looked every part a lady, which she now was. Her refined voice and classic Victorian good looks made her stand out from the crowd whenever she left her home.

'Edith, I will not be long,' she called to her maid, who was hurrying down the stairs.

'Yes ma'am,' the young woman answered, shutting the door gently behind her mistress.

Lily walked smartly up onto Queen Street and along to Cardiff Castle. She could have taken a pony and trap, hailed a horse cab, or a two-horse brake, but she wanted time to think. Many a gentleman nodded to her as she passed, but she had only one thing on her mind: her brother Moses Tarr.

She turned into High Street, walked with a pace down into St Mary Street, observing the crowd amassed outside the Town Hall, then turned into Church Street. She stopped at the door of H.J. Jones, Solicitor, pushed it open and entered.

Part X

Scott assembled his witnesses in the wood panelled waiting room of the Town Hall. He and his small squad had witness trawled everywhere they could. It was in Stanley Street he learnt most and had discovered the residents at number twenty-four. The telecommunications to Cardigan had discovered more about Moses Tarr's domestic and work situation over the years. Scott asked for a statement to be taken from the Workhouse cook that Moses had insulted and assaulted; this had been done and Scott was in possession of the details. The woman was not to be called at the early stage of the trial unless the recorder, or Grand Jury, desired it. Tarr was not represented and his lack of answers to questions would make life easy for the prosecuting team. He would evidently be incapable of representing himself.

The only worry for Scott was that, if Tarr continued in an unusual manner in the court, together with the odd "yes" or "no", then the recorder might deem him criminally insane and unfit to plead and send him to an asylum, such as Broadmoor. However, he was sure that Dr Buistin, who had examined Tarr on several occasions, would confirm the prisoner was perfectly sane, and responsible for his actions.

He looked round at the witnesses, all sat on chairs in an ante room:

The Warden from the Cardigan Workhouse.

Tom Glazier, the grave digger who found the glove.

William Jones, the boy who found the body.

Miss Clarissa Cadence, giving evidence on her father's regular morning walk.

Master Humphrey Cadence, the last person to see Charles Cadence alive.

Police surgeon Buistin, who had undertaken the examination of Charles Cadence's corpse.

Joseph Whetstone and wife from 24 Stanley Street, who had heard Moses shout, 'I'll kill you, I'll kill you all. I'll kill the bastards who killed my ma, I'll shoot you all dead!'.

Harold Tierney, warden from the Cardiff Workhouse.

The Cowbridge police officers who arrested Moses Tarr.

Rose James of Number One, Stanley Street, of whom Moses Tarr had enquired about his mother.

The gunsmith who identified his stolen gun as the gun used to murder Charles Cadence.

The detective officers who had dealt with the defendant and noted his words and behaviour.

Scott had interviewed and charged Moses Tarr and he would be the last witness to give evidence. All was ready. Scott turned to his fellow officers and whispered in their ears, 'If this lot doesn't convict the bastard, I'll eat my hat.' His case was watertight.

Scott would know many of the men who had been chosen for the Grand Jury, if not by name, then by sight. The Mayor of Cardiff, Henry Timmons, had been chosen to be the foreman.

**

At the same time, Mrs Lily Spencer was sitting in a waiting room at Jones' solicitor's office in Church Street. She was eager to see the man she had known for several years, through her husband's employ. He had dealt not only with their business responsibilities, but also with their personal, financial needs.

She sat upright in the high-backed leather armchair, her pose and style making her look the definitive, upper middle-class wife. Lily's feelings and knowledge about her background had been hidden deep inside. She had escaped through her assets: beauty, bearing and God's blessing. She had taken to reading to further her education and Walter Scott's 'Guy Mannering' had been a difficult study, but one sentence had stayed with her, a line she was now quoting over and over in her head. "Blood is thicker than water." Her brother had not been so lucky; his escape was to hell, but she was about to put that right.

**

The main Courtroom at the Town Hall was bursting at the seams with as many onlookers as authority would allow. The public gallery had filled to capacity as soon as the double doors opened. The reporters raced to their seats, as did the clerks, the barristers, their commissioning solicitors and the designated runners. The cartoonists laid out their papers, eager to start sketching the main personalities within the court room. Moses Tarr would be the centre of attraction, his profile soon to go across the country, via various newspapers and journals. The recorder had been sketched numerous times in the past, as had been Detective Scott, but it was people unique to this case the cartoonists wanted. The Cadence family would be mandatory, a sketch of one giving evidence, extremely valuable to editors. They were all soon to find a totally unexpected inclusion into their sketch pad: a woman who was about to cause a sensation.

Moses Tarr stood in the dock. His plea of "Not Guilty" to the charge of murdering Charles Cadence had been a convoluted affair. When the clerk asked how he pleaded, Moses simply stared at him and said nothing. He was asked again, and, once more, said nothing.

Recorder Williams spoke. 'Moses Tarr. You are not represented here in this court, and you should be. It is a serious crime with awful consequences for you if there is a finding of guilt. Now, how do you plead to the charge of the murder of Charles Cadence, Guilty or Not Guilty?'

There followed another period of silence. Reporters with pencils at the ready added to the drama as they stared into the eyes of the unfortunate accused.

The recorder leant over and whispered to his clerk, but straightened up when he heard the defendant say, 'Not Guilty. Not guilty to anything. Why am I here?'

The clerk, while he had the chance, quickly spoke, 'Moses Tarr. You are charged with the murder of Charles Cadence. How do you plead, Guilty or Not Guilty?'

'I plead I don't understand.'

'How do you plead, Guilty, yes or no?' asked the exasperated man once again.

'No, I suppose,' answered the confused Moses. The recorder leant forward, staring directly at him, wanting a straight answer to a straight question.

'We take that as "Not Guilty", Mr Tarr,' the recorder said. He waved the proceedings on. At that point Inspector Scott left the courtroom. He had come in to witness the plea and gauge the atmosphere within the crowded courtroom.

The preliminaries to get to the meat of the trial took another full hour and a half. The recorder's instructions to the Grand Jury, with a description of the exhibit table, came next. The opening witnesses were interrupted by the defendant leaving the court twice to attend to bodily functions in the small cell block situated below the dock.

There was time before the luncheon adjournment to hear the testimony of the murdered man's son, Humphrey

Cadence. He was the last person to see his father alive. At the age of twelve it might have been considered a difficult assignment to undertake, to appear in a Crown Court witness box, but not for Humphrey. He was his father's son: confident, with an attitude of maturity far beyond his age. After swearing the oath, Humphrey Cadence told the court that his father would always take a morning walk through Cathays graveyard, except Sundays. 'It was his way of facing the tribulations of the day,' Humphrey said.

Prosecutor Barley spoke to Humphrey Cadence in a mild and pleasing manner, which was unusual for him; gruffness being his trademark. 'Who else would have known that your father walked through the graveyard in his daily routine?'

'My mother and sister, all our servants and underlings knew Sir,' Humphrey replied in a superior manner. 'I expect one of them told Tarr. I do not trust any of them.'

Recorder Williams turned to the Grand Jury and said, 'Please ignore that last comment from the witness. Take it out of your mindset for this case.' He turned to Humphrey Cadence, 'Young man, answer only the question being asked. The court shall not be interested in your suspicions or criticisms.' He followed his words with a smile towards the twelve-year-old. 'Back to you Mr Barley.'

'Thank you, Your Honour,' the prosecuting barrister replied. 'No further questions. You may stand away from the box Master Cadence.' A court official led Humphrey from the box into a reserved seat adjacent to his sister Clarissa in the public gallery. As he passed the dock he stared at Moses Tarr and whispered under his breath, just loud enough for the clerk to hear, 'I hope you hang.' The clerk hurried the young man to his seat.

Detective Scott had returned to the courtroom with Hayward, to hear Humphrey's evidence.

'He's a mouthy one,' Scott whispered to Hayward. 'Way beyond his years.'

At half past one, solicitor Harold Jones and Lily Spencer walked into the Town Hall foyer. She sat down in a waiting area and Jones disappeared through an ornate wooden double door. He was used to the Hall and its logistics. For Lily, it was the first time she had set foot inside. Jones reappeared within a few minutes, with him an elderly man with white hair and a full white beard. He was attired smartly and had the look of a professional man.

'Mrs Spencer. This is Archibald Hutton. He is a legal man who has represented my clients in the Sessions. He is free this afternoon. He wants to speak to you. Now tell him what you told me.'

'Moses Tarr is my brother.' She paused as the two men looked at each other.

'Go on, go on,' said Hutton.

'I want him represented in his trial. He did not murder Charles Cadence. He could not have done. He was with me.'

This time the two men looked at each other quite differently, Jones shaking his head, and Hutton with his mouth open.

'My brother called to see me in the evening. The date was the thirteenth of June. I had not seen him for many years, and I was surprised that he had even found me. Our paths had gone separate ways.' Lily stopped speaking as a group of people walked past with much shushing and pressing of fingers to their lips.

'Doesn't start again 'til two' said one of the crowd, 'no need to whisper.' With that, the sound of voices grew louder as they established themselves outside the main entrance of the Crown Court.

Harold Jones indicated for Lily and Hutton to follow him. They left the confines of the Town Hall building and stood against one of the pillars outside, and ignoring the comings and goings, he spoke. 'Go on, Mrs Spencer. Our words here will not be overheard, and I want Mr Hutton to be told everything you know. I may have to call on the recorder to adjourn the trial of your brother, or at least put you in the witness box, but that would not be today, of course.'

'My husband is away at sea, and I am therefore currently alone in the house with my maid, Edith Collins. My brother was obviously not well. He seemed distant. He was poorly dressed and quite obviously poor in health. It took me a few seconds to actually believe it was my brother. We have a basement in the house, which is not used, but to all intents and purposes habitable. I took him to that basement. I lit candles and he sat on a sofa. His conversation was mostly unintelligible, but it was my brother. He told me that our mother was dead, and I made him aware that I already knew. I eventually went back upstairs as he fell asleep. I said nothing to Edith. In the morning, at about eight, I took him some porridge and coffee. He told me he had slept well and thanked me generously for the love I had given our mother. He eventually left the basement around noon, saying he wanted to find out more about our mother's death. That's all I know.'

Hutton said eagerly, 'How about the maid Edith? Can she verify these facts?'

'I do not know. You would have to ask her. She is home now, if you want to speak to her'.

With that, Harold Jones asked that Lily walk with him back to his office, and suggested Archibald Hutton go to Windsor Place to speak to Edith.

'We should tell the police about this,' said Hutton.

'Yes indeed,' Jones replied, 'but we do our enquiries first.'

As Lily Spencer and Harold Jones walked off, Hutton turned and caught them up. 'One question Mrs Spencer. Why has it taken you so long to tell your story?'

Lily stopped walking and replied immediately, 'Because Mr Hutton, I have made a new life. What will come out once I tell the truth about my brother and my past, could destroy me, my home and, more importantly, my husband's fine reputation. I will be Lily Tarr from Stanley Street, a back street girl, a whore. The newspapers and the Cadence family will castigate us, but I feel I must do it, or there may be, or will be, an injustice.'

Her erudite and candid answer promoted a feeling within both men that Lily Spencer was telling the truth, and Moses Tarr could not possibly be the killer of Charles Cadence.

Hutton and Jones had to move fast. They were on a mission to bring justice to the Tarr family, and more than a little prominence to themselves. Jones entered his office and indicated to Lily to sit. He spoke with his senior clerk, who motioned Lily to cross and sit at a table. He was going to write out her statement of facts relative to the Moses Tarr accusation. It was to be a full record of events, both historically and currently.

**

'All rise!' The door opened, and Recorder Williams entered the Crown Court chamber. He took his seat with the Chief Cardiff magistrate seated on his right. He looked down at the packed courtroom and signalled to the Prosecutor, Mr Barley, to commence.

'I call Mr Tom Glazier'. The clerk hurried out into the waiting room and called out the witness's name. An elderly man, around 75 years of age, dressed in a shabby overcoat and breeches, stood up and followed the clerk into the court.

'Go into the witness box and take the Holy Book in your right hand.' Glazier slowly climbed the steps into the box, something he had never done before. He was visibly shaking.

∗∗

Edith Collins opened the door at Windsor Place, to be confronted by the imposing figure of Archibald Hutton. She curtsied, nodded her head and said, 'Yes Sir. How may I help?'

'Is this the Spencer household, and is Lily Spencer your mistress?'

'Yes Sir. That's correct. How may I help?'

'May I come inside? I want to speak to you. I have come from your mistress.' Reluctantly Edith opened the door and beckoned the man into the drawing room. 'Your mistress is with Mr Jones, a solicitor. I am a legal man and am going to try to assist with some information that Mrs Spencer has given to us. It is vital information, and I have been asked to quickly ascertain how you could help your mistress by verifying certain facts she has told us.' Edith was concerned, still a little in awe of rich and powerful men but had been instructed well by Lily into the eccentricities of her betters.

'What do you know of Moses Tarr?'

'Nothing Sir.'

'Were you aware that he is your mistress's brother?'

'Yes Sir.'

'Have you seen him recently?'

'No Sir.'

'Your mistress says something different. She says he was in the basement here some time ago, on a certain night.'

'Was he Sir? We do not use the basement, but I keep it clean and tidy.' She paused. 'I do know, Sir, that my mistress was talking to someone in the basement room a few weeks ago. I heard a man's voice. Other than that, the basement is left open for guests, mostly the Master's. But he is often away for months.'

'Can you remember the date you heard this voice?'

'Oh yes, Sir, it was in the early morning of my master's birthday, as I was baking a cake for the mistress to singularly celebrate the occasion. I thought it was something to do with that. I do not ask questions of the mistress, Sir.'

'What day is your master's birthday?'

'14th June Sir.'

'Did you see this man in the basement?'

'No Sir. All I can say is that there was someone downstairs. A man, I did hear a voice. My mistress was back and forth to the basement the previous evening too. I do not know who it was. Please Sir, I have chores to undertake.'

Hutton had heard enough. 'Thank you. Thank you. I will be back to see you again very soon.'

'Why Sir? I know nothing else other than what I have told you.'

'We will need to see you at Jones' solicitor's office. Your mistress will no doubt arrange.'

Part XI

NEWSPAPER HEADLINES
Thursday 27th/28th/29th July 1893 ad infinitum

CADENCE MURDER – NOT GUILTY VERDICT
Sensational new evidence sees Tarr released
Tarr shows no emotion

MOSES LEAVES COURT AN INNOCENT MAN
His sister refuses to speak to The Gazette
Humprey Cadence screams 'murderer' as Tarr is released from the court

UPROAR IN THE TARR TRIAL WITH CHEERS FROM THE PUBLIC GALLERY ON TARR'S RELEASE
We try to interview Tarr but he refuses to speak

MOSES TARR HAS BECOME A HERO TO MANY
So – who did murder Charles Cadence?

WAS IT AFTER ALL A SUICIDE? "NO" SAY POLICE
Detective Scott refuses to speak to reporters

TARR SHOWS NO EMOTION AS HE WALKS FREE

Lily Spencer and maid verbally attacked by Cadence solicitor over Tarr verdict

Captain Nathaniel Spencer, who was currently at sea, received a telegraph from The Gazette, asking for a comment from him on the day of Moses' release. After eight hours in the witness box, beginning on the afternoon of Friday 27th July, ending at lunchtime on Friday 28th July, Lily Spencer stuck to her story that Moses Tarr came to see her on the evening of 13th July, and she put him straight into the basement area of their Windsor Place home. She was with him from early morning on the 14th through to noon. He then left, and she was unaware of his proposed destination.

In answers to questions by Mr Barley, the prosecutor, she said her brother was not very communicative, his speech was laboured, and he appeared dazed. She was worried about him. He had told her all his belongings were lost. She told the court that when she asked him about his belongings, she could not get anything from him other than, "lost". Under the most intense scrutiny and questioning, she did not deter from her story and made a good witness.

It was ascertained that her maid, Edith Collins, was another girl from the back streets. She also made a strong witness, despite bursting into tears sometimes and weeping at the savagery of the questioning by Mr Barley. She said she heard a man's voice downstairs in the basement of the house but did not know whose it was. Mr Barley said to her, 'Didn't you ask?' Edith Collins became quite feisty in answering that question and said in a loud voice, 'My goodness Sir, I don't expect you've ever been a maid (laughter in court) but if you had, you would know you would never ask that type of question of your mistress. It is none of my business.'

THE GAZETTE
Editorial Comment

The jury accepted the witness of two back street girls, two girls from the hovels of Stanley Street, and Moses Tarr was released. How can you trust such women to tell the truth, whoever they are married to? We do not take their looks, delivery and bearing to be anything other than wafer thin. Their kind always stick together, and the truth often is jettisoned. Should Recorder Wiliams have allowed their evidence? The jury should not have believed everything they heard and should have examine the evidence and not listened to the words of back street women. Why didn't they come forward earlier? Why wait until the trial had commenced? These questions were not answered at all well. We all heard and saw the disgraceful scenes in court when Tarr was released by Recorder Williams. Whooping and caterwauling. That is what we have to deal with here in Cardiff from the working classes. It was Lily Spencer who called on, and paid for, legal assistance to her brother, and Mr Hutton did his job! He got Moses Tarr off.

The Cadence family are deeply distressed over this verdict, and I agree with them. There should be a retrial.

I, on behalf of the Cadence family, am going to appeal to the highest court in the land to rearraign Moses Tarr for the murder of Charles Cadence.

THE GLOBE
SHOCK APPEARANCE OF DEFENDANT'S SISTER LILY SPENCER! RESULT: AN "OPEN AND SHUT" CASE COLLAPSES

Detective Scott tells The Globe he thought the case against Moses Tarr was watertight. If he had known of Tarr's sister's evidence, perhaps, just perhaps, Moses Tarr would never have appeared in the Crown Court. Scott also said it was down to the Grand Jury to decide and decide they did. 'Not Guilty'.

THE SOUTH WALES REPORTER

BOROUGH POLICE "DON'T KNOW WHAT THEY ARE DOING" CLAIMS CADENCE SOLICITOR.

Was it suicide, or was it murder? We believe the Cadence death affair has been referred back to the coroner. Total confusion, as our reporters try to get to the bottom of the story. Meanwhile a memorial plinth is being constructed in remembrance of esteemed Alderman Charles Cadence, to be erected at the head of his surface gravestone in Cathays cemetery.

Part XII

Lily Spencer and her maid Edith Collins had become prisoners in their own Windsor Place home. It was not just local reporters who wanted to speak to them, but officers from her husband's company as well as curious neighbours. All were refused entry. Captain Nathaniel Spencer had been telegraphed, not only by the press and his wife, but by his company. He was due to sail into Liverpool at the end of the week, then, as usual, would take the train down to Cardiff. In verification, a letter arrived at the Spencer home, giving exact detail of his movements. Lily and Edith were closer than ever. Each was scared and in fear of her future, but for different reasons. Lily enjoyed the lifestyle and was in love with her husband. Edith had never been so happy, having the best job in the world, she often thought. The fear was, as they discussed endlessly, whether Captain Nathaniel would be angry, and in that anger might make decisions that would affect them both.

What the reporters did not know, what the police did not know, what the Cadences did not know, what the Windsor Place neighbours did not know: Moses Tarr was now resident in the Spencer basement.

**

Captain Nathaniel Spencer arrived in Liverpool on 10th August and could not wait to get home to his wife. She, in his eyes, was the most beautiful woman that ever walked the earth. She was also the kindliest and most loving. Whilst he was away his every thought was of Lily and how lucky he was. He knew about her background, and it mattered little to him. His roots were not the best either, or certainly not in the upper classes. He would never find another Lily.

Before Captain Nathaniel returned home, he had been briefed on the circumstances surrounding his wife's problems, her maid's witness and the arrest of his wife's brother. He had also been made aware of his wife's evidence in court and Moses Tarr's subsequent acquittal. The "sorry tale", as the captain had labelled it on his return, seemed only to enhance his relationship with his spouse. He believed her implicitly and was proud of what she had done. The belief stretched to a goodly sum of money being paid to Edith as a bonus. She had stayed behind in Windsor Place as the housekeeper, as the captain now described her.

Lily Spencer, for her part, was both delighted and relieved to have her husband home, as was Edith Collins. Lily did genuinely love him and felt a great weight taken off her shoulders now he was back.

A few days after her husband arrived back to his home, things moved quickly; events that Lily Spencer could not have deemed possible in her wildest dreams. All the arrangements had been made. Letters to Cardigan sent and replies received, hotel booked, and a trap to take them to Cardiff General railway station. Just after nine in the morning, in a private compartment, Captain Nathanial Spencer, his wife, Lily and her brother Moses Tarr sat waiting for the train to depart. In the Captain's purse were three return tickets to Cardigan, changing at Whitland.

Moses had been struck dumb by all and everything that had gone on in recent months, and his conversation was reduced to one-word answers. The nodding of his head was becoming constantly used to signify 'yes' or 'no'. His physical appearance was a shadow of how his sister had remembered him. His one attribute, that had endeared him to not only Lily, but Edith and the Captain, was his smile. "*Not exactly radiant but full of tenderness*", was how his sister thought of it.

Nathaniel and Lily sat together, facing the locomotive, with Moses facing them. Lily had various pieces of paper on her lap, messages from Moses. The most important, and the primary reason they were 'en route' to Cardigan, was a scribble that said, "Lily. I have a son. He is beautiful. He is with the Parson. Please, Lily, I want to see my son". Notes that followed brought forth a parental urge within Lily, matched with a brotherly love. She could not wait to see little Joseph Moses Tarr. She was without children, which had been an aching to both her and her husband. They were about to rescue Moses's son.

When the train reached Whitland, the message of "change for Cardigan; Passengers for Cardigan change trains here", was shouted out by several male voices along the platform. Nathaniel Spencer alighted first, then helped his wife out onto the platform. One or two gentlemen, and some working men on the platform, gazed at Lily. She had dressed in fine clothing and looked radiant. Nathaniel shouted for a porter with a luggage trolley, with immediate effect. Moses lifted the luggage from the compartment and onto the trolley. Soon they were away on the little single line country railway to Cardigan. The journey was slow, there being numerous stations. The train dawdled at Login, but as soon as Cilgerran was passed, Moses knew they were close. They finally alighted at the only platform that was Cardigan station. A horse and trap took them to their out-of-town destination, the Parsonage, home of Algernon Williams.

The Spencers and Moses Tarr were expected but were not a welcome sight to Parson Williams and his wife. In fact, they were not a welcome sight to the maids, the gardener, or other members of the tight local community. Little Joseph Tarr, now two years old, was loved, in some cases, adored, by everyone. He was handsome, jolly and "a fine little chap", as the Parson told Lily Spencer and she had fallen instantly in love with the child, an emotion not unnoticed by her husband.

There was simply nothing the Williamses could do. Moses Tarr had every right to fetch his son. The parson's wife noted how well to do and kind the Spencers were, but it was with a heavy heart the maid packed a small bag for him. Parson Williams asked Moses if he would like to visit the grave of his wife Branwyn, while he was here. The question was answered by Lily Spencer. 'We have no plans on this visit, but we intend to come back and attend to the plot.' What the residents of the parsonage couldn't fail to notice, was that Moses Tarr did not speak, his smile and nods seemingly sufficient to communicate.

After a pot of the finest tea, Captain Nathaniel Spencer, Mrs Lily Spencer, Moses Tarr and Joseph Moses Tarr left for their overnight stay at The Lion Hotel in Cardigan. Tomorrow, they would be home in Cardiff with a beautiful little boy.

Edith Collins bought all the ingredients for a special evening meal to welcome the family home the following day, knowing they were on their way back to Windsor Place. Edith had already prepared the basement as a home for Moses and his son. She had been ordered by the Master to tell no-one of the arrangements, which she observed faithfully.

**

Captain Spencer received orders in early September to join a ship in Bristol docks. Three weeks had passed since his train ride down from Liverpool and the revelations around his domestic life. He was sure his wife could cope, and with housekeeper Edith always there to assist, his assurance was complete. With his trunk packed full of well ironed clothing and all the personal items he would need to take him through his journey, he made his way via horse cab to the railway station, his darling wife Lily alongside him. The porter at the station placed the trunk on a cart to be pulled up to the platform. The cab driver waited as Nathaniel and Lily hugged, both with tears in their eyes. She stared until he disappeared into the bowels of the station and out of sight.

Climbing back into the Cab, she gave a smile to the driver, who commenced the short journey home. On arrival, Lily hurried down the steps and knocked on the basement door. There was no answer, so she slowly made her way back up to her front room and pulled the bell. Within an instant it was answered by Edith, who could see her mistress was upset. She put an arm around Lily and walked her to the lounge.

'You sit down ma'am, and I'll get you a nice pot of tea'. As Edith pushed open the lounge door, little Joseph Tarr looked up from his paint brushes and paper, then ran towards Lily. They hugged and laughed. *"More like a mother and son"*, Edith thought. She curtsied out of habit, then departed the room to fetch the tea.

Lily brought the table forward, sat Joseph in his little chair and placed his drawing paper on the seat shelf. Edith entered and lay the teapot, cup, saucer and milk jug on the side table. 'Where's Moses?' Lily casually enquired.

'Don't know ma'am. He brought Joseph up earlier, just after you and the master had left for the station. He's probably downstairs.'

'Go and look Edith, will you? Tell him if he wants tea to come on up.' Edith left. Lily could hear the basement door being knocked, then once again more loudly than before. Edith re-entered the lounge.

'He's not there ma'am.'

Moses Tarr had gone and was never seen again.

17

I put the sheaf of papers back down on the table, as a knock comes on the door. It's Norman with a cup of tea and a hangdog look. 'Thought you might want this,' he says, tentatively. 'You've been reading for over an hour.'

'Come in and sit down,' I say, 'and yes, thank you, I'll take the tea.'

He sits. I sip. He waits.

'OK, Norman,' I say eventually. 'This is an interesting story, beyond interesting, actually. And I think it's where the family line of death started, but I can't make the connection between Charles Cadence's death and the subsequent murder – because that's what it's been – of three generations of Spencers. At the end of this story, you say Moses Tarr walked out of his sister's basement and was never seen again.'

A smile lights up Norman's face and kills off the worry lines. 'I'd put money on it being something to do with Humphrey Cadence.'

'What, the twelve-year-old kid?'

'I haven't done much research into Humphrey, but I do know he became obsessive about finding Moses Tarr, as soon as he learned the man had disappeared.'

'He was found "not guilty" though, wasn't he?' I ask.

'But he was guilty. Lily Tarr, or Spencer as she was, lied. He wasn't in her basement on the morning Charles Cadence was shot.'

'How do you know that?' I ask.

Norman shrugs. 'I was a police detective, wasn't I? Everything about her testimony, and that of her maid, screams "liars" to me. They blindsided Scott, but he hadn't done his homework properly either.' Norman is grinning now. 'There's an outrageous lie right at the heart of her story, and not one member of the detective force picked it up. Not one of them.'

'I couldn't see anything that obvious,' I say, thinking hard. 'I mean, the maid said she never actually saw him. She thought she heard Lily speaking to someone the night before and on the morning of Cadence's murder and remembered the date because they made a birthday cake for the Captain, and—' I stop, my mouth forming an "oh".

'You got it,' Norman says.

I close my eyes and hit the side of my head with the palm of my hand. 'It wasn't his birthday, was it.'

'No. His birthday was a week later. Lily Spencer probably had a plan to explain that away, but as it turned out she never had to, because no-one checked. She was such an imposing figure, from all accounts, an exceptionally beautiful woman with such regal bearing, that everything she said was believed.'

'Did anyone ever find out the truth Norman?'

'Oh, yes. One man did.'

'Of course,' I say. 'Humphrey Cadence.'

'Completely raving, poor boy. He was obsessed to the point of madness, with which he eventually became fully afflicted and ended up in the Cardiff asylum at the age of thirty-eight, where he died.'

'What happened to the Cadence business empire?'

'Ruined,' Norman replies. 'Humphrey was twelve when his father died. His mother married again and the new stepfather didn't want Humphrey. His sister married some Lord or other and went to live in London. Humphrey was left in the care of an elderly grandmother who didn't want the responsibility, so he had nothing to do except grieve.

Cadence's deputy took over the business, but pretty much ran it into the ground. He was a man called Rupert Evans, a real crook, who married Mrs Cadence. He syphoned off a lot of the money, left Humphrey with barely enough to exist on. Humphrey took over when he turned eighteen, but there was nothing much left to run. He married the following year, a girl from a good family, but without a big dowry that might have helped. Evans had sold off most of the slum housing to Cadence's former colleagues, who'd been happy to grab it at a favourable rate. Humphrey and his wife had a son. But the young man was still obsessed with finding Moses Tarr.' He leaned forward. 'What I'm going to tell you now are my suspicions on what happened. Some of it's fact, some supposition and deduction. I'll leave it to you to decide what really happened.'

'Go on,' I say. I need to hear this. It might turn out to be rubbish, but my reporter's nose is telling me the parts that are true will take us a long way to understanding why Agnes Hunter ended up dead.

'In his obsession Humphrey did two things. Before I tell you what they were, you need to know that Humphrey didn't care enough to try to re-build his father's business. He used what there was of his wife's money to employ private detectives to try to find Moses Tarr. He travelled around South Wales himself, asking questions about Tarr. He involved Detective Scott, who also became convinced Lily Tarr Spencer lied when Humphrey told him about the false birthday of Captain Spencer. Now, to the two things.'

By this time I am sitting on the edge of my chair. I have to admit Norman is a good storyteller.

'He indoctrinated his child – a boy called Vincent.' The shock makes me jerk up in my chair.

'What's the matter? Norman asks.

'Just something I thought of,' I say. 'Nothing important for now. Carry on.'

He gives me a suspicious look but continues his story. 'Vincent was born in 1911, when his father was twenty-seven years old. It came as a shock to both Humphrey and his wife Susan. Humphrey was already close to being a pauper. It's surprising Susan hadn't left him. For the first five years of his son's life, he marched the boy around Cardiff, taking him to the places his grandfather used to own, showing him the statue of Charles Cadence in the centre of the city, and to the street named after him – Cadence Place. He told the boy that they had been a wealthy, important family until Moses Tarr murdered his grandfather and took everything from them. The latter isn't true, of course, but Humphrey had told himself this story for so long, he believed it. His madness increased. He became known for walking around without shoes or a coat in winter, dragging the boy with him. He took to standing in front of the Spencer house in Windsor Place, screaming abuse and obscenities and vowing vengeance. The police had to remove him on many occasions. His fury was exacerbated when he found out, possibly from Detective Scott, but again I'm surmising it was him, that the Spencer's son Joseph was, in fact, the son of Moses Tarr, having been taken in by Nathaniel and Lily and given their family name after Moses disappeared.

'The crunch came in 1917. Humphrey must have seen in a newspaper that Joseph Moses Spencer, who had been born Joseph Moses Tarr, had died at the Ypres Salient. He laughed and screamed with joy outside the Spencer's house, saying it was proof he was right about Moses Tarr, and this was God's revenge. It was the last straw for Susan Cadence. She had Humphrey committed to the asylum. This should have been her chance to remove Vincent from his father's malignant influence, but she didn't. She allowed the boy to continue to visit his father, right up until Humphrey died in 1932, when Vincent was 21.

'The second thing Humphrey did was to compile a scrapbook. He had every newspaper report about his father's death, a copy of everything relating to the court proceedings, every letter of condolence written to his mother, in fact, everything he could find relating to the Spencer family, including the birth of Joseph Spencer's son, Gabriel, in 1913. If he'd obsessed before, he was now completely fanatical. I found records from the asylum. He would pace about the grounds, muttering about how he'd make sure no member of the Spencer family would escape God's divine justice. How was he going to achieve that? Through his son, of course.

'Apparently, on the boy's twenty first birthday, they met at the asylum. There's a note in the Visitor's book. Now I'm surmising. Humphrey made Vincent swear an oath that he would kill Gabriel Spencer and restore the family fortune. He gave Vincent the scrapbook, extracting the promise that he would continue to collect everything he could find about the Spencer family and – here's the worst part – that if he, Vincent, didn't restore the Cadence fortune, he would make sure that his own son or daughter, would continue to hunt down the Spencers until the Cadence fortune was restored.

'The final records from the asylum say that, two weeks after that meeting, Humphrey had one of his raging attacks, beat a warder almost to death and had to be confined in a straight-jacket. Back in his cell, he yelled out that his job was done, collapsed and died.'

'What did he die of?' I ask.

'Probably a stroke,' Norman says, in an uninterested sort of way. 'In the old days they would have called it a "Visitation of God." Silly nonsense, eh?' He laughs.

'Who knows about the scrapbook?'

'Whoever was his warder, I presume. Must have known. Couldn't have put it in the asylum death notes otherwise.'

'Didn't anyone try to intervene? After all, it was a death threat to Gabriel Spencer.'

'I only know what's in the notes. Who else could have heard it, unless they were spying? Perhaps the Warden, who didn't care much about the ravings of a madman. Go see them yourself if you don't believe me.'

'What happened to the scrapbook Norman?'

'No idea.'

'Didn't you follow it up – at all?'

'Why would I?' He shrugs. 'It wasn't a murder, so not my area of interest. The notes don't mention any further action to be taken.' He sits back in his chair. I am still sitting upright.

'First of all, thank you Norman. Second, I want those police files back. Now. Like I said, the new DCI will arrest you first and ask questions later, and I don't think any reputable publisher would ever publish a book based on material stolen by a man who's since been arrested for stealing it. However,' I see the panic in his eyes, 'if this material turns out to be useful in my investigation, you'll get your favourable comment. I can't speak for the police, but I'll do something on behalf of the paper.'

He jumps up and runs out of the room. This time, he comes back with a box, which he shoves at me. I stand up, take the box, and head to the door, when I have another thought.

'Norman, do you have copies of everything in here?'

He grins but doesn't answer.

'If you're keeping anything back, it will not go well for you.' With that I leave Norman Price's cottage without saying goodbye and hoping this will be the last time I have to see him. I want to get back to my murder room. I want to re-examine the paperwork that came from the army. If I'm right, Vincent Credance was a spelling error; deliberate or not, I can't tell for now. What I am sure of is that the man who shot Gabriel Moses Spencer in the back in Normandy in 1944 was Vincent Cadence. Did he ever get his hands on any money, which, according to Norman, would have been his plan? That's the direction my investigation will take, because, eventually, it will reach the person who killed Agnes Hunter. I know where I am going. That person has to be another Cadence. I am surmising that, as he died in 1955, Vincent Cadence never got his hands on any money. I will have to check out his marital status and any children born into that marriage. What am I expecting to find? If my reporter's instinct is correct, there will be another Cadence, a son or daughter of Vincent, who will turn out to be the murderer of Joshua Spencer. And again, I am guessing that another one followed him. A dangerous one, but definitely a Cadence and whoever it is, will have the scrapbook. But not yet the money. Not that there was any Cadence money, but the current Cadence will believe that the money Joshua Spencer had hidden away was really Cadence money, should he or she ever find out about Joshua Spencer's will. If they haven't already. They will also believe it belongs to them.

    I am thinking so hard on all of this that I don't notice the other Uber with its engine now running, until I see a woman, who looks vaguely familiar, running out of the cemetery in the direction of that other car, crossing the road in front of my car, which slows down to let her pass. I try to place her but can't and return my thoughts to my investigation.

18

At eight exactly Hayden enters the office allocated to DCI Evan Broderick. The office, previously the domain of Harry Morgan, is in a corner of the main open plan room, with two walls facing outwards, the top half of both being glass, so Broderick can see out and the team can see in. Hayden is calm, confident and ready. The team members are waiting for her and Broderick to emerge. They are at their desks, all surreptitiously watching this first meeting.

It begins well enough. Hayden has planned the story from her and Gareth's first suspicions through every event up to the arrival of the letter to David Hunter yesterday. Broderick makes notes as she speaks, never once looking up at her, asking no questions. When she is finished, she sits and waits. He's bound to have questions.

He doesn't ask any questions. He sits back in his chair, folds his arms and directs at her the piercing, no bullshitting, repellent gaze with which she will become uncomfortably familiar in the coming days. He speaks just one sentence. 'Tell me the truth about the involvement of the press man.'

'I was getting to that Sir.'

'Not quickly enough,' he says. 'Chief Superintendent Malcolm told me last night of a man called Trevor Gwyn Jones who, it seems to me, has inserted and ingratiated himself into this case and needs to be urgently removed from it.'

The plan to introduce Trevor's involvement in – not insertion into – an already proceeding case – has gone horribly wrong.

Hayden has to do some of the fastest thinking about her career thus far. She decides the only option available to her, to avoid resignation, or just demotion if she's lucky, is truth. 'It was Trevor who, from the time he first saw the body lying on the gravestone, didn't believe Agnes Hunter had committed suicide. It's been Trevor who found the leads back into the past. It's Trevor who had thought the unthinkable and got us to where we are, by connecting sympathetically with the Hunter family.' She feels anger rising. 'He hasn't disclosed a word of what we've been able to find, despite the disdain of Harry Morgan—'

'Inspector Morgan,' Broderick interrupts.

Hayden decides to throw caution to the winds. 'You're asking me to show respect for the man who publicly belittled me and sent me out in shitting-down rain, to look for a couple of boys he knew were over the other side of town?'

Broderick sits up. 'So who hit you on the head?'

'A woman,' Hayden replies, 'someone tied to the death of Agnes Hunter. This woman is now the person threatening David Hunter and there's more to come.' She bites her lips together and continues to sit up in a rigid pose.

'Do you have any suspects you haven't already interviewed?'

'Not yet Guv,' Hayden replies. 'But we're looking closer into Reg Hunter. He's had a mistress for several years, who he keeps in the background. There's the girl who was about to be fired, who'd been publicly rebuked and humiliated by Agnes Hunter, but I can't see how she could have got to the cemetery before Agnes, although we only have her word for her seeing Agnes arrive at the Senedd then get into an Uber without entering the building. And I'd like to go deeper into Agnes Hunter's colleagues and political opponents, plus her neighbours, with one of whom she was in a dispute that was about to go legal. Then there's the possibility of ID from people whose houses are opposite the entrance to the graveyard.'

'I thought they'd all been checked out Inspector.'

'Yes, Guv. But some of them have door cameras, which were checked for the approximate time of the shooting, but not before or after. Someone we haven't yet considered could have passed by either earlier or later. The front gardens are small and some of those cameras pick up people just passing by. They need checking again.'

Broderick nods. 'Agreed. We seem to have moved away from the subject of the newspaper man. My position hasn't changed.'

'That's a mistake Guv. He's an honourable man. I know the rep of the press these days is that they're all self-serving scum, but this one isn't like that. But, if you insist, he'll continue to investigate alone, and he'll remain one step ahead of us. I'd prefer to have him on side, as a consultant, perhaps?'

Broderick removes one hand from his tightly folded arms. 'I'll think about it. In the meantime, continue to dig. What about witnesses inside the cemetery, perhaps entering from the opposite side? Did we check for them and CCTV and door cameras at each entrance?'

'No, Guv. Inspector Morgan said it took up too much manpower.'

'Then go back and canvas again. Someone must have seen something.'

'Yes Guv,' she replies and stands up. She wants to get out of the office. Trevor isn't exactly off the team yet, which is as good as it gets, for now. Broderick stops her at the door. 'Acting Inspector Wilkins, I want twice daily updates and strategy meetings, and morning and evening team briefings. For the time being you are not to have any interaction with Mr Gwyn Jones.' Hayden grimaces, but she's done arguing for today. Together they go out to brief the team and allocate tasks.

Broderick begins the briefing with, 'I know this must be a shock for you. You were set up with an incorrect expectation and it might feel embarrassing to have to go back and re-do what you've already done. But remember, we owe the family of Agnes Hunter the truth about her death which is now looking more like a suspicious death than suicide. I'm not saying murder, not yet. That's what we have to find out with the new evidence we have. I urge you to all be diligent, uncompromising and seek out that truth. Acting Inspector Wilkins is going to allocate tasks, and we'll all gather here again at six for a further briefing.' He nods. The team nod back.

Hayden sorts out who's doing what. Then she indicates to Gareth that he is to go with her. She doesn't explain where she is going. Gareth knows what's up and sees Broderick watching them.

**

The call comes from Hayden at nine. She and Gareth are on their way to see me, can I wait in for them?

'He hasn't gone for it, then?' I say, knowing the answer already.

'Not yet Trevor. He's going to take some convincing. I want to speak to him again at the six o'clock briefing. That's the best I can do for now.'

'So why bother coming to see me, if that's all you have to say? In fact, don't come here. If Broderick finds out you've come straight here after him telling you to have nothing more to do with me and to keep me away from the case, then best you don't come here at all.' I go to end the call but am interrupted by a knock on the front door.

'Hayden, I have to go. There's someone at the door. Speak later.'

Out in the corridor I can see the shape of a man. Not certain who this might be, I approach the door carefully and glance through the peephole I've had fitted. I open the door immediately, to a worried looking David Hunter. He's glancing around nervously. I bring him in and lead him through the kitchen into the garden. I don't want him to see the murder room.

'What brings you here David? Are you feeling OK? You're pale.'

'Can I have a glass of water please Trevor?'

'Of course.' I get up to go inside, from where I can see him put his school bag down at his feet, then rest his arms on the table and play with his fingers, pulling at them, cracking the joints.

I shudder at the sound of another crack as I carry the glass outside and put it down in front of him. 'Would you mind not doing that David? It's one of those noises that makes me wince, like fingernails on a blackboard.' I smile. He probably has no idea what a blackboard is.

'Sorry,' he mutters, picks up the glass and takes three large gulps.

'Tell me what's happened David. Don't beat about the bush. Out with it.'

He nods. 'I think my father may have killed my mother.'

19

It takes me a few seconds to fully take in what the boy just said. How do I reply to that? Only one way. 'Why? And have another gulp of that water before you answer. Sounds like you have a story to tell.'

He nods. 'You know they didn't… they lived their own lives?'

'I know your father has another woman and has for some time.' No point in tiptoeing around this. 'Is it to do with her?'

'Yes and no. Two days before mum died, he asked her for a divorce. She was furious. She knew about the other… about Liz. But she said she had no intention of being made a fool of before she became Leader of the Council. You see, she's younger than dad, like, twenty years younger. Mum knew that too.' His head is bowed, his eyes boring into his intertwined fingers.

'What did your mother say David?'

'She said, "over my dead body". Then dad yelled back at her "well it might just come to that". They didn't know I heard. Dad still doesn't know.' He looks up at me. 'What do I do Trevor?'

I sit back in my chair, rub a hand on top of my sparse hair. At this rate I will be bald before we crack this case. How the hell do I know what he should do? I've never had children. I swallow, try to think calmly – and cynically. I am a reporter. I want a story. What if I'm wrong about the history angle and this is a straightforward case of wife murder by a man who wants to get rid of the ball and chain around his neck, on which his wife had been pulling hard?

My editor won't like it. I close my eyes. I'm not wrong about the history. I take the biggest leap of faith I have ever taken in my career.

'David, I understand why you're so upset and why you've come to me. This has been a secret and it's now too much for you. Secrets, bad secrets, any secret that affects you, are so hard to keep, they eventually overwhelm you and you have to tell someone. I'm pleased you've chosen me. For me, it means you trust me to give you good advice. But that's hard for me, too.' I pause to think. 'Look, the police are now re-investigating your mother's death, and this relationship of your father's will come out. When it does, he could well be a suspect, as he probably was before they concluded it was suicide. He must have had an alibi that eliminated him quickly. Closest family members are always top of the suspect list and cleared as quickly as possible. So, I would honestly and truthfully say that I don't think your father personally killed your mother. But, and it's a big but, I can't say that of this Liz. Nor can I say that they didn't collude. My suggestion to you is that you speak to your father as soon as possible, before the police do, if they haven't already by the time you get home. I'll come with you, if you want me to. Reg has to have the chance to hear about what you heard, so he can decide how he wants to deal with it. He said the words, it's his responsibility to decide how to act next, not yours.'

'I can't,' he wails, shaking his head so rapidly he'll give himself a headache.

'Up to you David,' I reply. 'When it does come out, which it will, at least the relationship details will, it's possible the police will want to speak to you. Think about this. Are you prepared to lie to them?'

The boy closes his eyes and shudders. I feel so sorry for him. This is a heavy burden for a sixteen-year-old and I'm probably making it worse.

There's about thirty seconds of silence before he replies, 'No Trevor. I can't do that either. But why would they even ask me?'

'Try this. *"David, what was the relationship like between your parents, given your father was seeing another woman? Did you know about her, by the way? Did your parents ever discuss this, as far as you know?"* You're sixteen. They can ask you these questions without your father being present.'

His head goes down again, this time right onto the table.

Another thirty seconds pass. 'OK, I'll talk to him, but I would like it if you're with me Trevor.'

'Then let's go,' I say. 'I'll call an Uber. We need to get to him before the police beat us to it.'

The car arrives ten minutes later. We undertake the ride in silence. I don't want to speak in front of the driver, and it's better if David works out for himself what he's going to say.

Reg is in the front garden when we arrive. He looks puzzled, then shocked.

'David needs to talk to you about something Reg. It's both important and urgent. He came to me for advice, and I've told him to come here and talk to you.'

Without asking anything, Reg leads us into the house and the sitting room. David takes an armchair, as do I, leaving Reg alone on the couch. David looks at me and I nod. 'Begin wherever you like David but tell him.'

David has two choices, the slow route or the fast-as-possible route. He chooses the latter. The story is blurted out in a couple of minutes.

Reg looks shocked, but then he smiles. 'I'm sorry you had to hear that, son. Your mother and I had many fights, and we said horrible things to each other on more than one occasion. What you didn't hear, because you were out at orchestra practice later that day, was the follow-up conversation we had. Much more civilised.' He smiles again. 'She agreed that we should have a separation to start with, but not until she'd become Leader. She would announce this shortly after her elevation to the top role. We'd then leave it a couple of months, before confirming that we were to divorce. It was to appear amicable, and we were going to tell you and Louisa before we announced anything properly. I was going to move out of here and move in with Liz.' He pauses and indicates to David to come over and sit beside him, which David does. Reg puts an arm around his shoulder. 'Davey, I'm so sorry you heard that, it must have been horrible for you when your mother died two days later. You could have talked to me, but,' he glances over towards me, 'I'm glad you told Trevor. This is not a burden for you to carry.' He hugs David in towards him. 'Just so you know, neither I nor Liz had anything to do with your mother's death, however it occurred. I will tell the police everything, so you don't have to.'

They hug each other and David whispers, 'Thanks, dad.'

'You need to concentrate on your studies with your exams starting soon. I'll give you both a lift, back down to town for Trevor, and to school for you.' He stands up and takes David's hand to pull him up.

'Thank you Trevor, for persuading him to come to speak to me.' He smiles at me. It's a reassuring smile. Am I reassured? No. I don't know why, but I am not. Perhaps because it was too smooth and there's no-one left to confirm

Reg's version of events. He hasn't asked me anything, either. No advice wanted this time.

**

We take David to school first and Reg goes in with him to make the prepared excuse for his lateness. Then he takes me home. It's only a ten-minute journey, but plenty of time for him to open up. He doesn't.

I've just taken my coat off when my phone rings. It's now eleven and I need to get on, with a feeling of urgency that has been growing exponentially and has speeded up in the past two hours. I decide I have to continue with the historical aspect, but I know it's Hayden calling.

'I'm back home,' I say, 'but I'm about to go out again.'

'You're avoiding me Trevor.'

'Yes, I suppose I am, but you're going to need what I hope I'm going to find, so I'll call you when – if – I find it.' I end the call quickly, put my coat back on and head down to the Glamorgan Archives.

I haven't been here before so there's the kerfuffle of having my photo taken for my ID document. At one point the receptionist leaves the desk to find some piece of paper or other. I have already signed in, but on a hunch, as the book is facing me, I start to look backwards towards the beginning of this year and the end of the previous year. I find multiple entries for Norman Price. Some weeks he's here every day. I manage to get back six months when I hear the receptionist returning. I quickly turn the book around, and as I do I catch another name I recognise, Agnes Hunter. What was she doing in the archives back in September last year? Then I spot another Hunter name, prefaced with just and initial, "P", but the receptionist enters the room and I just manage to turn back to today's page. I give her an innocent smile and she gives me my ID entry card. I know

Agnes knew about her father, so she was probably here looking for any details she could find about him.

'Go through and talk to the archivist,' the receptionist says. 'If you tell her what you're looking for she'll be able to tell you where to find the documents.'

In the main research room, I find the woman named Dora at a desk, going through a pile of files. I explain what I need. She doesn't offer to help but directs me to a desk where I can check out available files on the Cardiff Lunatic Asylum in the 1930s. I note the references I need and take my little slips of paper back to her desk. Then I sit and wait. Whilst I wait, I think about Reg Hunter and why he would visit here? It could be coincidental, but I don't believe in coincidence. Could he have been checking out some family history? Possible. But – whose? I wonder if I can find out what documents he looked at.

When I get the files, I ask, 'A friend recommended I check out these and some other files for a story I'm writing,. Could you take a look to see what year he ordered?'

My best smile has no effect whatsoever. She walks away muttering "data protection". There's nothing I can do, and anyway there are plenty of people in Cardiff called Hunter so I'm probably over-reacting and I only got a fleeting glance at the book. I start to go through the half a dozen files she had put on my desk. It's an hour before I come across what I'm looking for. The asylum visitor's log still exists, and I see the monthly visits of Vincent Cadence to his father. It appears Humphrey's wife never visited him. In the asylum record book there are a few records of Humphrey's fits of madness. Then, finally, after an hour and a half I find the first reference to the scrapbook.

20

The first entry is written by a warder who looks after Humphrey, a special arrangement paid for by his wife. He notes that the "large book" that Humphrey brought with him when admitted, and in which he writes feverishly almost every day, is filling up. Humphrey has asked for another one, a wish that has not been granted, for it is believed that his fits of mania often coincide with his having completed an hour or so of writing in this book. In another entry the warder notes that Humphrey is again filled with rage against the Spencer family and that his latest entry contains pictures of evil, satanic creatures, all named Spencer. The warder is alarmed by this and has spoken to Humphrey's son.

I find a note about a further five entries up to the time of Humphrey's death written by the same warder. He notes that Humphrey gave the scrapbook to his son and died shortly afterwards. So, Vincent Cadence definitely inherited the book. I am assuming he also "inherited" his father's hatred of the Spencer family.

I ask for copies of each of the entries, which are produced, and I leave the library deep in thought. I am now certain that Humphrey Cadence began a vendetta against the Spencer family, which passed down from generation to generation.

Could they all have accepted so easily and straightforwardly that the Spencers took everything the Cadences had, stole it deliberately? Such craziness hardly seems possible. I admit I know little about such mindsets. Could a child be so indoctrinated as to believe his or her father's story without question; not only that, but be prepared to carry on the vendetta, and kill the next generation of another family? After all, Humphrey himself did not kill Joseph Spencer, but according to Norman's story he did sing and dance and rejoice outside the home of Joseph's grieving parents when Joseph died, or rather adoptive parents as I now know them to have been.

I need expert advice on child psychology and the possibility of such thorough indoctrination, so intense that a child could be brought up to kill. I wrack my brain to think of any psychiatrist I know who could advise me on such matters. I will speak to my editor, who might know the right person. I call up and she gives me a name and phone number.

It's time to face Hayden and Gareth, literally. As I walk back home, I call Hayden.

'Sorry about that, but something came up that I needed to confirm immediately. When can we get together? You need to tell me about the new Chief Inspector.'

'Can't talk now.' Her reply is muffled. 'About seven this evening.'

It's now almost midday, so I have about seven hours to wait to find out if I am no longer wanted. I have a story to write, with plenty of material, so I am going to carry on with my research of the ancestry of the Cadence family.

I spread out everything I have on the desk. I can see the picture clearly now, but I still have at least two generations to find, and I have to, somehow, confirm with absolute certainty that Vincent Credance was Vincent Cadence. I need to think laterally here. What would he have done after being demobbed, given that he died in 1955, when he was just forty-four years old, of the after-effects of war wounds. I pick up my phone to call Jack Hamilton again and tell him I want to check the spelling of Vincent Credance's name when he was demobbed.

'The only way to find out is to get his army record,' he says.

'How long will that take Jack?'

'Difficult to say. If we can find it, probably a week.'

That's too long for me. I thank him and end the call. I need to know today. I have a brainwave, in my own opinion. If this whole family vendetta thing is real, then Vincent must have married and had a son or daughter. Probably a son who then had his own son or daughter, if the story of the giggling man with a small child is true. I begin to search for a Credance or Cadence born in Cardiff after 1939 when Vincent either signed up or was drafted and up to 1945. After an hour there is nothing. I make myself a cup of tea and try to think creatively. Marriage. I go back to the laptop and begin to look for a marriage between Vincent Credance/Cadence and a woman. Once again, nothing. What could that mean? The most obvious choice – there wasn't a marriage. The child was born out of wedlock when Vincent Credance/Cadence was at home. But if he or she was illegitimate and therefore given the mother's family name on its birth certificate, he or she must have changed it by Deed Poll.

When I check there is no register of names changed by Deed Poll. Bummer. However, another site suggests that some people make their change known by announcing it in The Gazette. No harm in trying. I pull up The Gazette and enter "Cadence" in the search bar, with a time frame of 1938 to 1958. Immediate success! In 1958, at the age of eighteen, a teenager by the name of Paul Wish became Paul Cadence. Going back to the BMD site, I enter into the Births search the name of Paul Wish. Got him! Born in 1940. A short hop onto the GRO and I find Paul Wish. With mounting excitement, I pay the fee and receive the pdf. Paul Wish was born on 14th July 1940 to Marie Wish. No father listed, but the informant is Susan Cadence, grandmother. Solid proof.

I am about to go on when my phone rings. It's Gareth. He asks if he can come around, which I reluctantly agree to. He must have been outside my front door, as it opens as soon as the call ends. He grins at me. 'How's it going Trev?'

'Well,' I reply. 'You?'

'Interesting. The new man isn't keen on the theory of ancestral spats. He wants to know about the present. We're going to have to re-interview all of the people previously seen and check out their alibis more thoroughly. Turns out Harry Morgan did a real crap job. Not one of their claims of whereabouts, who they were with, and so on, was verified. He's also got an eye on Reginald Hunter. Seems he's had another woman for a couple of years. Lots to do.' He frowns. 'Are you still on the history thing?'

I nod.

'Anything of interest?'

'Probably yes.'

His eyes widen. 'Hayden wants you to keep going. She's up to her eyes in paperwork, but she'll get around later, probably come in at the back. She's going to interview Reg Hunter,' he glances at his watch, 'about now. We nearly got to you this morning, but Broderick called us back, to talk about Reg. He really likes the man for some kind of involvement.' He pauses, 'Trevor, what's wrong?'

'When were you going to tell me I'm out, no longer wanted, not someone to share what you've found out with?'

'Come on, mate, you knew already, and I just did.'

I relent. 'Let's get a cuppa,'

'Fine by me. I'm supposed to be confirming alibis, but I can spend half an hour, say I've had to take more time than I expected to track some people down.'

Over tea, I tell him about what I believe is where it all started – the murder back in 1893 of Charles Cadence by Moses Tarr. He looks at the line of descent on the white board, mug in hand. I see the frowns and creases around his nose. 'Well, I ask?'

'I can see the logic of what you're saying, but—' here it comes, 'it's fantastical to think that a grudge could be carried down through generations – four generations – who've been so indoctrinated they're each prepared to do murder.' He shakes his head. 'It's a great theory, mate, amazing, but I can't see it in reality myself. Do you really believe you can indoctrinate children, young children, to this extent?'

'I don't know,' I reply. 'If my theory is right then I have to talk to a psychiatrist or a psychologist who could confirm it for me. And remember, we now know a lot of money is involved too. I think the revenge murder has become the revenge with money murder, from Vincent Cadence onwards. I can't think how he intended to get hold of the Cadence family's supposedly stolen money. This would have to keep going down to Paul Cadence, who would have had to find out that Joshua Spencer had stolen his firm's money and hidden it, and to the present Cadence, who for now I'm calling "X". He or she is also looking to get his or her hands on that money, which we now know has gone to David and Louisa Hunter. But I do believe that each Cadence has been indoctrinated in the belief that both revenge and recompense are rightfully theirs.'

'What is it you're stuck on? Perhaps we can do something to help?'

'It's here.' I point to the line of descent again on the whiteboard, which stops at the birth of Paul Cadence, the giggling man who killed Joshua Spencer and put his body on the gravestone of Charles Cadence, and X Cadence, Paul's son or daughter, who did the same for Agnes Hunter.

'Do you think Agnes knew?' Gareth asks.

'What, about her relationship to and descent from Moses Tarr? Yes, she'd done some investigating in the archives for definite, and I'm guessing whoever killed her revealed themselves to her shortly before she died. She knew what and who she was facing when she went to that early morning meeting on the day she died, as her letter to Reg confirms.'

'I see that,' he says. 'You've told me about the letter, but if she knew this person wanted to kill her, why the hell did she go? Why not just tell us?'

'God knows,' I say. 'She was an arrogant woman, so perhaps she thought she could easily deal with this person. She hated the police, believed the force does a terrible job, don't forget, she'd threatened the Police Commissioner and told the Chief Constable he was a total incompetent. Having to go and ask for help would have been humiliating for her. I think the prospect of humiliation and the effect it might have had on her chances of getting the top job were the deciding factors in her not telling anyone. And of course it would confirm that she'd known for a while who her father was and what he'd done.'

'Stupid cow,' he says.

'No point calling names now Gar. She miscalculated and she's dead.' I see him glancing at his watch. 'You need to go, and I need to get on figuring out when X Cadence was born, and under what name, because I don't know if he or she was a Cadence by name, not just by nature.'

'I do need to go, but two last questions Trev. Who did Paul Cadence marry and when?'

'That's my next line of enquiry. If I can find out, I'll be able to find his son, or daughter. Then, we'll have the likely killer of Agnes Hunter. What's the second question?'

'If Paul Cadence was born in 1940, is it possible he's still alive?'

'A good question. I'd assumed he was dead. That has to be my next focus. If he's alive, then he'll need questioning, but he was born in 1940, so he'll be eighty-three.'

I walk with him to the front door. 'I'll tell Hayden about what you've found out. I know she'll want to know, but she's walking on broken eggshells in bare feet, as far as convincing DCI Broderick this isn't just a pile of wishful shit.'

'Will you let me know what happens with the girlfriend?'

He pauses for a moment, then says, 'Yes Trev, I will. Must go.'

I watch him walk to the end of the street. He's risking his job to let me know about Reg's girlfriend.

For the next hour or so, I search for a marriage of Paul Cadence and eventually find it, in North Wales, in Rhyl, in April 1966, in a Welsh Chapel record. His wife's name is or was Martha Bronwyn Llewelyn. I can only think he met her on holiday, or something like that. I can't get the actual certificate quickly, as the General Register Office hasn't yet digitised marriage records, but I make the application. However, what I try to find, again in Rhyl, is the birth of a child ten months after the marriage. I get it. It's a daughter and she is called Elisabeth Mary Cadance – incorrect spelling again. You'd think by now they'd get it right, being literate people, unlike in the past. I search for more children under both spellings but there are none. Elisabeth Mary was born on 6th June 1970 and registered on 8th June by her mother Martha.

I cannot tell when or why they moved back to Cardiff, not that it matters. What does matter is that Paul Cadence does not appear to have had more children.

It looks like I may have found the murderer of Agnes Hunter. Elisabeth Mary Cadence, who probably now has a married surname, but there's a good chance she did it. I just have to find out what is her married name, if she married, and I'm praying it's not Smith or Jones.

I am excited and frustrated. If I were a professional genealogist I'd know exactly where to look to find more information about Elisabeth Cadence. But I'm not and I haven't a clue. I could try the Free BMD for a marriage but the records only go up to 1998. No census records are available, or indeed any other public record – unless she has a police record. Hayden or Gareth could look this up for me, but I don't know if they will.

It's almost five o'clock now. I'm thrilled by my discoveries, but at the same time I know I must tread carefully. Two reasons: this is a dangerous killer, and I want the story intact, from the horse's mouth, so to speak. My gut tells me I am close, but what else can I do? To whom might I speak? I recall the invitation to join the inquest groupies for the quiz night, which is at The Wharf pub. They've lived in central Cardiff all their lives and I could go and ask some questions, in a casual sort of way, to see if the name Cadence rings any bells. I might just get lucky.

Still no word from Hayden or Gareth.

I shower and change into something smart/casual. I need to look like I'm there for the quiz.

I am just about to leave when my doorbell rings. It's Gareth.

'Sorry mate, but there's some news I think you ought to know. We've brought in Reg Hunter and his lady friend for a "chat", not official yet, but it turns out she doesn't have an alibi for the morning Agnes Hunter died.'

'Do you like her for it?' I ask, my heart sinking.

'She certainly hated Agnes Hunter, she's made that clear, but swears she was at home all morning. Reg is having a nervous breakdown in the waiting room. His turn next, to see how closely their stories match.'

'I don't suppose that will bother Broderick. What's her name, by the way? Reg may have mentioned her, but I can't recall. I know her first name is Liz.'

'It's Comley.'

'OK. Where's Hayden?'

He leans in, to whisper.

'This is my house Gar. There's no-one else here. You don't need to whisper.'

'OK, she's gone back to speak to John Harries, see if there's anything else he remembers. She says she got the feeling last time, there was something else.'

'I don't know if he'll talk to her without me being there,' I am miffed, surly, upset.

'She's just going to give it a go. She's still trying to identify the giggling man,' he says. 'She thinks even the smallest detail from John might help. She still believes in the theory of the bloodline, never mind what Broderick says.'

I perk up. 'We're still a team, then?'

'Of course we are. She just needs time to pull Broderick in. He's fixated on Reg and the Comley woman for now.'

His phone rings. 'It's Hayden,' he says, 'have to go. Call you back in five if it's something significant.' He dashes off.

Whilst I wait, I go over everything, yet again, we've learned from the bloodline of the Spencers and the Cadences. Gareth calls back. I tell him about my discovery that Paul Cadence had a daughter called Elisabeth. 'I think she's the killer. I just have to find out who she is.'

'She won't be called Cadence.'

'I know that. But I'm hoping you could use your resources to just check out if there is an Elisabeth Cadence on a database somewhere.'

'Probably can,' he says. 'Leave it with me. What about Paul Cadence?'

'I was about to check when you called. Hang on.' I open up a couple of sites. Nothing on either. I'd have to send for a certificate, and we don't have time for that. 'Do you have anyone you trust back at HQ who could have a quiet look for us? Maybe criminal, or pension records, or some such?'

'Maybe. Give me a minute. Stay on the line.' He puts his phone down and leaves the room. There's a voice in the background. Whoever it is, it's probably someone I already know, and he has no intention of dragging them in. He's back within five minutes. 'Paul Cadence died in 2019. He was sixty and living in a dementia care home. His next of kin was his daughter, Elisabeth. I had her checked too. There's no Elisabeth Cadence recorded on any database we have access to, anywhere in Wales.'

'Can you access the latest census?'

'No, I mean we could try for a court order, but probably wouldn't get one.'

The kitchen door opens and Hayden rushes in. 'I was calling Gareth from the car, but I have to get back to the station to brief Evan—'

'He's still on the phone with me. Hang on Gar. Evan now, is it?' I interrupt. 'I assume you mean Detective Chief Inspector Broderick?'

'Oh stop it,' she snaps. 'Relationships are good on the team. What I came here to tell you is that John Harries thinks he remembers a name from his encounter with the giggling man at Christmas '73. He thinks he called the child "Lizzy".'

'Correct, Hayden. Elisabeth Mary Cadence, born 6th June 1970. Daughter of Paul Cadence and his wife Martha.'

I expect Hayden to be annoyed, but instead she laughs. 'Ahead of me again. I presume you have more to tell me?'

'A lot, but you'd better get going. Gareth knows the whole story of the Cadence vs Spencer saga, right back to the beginning and where, how and why it started.'

She looks startled. 'Very much ahead of me.' She glances at her watch. 'Tell Gareth I'm on my way.' She turns to me. 'How about seven tomorrow morning. I'd like to hear it all from you, please Trevor.'

I am mollified. 'No problem. I need to go too. I'm off to do some gossiping and snooping. See you in the morning.'

We leave the house together and go our separate ways.

21

At the pub, the excitement is palpable. Fifty pounds prize money is at stake. This pub used to be a dive, a smokers' paradise, but since smoking's been banned indoors everywhere, it's more upmarket, with comfortable armchairs and printed menus. Many of the old crowd remain, although it still looks like the combined average age has been reduced from ninety to about sixty. The standout is old Bob – no-one has any idea of his identity or his surname. He's been occupying the same barstool for longer than I have been alive, so I calculate his age to be around ninety-seven. When the pub was gutted ten years ago, they kept Bob's stool. Anyone else who attempts to sit there does so at their own peril. I give him a wave. He ignores me. Same old, same old.

The usual crowd is delighted to see me stroll in. Each team in the quiz can have up to six players. Mary Ann rushes up to me as I wait at the bar for my pint.

'Trevor!' she throws her ample arms around me, and I get a whiff of fried eggs and cheap perfume. 'Terrence couldn't make it, so it's just me, Betty and Billie so far. You'll make a lovely fourth.' I smile, graciously, accept and take my pint glass from the scowling landlord who knows about my eidetic memory.

Bert and Ernie – that's Sid and Harry with Marcus the ever-starving dog – are at the next table. Marcus wanders over and gives me "the look". I've brought a couple of pieces of leftover sausage for him, which he devours instantly, then wanders back to sit at Harry's feet, looking hungrier than pre-sausage.

Betty has her bag of toffees ready on the table and is looking unusually well got up this evening.

'You're looking smart tonight, Betty. Done something with your hair?'

She preens.

'Got a hot date?' I joke. Except it turns out it isn't a joke.

She nods in a knowing kind of way, with an embarrassed little smirk. 'My Peter is picking me up and giving me a lift home.'

'Good for you, Betty. He's new on the scene, isn't he?'

'I met him at the library, about two months ago. We've been seeing each other ever since.'

'Good for you,' I repeat. 'You deserve someone nice in your life.' Peter must be keen on crimplene and toffees.

'What about you Trevor?' Mary Ann asks.

'No,' I reply, picking up my glass. 'Nia was the only one for me. Besides, work is busy at the moment. Actually, I thought I might ask around here tonight. Have any of you ever heard the name "Cadence"?'

'Of course,' Mary Ann says. 'You know, the statue down in High Street, and there's Cadence Place, down by the City Hall. Posh end of town, of course.'

'Who was he?' I ask, with my best astonished look. 'He must have been someone important.'

'Some councillor or other, back a hundred years ago, I think. He was murdered,' Mary Ann says.

'He was more than just some councillor,' Betty chips in. 'He was an Alderman and was going to be Mayor, some say a Member of Parliament, before he was murdered.'

'Wow, Thanks ladies.'

'Why are you asking about him?' Billie asks, her long nose growing.

I have my answer ready. 'It's for a friend who's writing a book on the biggest unsolved crimes in Cardiff. He asked if I could ask around.'

'I thought you said it was for work?' Billie chips in.

'If it turns out to be an interesting story, I thought I might change it into a historical piece for the paper. I've collected some notes but haven't got far yet.'

The Question Master calls for quiet and we all settle down with our paper and pens, ready to begin the first of the ten rounds.

There's a pause for refreshments and toilet breaks, and the purchase of more drinks of course, after the first five rounds. The ladies all depart, leaving me alone at the table. I move along the bench to join Sid and Harry and the others on their team and ask about Charles Cadence again. I get the same replies about the statue and the cul-de-sac name, but Fred, also on team "Sid and Harry", knows a little more.

'They say his son went mad,' he says. 'Ended up in the asylum.'

'Really?' I say. 'Why?'

'They say he vowed vengeance on the family of the man who killed his father but got away with it, drove him mad. The murderer got away with it, wasn't it. Then disappeared. I'd be interested to read that book when it comes out. I like murder stories.'

'I'll make sure you know, Fred.'

The ladies arrive back as I finish speaking to Fred.

'What will you let him know?' Betty asks. Nosy old cow.

'I'm going to let him know when the book about the Cadence murder comes out. He likes history.'

'He ought to be in it,' Billie mutters, sipping her gin and something. She leans forward. 'His wife left him suddenly and was never seen again,' she says, loudly enough for Fred to hear. His face turns red. This woman really is vicious. She gives out a great honking laugh.

'I heard she's in Gloucester,' Betty says. 'Living with another woman. Anyone ready for another round? I can see your glass is empty Trevor.' A few are, mine included, and I offer to go to the bar.

As I'm waiting, I catch something above the general noise. It's a high-pitched giggle, quite shrill and, for me, disquieting. As I return and set the tray down on the table, I ask, 'did I miss a funny joke?' The three women look at me and shake their heads. 'Just a women's thing,' Betty says, blushing. The Question Master announces the start of the second half of the quiz and we all scramble for papers and pens. I deliberately give a few wrong answers, enough for us to come in third. Billie is furious and Mary Ann looks despondent. 'I was sure we could win with you on the team Trevor.' Billie sends me hate waves. I don't react, but I can't help myself giving Billie a quick smirk. Betty doesn't seem to mind. She's out of the door before me, calling a quick 'Bye' without looking at us.

'Who's this Peter?' I ask Mary Ann.

'She doesn't talk much about him,' she says. 'Except that he's handsome and well off.'

'Probably married and stringing her along,' says the witch bitch Billie, giggling and I feel a tingling in my fingers accompanied by a need to put them around her throat.

'I'm off too,' I say. 'Tell Terrence I was sorry not to see him.' I turn back to Mary Ann. 'Are you sure Betty's OK?' I ask.

'Of course Trevor. Why wouldn't she be?'

'I don't really know. Just something about… never mind. See you all again soon.'

I leave the pub and wander home, my mind on Betty. I don't know why, but I have the feeling she may be the victim of a scammer. Or am I being biased because she doesn't seem like a woman a rich, handsome man could fall for? At the edge of the carpark a hand on my arm stops me. 'I want to talk to you,' says the voice behind me. 'There's something you should know.' It's Billie Everard. She begins a diatribe about Betty and her new man, but I interrupt her, not really listening to what she's saying. I shake her off and walk away, annoyed. What an evil bitch that woman is.

Forget it. I didn't get anything useful regarding Charles Cadence. I'd been hoping someone would mention the name of a person in the present, but it was an exceptionally long shot. Back at home, I make a cup of cocoa and head up to bed, as I have to be up in the morning and ready for Hayden at seven.

For a while I think, as I finish my cocoa, about that giggle, but many people have strange laughs and I'm probably over-sensitive. Yet something about it bothers me. Maybe I did catch something Billie Everard was spewing out. Perhaps I'll find time to listen to her, but she's not an immediate priority.

I sleep immediately, a deep sleep, but at about two o'clock something wakes me up. A noise? No, something else. I was so deeply asleep that it takes a few minutes before I realise what has disturbed me. It's a rattling noise, coming from directly below me – the murder room! I creep out of bed, grab my phone and the baseball bat that has been sitting next to the bedroom door gathering cobwebs and tiptoe down the stairs. I had closed the murder room door before I went to bed. With a shaking hand I gently turn the handle, praying it won't squeak, open it a few inches, enough to see outside through the old French doors that lead to a path down to the garden and back gate, a figure dressed in black, standing, fiddling with the lock. Blood is pounding in my head. What to do? Within seconds they might succeed in getting the door open and I will be no match, even if I get in a swing of the bat, for what they might do to me. I make a quick decision and flick on the light switch, whilst yelling out, 'Who's there? The police are on their way!'

The figure freezes. I can only see black clothes and a balaclava with the eye holes and mouth cut out. Without thinking I walk into the murder room with the bat held over my shoulder. I see the look of surprise in the eyes, then – fear. The intruder turns and runs. Something comes over me, some kind of super-hero fury and I run to the door, unlock it and charge out, as the would-be intruder legs it down the path to the gate. They are not running that fast, being hampered by something heavy in their right hand. The gate has been left open – quick escape. I'm catching up. As soon as they are in the lane, they swing the object high and throw it into the trees and bushes that line the opposite side of the lane. A car is waiting, passenger door open. The intruder jumps in and the car speeds off. I run after it for a few yards until I am out of breath. I bend, drop my weapon and put my hands on my knees as I lose sight of the car. I didn't even catch the number plate.

It takes a few minutes before I can walk back down the lane. A couple of lights come on: the ones fixed on back door gates. I turn on my phone torch and stop to see if I can find the object that was thrown. The adrenalin is dying down now, and my legs are turning to jelly, but I see it, lying behind a bush, easy to spot because it's bright red. I make my way towards it and tentatively pick it up. It makes a sloshing sound. No need to take off the top, as its pungent smell gives it away. Petrol.

Someone was going to burn my house down, or was it just the murder room they wanted to get rid of? I walk to my back gate and lean against the open door, memory of the incident step by step returning as I remember the only sound from the intruder as they leapt into the car.

A high-pitched giggle.

22

I am still awake at seven when Hayden and Gareth arrive.

'Trevor? What's happened?' Hayden asks as she looks at my now ashen face, swollen with distress and lack of sleep.

'Someone wanted to burn my house down Hayden.' I take them through the incident step by step.

'But they didn't get in,' Gareth says, without any suggestion of doubt. 'Or did they? Has anything gone? Maybe they were just on their way out when you woke up.'

I smile, and he looks at me as if I've gone mad.

'None of the files have gone,' I say. 'Call me "Mr Paranoid", but after the attack on Hayden I've been extra cautious.' I stand and walk towards what looks like a second small fridge and open it to reveal a safe. 'I had it installed when Hayden came out of hospital. I put the files in here every night before I go to bed, just in case. There were a few random pieces of paper on the table, but they were nothing to do with the Cadence/Spencer investigation. They can't have been in, because the petrol holder was full.'

'What else?' Hayden asks. 'There was something else, wasn't there?'

Is a certain part of my head transparent enough for her to see in? Or maybe it's my body language. I tell them both about the person running away, and the giggling. Hayden shakes her head. 'I have to tell Broderick about this. It's serious.' She pauses for a moment. 'We're going to formally question Reg Hunter and Elizabeth Comley this morning, not arrest them yet, but take formal statements. They'll have a lawyer present.'

'You'll come and stay with me,' Gareth says, 'and no arguing.'

I nod. The adrenaline has left me now. I'm feeling shaky and nauseous. I won't argue with him. My bedroom is above the murder room. I could have burned to death.

'I'll call my editor, I'll tell her I can't work today. I was supposed to go up to an inquest, but she'll have to get someone else to cover for me. But I'm not sure about reporting this formally.'

'Oh yes you will,' Hayden says. 'This was an attempt on your life. Someone will come around and check for fingerprints.

'They were wearing gloves.'

'No matter. It's important we have a formal investigation.'

There's a knock on the door. It's my neighbours, Alf and Daisy. They want to know if I'm OK. They had heard the kerfuffle in the night, but it seemed to be over by the time they got up and dressed. I explain that it was just an attempted burglary, and no-one got in. Then they spot the can of petrol. 'Did they try to set a fire?' Alf asks.

'No,' I reply. 'I just found this in the bushes out in the lane.'

They look at each other, then at me, as if somehow it's my fault, and back off. I wouldn't be surprised if they put their house up for sale. I am no longer the "cool" neighbour, the person on the pedestal who is on first name terms with the First Minister.

'There's something else I have to do,' I say to Hayden and Gareth. 'You need to get away for your briefing. I'll be fine now.'

'Don't you want to talk about what's happened, how it's connected to the Hunters; because it is,' Hayden says.

'Later,' I reply. 'There's something in the air, something that bothered me all night as I sat in the dark waiting for dawn to break. I'm getting the trembling feeling I always get when I'm close to something. I have a visit to make.' I stop for a second, then add, 'Please let me know the outcome of the interview with Reg Hunter and Elizabeth Comley. I know it's connected, but right now I don't know why or how, but it is connected.'

**

As soon as the shops open, I head into town, to a shop that sells security equipment, and buy cameras for the front and back entrances, and one of those doorbell cameras, so I can see whoever's approaching, on my phone. I buy extra locks for the internal doors and discuss an internal alarm system for the whole house. Whoever tried, and failed last night will try again. I am certain of that.

For the next two hours I walk around the city, down to the Bay and back again, stopping several times in cafés to check my notes. There is just one thing on my mind. Whoever tried to get into my house was at the pub last night at the quiz. That giggle is imprinted on my mind. I wonder how clearly John Harries heard it all those years ago. I will call him later. There were seven teams of four. Each time I stop, I add to a floorplan of the seats in my notebook and try to put names to faces. I know the giggling came from behind me, not to the side, so I can discount four tables, which leaves three, each of four persons. Twelve people, eleven excluding myself. Eight of them are men, so just three women. I go home, because an idea is forming in my head – one I don't like at all. I suppose I should tell Gareth and Hayden where I'm going, but I'll text them later.

An hour later I don my overcoat and head out, walking at a fast pace to the house of the person I want to speak to. The house is in an old working-class area of

Cardiff: steel works and the like. It's still terraced street after terraced street. Many have been done up, but not all. My subject lives at the scruffy end of one particular street.

I pass a house from which emanates a deep throated bark and a menacing thump against the front door, followed by a scream of 'Brutus get back in here' from somewhere inside. I pick up my pace. The door shudders with the impact of another thump and more barking. *'Yes Brutus'* I think, *'get back in there before you actually break through the door and rip my throat out.'*

I arrive at number 106 Garden Street. These houses open straight onto the pavement.

I give three hard knocks on the door, which has two frosted glass windows on its upper half. I see a figure heading down towards the door. I take a deep breath. If I'm right, this is the beginning of the end.

The door opens. The woman looks amazed. 'Trevor, what are you doing here? Is something wrong?'

'Not at all Betty,' I reply. 'I hope you don't mind my unannounced visit, but I need to ask you some urgent questions about the death of Agnes Hunter. The questions are about Billie Everard.'

23

Betty has paled and appears to have stopped breathing. After a couple of seconds, she recovers herself. 'Of course Trevor. Come in, come in.' She stands aside and as I pass her, she wrinkles her nose.

She ushers me into the first door on the right, the ubiquitous, barely used best living room, where I take an armchair and Betty takes the seat opposite me.

'Someone tried to burgle me last night Betty. They were going to try to burn my house down.'

'Oh! Trevor, that's terrible.' She pauses to breathe. 'Why would anyone do that?' She has thrown her hands up to the sides of her face, a picture of concern.

'I want to know more about Billie,' I say. 'I find her… strange.'

'I don't know about "strange" Trevor. She's a nasty piece of work.' Her lips pull a moue, then her bottom lip turns down. 'I don't often speak ill of people, but she has a mind like a sewer and a mouth to match.' She sets her face in an arch expression. 'There, I've said it. I wish she'd go away Trevor, I really do. I don't know why she's latched onto us, but whatever name comes up, just in the course of conversation, you know, she has something nasty to say about whomever it is. Really nasty.'

I want to ask what Billie has said about me, but I refrain. It really doesn't matter to me.

'Agreed. I want to understand why she's so vitriolic. Is it directed against one of us, in particular, or just the world in general?'

'The latter,' Betty says firmly. 'But let me get you a cup of tea and a biscuit.'

I go to protest, then nod my head. 'I could do with a good cuppa,' I reply. 'Thanks Betty.'

She jumps up and leaves the room. As soon as I hear the kettle filling, I get up and look around. There's just one family photo hanging on the wall above the fireplace. It's of a middle-aged man with a child and framed, with what looks like a birthday card attached to the frame. I get out my phone and photograph the card and the man and child, then sit again, seconds before Betty comes back into the room with a mug of tea and a plate of biscuits.

'I was just glancing around Betty. Was that your husband?' I say, pointing to the framed photo.

'Hell no, he ran away and good riddance. I never want to see his ugly mug again. That's my late father: my daddy.' Her expression softens into nostalgic, soporific smiling admiration. 'That's the last card he sent me before he died. He never forgot my birthday.'

'Has he been gone long?'

'Just a few years. I still miss him terribly.'

'Can I take a look?' I ask, 'and could I have some sugar for my tea? Sorry Betty.'

'No problem,' she replies, 'jumping up again and going into the kitchen. I have to be quick. I whip out my phone again and take a picture of the words. *"To my darling Lissy, from her adoring daddy"*. Sounds childish from an old man to his almost fifty-year-old daughter. I am back in my seat before she returns with a crusty sugar bowl. I help myself, smiling thankfully. I hate sugar in tea.

'So Betty, why does Billie hate the world?'

She leans forward in a conspiratorial way. 'You remember what she said about Fred's wife leaving to live with another woman?' I nod. Betty shakes her head. 'Not true. It was Fred who left Billie, to live with another man.' She sits back, looking pleased with herself.

'Fancy that,' I say in my best gossipy voice. 'I'd never have guessed from the way they were at the pub quiz that they were once married. Anyway, do you know why she was at Agnes Hunter's inquest? I'm certain I've never seen her at an inquest before, not like our little group.'

'No, that was when she joined us. She had a run-in with Agnes, who gave back as good as she got. That woman could out-spite anyone. They say Agnes, when she could see Billie wasn't going to stop, referred to Billie's "marriage difficulties".' She says this with air quotes, 'and Billie went red and backed off. She was humiliated.'

'Hmm.' This time it's my turn to lean forward. 'Do you think she might have been the person who tried to break into my house?'

'Why would she do that Trevor?'

'Be honest Betty, she's said some terrible things about me. But that's not the reason. I've been investigating the death of Agnes Hunter since before the police re-opened the case. I wondered if my mentioning the name Cadence when we were in the pub worried her. Perhaps she knows something I don't. Perhaps Agnes humiliating her made her crazy, and angry with me because the case is related to the Cadence family. But you mustn't tell anyone that,' I add. 'Could that be the reason she might have killed Agnes? Did you know the case has been re-opened Betty?'

'Of course, everyone knows. Word travels fast.' She seems flustered, pink spots appear on her cheek bones, and she rubs one palm with her thumb. I don't think she's told me the truth. There's something about the atmosphere in the room. Cold has descended.

'Excuse me for a moment Trevor. I just need the bathroom. Do drink your tea before it gets cold.'

'Of course,' I say, smiling blandly. As soon as she is out of the room I stand, take one mouthful, then pour the disgustingly sweetened tea into a plant, and begin to look more closely around. There are many artifacts, knickknacks and china in a cabinet. I go to look at the china, because I can see that the cups on the bottom shelf are sitting on something flat to raise them up to the level of the glass in the door. I open the door. I can see it's a book of some kind, quite large. I move a cup to get a better view of the front cover, and my heart explodes in my chest. It's a scrapbook, and the name on the front is Humphrey Cadence. Oh God. I knew there was something strange about Betty when she began to talk about the new man in her life. I thought I was just coming here to try to feel out the circumstances.

I quickly take the scrapbook out of the cabinet, find another one from the bookcase to take its place, close the door, stuff the book down the back of my trousers and cover it with my jacket. I have to get out of here. Fast. I am shaking, but I take a deep breath and pull out my phone. I type a fast text to Gareth and Hayden: "*Call me NOW! URGENT!*" I hear the sound of footsteps on the stairs. My mouth is dry, but the tea is gone. Betty steps back into the room. She sits and is about to speak, when my phone rings. Almost crying with relief, I answer.

'Hello… Is it important?' I pause a few minutes, appearing to be listening, the phone pressed tight to my ear to ensure Betty can't hear what's being said.

'What! An arrest? Well, OK, a formal questioning. Is there a solicitor present?'

A short pause. 'Yes, I'm on my way.' I end the call to a puzzled Gareth, and stand up, praying the scrapbook doesn't slip.

'Sorry Betty, I have to go. There's about to be an arrest in the Agnes Hunter case. It's a woman called

Elizabeth Comley. She's Reg Hunter's new girlfriend.' I watch her closely. She is struggling to hide a look of horror. 'I must make sure I get there first before the other reporters. Thanks for the tea and biscuits. Looks like my theory about Billie Everard was wrong. Can we talk again later?'

'Yes, looks like it,' she says and opens the front door for me. 'Do let me know if there's anything further, and yes, do please come back again later,' she says, with a nervous high-pitched giggle.

**

I run to the end of the road and order an Uber, which arrives in minutes. I call Gareth and ask where he is, which is at the station with Hayden. I tell him I need to speak to him and Hayden immediately.

'Why Trevor?'

'Because I know who killed Agnes Hunter.'

24

As the Uber reaches the entrance to the police station, I see Gareth waiting inside the front door. He rushes out and yanks me out of the car.

'What the hell is going on Trevor?'

During the ride I have taken the scrapbook out of my trousers and flicked through it. I feel so sick, physically sick, I cannot answer him. He steps back as he sees my face, then his eyes descend to the object in my shaking hands, which I give to him before I drop it. He takes my arm and leads me into the station and through to the main investigation office. A couple of officers I don't know are conferring at a desk. Gareth takes me to a desk in the corner, sits me down and calls to the pair. 'Lilly, fetch a mug of tea, would you please? Strong, just a little milk and no sugar.'

She starts a reply, which begins with, 'Make it yours—' and is stopped abruptly by the sound of me retching into a waste paper basket. Gareth stands by until I am done. Betty's tea has made a return. I am dizzy and confused. How did I get here? My head is spinning. Somewhere above me I hear Gareth calling for an ambulance. I retch again, then the world turns black.

**

I come to. I am horizontal, lying on a bed I don't know. My head is pounding. My eyelids each weigh a ton. I groan.

'He's awake. Trevor, can you hear me?' It's Hayden. I manage to move my pounding, three-ton head in the direction of her voice and attempt to open my mouth. No sound comes out, but the attempt is enough for her to say, 'He's awake. Trevor, don't try to move. You're in hospital.'

I try again and manage a miniscule movement of my head. I hear a sigh of relief.

'You're going to be OK, but it'll be a couple of hours before whatever it is wears off. The doc thinks it's something like Rohypnol, not serious, but bad enough. Gareth and I are going to stay here until you can talk. Go back to sleep now.' I feel the touch of her hand on mine, and I manage a smile. Then, blackness returns.

**

My eyelids have lost weight. I open one, then the other. For a few seconds, I have double vision, so I can see two Haydens and two Gareths. I blink a few times and they are each back to being one person.

'What's happened?' I croak.

'You were drugged,' Gareth says. I can see tears in his eyes.

'Stop blubbing, you wuss, and tell me about it.'

'He's on the mend,' Gareth says to no-one in particular.

Hayden tells me the story.

'I really threw up in the investigation office?'

'Yeh,' Gareth says, 'then you collapsed. Scared the shit out of Lilly Page. We had you here in under fifteen minutes. In case you're wondering, you've been unconscious for two hours.

'But you have got her,' I say.

'We had to let Comley go, but we had, and have, no idea where you called us from, although you sounded like you were in trouble so I started working on it after you rang off. The scrapbook is incredible, though. Who had it? How did you get it?'

I try thinking for a few seconds, but my brain seems to be full of fog. I shake my head as a nurse enters and tells Hayden and Gareth they have to leave. I shake my head and think I am going to throw up again.

'Wait five minutes, please. I'm going to close my eyes and see if I can work it out. You need to get her. She's Elisabeth Cadence. It must have said something in the scrapbook.'

'No, Hayden says. It confirms she is the next Cadence, the daughter of Paul Cadence, but we don't know who she is right now. I know this is difficult, but please, Trevor, is there anything you can tell us? If there is another woman out there, she tried to disable you, then God knows what she would have done to you next.'

I close my eyes and a series of flashing images flood my brain. A sugar bowl. Why did I ask for sugar? Because tea was too strong for me. And I wanted her out of the room. The room begins to take on focus. There's a photo on the wall above the fireplace – a man and a child, with a birthday card. I can't remember what's on it, although I know it's important. There's something about the picture and the card that's both important and troubling. There's a cabinet with a glass case, with floating china. Curiosity takes me to the cabinet. The china isn't floating, it's standing on a large black book. It's a scrapbook. I see my hands taking it out and seeing the name Humphrey Cadence. I stuff the book down the back of my waistband. I must get out of there. She comes back with the sugar bowl and sets it down on the table. My phone rings. There it is! On the table, a dish of toffees. And I see her face – Betty Connolly. Betty the inquest groupie. I must go. She tries to stop me, but I tell her someone has been arrested and she smirks. I remember an Uber and feeling sick. Nothing more.

'It's Betty Connolly,' I say. 'There were toffees. She's the one who giggles.'

Hayden looks puzzled, Gareth amazed. 'What, old Betty with the bag of toffees? You can't be serious.'

'It's her,' I say. My voice is getting weaker. 'I need to sleep now. Gareth, tell Hayden who it is.'

**

I come to again, and I must have been out of it for another couple of hours, as it's dark outside. For a few seconds I have that strange feeling of nothingness when you wake up and have no idea where you are. It comes back after what feels like trying to re-start an engine that keeps turning over but just splutters. Then the engine explodes into life. I sit up and this time I am not sick. Whatever she put in the tea is wearing off. I am still foggy, but I can see the whole picture clearly now. Betty Connolly. Never for a single minute would I have believed it could be her, at least not since I heard the would-be arsonist leave my garden with that high-pitched weird giggle, the same one I had heard in the pub the previous evening. It gave me a scintilla of doubt, although I didn't really believe what I was thinking. But there were just three people I wasn't sure about – Betty, Billie and a man. I knew it was a woman, so that left Betty and Billie and I already knew Billie had a deep, honking laugh because I heard it in the pub. But I still can't believe it was Betty. I've known her for such a long time. I search around for my phone as a nurse comes in.

'You're awake,' she says. 'Your guard outside wants to know when you wake up. I'll let him know.'

'I have a police guard?' I don't understand this.

'Seems the police are worried that someone might try to kill you.'

Now that does come as a shock. 'Where's my phone?' I ask.

She opens the standard-issue hospital cupboard next to my bed, takes out the phone and hands it to me. I call Gareth.

'Already on my way,' he says. 'Five minutes.'

I try to get out of bed and am delighted to find my legs work. The nurse checks with the guard and walks with me to the men's toilet, where I suffer the indignity of having to pee in a bowl, which she takes away.

'Needed for analysis of the drug,' she says. 'People think Rohypnol leaves the system and can't be detected. Wrong – bad for them, good for us. We'll know soon enough if that's what it was. She must have given you enough of a dose to knock you out,' she adds with a scowl.

'But I only took a mouthful, then poured the rest away. Someone should go to her house and test the plant I poured the remains onto. It's probably dead as a dodo by now.'

'Must have been a very strong drug,' she says. 'I'll let the doctor know.'

When we reach my room, the policeman on guard nods and before I can get back into bed, Gareth arrives. I sit on the edge of the bed feeling silly in my hospital issue gown that doesn't do up properly at the back. He takes the armchair.

'Before you can ask, she's gone,' he says. 'She must have realised you took the scrapbook. The photo on the wall and the card you described, also gone.'

'I have a picture,' I say and hand him my phone. He sends it on to Hayden.

'She'll be delighted,' he says. 'This should convince Broderick. He's still sceptical, but this should do it. He'll have to eat a shit load of humble pie.'

'So, what's happening?'

'There's an APB out for her. No sighting yet. Do you have any idea where she might go?'

I shake my head, then get a gut punch of panic. 'Would she go to my house, try to burn it down again?'

'Covered already, mate. Two officers stationed.'

'You should try Terrence and Mary Ann. But if she went there, her cover story would have to be good, because Mary Ann is captain of the Welsh Olympic gossip team and Betty knows that. Mary Ann'll promise her undying silence, then tell just one close friend. Half an hour later the whole of Wales will know. "Keep this to yourself, but…" is a highly overrated method of secrecy.'

Gareth calls it in anyway and Hayden sends back best wishes and says she and Broderick would like to talk to me as soon as I get out of hospital and they are going to dispatch a couple of detectives immediately to Terrence and Mary Ann's home. Mary Ann will be dining out on this for years.

'I'll need some clothes, Gar.'

He hands me a bag. I get dressed into what he's brought, including my coat.

'That's better,' he says. 'Back to the bald Welsh version of Columbo.'

'I'm not bald,' I mutter as I put on my lucky overcoat. 'Let's go.'

'You need to be discharged.'

'Then go get a doctor.'

He's back in five minutes. 'They say you need another twenty-four hours. The after-effects of Rohypnol can be nasty: dizziness, memory loss, confusion, vomiting etc., and you really can't do that in the investigation room again. Lilly Page will resign.'

'I'll sign myself out. I can't lie here whilst Betty is out there.'

The doctor enters the room. He puts up a hand, but I interrupt the coming diatribe. 'I'm going,' I say. 'I'll sign whatever's necessary.'

'It will be against medical advice, Mr Gwyn Jones,' he snaps.

**

Ten minutes later we are in the investigation room, where Lilly Page is giving me the dirtiest of looks. I go through the story again, this time with the whole team, including Broderick.

'Has she been spotted anywhere yet?'

'No,' Broderick replies. 'She's not with your friends Terrence and Mary Ann Rafferty. Any other ideas?'

I am about to say "no" when an idea does come to me. 'She's recently had a man friend, called Peter, but I don't know his surname.'

'Mary Ann volunteered him, described him as mid-fifties, with thick blond hair and a beard, but she never got close enough to get a good look at his facial features.'

'Deliberately, I suspect, Chief Inspector. Sounds to me like a bad disguise from an old Inspector Clouseau film.'

He gives me a sharp stare. 'Do you have any idea who this man might be?'

'Sorry, no.' Another thought. 'Have you arranged protection for Reg Hunter and his family? If Betty's as mad as her father, she might go after Reg and his children, but only if she knows about the trust fund.'

'Hayden and I are on our way to see him next,' he replies and stands up. 'If you think of anything else, please let us know immediately. Otherwise, please go home and rest.'

'I'd like to take a proper look at the scrapbook, if that's OK with you. It might jog something in my memory.'

He nods to Del Smith, who takes me out to a table in the corner of the room and puts the scrapbook in front of me. Now I can see it's a different shape and size to A4, what I remember used to be called Quarto, and I can see at once that it's old and worn.

Hayden rushes in, runs straight to me and gives me a hug, which hurts my head, but I don't say so, and I hug her back. 'I'm so pleased you're OK,' she says. I can see a glistening in her eyes. 'We have to go see Reg Hunter, but I'll be back soon.'

'If I'm not here I'll be at Gareth's,' I whisper. 'Come around later. And give Reg and David my best wishes and tell them to be careful.'

She nods and leaves with Broderick. I open the front page of the book.

25

25 December 1893

My name is Humphrey George Cadence. I am twelve years old and an orphan, more or less. My father, the Honourable Charles Cadence, was murdered by a vicious scoundrel, one Moses Tarr, four months ago. My mother is already engaged to be married to another man, our former property manager, Rupert Evans. I am left alone. My father was the greatest man in the city of Cardiff and was about to become Mayor. He would also have been honoured with a Knighthood by her gracious Majesty, Queen Victoria, Empress of India and Sovereign of our British Empire. The evil Tarr took all of that away from me, from us. Mr Evans is now managing my father's properties on behalf of my mother until I come into my inheritance at the age of eighteen. He says I must learn everything about my father's property empire, but I do not care. My only wish is to find the monster Tarr and have him hanged. I will also exact my vengeance, which is God's true vengeance, on the family of his sister, the slut Lily Tarr, or Spencer as she is now known, for I know she lied to ensure her murdering brother was found not guilty.

I have persuaded Mr Evans to release funds to me so as to pay for the services of two private detectives. They will surely find the criminal murderer in whichever hole or under which stone he currently hides and return him to justice. And I will prove the Spencer slut lied to the court. This is now my only mission in life.

In this scrapbook I will retain every piece of information I can find.

I look up at DC Lilly Page, the new member of the team, who is now sitting next to me picking at her nails whilst Del is across the room answering a phone. 'Is there any evidence that Charles Cadence was about to be made Mayor and knighted?'

'No idea,' she says. 'Doesn't really matter, does it?'

I ignore her comment, read the newspaper articles and details of the trial, the same ones I have already seen in Norman Price's manuscript. Nothing new here, so I move onto the next significant hand-written entry. The intervening ones are mostly rants and lurid details about how Humphrey would go about killing Moses Tarr.

January 1900

I have today reached my eighteenth birthday. Mr Rupert Evans has been selling off properties of my father to his former colleagues – Aldermen and Councillors. Mr Evans says the accounts are in a bad way. But I do not care. After six years of searching for the monster Tarr, there have been no sightings of him. I have spent almost five hundred pounds, to no avail. I am heartsore. My mother, who is now Mrs Rupert Evans, says I must hand over full power to Mr Evans, as I seem to have no interest in the business. She is right, but nevertheless I refuse, even though it seems there is little money to spare these days. But I have heard of a new detective agency in London, which has, according to the reports in the London Daily News, superlative results in tracking down missing people. They are costly, but my fervour remains strong. I will do whatever it takes to ensure that Tarr will hang for his crime. I have the evidence to show that the whore Lily Spencer, lied in the witness box, having sworn by Almighty God to tell the truth.

June 1900

Wallis and Bailey Detective agency of Mayfair have informed me there is no news of the murderer Tarr and that in all likelihood he is dead. A body found on the shore at Pembrokeshire might well have been him. I am destroyed by this news.

January 1911

I am a married man now and my wife has given me a son. I have given him the name Vincent after my revered grandfather. As my heir he will take on the mantle of saviour of the Cadence family. I will begin his introduction to the family story when he is five years old. My wife forbids it, but I tell her to keep to her role of wife. I will take the boy from her if she continues to insist.

I will take him on daily walks and show him the magnificent house in which the Spencer family now resides, thanks to stolen Cadence money.

My protestations at the police headquarters and the courthouse have led to my being threatened with incarceration. But I am no nuisance, I am a wronged man. And I will have my revenge, whether through my own devices or those of my son.

November 1917

A day of great rejoicing! Joseph Tarr who calls himself Spencer is dead. I read that he was killed at the Battle of the Ypres Salient. This is my and God's vengeance on this terrible family. I take Vincent and run to the Spencer home, where I dance with joy and sing outside their gate. Vincent dances with me. The police come to take me away. At the station Vincent's mother comes to take him.

They take me before a magistrate, where a doctor says I am a madman. I am to be confined for my own safety and that of others. I try to explain that I am quite sane, that it is the Spencers who are the villains, and that God has blessed me and brought down His divine vengeance on those evil people by taking their only son. What better sign could there be of my righteousness?

Christmas Day 1920

My wife is dead, of the Spanish Influenza. Vincent has been taken by her sister, who does not care for him. He has made the occasional visit, when he is able. I wish to leave this terrible place, where devils taunt me. I have petitioned to be removed and allowed back to my home, but the husband of my wife's sister, who beats my son mercilessly, will have none of me. And the Spencers have made certain I cannot be released. Each time I petition they object; they say I am a danger to them. The devils inside my head give me fits of madness wherein I attack the warders and am placed in a jacket, unable to move my arms. My father appears before me at these times, urging vengeance on the Spencers for all time.

October 1932

Vincent is twenty-one years old today. He has been a frequent visitor, and we talk about his grandfather, and what has been taken from our once prestigious family. He has told me that, before he died, Joseph Tarr Spencer produced a child, Gabriel Moses Spencer, who is now nineteen years old.

In a solemn moment we agree that Gabriel Spencer must die, and that Vincent must find a way to remove the vile spawn from this earth and regain the stolen fortune. My boy accepts his role as a Cadence, and I hand on to him my scrapbook.

This is the final entry in the scrapbook by Humphrey Cadence. I know already that he had another fit, as a result of which he died, shortly afterwards.

Next, there are a few entries by Vincent Cadence, where he writes various scenarios about how he might dispose of Gabriel Spencer. His writing is grammatically poor with frequent misspellings. Interestingly, none of his ideas include how to regain the so-called "fortune". He eventually has a child with a woman called Marie Wish, in 1940. I know Vincent did not marry this woman and I know the history of this era of the family, which produced the child Paul Wish who changed his name by Deed Poll to Cadence. An important fact is that Vincent reports that he has joined the same regiment as Gabriel Spencer and has altered his name so there is less chance of being recognised as a Cadence. There are many rants of pure bile against the Spencer family and countless threats.

The crucial piece comes also in 1944, in September that same year, when Vincent writes with immense joy, that he has killed Gabriel Spencer after landing at Gold beach in Normandy. He is pleased with himself. He then discovers later in the year that Marie Wish has married an American and gone away to the States. He is not sorry. But his son, Paul, is being cared for by her mother, Muriel Wish.

As soon as he is home, in 1946, he reports that Gabriel Spencer was married and had a son, named Joshua, born in 1944.

When Paul is six years old, he takes the boy back and begins his "education" in the family history. The boy has been neglected by Marie's mother, beaten and abused, starved and kept in a shed in the back garden. On questioning Paul, Vincent discovers that Muriel Wish has been renting out Paul to older men. Two weeks later her body is discovered in the River Taff, beaten to death. The police had failed to find her killer, probably because she was a well-known prostitute, so they just went through the motions.

He notes that Paul is a strange boy, often withdrawn, angry and cannot attend school, as he bites any other child who tries to speak to him. He also likes to torture animals, cats in particular. One sentence stands out for me:

"Paul has come home in tears with another cat to bury that he says he found by the riverside."

But nevertheless, he begins the "education". This time the target is Joshua Moses Spencer, born in 1944, four weeks after Joshua's father Gabriel died. Vincent also points out that Paul can be charming and helpful when he wants something. That includes his relationship with his mother, Marie, who sends him gifts from Georgia in the US, where she is now living a happy life with a husband oblivious to her former profession.

In 1955, aged forty-four and now seriously ill from his own neglect of the management of his war injuries, he writes that Paul is ready. He hands over the scrapbook to his fifteen-year-old son. He tells the boy to watch and wait, to find the right time. This is his final entry, shortly before death.

I turn to the page beginning with Paul Cadence's entries and am shocked. The previous three Cadences had been motivated by vengeance. Paul is motivated by killing, not just Joshua Spencer, but anyone he doesn't like. I look up at Lilly Page, my mouth open.

'Yeh, we've just handed over a series of deaths in the 1960s and 70s to the Cold Case squad. Good, eh?'

'It seems to have stopped around 1973, when he killed Joshua Spencer. I see he writes of this as his greatest achievement, but a serial killer will normally go on until he or she is caught. They can't help themselves.'

'Who cares? These are cold cases now. We've got the person we want, the woman who killed Agnes Hunter. Job done. Brass will be pleased with the boss.'

'You mean Acting Inspector Wilkins?'

Lilly laughs, and I like her even less, if that's possible. 'DCI Broderick, of course. He was brought in to solve the mess left by the previous team and he's done it.'

I slam the scrapbook shut and stand up. 'He hasn't done a bloody thing,' I growl at her. 'The lead came from me, which I passed on to the police.' I turn to walk out, then realise I haven't looked at Betty's entries. I open the book again. Betty has written only two sentences.

My name is Elisabeth Cadence, now Betty Connolly. My daddy told me that my job is to kill the woman whose ancestors stole our family's good name and money, but I don't know how to do it. My daddy didn't tell me what to do, or when.

Thank goodness for Peter.

26

Him again. Who is this "Peter", who has been so helpful? Did he help her or advise her on how to kill Agnes Hunter? Is he in it for the money? How did Betty meet him? Or is he just an innocent bystander with no idea of who she really is? That she adored her father is undeniable, but did she care about her family history? I suspect not as much as the previous generations, although I do wonder how much she really knew about her father's murderous personality. The father she adored was a serial killer, it seems. It would be interesting to know and would make a fascinating addition to the article I am almost finished writing.

Betty is the only one who has made no mention of the infamous Moses Tarr. I had skimmed through the newspaper articles at the front of the book, all meticulously pasted in and annotated by Humphrey Cadence. I turn back to them but decide instead to visit the library and get my own copies. However, I would like to have Humphrey's notes as well, so I go back and memorise what he had to say about each article written at the time of his father's murder. As I close the scrapbook again, something hits me, the significance of which may be crucial. Agnes Hunter died exactly one hundred and thirty years after the death of Charles Cadence and her body was placed on his gravestone. Joshua Spencer's body was found on the same gravestone eighty years after the Charles Cadence death. Agnes Hunter's body was found on the same gravestone fifty years after the death of her own father. Betty should have known the significance of how the body should be placed on Charles Cadence's grave, where to put the gun? I realise I have been trying to make her less culpable, based on her short entry in the scrapbook. She didn't know how to do it. But maybe "Peter" did.

I close the scrap book again as Broderick and Hayden enter the room.

'That didn't take long,' I say.

'Didn't need to,' Broderick says abruptly. 'Hunter doesn't want extra security. He's happy to have a PC outside the house, but wants the FLO taken away, says it's too intrusive. The lad will still have a plain clothes officer with him until his exams finish.'

Hayden shrugs. Lilly Page goes immediately to Broderick and talks in a muffled voice. When she's finished, she throws Hayden a look that could melt steel. It bounces off as Hayden grins and turns to me.

'I'm interested in this "Peter" character,' she says. 'My gut tells me he's not just an innocent friend of Betty's, he's more to her than that and somehow – don't ask me how – he's involved. Have you read the book?'

'Yes,' I reply, happy that she's consulting me in front of Broderick. He walks over to us, as I say to Hayden, 'I only looked at the direct line of descent. I tried, in a small way, to see if there were any siblings. Agnes didn't have any, we know that, but what would have happened if the only child died? Who would take over the vendetta? From the scrapbook it reads as if there was only the one offspring in each generation, but we should take a wider look.'

'I agree,' says Broderick. 'Page, Smith and Khan can get on with that.' He shouts over to them, and they rush to his side. 'Go through each generation, see if there are siblings for each of the killers. As far as we know,' he gives me a quick sideways look, 'there aren't any, but we need to be sure, especially in the case of Agnes Hunter. Is this Peter a friend, a lover, or even a half-sibling of Agnes's; someone who's been hiding in the shadows up to now?'

I thank him, which he ignores, turn to leave the room, when my legs buckle. As I fall forward, Gareth catches me. 'Home,' he says. 'Don't even think about arguing.'

I don't. A wave of exhaustion washes over me, and I close my eyes. He leads me out of the room, holding me up with a strong arm under my armpit. He shoves me into the car and we are at his house in five minutes. He makes me a cup of tea and deposits it on the bedside table. The bed is comfortable, and I am asleep within five minutes.

When I awake it's dark outside. My watch says I've been asleep for seven hours. Before I can get out of bed Gareth comes in with another cup of tea. He shakes me gently. My eyelids feel like they are made of iron and a sudden wave of nausea keeps me still for a few seconds.

'How are you?'

'Better,' I lie. 'Bit sick still. Any news?

'Plenty,' he says.

With a struggle I sit up. The room is spinning but settles down if I concentrate on one spot on the wall.

'Go on then Gar, tell me.'

He gives me a dubious look. 'Drink the tea and tell me when your head and the walls are moving at the same speed.' Gareth doesn't miss much.

I wait a few minutes, drinking tea, before I nod.

'The good news first.'

'There's bad news?'

'Oh yes. The good news is we got Betty. We took her in and questioned her. Of course she denied everything. We asked her how she came to have the scrapbook and she said it was just some old thing her father gave her, that she'd never really looked at. We pointed out that she'd written a couple of very damning sentences in it. She began to cry then. She said Peter had read the book and it was all his idea. He said she deserved the money, because, if her three times great grandfather hadn't died, she would be a rich woman. Peter told her the Spencers really did destroy her family, so the money was rightfully hers.

'We told her about her father potentially having murdered others. This upset her and she refused to believe it, said he was a kind man, a wonderful father and she had adored him. She believed he wouldn't hurt anyone.

'Now the bad news. A solicitor appeared and after that she didn't say any more. He said Betty had an alibi for the morning of Agnes's death that should have been checked out. Apparently, she was in a café down at the Bay, from seven thirty, until midday. Broderick sent Lilly Page down immediately. Lilly came back an hour later with the news that a waitress was prepared to ID Betty; but Lilly thought the woman seemed nervous, especially when told she would have to come into the station to make a formal statement. Betty's solicitor said it was enough to release her. Broderick was reluctant, and checked with Jimmy Malcolm, but they agreed they had to release her pending further enquiries. Lilly's gone back down to bring in the waitress to make her statement.'

His phone rang and he answered it. 'Lilly? What's up?' He listened and, as he did so, put his non phone hand to his forehead, closing his eyes. 'OK, try to get into her bank account, see what's been deposited over the past couple of days.'

I fall back onto the pillow and groan. 'Don't tell me. She's done a runner, with Peter,' I say. 'Broderick should have waited for the waitress's statement.'

'They won't get away from us Trev, and…' he pauses, 'the neighbour next door doesn't think she did leave permanently with Peter, nor with a suitcase or anything else beside her handbag. She says Betty was walking up and down her garden, looking agitated and shouting into a phone, which she threw into a bush when she was finished. We've retrieved it, but there's nothing on it except lovey-dovey messages, calling each other "sweetie pie" and "my darling" and such like.'

'Then I'll assume this Peter isn't a relation, yet he knows about the money?' I've closed my eyes. 'Give me an hour, could you Gar? I want to think.'

'About what?'

I shake my head, which causes a ringing in my ears. 'I just want another hour of peace and quiet. What time is it now?'

'Nine. I have to get back to the station. Are you thinking about anything I can share when I get there?'

'Occam's Razor,' I say.

He flashes me a puzzled look, assuming I am still a bit fuzzy in the head, then departs, shaking his head.

As soon as he's gone, I sit up, drink the tea. Occam's Razor is well beyond Gareth. He'll probably tell them I was mumbling about having a shave.

An hour later I am following a trail down a dark, winding, difficult to navigate rabbit hole. My head is hurting, with a headache not caused by anything that has happened to me, just by the outcome of my thoughts, having taken everything I have heard since Agnes Hunter's inquest into consideration. I take some painkillers left by the side of the bed and drift off back to sleep.

**

I am awakened by the sound of a front door slamming, then boots running up the stairs. Gareth bursts into the bedroom. I push myself up on my elbows. The expression on his face tells me that something significant has occurred.

'What's happened Gar?' I slur.

'She's dead,' he says, speaking fast. 'Killed herself on the same gravestone, Charles Cadence's gravestone, shot herself with yet another of those German pistols. Someone reported a shot coming from the cemetery. A patrol car was sent out to check and they found her. She's done exactly what we think she might have done to Agnes, blown off the top of her own head.'

'She did that herself?' I'm struggling to understand.

'She left a note,' he says, 'addressed to her father, of all people. She confesses to killing Agnes Hunter and says sorry to him for not successfully restoring the Cadence family fortunes, which she'd promised him she would do. She says that Peter has let her down, and run away, like so many other men in her life. When he understood what she had done to Agnes and that she was now trying to steal money from Agnes's family, he called her deranged and said he could have nothing further to do with her.'

'Are you sure it's genuine Gar?'

'Absolutely certain. She signed it herself —*Your loving daughter, Lizzy* — in her own handwriting.'

I know now, the final piece in the puzzle has just landed, but I must ask a couple more questions. You mean, Lizzy — I spell it out — not Betty.'

'Yes. Is there something in that?

I don't answer but ask my next question. 'How do you know it's her handwriting?'

'We took a few documents from the house on which she'd signed her name. Of course, she signed Elisabeth Connolly. We also found her marriage certificate to Cyril Connolly and it confirms her father was Paul Cadence. His profession is listed, "Unemployed due to War Injuries". We have the right person, Trevor. Why do you sound sceptical?'

I think about how to say what I now know for certain. 'I'm not sure, but that is how I feel. It sounded like she thought she was going to run away with this Peter, but he let her down, so that would mean she had nowhere else to go.' I am sitting up now. I glance at my watch. It's almost five in the morning. 'Are you going back to the station?'

'No, I'm going to grab a couple of hours sleep, then go back in at ten.'

'Who's going to formally identify her?' I ask. 'She has no family, at least none I know of.'

'Lilly Page and Khan are working on that, if they can't find anyone, it might have to be a neighbour, although they'll be reluctant.' He pauses and coughs. 'You knew her. You were with her a couple of nights ago. If no relative can be found, could you do it?'

I ponder. 'Is there enough of her face left for an identification to be made?'

'I think so,' he says, 'but it'll be up to the DCI, I suppose.'

'Who is not my greatest fan,' I say, with a wry smile.

'Did your Razor thing go anywhere?'

'I think so. How are the rest of the team taking this?'

He shrugs. 'I think the boss would have preferred an arrest, but he's happy enough. She confessed. She's been identified as the killer, confirming her guilt through her note. There's drinks in the pub later tonight.'

'I won't be welcome,' I say. 'It'll be easy enough for him to paint my contribution out of the picture. How's Hayden doing?'

'The Super is delighted with her. I'm thinking that she won't be Acting Inspector much longer. It will be Inspector Wilkins.'

'What about you Gar?'

He folds his arms and shakes his head. 'If Hayden does get the promotion, and I'm on her team, that's good enough for me for the few months I have left before I can get my pension.'

'Well, if you don't mind, whilst you're sleeping I'll go back to my place for a shower and some clean clothes.

'Fair enough,' he says, yawning. He takes himself off to bed.

I am out of there as soon as I can dress and put shoes on. I run to my house, shower, dress, grab my overcoat and my laptop and take an Uber to my office. It's just after seven now and the sun is up. The cleaners are in. We exchange quick greetings, and I get to my desk and get going. But before I start, I look up one final piece of family history. My shoulders sink and I take a deep breath. But this is, at last, my big scoop, the one I've waited for, for years. I have to finish before my editor gets in, which is usually around eight thirty. I want the piece ready for her to sub, approve and edit, so it can go to the lawyers in time for the evening edition. But with which ending? The truth or the lie?

27

I know what I know. But can I prove it?

After hours of arguing back and forth, my editor decides on what I mutinously insist on referring to as "the lie". This is on the advice of the cowardly lawyers. OK, I know they are doing the right thing. To tell the truth would mean months more of investigation that might come to nothing, with a law suit hitting the paper. The story would be lost, and I would probably be sacked. As it is, it's a brilliant story – even though I say so myself – of a one-hundred-and-thirty-year-old murder, and the vendetta that followed it down to the present day and the final failure of the last perpetrator to restore what they thought was once a great Cadence family fortune. I also manage to include a few remarks on the true villain which cast that person in a dubious light, but that has been the only part the lawyers insisted be removed. They won.

I am frustrated and angry, but there is nothing I can do. 'Suck it up,' my editor says. 'Karma will triumph eventually. The owner's thrilled with the piece. It really is remarkable, Trevor. You may even get an award for this.'

'Not if the police can help it,' I reply.

'Fuck them,' she says, which shocks me, as she is generally deferential to the brass and ordinarily doesn't use the "F" word. Not this time. She's practically jumping up and down with excitement.

'I have to let the police know we're going to press,' I say. 'There's no more investigating for them to do, but I want to let Hayden and Gareth know and they can tell DCI Broderick, who can tell Jimmy Malcolm.'

'They can't stop us,' my editor says, the lawyers are clear about that, given you've barely referred to the police involvement.'

'They'll be furious,' I reply, 'but you're right. Too much at stake involving the likes of Harry Morgan. They'll probably have a comment, but I expect it will be very anodyne. They'll have closed down the murder enquiry now.'

I can't reach Hayden or Gareth, so I leave them a message, telling them what's coming.

By midday, the presses are ready to roll. The five o'clock edition will be on the streets, in the news agents, and on the internet. "The True Story of the Death on a Gravestone", sub head: "How and Why Agnes Hunter was Murdered".

There is nothing more for me to do now, except to let the real villain know that I know and that one day, Agnes will have true justice. She may have been a spiteful, conniving, all around nasty bitch, but, like everyone else in this world, she deserves justice for the terrible wrong done to her. This is the foundation of democracy.

Once the final proof is approved and the story is set in stone, I call for an Uber. This is the one last thing I need to do. I hate confrontation, but this one has to be done for my own satisfaction and for my mental health, as I know I will torture myself if I don't do it. I am shaking with nerves, so I take a large shot of whiskey. It burns in my stomach but calms my nerves and gives me false bravado.

When I arrive, I bang as loudly as I can on the door. Up to this moment I have felt confident, buoyed along by my righteous indignation, but as a silhouette appears, features masked by the frosted plate of glass in the upper section of the door, my palms begin to sweat as I feel a quickening of my heart. He reaches the door and opens it, stares in surprise at me for a few seconds, then a wide smile lights up his face.

'Trevor! Wonderful to see you. Come in, come in.' He holds back the door. 'We're in the garden.' He leads the way to where the woman sits with a glass of champagne in her hand. I take the third armchair and he, sitting next to the woman, goes to pour another glass, but I stop him with a hand over the glass and a shake of my head. My breathing has increased rapidly. I wonder if they can see. Is this a catastrophic mistake, borne and about to be delivered on the wings of my ego and professional dented pride?

'What's the matter Trevor? The police haven't long gone. They told me about the suicide of the woman, Betty Connolly and about how she tried to poison you. So, it's all over. I have to say, I'm shocked and surprised, but immensely relieved. You must be too.'

He stops and smiles again, waiting for my agreement. I remain silent. The woman fidgets in her chair. 'It's a big relief for Reg, Trevor,' she says, taking his hand. She reminds me of Margaret Thatcher, with the same deep throat voice spewing out its false plummy accent. I still say nothing, but glare unblinkingly at them.

'Why are you here Trevor?' Reg asks.

I go for a superior smile, but I'm not sure it comes off, as I can't get it past my mouth. 'You know why. I'm here to speak to the man who called himself Peter, the man born Peter Reginald Hunter. The man who deceived a woman into killing, with a promise of marriage and money, because, Peter, she didn't want to do it, did she? A poor, abused woman who knew what her fate was supposed to be, but wasn't going to go through with it, until you persuaded her.'

Reg Hunter moves his champagne glass to the table in front of us, never taking his eyes off my face. 'Have you had a bang to the head, Trevor, because I have absolutely no idea what you're talking about?'

I desperately want to take out a tissue to wipe my palms, but I don't, keeping them clasped together in front of me as they slip and slide. I move forward to sit on the edge of my armchair as I continue to look straight at him, unblinking, which is now an impossible struggle.

'I worked it out, after you picked Betty up after the pub quiz last Friday. I was wondering, idly at the time, about this man who had so suddenly come into Betty's life and changed her personality. Billie Everard noticed too. She's a nasty piece of work, is Billie, but she's observant, and very, very nosy. Her husband left her for another man, you see, and Agnes humiliated her in public about it when she once challenged Agnes. She's vindictive too, so she decided to research Agnes's background, to see if she could find something equally embarrassing, to bring up at an inconvenient moment. She went to visit Betty, brought up the subject of Peter, and got Betty to talk about her "wonderful Peter". She was intrigued, as he seemed too good to be true, so she made it her mission to find out more about him. You had Betty well-schooled, mind, she rarely gave anything away, anything that could identify you, but like everyone on this earth with a secret, she just had to let some of it out. She couldn't hold onto it. She had already made the mistake of telling Billie that her new man was called Peter, and they were going to be married once his divorce was final. Billie never misses an opportunity to put someone in a difficult spot, so she snuck out after Betty on the night of the quiz, and saw Betty run down the road towards a parked car that blinked three times at her. She saw you as you drove away and thought she recognised you, but she wasn't sure because she didn't recognise the car, so she approached me in the pub carpark and told me, in that smug whispering of hers, of her suspicions.

'In my stupid hatred of the woman I didn't listen properly to what she was telling me. My bad. I remembered later.' I turn my head a fraction to look at Elizabeth Comley. 'Your car, I presume?' The woman pulled in a sudden deep breath but clamped her lips together.

'In the end it turned out to be the oldest story in the book – two lovers kill his wife for her money. You must have spent months, years even, working it all out, both of you. Get rid of Agnes, find a patsy. Make sure you always have alibis, and so on, and so on, so that, if the police ever came to suspect you, as they did Mrs Comley, you could respond with righteous indignation. But that's where you started making mistakes Reg.'

'Trevor, I'm not liking what you're insinuating. This is the biggest, most insulting pile of rubbish I've ever heard.' He slowly stands up now, walks around the table and puts his hands on the arms of my chair, too close and overbearing. I instinctively sit back. I've always realised he is big and tall, but then I saw a jolly giant. Now he's leaning over me, too close to my face, and I realise what his size and strength are. I am feeling a stomach clenching fear, despite the alcohol.

'Trevor, I will have your job for this, if you ever repeat a single word of what you've just said, in your crazy attempt to destroy both my and Elizabeth's good reputation. I thought you were a friend.'

'No Reg, you kept me close to see how much I was finding out.'

The spittle flying from his mouth has landed on my face, and I feel a quick punch of nauseated disgust. I am sweating from my forehead now, as well as my hands, but

I'm going to get through this, then get out as quickly as I can.

'There are always mistakes Reg. Your first one was the leather glove you put on Agnes's grave. It was an oldish glove but not as old as Moses Tarr's glove, but without knowledge of the history it was meaningless, except to you and, I suspect, to Harry Morgan. He insisted, too strongly I gather, that it wasn't important. You must have paid him a handsome sum to steer the inquiry away from it the way he did. He made sure that his sergeant's concerns went unchecked. If she'd continued to investigate, she would eventually have been able to discover the glove's date of manufacture, which was around 1973 and purchased by Paul Cadence, just before Joshua Spencer died. That was the left-hand glove. Cadence gave the right hand of the pair to his daughter Betty. But by 2023, when you'd found out about the legacy and "accidentally" met up with Betty and got her to tell you her story, she wasn't that keen on killing Agnes. You persuaded her it was the right thing to do and that, once it was done you and she could get married. You knew how miserable she'd been with her previous abusive husband. You told her it was justice. That's the "justice again" murmur I heard as you left the inquest. It was you to her. You thought you spoke in a whisper of a voice for her ear only, but I caught it. Now, putting a glove on Betty's body when you killed her was a real whopper and your second mistake. It was a new glove, which I'm sure will yield something in the way of DNA or maybe a partial fingerprint. For a police inspector on a mission, its purchase will be discoverable. I don't understand why you did that. It was completely unnecessary. Also wrong family. She was a Cadence and it's the Spencers who were the victims of the revenge killings.'

Reg flicks his eyes at Elizabeth Comley, only momentarily, but her eyes bulge in a double take and her mouth opens. 'You were the one who thought that was an extra symbolic touch Mrs Comley? Wrong.'

This time he turns his head to stare at her gaping mouth and hisses 'shut up'. Then he's back to me, but his unease shows as he begins to unconsciously tap a heel on the floor.

'And I know about the lack of follow-up in finding a door cam. Harry Morgan again. They've been looking again, not just around the entrance closest to where Agnes was killed, but both before and after, to check out anyone who entered the cemetery from any of the entrances, in the hope it might bring up a familiar face or two.

'You think that by killing Betty you'll have stopped that investigation, but I can revive it again.'

I decide to stand up and this forces him to move back a couple of steps as I push myself to my feet. One more piece of information and I can leave. My legs are shaking, my mouth is dry, and I want to pee.

'Now, the third mistake. It's in a name, Reg. This woman here is called Elizabeth. You call her Lizzy. Betty Connolly was also Elisabeth, but spelled with an "s", not a "z". L-i-s-s-y. Small detail, but you missed it. When you wrote the suicide note for Betty, you ended it with "Lizzy". When I visited her house I saw the little shrine to her father, which includes a birthday card, on which he's written: *to my darling little Lissy*. She took the card when she made a run for it. I could only snap a photo, so it probably won't ever be useable as evidence in court, but the spelling error will stand out. Finally, your last mistake, your supposed astonishment when the will of Joshua Spencer was read out. Your major concern was that you'd be able to manage David's share of the money. How did you find out about Joshua Spencer's will?'

His stands up to his full height. His face has turned a shade of red approaching purple, like a plum with worms inside it. 'I want you to leave my house now, or I will throw you out,' he snarls. He reaches out to take my arm, but my recent boxing practice comes in handy. I duck down and avoid him, so that he is left stumbling and clutching air. This makes him even angrier. He looks as if he could have a stroke any minute.

I carry on. 'I'm speculating now, so do tell me which bits I got wrong, won't you.' I'm talking too fast but my tongue seems to have taken on a life of its own. 'Agnes knew far more than she ever let on about the history of her family, but not about the exact amount of money her father had stolen. That was something you found out, Mrs Comley.' He turns to scowl at her and shakes his head. 'You worked in the same office building Joshua Spencer used for his financial company. It was easy enough to find the file and read it. I must admit, the amount amazed me. You'll be managing David's share until he reaches twenty-one. He'll have enough, but you'll find a way to make sure the two of you will be able to live a life of ease and comfort.'

I pause and look at the woman, whose face, I am pleased to see, is a picture of shock and fear. I have hit the target on this one and she wants to know how I found out.

'Now, moving on to more speculation. Agnes was not a woman to sit back and allow someone to get the better of her. She already knew about Betty Connolly. That's why she went to the cemetery that morning, to confront Betty. The girl Cerys, told the police Agnes looked a little unsteady on her feet, swaying. Had you slipped a little something in her coffee Reg, to put her off balance? You were at the cemetery, too. By the time she reached the grave her brain would have been muddled. You and Betty were both waiting. But, when it came to do it, Betty couldn't pull the trigger. By this time, Agnes must have been almost unconscious when you laid her on the gravestone. Did you show her the gun before you shot her, because it was you who shot her, in the end, wasn't it Reg?'

I begin to shuffle my feet to be able to turn quickly around the armchair and head to the door. 'I've wondered why you didn't accept the verdict of suicide. Was it because it wasn't in Agnes's character to kill herself and it would have looked odd if you'd just meekly accepted it? I'm guessing you had to show some outrage and overdo it just enough to make people think you were a man sunk in grief, who had taken to drinking. But then I showed up in person and became a nuisance. What's that saying? "Keep your friends close, but your enemies closer". You welcomed me in, allowed me to get close to your family, all so you could keep an eye on me. When I found out stuff I wasn't supposed to know, you tried to get rid of me, twice, but I'm like one of those cockroaches you can wound but can't kill. By the way, I realise now it was you, Mrs Comley, who followed me to Norman Price's house. You found out from his frequent visits to the library that Norman was writing a book about unsolved murders in Cardiff. You told Reg, and he used Betty to try to set fire to my house, to get rid of any papers Norman might have given me. You needn't have bothered. I have an eidetic memory. But would you have tried to silence Norman next?'

A smile comes over his face. And my hands begin to shake. 'A cockroach is easily squashed.'

'Don't even think about it,' I say. 'One police officer knows I'm here and if I don't text within the next – I stop and check my watch – ten minutes, it'll be like those American cop shows, where dozens of armed police screech to a halt outside your front door.' I need to finish up and get out of here, in case he decides to risk the fact I'm lying through my teeth.

I am clear of him, and I start to walk towards the door. He is close behind me. Too close. As I quicken my pace I say, 'Who was following David? He was being followed, wasn't he?'

He doesn't answer. He can't be sure this isn't just more guesswork.

'Did you do that to your own son? What a disgusting, vile creature you are.'

My walking pace becomes a slow trot. 'I've already asked questions about whether or not that inheritance would be subject to the "Proceeds of Crime" Act, even though you didn't commit the crime.' There's a short hoot of laughter in my ear. It tells me he's ahead of me on this, too.

I have almost reached the front door and, to my enormous relief there is a shadow of a person outside. I turn to face him. 'As I said, I've already had a quiet word with one of the police squad involved in Agnes's murder, who now knows the real story. This officer won't just let it go. He's like a dog with a bone, he'll keep on gnawing at it until your other mistakes are uncovered. Because they will be, Reg. Karma will get you, no doubt about that. Oh, and you should read the evening edition of The Cardiff Sentinel. The whole story's in there.' My voice is shaky and whimpering. As I reach out for the handle to open the door, I catch a glimpse of his smiling face. He can sense the fear coursing through me. He can probably smell it too.

He grabs my arm, but I manage to pull it away. 'You can't do that. It's slander Trevor. And more. You really should not have done that.'

'You barely get a mention Reg, nor you,' I fling at Elizabeth Comley. 'You don't feature at all. But I'm hoping the press are going to be bothering you for some time to come. Enjoy.'

My shaking hands pull the door open, and I get one foot over the doorstep as he grabs me and tries to pull me back in. Standing in my way is an astonished David. Reg spins me around as I look desperately at David for help. I have allowed my concentration to slip and Reg swings at me. This time my boxing practice has not been enough, and a punch connects with my eyebrow. I am stunned, disoriented, as his ring opens up a gash on my forehead and blood runs down my face. I stagger against the doorframe as David tries to hold me up and screams at his father, 'Dad, what are you doing? What's going on?' Reg still has a grip on my upper arm, which David attempts to pull off. He fails, of course, but the distraction in those few seconds of shouting and yelling and confusion, of Reg trying to hang onto me as David pulls on his arm, are just enough to loosen Reg's grasp. The vice-like grip that would have dragged me back into the house slackens as Reg yells something indistinguishable back at David. I pull at his fingers and the hand comes away. I am free!

I turn to run down to the path, blood streaming from my head to the Uber, which I must have some premonition I would need in a hurry and for which I agreed to pay the driver a huge bribe, jump in and scream, 'Drive! Drive!' The astonished driver takes off at speed not unlike an aircraft hurtling down a runway. My last fleeting look back reveals the three of them standing in the doorway, David, mouth open, pushing at his father's chest, Elizabeth Comley screaming, Reg Hunter with his mouth ominously set, holding off his son.

This is not the end. What the hell have I done?

28

When I reach Gareth's house, I pour myself an almost full tumbler of whisky and down it in one go, then a second. The shock hits my head, and I stagger down into an armchair. What now? It's just after five and the papers will be hitting the streets. I call my editor and tell her I have been to see Reg Hunter because I know the real story. She explodes.

'There was no reason not to tell him,' I say. 'He knows he's hardly mentioned in the article, which I hope he's now seen, and is giving him grief. And fear. A lot of fear, I hope. He's probably plotting my demise right now. It's not over between him and me.'

'Trevor, leave it alone for God's sake; don't go anywhere near the rest of the family.' I consent and she ends the call. She'll be rushing off to speak to the lawyers. A quick visit to the bathroom for me to throw up the whisky before I return to my armchair, falling down into it as the enormity of what I've done hits me. Some of what I said was true, but the rest was just speculation. I can barely prove any of it. The ball is now firmly in Reg Hunter's court.

What are my options? Just sit here or answer the persistent ringing and knocking at the door, which has been going on for a couple of minutes.

Hayden stands there, stony faced. Some of the whisky has got through and she backs off, wrinkling her nose at the mixed smell of alcohol and vomit coming off me. 'I've been calling you for hours,' she starts, and marches past me into the living room. 'There's uproar down at the station, about what you've written.'

'Let's go into the garden Hayden. If I need to be sick again, I can do it in one of Gareth's flower beds. Gareth and Nia talked about gardening all the time. Vera left him because of the flower beds, you know, and Tracey's gone too. Am I rambling?'

'You're drunk as a skunk.' She takes my arm, leads me over to the pergola, and pushes me into one of the large, comfortable garden chairs. The smell coming from a fragrant wall climber makes me feel sick again.

'I'm going to get you a cup of tea and a glass of water, then you can tell me what the hell's going on.'

I visit the flower bed once her back is turned. This is no longer the reaction to the whisky. It's terror heaving in my stomach, as I look back at what I've just left behind. I manage to find a spot that Gareth won't see. When she comes back, I'm feeling better, but my mouth is like the bottom of the proverbial parrot's cage. I grab the water, swish it around in my mouth then spit it onto the lawn, and down the rest of the glass.

She gives me a few minutes, then says, 'So what's up, and what's happened to your face? Who hit you?'

I shake my head. 'It doesn't matter,' I say. 'Not as bad as it looks.'

'You should get it checked out at the hospital Trevor.'

I shake my head again and this time the garden doesn't stop spinning.

'Up to you,' she shrugs. I've seen the paper, by the way. It's a good piece, very professionally written. You might even get a prize, it's that good. Broderick and Malcolm are fuming, needless to say. The Chief Super has already made a call to your Editor. Last I heard, lawyers were involved.' She pauses and waits for me to say something.

Eventually I do, keeping my head still until the walls have calmed down. 'I have nothing to say to you or anyone else Hayden. Broderick can go shove it.'

Hayden purses her lips to make sure she doesn't grin, drinks some of her own tea, then gives me a look that would bend a fork. 'It's about Reg Hunter, isn't it? He's involved, somehow, isn't he? I saw something I didn't like when we visited him to tell him about Betty Connolly, something like a smirk, for just a fraction of a second, but I know I saw it.'

My head is spinning, and I know I'm slurring. 'Ever since I met you Hayden, I swore you could see through bone into the intermost, I mean inmost, whatever, workings of my mind. What else do you know?'

She puts her elbows on the table. 'I could see in the past twenty-four hours, just exactly how troubled you were – are. You've been to see Reg Hunter today?' I nod and the table looks like a ship plunging down and up in heavy waves. 'Anything to tell me?'

I stop and think, as far as my head will allow me. 'No. Don't want to hold you back from your cebre, cebrel, celebrations—' three attempts at that word. 'Off you go. Your colleagues are waiting. I'm off to bed, sleep this off. I'm going to talk to Nia.'

'But why did you go? Why is there blood on your shirt? And how did you get that cut on your head? It might need stitches. We'd already been there to tell him about Betty Connolly, that he and his family could relax, now it's all over.'

'No stitches. Occam's Razor. In looking for an answer to a thing, no more assumptions should be made than are necessary, or something like that. Most obvious answer is the simplest one. I'm getting confused.'

I shrug, stand up and head for the living room, where I fall back down in the armchair. She follows me, watches me close my eyes, and leaves. I wait five minutes after the door slams shut. I go upstairs, shower, check the cut, which has stopped bleeding, put a plaster on it, and put on clean clothes. Back downstairs, I lock up the back door, head out the front, down to the nearest pub, which is The Lion on the green.

I order a pint of lemonade and go over to sit in the corner. The sickness has subsided, and my head is no longer spinning. I am weary, but clearer headed.

From the confronting of Reg Hunter and Elizabeth Comley I know that Betty was present at Agnes's death, but she never actually killed her. I have also realised that the person who hit Hayden over the head was Elizabeth Comley. It was definitely Betty who roofied my tea, but on instruction from Reg Hunter. I wonder, briefly, how he is explaining to David why he hit me.

I have to acknowledge he has won, for now. I saw what they wanted me to see. What a fool I've been. I think of that expression used by outraged people: "it made my blood boil". I have always thought it hyperbole, badly used embellishment. Not today. As I sit here, with the sun streaming in through the windows, people arriving for a drink after work, happy, smiling, ignorant, taking their drinks outside to watch their children playing on the green, I feel the thumping in my neck, the heat in my face. This is not anger. This is incandescent fury. My blood is boiling.

A mile away somewhere in the centre of town, the police drink their way through bottles of champagne (Broderick) and pints of beer (Gareth, supplied with a tab by Broderick), patting each other on the back, bathing in the glory of their success, with the suicide of Betty Connolly and her confession to the murder of Agnes Hunter. The case now closed, or so they think. I am deep in thought, of how I will eventually find a way to expose the monstrosity of Peter Reginald Hunter and Elizabeth Mary Comley.

Footsteps approach my table. Looking up, it's Gareth and Hayden.

'I thought you'd be knee deep in champagne,' I say.

'Your article put paid to that. Broderick is still spitting tacks and you'd better keep out of your old mate Jimmy's way for a while, probably the next year, I'd say,' Hayden replies.

'I'm a reporter and it was a great story. We didn't make the police sound bad, in fact I hardly mention you. It's a historical story and not written from a police point of view.'

'The Chief Super doesn't agree, but I think he'll try to play it down. He has to brief the press tomorrow about Betty Connolly's death. My advice – don't go. He'll probably be armed, in case you turn up.'

I shrug. 'Of course I'll go. It's my job. Anyway, why are you two here?'

'Because we both know the culprit is Reg Hunter and has been all along. We don't like him getting away with it, any more than you do. We think a plan may be necessary,' Gareth says. 'We thought you might like to be involved.'

For the first time today I smile a genuine smile. 'Bring it on,' I say. We put our heads together and start to talk.

Thanks and Acknowledgements

Writing a book is a huge undertaking. Coming up with the concept for a new book to be written by two people, with everything such an undertaking entails: new characters, settings, plot, etcetera, that both writers can buy into with enthusiasm and enjoyment, from the outside looks impossible. Yet for both of us the experience has been entertaining, innovative and most important of all, good fun.

We have, of course, had many differences of opinion along the way but never an argument. We have solved problems with mutual respect for each other's knowledge and the skills we have brought to the project. So, we want to acknowledge each other's professionalism and ability to collaborate in a peaceful way to produce a successful novel.

Along the way we have used and relied on the support and skills of others who have brought to the table their particular brand of skills and expertise, to help us reach the finishing post.

Rose Bell has been our first reader and editor, collaborating on the formation of characters and helping to ensure the people who inhabit this world are both believable and interesting. She also supports us with marketing and publicity, plus constant enthusiasm and encouragement.

Enez Bosley's eagle eye has also helped us with continuity and enthusiastic support.

Copy editing and proof reading have been done by Ellen Morrow, in the US. Ellen's eagle eye ensures that not only are plot holes and errors in timelines called out, but spelling and punctuation are as close to perfect as they can be. (Mary is hopeless at remembering which quote marks are applicable to which type of quote!)

John's expertise in matters relating to police procedure in the 19th and 20th centuries is exceptional and has been vital, as has Mary's knowledge of genealogy research.

As always, we thank our families for the advice, the eye rolling, their perpetual loving support and their expressions of pride in our efforts.

And to you, readers and supporters, we are so grateful that you have chosen to put your faith in us and read the first book in what we hope will continue in a successful collaboration, as we invent new stories for Trevor, Hayden and Gareth.

We welcome all feedback and if you would like to endorse your enjoyment by leaving a comment on Amazon, it would be gratefully received, as it helps other readers find us.

John and Mary

John F Wake

John F Wake has written numerous books on historical, social injustice and crime in Cardiff, together with examining several sensational murder investigations of the past. His novels include 'Mad Jack Matthews', the bio/story of Cardiff's most outrageous criminal of Victorian times. He also has penned a Drama performed at the Edinburgh Festival. John was a police detective officer in Cardiff and South Wales for 20 years, serving in several specialist departments. He also undertakes lectures/presentations on his books

Mary Kathryn Jones

Mary has two series, Maze Investigations, which is genealogy mystery based, and The Curiosity Club of St Foy, a Cornish Cosy Mystery series. Originally from Cwmbran in South Wales, she relocated to North Wales and now lives close to Conwy and the sea. She has been writing full time since retirement and next year will see the 10th anniversary of the publication of her first novel, Three Time Removed in the Maze series, which is now available in ebook, paperback and audio versions.

Website: www.mkjonesauthor
Email: mary@mkjonesauthor.com

Mary can also be found on Instagram, Facebook and Threads as MKJonesauthor.

Printed in Great Britain
by Amazon